FLINT'S HONOR

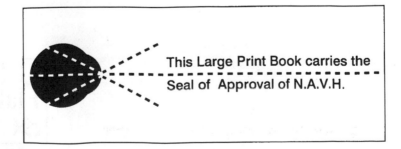

This Large Print Book carries the
Seal of Approval of N.A.V.H.

FLINT'S HONOR

RICHARD S. WHEELER

G.K. Hall & Co. • Waterville, Maine

Published in 2001 by arrangement with
Tom Doherty Associates, LLC

G.K. Hall Large Print Western Series.

The text of this Large Print edition is unabridged.
Other aspects of the book may vary from the original edition.

Set in 16 pt. Plantin.

Printed in the United States on permanent paper.

Library of Congress Cataloging-in-Publication Data

Wheeler, Richard S.
    Flint's honor / Richard S. Wheeler.
      p. cm.
    ISBN 0-7838-9503-8 (lg. print : hc : alk. paper)
  1. Flint, Sam (Fictitious character) — Fiction. 2. Newspaper editors — Fiction. 3. Arizona — Fiction. 4. Large type books.
  I. Title.
  PS3573.H4345 F58 2001
  813'.54—dc21   2001024482

Try not to become a man of success, but rather try to become a man of value.
— Albert Einstein

1

Sam Flint knew he was making the dumbest move of his life. He had argued with himself for weeks, trying to talk himself out of going to Silver City. The place already had a newspaper and didn't need another. It was a county seat, but he would get none of the legal advertising, the lifeblood of any small weekly. He'd go broke in a hurry.

But he was drawn to Silver City, a boom camp in the newly minted state of Colorado, by a hunger he couldn't resist. His entire motive was to free the mining town from a scoundrel named Digby Westminster, editor of *The Silver City Democrat*. Flint had been studying that repulsive paper for six months, waxing indignant at Westminster's arrogance and cruelty.

Flint knew exactly what sort of mortal inhabited the editorial sanctum of *The Democrat*. The man would be a cunning political manipulator and familiar with the jug, pulp-nosed, the veinous insignia of his boozing all over his puss. He would be barrel-shaped, coarse, grossly dishonest, and possessed of a low and snakelike view of the world. Flint was sure that Westminster would be mean. What manner of man would make a woman's tragic suicide an occasion for editorial wit? What manner of editor loaded his columns with endless flattery of the merchants who advertised on his pages, lauded his pitiless pit bull sheriff and courthouse cabal, and oozed contempt for those whose stations were humble?

Flint was angry. Someone in the newspaper fraternity must rescue Silver City. And Flint, war veteran and tramp editor, appointed himself to perform the thankless task.

He discovered the power of words back in the war, when he began writing a column called "View from the Trenches" for James Gordon Bennett's famous *New York Herald*. A foot soldier's view of the stupidities and blunders of the men who led armies, it had sometimes made life a little easier for the men around him, winning a few comforts as humble as gloves and soap and vegetables and hospital cots and even blankets that didn't unravel in two weeks. By the time he was mustered out, he had become a crusader and dreamer.

All very idealistic, he thought, but it didn't make any financial sense. He pulled aside on the muddy trace to let some big Murphy freight wagons pass. He needed to rest his mules, Grant and Sherman, a giant pair crossed on Percheron mares. His weary plugs faced a ten-mile grade ahead. Eventually they would drag Flint's wagon, with its small rotary flatbed press, California case boxes filled with fonts, other printing paraphernalia, and his personal things, into the fevered gulch in the San Juan mountains where an incredible bonanza of silver glance, a sulphide ore combined with galena, had been discovered three years earlier.

Sam Flint preferred to start weekly papers in places that had none, but this time he itched to do the world a favor. It appalled him that journalism contained more than a few Digby Westminsters, men who had crawled out from under some rock to represent the alleged conscience of their victimized community. Flint laughed at himself. There were more than a few who considered Flint himself a species akin to Digby Westminster. Many a frontier town considered high-minded editors the brethren of rattlesnakes.

Maybe Silver City would be like that. There was something to be said for a town getting the newspaper it deserved. If this brawling place enjoyed Westminster's condescending jokes about pathetic women, or his ridicule of working men, then Flint would not survive long. But he was used to that. He'd started up weeklies in seven or eight places in a dozen years, never putting down roots. He rarely lasted long. Sometimes it was because the town defeated him. Once in a while he got bored after transforming a cowtown into something almost civilized. More often it was because he grew restless, the itch upon him again to move along, and then he would sell out if he could — or shut down if he couldn't — pack up his wagon, and hit the road.

The big, lean editor gave the mules twenty minutes and then slapped his lines over their croups. They lowered into their harnesses and tugged the creaking wagon forward, their tails mowing down flies and their long mule ears rotating this way and that. With each mile the mountains grew. To a son of Cincinnati, the western mountains were always a source of awe and visual delight. These had arid, brown lower reaches, but dense green timber, often appearing black from a distance, crowded their upper slopes almost to the rocky escarpments that formed their rugged peaks streaked with the first snows of fall.

He had never been to western Colorado, and he found its southern precincts almost as arid and rough as New Mexico, and with the same grand vistas. A traveler could see into tomorrow and drive into the week ahead, always with the same vast landscape in view. But as much as Flint loved the sight of noble distant ranges, he didn't much care to live in the mountains, hemmed in by steep walls of rock. The trace followed a murky creek that exuded sharp odors and carried green scum along its surface. He didn't doubt that this was the cloaca of Silver City, carrying out of town the sewage of four thousand people.

The gulch's yellow walls catapulted upward hundreds of feet and grew ever closer together, like a giant vise clamping life between its jaws. In places the trace narrowed to the point where opposing traffic could not pass, and more than once Flint stopped to let travelers by: a Concord stagecoach drawn by three spans of mustangs, Pittsburgh wagons drawn by six yoke of slavering oxen, ore wagons tugged by pairs of mules, a one-horse spring wagon. He didn't mind; he was in no hurry, and the stops gave him a chance to study the men of the silver camp.

When he reached Silver City itself, the gulch narrowed into a shadowed canyon immersed in gloom. He judged that the sun had vanished behind the slopes at about three o'clock on this autumn day, and he doubted that Silver City would see sunlight again before nine the next morning. The town announced itself simply, with clapboard residences that crawled up the slopes from the road, often on stilts, one house almost atop another. Small steep alleys gave foot passage upward. It seemed wondrous to Flint that people actually lived in homes where front ends stood on ten-foot poles, and from which one could look straight down on a neighbor's shake roof. He spotted more than one double-decked outhouse, and one triple-decker serving three cottages that clawed their way up a fierce and intractable slope. Obviously, level land was at a premium in Silver City.

This savage, raw gulch was a far cry from green and hilly Cincinnati, where he had grown up on the banks of the Ohio River. A head-master's son, pale and brown-haired and serious, he had been bent on becoming a classics scholar. But the savagery of war had changed that, annealing his spirit and forging a man's soul. He had been discharged not into a peace but into a restlessness that ran through his flesh like a perpetual itch, a hornet swarm that drove him west into the unknown. Now some sort of merciless flame burned in him, driving him to remake a world he found wanting.

Traffic on the jammed road stopped him frequently. Everything from pedestrians to freight wagons crawled in both directions, and men bawled at each other or laughed or sat patiently. It seemed odd and disturbing to Flint that in the space of a few miles he could travel from vast hundred-mile views of mountain wilderness to a city so compressed and dense that passage was acutely difficult. He did not think much of this place and pondered a hasty exit.

But the loathsome image of that vile newspaper drew him onward. Somewhere in this warren, a cruel wordsmith put together his weekly rag. So Flint plugged on, up the gulch that twisted into the mountain like a snake. He saw no side streets, nor could there be any. All the life of Silver City existed in this chasm.

He passed a few neighborhood groceries, numerous small corner saloons with names like Miner's Rest and the Silver Dollar, a smithy, and even a livery stable jammed into a side coulee — every precious inch of usable land claimed and jealously defended. A mile or so later, still traveling beside the foul creek, he came to a widening, a few precious acres that bulged from the creek like a rabbit inside a snake's belly. This, it turned out, was the cramped business district, its every building cheek by jowl, often with common walls — perhaps to make fires as infectious as possible. Flint shuddered at the sort of holocaust that would inevitably happen here. There was no place to go.

But here, at least, were some short cross streets, and down one he spotted a sign announcing the *Silver City Democrat* in gilded letters on a green ground. Flint paused to study the red-brick building. It seemed to exude evil, a miasma worse even than that which rose off that infernal creek. Some cursing behind him announced that he had paused too long, so he hawed his nervous mules forward again, ever upslope, into an area crammed with three-story residences or apartments, their backs jammed against the vaulting bluff.

He would have a dickens of a time renting a shop or even living quarters; he had not seen a single For Rent sign. The hotels he'd passed advertised rooms at the rate of a dollar for eight hours. Every bed was apparently triple rented. He had yet to see a mine, or tailings on a slope, or a gallows frame announcing a shaft, but they had to be somewhere. Silver City had about a dozen fabled mines. He wondered whether tonight he'd be sleeping under his wagon, the mules' halter lines tied to his wrist to keep them from being stolen. He knew how to defend himself. Wrestling a cranky handpress for years had muscled him up. The drill sergeants in the Union Army had taught him a few things too.

He pushed grimly onward, rounding a bend that revealed the tawdry sporting district with its saloons and dance halls and gambling dens. Beyond that he discovered a Chinese quarter, an alley jammed with small wooden shacks and a joss house at the end of the narrow passage, against the bluff. Fronting the main road were Chinese laundries, white bundles on their shelves. Beyond that cramped precinct he came at last to the mining district, chock-full of head-frames and buildings, slack piles and tailings, all upslope from the road and in raw disarray. A stamp mill roared. He continued up the gulch through humble neighborhoods and emerged onto a mountain plateau where a sawmill steamed and whined and a road wound toward some distant ranches in the crannies of the towering San Juans.

That was the upper end of Silver City. He had seen nothing for rent, nothing empty. He turned the mules around and retraced his way into town, following a heavy wagon carrying timbers for the mines. He passed the mysterious Chinese quarter again and plunged into the sporting district. He studied a few dark saloons dug into the cliff, their snouts on the road: a dance hall called The Silver Belle and a gambling joint called The Bankers Club, both gaudy and gilded. Unlike the rest of the hurly-burly town, the area dozed

14

in midafternoon slumber, with scarcely a person in sight.

And there, much to his astonishment, he discovered a sign on a weary wooden building: ROOMS TO LET. He pulled the mules to the side and studied the layout. Through the naked window on the left side he could see a small flat consisting of a front room and a rear one, with possibly a kitchen beyond that. A brutally tight fit for a press and composing room and office, but he could manage. It was on the edge of the sporting district, which didn't suit him, but he had little choice. He clambered down and knocked on the other door, hoping the price wouldn't be too high.

2

Flint knocked on the adjoining door and found himself being surveyed by a sleepy blonde in a slinky black silk kimono, embroidered with dragons.

"You're early," she said, "but I'm always open."

"Uh, I think I've made a mistake," he said.

"Oh, come on in, sweetheart. I was just making breakfast. How about a cup of coffee first?"

"I was going to ask about that apartment next door."

She studied him. "You don't look like a pimp," she said. "Are you in the business?"

"No, I'm a newspaper editor."

She squinted ferociously. "We don't want those around here," she said. "Nothing but grief." She possessed a rowdy beauty, with unruly blond hair that had seen neither comb nor brush this afternoon, and a pouty, sensual face with bright, intelligent eyes.

"Well, I'll be getting along," he said.

"You new in town?"

"Just arrived."

"You want to find a place, is that it?"

"Yes. But not here."

"Well, you come on in and have a cup of java. I'll tell ya all about this lousy burg."

"That's all right. I'd better be going, Miss —"

"Chastity. That's my real name. Chastity Ford."

He grinned.

"It really is. I got two sisters, Forgiveness and Obedience. Only with me there was a little falling out over family philosophy. I'm in favor of virtue except when it gets in the way, so I took off. My name doubles my trade so I use it. You come in now."

"I'd better not."

"What's the matter. You some puritan?"

"This is simply business," he said amiably. "Nothing personal. Perhaps I'd better keep looking."

"Well, you're a case." She tugged his arm, and he surrendered. She led him through a gaudy parlor with green flocked wallpaper, a handsome wainscotted bedroom with a massive oak bed, and into a small rear kitchen, where she sat him down at a prim table and poured some coffee from a speckled blue enameled pot on the range.

Flint accepted gratefully, feeling travel-worn. It would be all right — not a soul knew him here. It wouldn't do, however, for an editor to be seen in the lair of an obviously expensive lady of the night.

"I hate newspapers," she said. "What's your name?"

"Sam Flint. I publish weeklies."

"We've got the biggest ass of an editor in the whole universe here, Digby Westminster."

Suddenly Flint was interested. "Why do you say that?"

"He's a hypocrite. He sneaks over here, but he's always making snide remarks in his rag. He despises the female sex. He's as kind as a rattler."

"I rather had that impression."

"You want to start up some opposition, is that it?"

Flint nodded. He sipped some excellent coffee and admired the curves under her silky kimono.

"We sure need it," she said. "Drive him out. String him up. He deserves a good, slow hanging."

"You know some district where a man could set up shop? Place to rent? Proper neighborhood?"

"Right here. This is the only place in town."

"I can't publish here."

"Then you can't publish anywhere. This gulch is so crammed full of people there's not room enough to squat. A vacancy doesn't last five minutes. People sign up months in advance for a place."

"What about that business area where the gulch widens? It's full of stores. Sometimes a merchant'll rent the rear part of a store."

"That's the courthouse."

"I didn't see any courthouse."

18

"It's there. Up against the bluff. They get rattlesnakes in there — probably because they're kindred souls. Hey, Flint, you can rent, you can build, or you can buy. Sometimes you can build by digging into the cliffs behind someone's place — if they let you. If you're gonna buy, you'd better have a pile of cash. This place is tighter than a banker's purse."

"I can't buy and can't build."

"Then you're stuck with me, sweetheart. But I'm not sure I'll rent. If you're another Digby Westminster, you can just pack up and vamoose."

"I can't set up shop here."

She grinned. "You go try somewhere else. I'll keep that flat open for one day. It's two hundred a month, but for you it's one-eighty. I think I like you."

"What? That's triple what I was hoping to pay."

She grinned and sipped. "People here make lots of boodle so I charge a lot. More java? I need a dose of coffee in the morning," she said. "It makes me wiggly."

"It's four in the afternoon."

"Morning for me, sweetheart. Look, I know everything there is to know about this burg. I'll share it all with you if you promise to be on our side."

"I'm an independent editor, Miss Ford. I run my news as neutrally as I can. I write editorials for or against things."

19

"Well, that's an improvement over Digby Westminster."

"Why do you want me here?"

"We need you. The town needs you. If I turn you loose, you'll drive up and down the gulch, try every place around the courthouse, and give up. There's no place for you, unless you want to build some shack way up above, in the mountain, or down below. Even if you find something down the gulch it'd cost you a hundred, maybe more."

"I'd like to look. This isn't a proper spot for a paper."

"Are you some prude? I bet if I offered you a free one you'd turn me down."

"I'm a man trying to start a reputable business."

She grinned. "I tell you what. I'm crazy, but I'll give you that flat for a hundred and a half."

"Are there strings?"

"Yeah. No anti-vice crusades. I've got a right to my living. I charge twenty a piece — that's the highest in Colorado, and I'm worth it. Most girls get fifty cents. Just think about it. These are three-dollar-a-day miners walking past here, and I ask twenty and get it. I'm gonna retire soon. I don't want to move; I don't want to be booted out or licensed or taxed to death. I've got the only rental in town, and if you rent, it's on my terms."

Flint sighed, suspecting she had painted a picture of ironclad reality. "Maybe I could have a look at the flat," he said. "But I'll want a day to look around. You know what this address'll do to my credibility."

"What's credibility?"

"A paper — well, it's got to publish in a way . . ." He gave up. "This address would turn my weekly into a joke," he said.

She grinned, so winsomely that he laughed. He couldn't help liking her.

"All you gotta do is put a post office–box address on the paper," she said.

It was a naive idea, but he nodded. "I'm going to look around for a day. If I can't find something in the business district, maybe I'll take you up."

"You won't find a thing," she said. "Where you gonna stay tonight? Everything's triple rented, the rooming houses and hotels."

"Well, that's a good question. I need to find a livery barn for my mules and wagon."

She snorted and slid into a knowing chortle. "Two dollars a night per animal, five for the wagon. There's no space, and every bit of hay and oats is brought into the gulch."

Dismay slid through Flint. "I need permanent pasture. . . ."

"That's easier. Up above, the town sort of peters out and you get into a hanging valley. You can rent pasture up there, not too bad. A rancher keeps a lot of the town horses."

"I've never been in a gulch this cramped."

"We call it Virgin Gulch, sweetheart."

Flint sighed.

21

"Are you all right?" she said, full of concern.

"I grew up in a different world," he muttered.

She laughed gaily. "So did I," she said. "Look, Sam, just relax. You come from back East somewhere. I can tell. This isn't the East. Life isn't serious here. We mostly live and let live. I mean, you're in the middle of the district, but no one'll care, know what I mean? It's the frontier. It's like there aren't any rules. If I weren't having fun, I wouldn't be in the business. God knows, I get a marriage proposal about twice a day. I could be married and on the evening stage to Durango if I wanted. What you need to do is just quit worrying. This burg needs a new rag. So what does it matter where you operate from? You could set type in my bed and no one would care." She laughed deliciously.

He subdued all the reservations rising from his soul and went along with her. "Maybe I will," he said. "What should I write about?"

"Write about the pirate that runs the biggest mines — Achilles Balthazar. He's worse than the devil. He's worse than a crook. He bleeds the miners. He cheats. He's mean to his family. Write about him and about Digby Westminster."

"Are the two connected?"

"Nope. Digby Westminster's in with the courthouse crowd. He tells the public who to vote for, and all the clerks and the judge pay him back. Westminster's in with the merchants. That's how he gets his advertising. But he

22

attacks the mine owners, especially Balthazar."
She stared at Flint as though he were dumb not
to understand.

Flint needed to get on with his search, and to
take care of his mules. "Thanks for the coffee,
Miss Ford," he said. "I'll let you know tomorrow
morning."

"Make it after three," she replied. "I'm a busi-
nesswoman."

He left, wondering about her. Was she as
happy as she seemed? It didn't seem possible.

3

Flint took reluctant leave of the engaging vamp and drove up above the mines, through a district jammed with miners' cabins. It looked like a bachelor town with its grimy windows, unpainted wood, tin roofs, and cockeyed stovepipes leaking suffocating woodsmoke. A queued Chinaman was selling drinking water from a handcart. Flint's big off-side mule, Sherman, was limping slightly, and Flint discovered a stone bruise in the left forefoot. It was time to find a place for his critters to rest. He spotted a livery barn jammed into a side gulch, and he boarded the mules for the night at the awesome price of two dollars a head, though it was only a dollar to park his wagon. A grinning, gold-toothed hostler took his cash and swore that he knew every thought that passed between a mule's big ears and that he would keep them happy. For an extra four bits he would curry the pair, but Flint declined.

Flint hiked downhill to the center of town, passing Chastity's place and vowing not to operate his newspaper from such tawdry precincts. He'd abandon the project before succumbing to that. He had standards and he'd abide by them, even though — he confessed to himself — Chastity had been an engaging diversion, not to mention a tempting one. He hadn't asked her about the upstairs flats, but he supposed they were rented to independent tramps like herself. All the worse for a newsman who cared about his reputation.

There were always ways. A favorite was to approach a merchant who had space and ask him to partition off the rear of his emporium for a printing shop and rent it to Flint. That would get him quarters, even in a jammed gulch. But when he reached the business district, he was smitten with doubt. The buildings crowded the two short sidestreets that stretched in either direction from the main artery. Many had been carved into the rocky cliff, so their rears were standing in an excavation. Others perched on stilts, which required customers to negotiate a long stairway. He saw no vacancies in this booming little precinct, and no real estate agents.

He discovered scores of shops, and he knew they'd all need advertising. Heartened by that, he tried a hardware store first, passing through its double doors into a gloomy warren of stovepipes, kegs of nails, wagon and carriage furniture, horse tack, saws and planes and augers, sheet metal, coal oil lanterns, ice chests, soldered kitchenware, knives, razors and shaving mugs. The place bulged with merchandise; even without a railroad, supplies weren't lacking in Silver City.

A bald man with a prominent Adam's apple and wearing a grimy white apron approached Flint. "You look lost," he said. "My name's Bill Hope, and that's what I offer. You probably need something I won't have to order. I have everything."

"Looking for space," said Flint. "I'm a newspaper editor, trying to start up a weekly. I'm looking for some floor space to rent. Maybe something to partition off."

Hope's eyebrows knitted, and he studied Flint suspiciously. "We've got a mighty fine paper, Flint, the *Silver City Democrat*. I'd say it's the finest little weekly this side of the Mississippi."

"Well, I'm going to start another."

"It don't make a lick of sense. You'll just go belly-up."

"There's merchants enough to support three papers. I don't even see cards — you know, the small boxed ads — in the *Democrat*."

Hope wove from one big foot to the other, squinted, hawked up some brown chewing tobacco, fired it at a cuspidor, and grumbled softly. "I don't have space. I'll guarantee there's not another merchant in Silver City's got space. That's the one thing we don't have and can't order, because Mother Nature decreed that this city would be three miles long and two yards wide. I'm so crowded I have to use this here hook to take things down from the walls." He stared at Flint suspiciously. "Do you favor the merchants?"

"I support honest commerce and competition."

Hope didn't like that. "Mr. Digby Westminster's as much of a sage as ever put together a thundersheet. He never misses putting in some good words about the merchants. Why, every time I advertise I get a free story out of it, pushing my new pocketwatches or pie safes. And let me tell you, Flint, he favors the merchants. He makes sure we don't get taxed. Town supports itself by licensing the sporting houses and saloons. That's proper justice, I say, taxing the scum. He's got a yard to say about the mine owners, none of it charitable. And he don't think much of the lazy miners, either. He supports the county officials and the merchants, and that's how it should be. I reckon you won't sell five cents of advertising if you don't agree."

Flint excused himself and stepped into the late afternoon of an autumnal day. The whole district hummed. The narrow street bustled with wagons and horses and profane teamsters while pedestrians, mostly male, darted from store to store. He found himself confronting a dirty, bearded man leaning heavily into crutches and clutching an upturned hat.

"Can you spare a dime?" the man asked.

Flint dug into his trousers and found a wad of shinplasters — paper coinage — and extracted two bits. These he dropped into the hat. The man grunted something that was supposed to be a thank-you, but it seemed too bitter. Flint surveyed him. He was young, unkempt, with a desperate look in his gray eyes and two wasted legs. The man's eyes darted everywhere, as if watching out for something. Flint suspected that the town constables drove beggars from this business area.

"Well, good luck," Flint said.

The man nodded, his gaze on other potential donors. "You're staring at me. You all do," the man growled. "All right. You all want to know how my life ended? It was the Silver Queen, Balthazar's richest mine. A timber fell on me, crushed both legs. That was that. Now are you satisfied?"

Flint recoiled. He had been curious but didn't mean to pry. "No help from the mine? No infirmary? No pension?"

The crippled man glared at Flint. "Jesus, you're pilgrim," he said, and spat. "Wise up."

Flint felt the glare strike him like a brickbat. He nodded and retreated. Life was brutal, especially in mining towns. Injuries were common; disease rampant, especially miner's lung and consumption; mortality common. Miners often died in their thirties, spending a brief life scarcely seeing the sun. No one was spared. Maybe he could do something about it. If the mine owner Balthazar oppressed his employees, then Flint would push for reforms.

He studied a larger emporium up the street, this one an apothecary shop on one side and a dramshop on the other, both announced by a gilded sign. A long, scarred mahogany bar with a scuffed brass footrail lined the dramshop side. An odd place — there might be enough room for a newspaper if the drugstore were cut in half. He corraled the beefy bartender who was alternately rinsing glasses in gray water and slapping at green-bellied flies with an ornate device that looked like a small rug-beater.

"I'd like to talk to the owner here."

"He lives in Central City, bub. Talk to me."

"I'm looking for business space. I could use that whole apothecary place."

"Forget it. That mints money. Only one in midtown."

"But it could operate in half the space. Those carboys and canisters and bottles don't amount to much. A few shelves —"

"Forget it. What do you want to put in there?"

"Weekly newspaper."

"We got one. It's a ripsnorter."

"I know. This is a big town, and there's room for more."

"You'd go broke, pal. This editor, Digby Westminster, he's got this whole burg locked up. He squeezes ads out of cigar-store Indians. Everyone likes what he says too. He really sticks it to 'em. We don't pay a dime in taxes here, y'know. He's got the sluts and tinhorns paying the freight."

"If I started my weekly, would you advertise in it?"

The barkeep paused, settled some glasses on his backbar, and stared. "I didn't get your handle," he said.

"Sam Flint. I'm an editor. I've got a printing outfit."

The bartender gazed into the busy street. "Best you could do is start a job-printing place. Everyone needs posters and menus and like that. But you'd just go bust if you took on the *Democrat*."

"So I gather." Flint decided on a calculated risk. "I don't much like what the man says, though. He picks on the poor, touts the county officials as if they could do no wrong, and has nothing good to say about anyone else."

The barkeep grinned. "In that case, Flint, you'd best forget about the job-printing shop."

"Well, I'm for fairer taxation. I bet you pay a stiff license to keep this saloon going."

"I do. You have a point, Flint, but not enough of a point. Westminster's doing a good job protecting the merchants. And we've got some friendly law enforcement, thanks to the *Democrat*." The man wiped his paws on his apron and turned to pour a Pink's ginger beer for a potbellied customer.

Flint didn't tarry. These stores would all be shuttered by six-thirty or seven. He hurried into a grocery and found it jammed, tried a yardgoods store and found it tiny, wandered into

30

an ice cream parlor and found it crowded, and peered into the streaked window of a cramped law office. He studied a second-floor millinery store, noted that a tailor worked in a half-basement hovel beside a cobbler, and that the ready-made men's clothing store had goods stacked to the pressed-tin ceiling.

No merchant with so little space was going to surrender a large quantity of it, even for a stiff rent. He sighed in the October twilight, pausing before his rival's darkened plant and peering through cut-glass doors into the gloom. Westminster had spent a pretty penny fixing it up. Beyond a fancy wallpapered foyer and front office, Flint could see the composing room. He spotted a composing bench, a good-sized Hoe Patent Number 3 press, two sets of case boxes to hold the fonts, a folder, a proofing table, some stones — the trucks on casters to carry forms — a big stencil machine for addressing copies, and a paper cutter. It was a modern plant with better equipment than his own, Flint thought. Digby Westminster was affluent and a force in the town's affairs.

Flint examined a few more stores, finding them all cramped. He talked to a blacksmith, a tonsorial artist, a fire-insurance salesman, a coal and ice dealer, and a housing contractor. None had room, and all applauded *The Democrat*. Most candidly approved of the iron triangle that ruled San Juan County: the paper, the merchants, and the courthouse gang, especially Sheriff Poindexter, who busted up labor strife and favored the merchants.

Flint began to get a sense of who in Silver City had power and who didn't. Oddly, the mining magnates didn't have much control of county affairs. Neither did the miners. The spider in the center of the web was Digby Westminster.

It all discouraged Flint. Miners didn't advertise. The politicians wouldn't. The mine managers didn't need to. The merchants all flocked to *The Democrat*. That left maybe a few tobacconists and restaurants, and he'd sell some cards on the rear page to small-time entrepreneurs, such as milliners, tailors, and dressmakers. Perhaps he could talk the banks into a few ads, or even a rival politician or two.

He wondered whether to quit the town. He found a smoky cafe, the Bottomless Pit, featuring a fixed-price four-bit dinner, and tackled some surprisingly good beef and spuds, all in a tangy gravy. The place was under the thumb of a dour, fat woman, who cooked while her husband served. Their clientele seemed to be bachelor miners, many still grimy from the pits and most dressed in canvas jumpers. They ate swiftly, didn't look happy, and seemed to have lost track of the future. In fact, most looked as though they had never dreamed of a better life.

He realized he was without a place to stay and that the hotels would be jammed. That was how it was. He walked wearily to the livery barn — the refuge of the roomless — knowing he could stretch his bedroll there. He decided to give

Silver City one more day: In the morning he would try to buy or rent at every private house that fronted the gulch road. He'd run a weekly paper from a few front parlors before, and maybe he'd be doing it in Silver City.

4

The next morning Flint hunted through the other districts along the gulch. Whenever he came to a likely cabin or frame house on a level with the artery he learned was Silver Street, he knocked, asked, and offered rent. Nothing came of it. Some of those little cottages were home to eight or ten miners. One gabby fellow sounded like he might rent, but when he learned Flint intended to compete with *The Democrat*, he backed off, announcing to Flint that it was a fool's enterprise.

From almost anywhere on cramped Silver Street, Flint could gaze upward upon virgin wilderness stretching toward the heavens, utterly uninhabited for scores of miles in any direction. Simply by scaling the steep bluffs, a person could plunge into a world of heady beauty, gaze at the towering slopes of the snowcapped San Juans, and see no sign of the bustling city at his feet.

By the time he was ready to tackle lunch, Flint knew he wouldn't be publishing in Silver City, and the despicable Digby Westminster would reign supreme. He briefly considered offering to throw in with the man and begin to reform *The*

Democrat from within, but the thought repelled him. Rattlers didn't reform.

Disconsolately he checked a few more shops that were distant from the business area. Finding them just as cramped as the rest, he headed up the gulch through a jam of wagons, resigned horses, and hurrying pedestrians. Silver City had defeated him. That was just as well: He shouldn't have come in the first place on such a quixotic mission. He would head for a town with no paper, where he could make a living. He stoked up on a bowl of chili at Ma's Eats, which catered to nightshift miners, and hiked through fall sunshine to the somnolent sporting district. He had time to tell Chastity and get out before he faced another awesome board bill for Grant and Sherman and the wagon.

Her place was only two blocks from the mines, and as he approached he could hear the rattle of ore crashing down the chutes, the hiss of steam escaping boilers, and the thunder of the half-ton stamps pulverizing ore in the mill. He climbed her two enameled steps and knocked, knowing he was early and he'd wake her. She answered, studied him quietly for a moment through squinting eyes not yet accustomed to light, and finally nodded. She looked sweet and innocent and somehow tender with her blond hair in wild disarray. It was as if he was seeing her without the paint that armored her against a hard world.

"You're the printer. I forget your name," she said.

"Flint. I've decided not to take you up on the rent. Just wanted to let you know."

"I need some Arbuckle's," she said. "You'd better wait until I brew some and then tell me."

"Nothing to tell. I'm not staying."

She yawned. Then, to his astonishment, she slid her arms around him and hugged a moment. "Come on in. I'm charging you too much rent. Let's talk."

It was a million-dollar hug, and he didn't have anything better to do, so he followed her through her rumpled, fussy flat to the kitchen. He watched her jam some kindling and an issue of *The Democrat* into the range, light it with a lucifer, draw some water from a pail with a dipper, set it to boiling, grind some roasted coffee in a hand mill, and throw it into the blue enameled pot.

"Humff," she said, adjusting her kimono over her curvy figure. The sunlight that caught in her hair dazzled him. "Don't ever use water from the creek," she said. "Buy it from the water wagon or the Chinamen."

He nodded. "I couldn't find a place," he said.

"I told you so."

"As I told you, I can't run a paper from here."

"Even for a hundred a month?"

"It's not the money, it's the place, the sporting district."

"So?"

"It wouldn't look good."

"Humff," she said. They sat silently while the water heated. Finally it boiled, and the lusty aroma of coffee tantalized him. She extracted two china cups and saucers from a shelf and poured. They sat silently again while they waited for the coffee to cool. "I never get up this early," she muttered. "It softens the brain. That's what they say to boys who abuse themselves. It softens the brain. Most men are soft-brained." She grinned winsomely.

"I think I'd better go," he said, slurping up coffee.

"What did you want to pay for a place?"

"Seventy-five maximum. Preferably less."

"I can't do that, but I'll do a hundred."

"Why, Miss Ford?"

She shrugged. "We're all afraid of that Digby Westminster. Everyone in the sporting district. We need you."

"You might end up more afraid of me."

She shook her head. "No, I know what kind you are. You might not like us, but you know we've got a rough life. There are two girls upstairs. Sarah, she ran away from her husband. He beat her, cut her, almost killed her. Marcella, she was orphaned at fourteen and almost starved to death. Westminster thinks it's all funny and we all deserve what we get. One girl next door, she died from drinking turpentine. Her pa had tracked her down and wrote her he was coming to put her in jail for taking his comb and hairbrush when she ran away. Westminster thought the death was pretty funny. He made jokes in the paper about new uses for turpentine. Called her a frail, and said the town was rid of a pest and maybe the sheriff should hand out a lot more turpentine."

"Do you employ the girls upstairs?"

"Naw, I just rent flats. They're on their own. This is the best place to come to. Men know that. I only rent to nice girls."

Flint nodded. He knew that very few unfortunate women chose the profession. He felt sympathy for the dead girls, but it didn't change his mind. He wouldn't publish from here.

She sipped. "Know something, Flint? I know more about what's happening in Silver City than anyone else in town. A lady in my business learns everything. Men simply babble when they're naked. If you stay here you'll have three reporters. You'll be so accurate and break so many stories you'll put Westminster out to pasture. That idiot! I've seen him. He sneaks over here some nights to Marcella. I wouldn't let him into my sack. A lady's got to draw the line somewhere." She sipped and smiled. She was dazzling when she smiled. Her kimono slid open a bit, and she absently tightened it against Flint's wandering gaze.

He shook his head.

"Flint, do I hafta spell it out? Just put a thing in your paper that says you're publishing from upper Silver Street because it's the only quarters available, and that people shouldn't, you know, draw conclusions, and that you're not anyone's mouthpiece."

"A disclaimer," he said, his mind suddenly alert to possibility: acknowledge the unusual address in the first issue, and explain that the paper was independent and would move to a better tenancy as soon as possible. He smiled. "It might work," he confessed.

"I thought it up before I even had a cup of coffee," she said, rising to fill his cup. "That shows I was straining my brain. I'm sort of a loner, but I sort of know people. I sort of know you."

"I suppose people are going to wander into my sanctum and ask where the girls are?" he said.

"What's a sanctum?"

"The place where the editor writes and thinks. It's an old newspaper term."

"I sit on my sanctum," she said.

He sighed. "You're going to be an unusual landlady," he replied. "I'll try it for a hundred a month. I'll probably go broke anyway — Westminster's got the advertising locked tighter than I've ever seen."

"I know some bankers," she said. "I'll make them advertise. They've got wives."

"No, Miss Ford, no! I won't have that."

"Well, I'll just lick their ear and put in a word."

"I don't want you to do anything of the sort! The day I hear that you're blackmailing your clients on my account, that's the day I'll pack up."

She grinned cheerfully. "All right. I'm awake. It always takes two cups. Let's go look at what you've got."

A dark hall with a stairwell divided the two flats. She led him across it, unlocked the door to the other flat, and ushered him in. He peered around a barren and chill parlor with a bay window, a bedroom that would barely hold his press, and a small kitchen with a cooking range, a few shelves, and a battered table with two chairs. The place would work. He would need to put a cot in the kitchen. The front parlor and bedroom would be jammed with equipment and composing benches. He didn't know where he could put a desk.

"Just a minute," he said. "Have you a tape measure or a ruler?"

She fetched a tape from her sewing basket, and he measured the front door, frowning.

"My flatbed press won't go through here. It's an inch wider."

She pouted, then brightened. "Chop it open," she said. "I'll get a carpenter. I know one who'll come running." She laughed wickedly.

He liked her derring-do but declined.

"Well, can't you pull off some moulding?"

He measured again. With the moulding off, the door off its hinges, four gorillas could wedge the Cleveland flatbed press through with a half inch to spare. He grinned. "I thought I'd escaped you for a moment."

"I thought you had too, Flint. I want you captive. I always wanted my own big galoot of an editor." She smirked. "I'll line up some bartenders and bouncers and general-purpose thugs whenever you're ready. There're twenty of them within fifty yards. You can tip them; that's all you'll need to do. They'll load this room with your stuff faster than, ah — you just leave it to me, kid. You'll like the sporting district. We're all friendly."

Alarm bells were ringing in Flint's skull. "Miss Ford, I can't promise I'll take your side. I think saloons and sporting houses should be licensed. I'll be frank: Vice doesn't help a town, and some of these people are dangerous."

She shrugged. "It beats Westminster. He thinks we should all croak." Her face darkened. "I'll feel safer with you here."

5

After a miserable afternoon toting gear, Flint found himself ensconced in the tiny flat and ready to begin business. His flatbed press — dragooned up two stairs and squeezed through the surgically enlarged door by five cheerful, mustachioed saloonmen built like bears — stood nobly in the bedroom. It occupied the exact spot where the previous tenant had made her living with her own version of a flatbed press. His composing bench and California type cases, along with a desk, occupied the parlor.

Following Chastity's advice, he drove up the gulch a mile beyond town, found a rancher named Austin Bean who would pasture Grant and Sherman and store the wagon, and hiked back past the mines, which he had scarcely studied earlier. They crowded the north side of the gulch, their buildings perched precariously halfway up the grade, and their piles of waste rock and tailings threatening to engulf the road below. Flint didn't doubt that within a year or two the slackpiles would overwhelm the Chinese quarter, and eventually the mountain of waste rock would threaten the sporting district and Chastity's four-flat building.

He could now name the major mines, after hours of banter with the saloonmen and sports. The glory of Silver City was the Silver Queen, a fabulous mine farthest upslope. Next was the Lucky Strike, almost as legendary, and then the Fickle Fiancee, the Toughnut, the Morning Glory, the Ace of Hearts, and the Shotgun. Three of them, the Silver Queen, Lucky Strike, and Toughnut, belonged to Achilles Balthazar, for whom the sports had no good words but a great many hostile ones. The Balthazar manse, a white palace, could be seen from the road, perched on a shoulder overlooking the gulch, where twenty laborers working with fresnos had leveled a spot for it.

When he returned, he found Chastity sitting on a stool in his sanctum. Her invasion seemed a little audacious, even for a landlady, but maybe a lack of privacy came with running a newspaper from a bawdy house. She wore her black kimono embroidered with the dragons and not much underneath, along with some slippers. She had either taken an eggbeater to her blond hair, or she was still in her wake-up dishabille.

"I bet you're tuckered out," she said. "If you want to come next door, I'll fix you up."

He grinned. "Miss Ford, our relationship is going to be strictly business," he said, while enjoying her sultry sociability. Something in her bright, wide gaze suggested intelligence, even if it had never been disciplined by schooling.

"Well, that's good," she said. "Any time, day

or night, that's what I always say. Are you gonna make a paper now?"

"No, I always begin with a flyer. It'll give my advertising rates and tell about the paper."

"Whatcha gonna call it?"

"I haven't even given it a thought."

"You mean you don't even have a name for your paper? I'll help you, sweetheart. You could call it *The Silver City Sport.*"

"No, thanks."

"How about *The Silver City Lark*?"

He shook his head.

"Well, I'm fresh out of ideas."

"I guess maybe I'll call it *The Silver City Sentinel*. How does that sound?"

She shrugged. "Too pompous," she said. "You should have a name that'll make people smile."

"A paper's a serious thing. I'm going to start the flyer now. You can watch if you want."

He donned his grimy apron, found his type stick and a galley tray, opened up the case boxes, and began setting the disclaimer. He was going to put it on both the front and back pages, just to make sure people understood.

Chastity watched as he whipped letters from their niches and slid them onto his stick, working upside-down. When he had completed a line he added the leading — typemetal spacers — and slid the stick of type onto the galley tray.

"What's all that lead in there for?" she asked.

"To make the line come out an even width, a

column width. It's called justifying."

"I can get you some ads," she said. "I'll make every saloon in the district buy an ad."

"Ah, that won't be necessary. I'll solicit them. There may be some places I'd rather not sell space to."

"I'll buy an ad."

"Ah, Chastity, I'd rather not, but thank you."

"I think I should. I've never tried an ad before. 'Your Happiness Guaranteed or Come Again.' How about that?"

"Chastity —"

"I know, I know. You're a worse prig than Digby Westminster."

That offended Flint. He dug into his work and ignored her, composing as he set type: "*The Sentinel* is an independent paper temporarily lodged on upper Silver Street. No inference should be made concerning *The Sentinel*'s views, politics, or the habits of its staff because of its temporary address forced upon it by necessity. Samuel Flint, editor and proprietor."

"What does it say?" she asked, eyeing the growing number of backward lines in the galley tray.

"It says I'm not connected with the sporting life," he replied. "Frankly, I have my doubts about being here, Chastity. You may as well know that."

"Hey, you've been shouting it. You're about as friendly as a cigar-store Indian."

45

"I'm sorry. I'm tense. Everything inside of me is howling."

"That must be an experience. My insides don't howl that often, but when they do, watch out!"

He began work on the nameplate, drawing big sixty-point letters from his small supply of display type. Both the nameplate and the disclaimer would go on the flyer he'd distribute tomorrow. He filled another galley tray with the letters that read THE SILVER CITY SENTINEL. Then he added a ruler line and turned to his type stick again and his ten-point Caslon. He set his name and title, editor and proprietor; the place, Silver City, San Juan County, Colorado; then Volume One, Number One; and the date, November 14, 1878; and finally the price, Ten Cents. Beneath that he ran another ruler line and then centered his creation with wooden "furniture," the filler material that held the letters tight in the form.

"That's the whole top of the paper," she said. "I bet I could do that. I'll come over between business."

"Uh, thanks, but it takes a journeyman compositor or an apprentice. They're called printer's devils."

"Well, I'm a devil, so I may as well be a printer's devil."

"Chastity, for the sake of my business, I —" He couldn't continue. He wanted to ban her from the premises.

"You sure are a stiff one. I hope I didn't make

a mistake. Aren't you friendly? You don't like women, is that it?"

"Uh, Chastity, it's your profession. I enjoy women. I was engaged once, and I'd like to be again, only I'm wed to this work. It's a calling."

"You're sort of peculiar, aren't you?" she said, abandoning her stool. "Well, I'm gonna get you some ads before it gets dark around here and I have to go to work. What do you charge? Never mind. I'll sell the ads for twenty dollars."

Flint gaped. "But it depends on how much space they buy."

"You sure make things complicated. You can work all that out, but I'm gonna hit up everyone around here for twenty dollars."

"Uh, I'd prefer to get businesses —"

"Well, saloons are businesses aren't they?"

"I mean, I want the first issue to have advertising from all walks of life — merchants, land offices, banks, stagecoach lines, freight companies."

She sighed. "Flint, sometimes I think you're dumb. You won't get a single ad from those people. Digby Westminster has them all locked up. Don't you want to make money?"

"Enough to sustain me. There are other things more important."

She looked at him as if he were daft, and he laughed suddenly.

"What's so funny?" she asked.

"Newspaper editors are a strange breed," he said. "Sometimes money isn't the most impor-

47

tant thing. Sometimes we dream of a better world."

She eyed him skeptically. "I shouldn't rent to you. You'll go broke and owe me money."

He ignored her as if she were a buzzing wasp. He had work to do. He hoped that no one would walk in just then to find a soiled dove in his sanctum. Tongues would wag. He sighed — tongues would wag anyway.

He began working on his "Statement of Principles," which he always included in his flyer. "*The Sentinel*," he wrote as he slipped the tiny letters from the case boxes, capitals from the upper case, "would be an independent and non-partisan weekly devoted to evenhanded and fair taxation, the impartial administration of justice and law enforcement, free markets devoid of collusion or monopoly, the improvement of transportation, telegraph connections with the world, a proper school system, fair and honest elections, the encouragement of mining and commerce, the nurture of family and religious life, the encouragement of charities and hospitals, the development of sanitary measures (such as clean water piped in), to protect life and health, and the humane treatment of the oppressed and poor and those without voice in the community. *The Sentinel* intended to be a moral beacon that would shine light into dark corners and stir consciences and, withal, make Silver City a splendid place to live."

He rather liked that. With each paper, he was

getting better at these statements of principles.

"Let me read it," she said, eyeing the lengthening lines of type in the galley tray. He silently obliged her, running a chamois ink ball over the type and laying some galley paper over the inked metal. He pressed the paper into the type with a roller and handed the result to her.

"Oh!" she squealed. She studied it. "My God, Flint, are you a bishop or something?" Her face radiated alarm.

It puzzled him. "No. I write a statement of editorial principles for each of my papers."

"I don't think I'm gonna like Silver City when you get done," she said. "What a mistake. I shoulda kicked your ass out."

"Why?"

"Whenever I run into someone with fawncy ideals, I reach for my derringer," she said.

He absorbed that solemnly. "I think you'll find me an improvement over Digby Westminster," he said.

The front door opened, admitting twilight and a skinny man with a bulbous red nose, dressed in a funereal black suit and a silk stovepipe hat. The fellow looked straight out of a Nast cartoon.

"Oh my God," said Chastity. She whirled away, and Flint caught a glimpse of throbbing Chinese dragons on her rump as she vanished toward her half of the building.

"Ah, here you are," the man said in a clipped voice. "I'm Westminster, editor of the one and

49

only newspaper in Silver City. I got wind of you just an hour ago. You're the one who's starting *The Bawdyhouse Bugle*."

6

Digby Westminster salivated at the thought of a rival. He had heard of the pipsqueak yesterday, moments after the man had tried to rent space in the first few stores. This morning he had heard from half a dozen people who said the fellow had tried to rent their homes. This afternoon several of his bartender spies — who got a dollar a tip for juicy news — reported that the new entrepreneur was setting up shop in a bawdyhouse near the mines.

Ah, it was delectable. He would crush the bug, but he would take his time about it, just for fun. The sporting district — oh, that was elegant. Now the skulking pickpockets, doxies, tarts, perverts, tinhorns, barmen, and thugs would have a champion. Some red-nosed half-educated guttersnipe printer!

He donned his black cape and silk stovepipe hat, grabbed his gold-knobbed Malacca cane, and braved the wind that howled along the gulch, sending up dust devils of whirling filth. He didn't like to walk much; rheumatism made his bones ache, even though he was scarcely an old man. He had a woeful predisposition to pain. In fact he had wrestled with his own tall, gaunt body all his life, mainly fighting the ague, which leapt upon him from time to time with icy cold, then fever, then sweaty delirium unless he remembered to take copious amounts of sulfate of quinine as an anodyne. It was said the ague came from miasmas that rose from swamps, though he couldn't remember being in any swamp in his life. Pain and fever only inflamed his soul, and he operated his press as if driven by a pitchfork.

He found the place all right, smack dab in the worst quarter of town, and he barged right in. A slut howled and fled, and the young fellow startled up, caught in flagrante delicto.

"Well, I was going to come and meet you. I'm Samuel Flint," the fellow said. "Welcome to *The Silver City Sentinel*."

Westminster sized up the man: thirtyish, big, serious-looking, but obviously dumb as a stump. Westminster could tell. He could fathom a man's intelligence in a trice. The forehead and eyes gave it away. This fellow had a dull, squalid look to him, the eyes uncomprehending, the forehead receding into an ape-like crown of brown hair. An obvious boozer, as well.

"That's the name, eh? *The Bawdyhouse Bugle* sounds better, and so it will be called in *The Democrat*. You'll last an issue or two, I imagine. A pity. I rather hoped you'd go six so we might have a contest of wits. You'll support all the scalawags, cads, bounders, and sluts; I'll support the businessmen and solid people. You'll come out for universal taxation; I'll continue to insist that the depraved should be licensed and bled of their booty to support the solid and moral citizenry."

"Well, you seem to know my policies even before I do," the upstart replied.

"You probably don't have any. Where've I seen your work? I get exchanges from all over the west."

"Oro Blanco. Payday . . . and a bunch in Texas and Kansas."

"Ah, yes, the name is familiar now. I should have known. Always supporting the depraved."

Flint stared. "There's no point in loggerheads, Mr. Westminster. I imagine I could brew up some Arbuckle's and show you my humble plant, such as it is."

"Plant." Westminster chortled. "Well, show me the plant, but spare me the staff." He laughed mirthlessly.

"I'm alone," said Flint.

"Except for the slut who fled when respectability walked through the door."

"My landlady."

"Your landlady. A famous tart. She turns up her nose at most men. She's a legend. Charges a fortune for her services. Comes from a noted family. Ah, yes, she'd be the type to start a paper."

"I'd never met her until yesterday. We don't see eye to eye on anything I know of. This is the only place I could find, as you must know."

"Why, you could have walked into my plant and made alliance with me. You could have spared yourself your beggar's journey, wandering up and down the gulch pleading for five square feet and a roof. We might have made common cause. I wouldn't have minded a little weekly using my plant. I could have shown you how this town works. Absolutely sound. I'm pleased to commend certain officials to the electorate at election time; they've been returned to office twice now. They're all for the merchants. Sheriff Poindexter drives the drunks and panhandlers and vagrants out. Judge Shreveport is the nemesis of slanderers and libelers and grousers. The county attorney, Solomon Drake, is a roaring tiger against chicaners, debtors, bail jumpers, seditionists, and grafters. I trust you have a license. Everyone in the sporting district needs a license."

He hoped Flint got that point.

"I'm not engaged in any of those businesses," Flint said.

"Well, I'll put Drake on it," Westminster said. "Where are you from, besides a lot of jerry-built blow-away frontier villages that needed some fourth-rate sheet purporting to be a paper?"

"Cincinnati. And you?"

"Why, the Empire State. I was in the wigwam of the Tammany Democracy until I wended my way west, looking for golden climes and silver opportunities and a release from rheumatism. I suppose you were a printer and got yourself a

54

press and some typecases and set up shop."

"No," said Flint.

"Well, it doesn't matter what you were, maybe the wastrel son of a wastrel father, for all I know. I hope you have money. I don't doubt that you'll suffer for want of advertising. It's simply a phenomenon the way the merchants flock to my standard. No sooner had you started canvassing them than they swore their allegiance to me in fiscal and fiduciary terms as well as the bonds of amity and congruent interest."

"You have a vocabulary," Flint said gently.

"Why, to a mendicant printer like yourself it must seem so. But it's a modest one, Flint. I simply have acquired a rudimentary facility with the language, and I try in my humble way to convey my ideas and visions to a skeptical world."

Flint smiled, and Westminster got the impression there might be some mockery in it. This loathsome young twit would soon find out who rules the roost, Digby thought.

"Well, where do your politics roost, Flint?"

"I'm independent."

"Ah, the refuge of the timid. I must say, if you don't stand for anything you'll not be counted. But if one is not alert mentally or is unable to trade jousts with the opposition, why, it's the safest course. Now, if you'll just get up the courage and take a position now and then, I'll have the pleasure of knocking it down. We need some opposition. I certainly do, to keep my wits sharp."

"I'm not in business for that, Mr. Westminster."

"Oh, you're in it to coin some boodle. I know your type. You won't need much advertising. For certain compensation, you'll make a case for anything. Even for the rascal mine owners who won't be taxed and won't timber the mines. Even for that prince of darkness Balthazar, whose dark shadow plunges Silver City into occasional gloom. Yes, I can see your ticket: You'll back the voracious mining magnates and the depraved classes. I'd wager Balthazar'd slip you a hundred now and then for a certain opinion on your pages."

Flint grinned. The young blockhead seemed to be enjoying the interview and wasn't properly impressed. Well, when it came to publishing and distributing the paper in the real world of Silver City, he would be impressed soon enough.

"I haven't met the man," Flint said.

"He doesn't make himself available to your class of person," Westminster said, silently adding that Balthazar didn't make himself available to any class of person, including Digby Westminster.

Flint yawned. "I don't suppose you have a rate card," he said. "It'd save me a trip to your offices to get one."

"What do you want a rate card for?"

"So I can set my space rates lower."

"Flint, you won't even be able to give away ads. And you won't get a speck of the county advertising. Don't count on any legals — I have that locked up. You have no circulation and won't get any."

"It'll be difficult," the young man agreed.

"Difficult! Who'd advertise in *The Bawdyhouse Bugle*? If you're going to go ahead with this, I can only presume you're in league with some hidden interest who's supporting you. Maybe the devil himself. Probably whiskey peddlers and distilleries. I'm going to say so in my paper. Maybe you've got a capitalist in your pocket. Maybe you'll be a mouthpiece. I'll know when I see what you say. The song you sing'll tell the tale."

Flint didn't reply, and Westminster suspected the young man was too slow-witted to think up a retort. The fellow was a plodder. Or maybe he was drunk. Gypsy printers were famous boozers. Westminster eyed the place, looking for the inevitable jug, but he didn't see one.

"I'll give you some advice, Flint. Forget the weekly. There's room for a job printer here. I have all I can handle, and I don't mind losing some of the trade, because it really interferes with the important things. I prefer to guide Silver City toward its destiny. The people need some direction. You've got a good Cleveland press here. You can gang-print posters, office forms, menus, and flyers. You can stay right here and make money. I'll leave you alone. I should add that a job printer needn't worry about a reputable address or making a public impression.

Don't start a paper. Now, be a sensible fellow and heed my advice."

Flint didn't say no, he just nodded amiably, and that pleased Westminster. But he wasn't pleased by Flint's silences. Westminster realized he'd given Flint a lot more information than the man had given him. He consoled himself with the thought that he had really come to make an impression and that he surely did.

"Well, I'll let you get back to your typesetting. You seem to be setting a rate sheet or something. I'll enjoy the sport, Flint. We'll match wits, eh? I dare say, during your sober moments, you'll find out how deep the water is."

"I guess we will," Flint said, extending a hand to shake. Westminster gave it a brief, limp squeeze. Handshaking always embarrassed him. He exited into the twilight of the sporting district. The place was just stirring, getting up on its haunches for another howl. It was tempting to tour the dives, take note, study degeneracy in its lair, but he resolved against it and strode purposefully back toward his offices. He had hoped to get more of a challenge out of the oaf, but it was going to be a rout.

7

Sam Flint sagged onto his work stool, feeling stupid. Only a knucklehead would tackle a hydra-headed monster like Digby Westminster. The editor of *The Democrat* held every card, with a few extra aces up his sleeve. Flint could scarcely imagine where his advertising would come from, or even how he'd circulate *The Sentinel*. People bought newspapers as much for the ads as for the news. The man obviously had a network of informants. Flint had scarcely gotten his equipment settled before Westminster had darkened his door. And if the man wanted to play rough, he could induce the law and the courts to harass Flint, confiscate his newspapers, prosecute him for libel and whatever else they dreamed up, and then take everything away.

The man's palpable conceits and oozing self-congratulation and casual cruelties had been Flint's reason to come here. If anything, Westminster's conduct affirmed Flint's whole mission. Publishing an opposition weekly here would be even tougher than he had imagined, but he intended to try. He had always been a stubborn fool, and now he would begin his greatest folly: turning over the stone and showing Silver City all the crawling maggots under it.

Westminster's quick, mercurial mind had already come up with a damning and ruinous barb. Calling Flint's paper *The Bawdyhouse Bugle* was a jibe so perfect it would scare away both advertisers and subscribers. Flint knew he would have to deal with it even in his advertising flyer, and then incessantly in issue after issue. Still, there might be ways. He could appeal to reasonable people. Everyone in Silver City knew about its cramped conditions. Thoughtfully, he picked up his type stick and began setting a simple explanation:

"The editor of *The Silver City Sentinel* canvassed all likely commercial and residential buildings in this town, looking for accommodations. None were offered, and most merchants wished their own buildings could be larger. This is a normal condition in the early life of a boom town. The editor finally located an empty flat in the sporting district on upper Silver Street, and decided on temporary lodgement there until a proper place could be procured. It was an act of necessity and temporary in nature.

"*The Sentinel* is independent, not beholden to any faction, least of all the denizens of the sporting district. The insinuation that it is in league with Vice is a slander that ought to be dismissed out of hand by all reasonable people. As soon as circumstances permit, the paper will move to permanent quarters in the business district.

"*The Sentinel*'s program for Silver City will be published in its first issue, but we can say right now that the virtues and morals of the community will be aggressively promoted on its pages. We hope you will advertise and subscribe, and help create a healthy and wholesome community. We welcome all news, especially church and club information."

Flint hoped that this would at least keep fair-minded people open to him. He laid the piece aside and began setting his rates. He didn't have Westminster's rate card, and decided he didn't need it. No matter what rate Flint chose, he knew that Westminster's would be temporarily lower until he drove Flint out. That sort of cutthroat competition was gripping the country, its purpose to destroy rather than compete. Instead, Flint set his rates high enough to give some life to the paper even if he got few ads. He added that payment could be in kind or for services. He locked up his flyer, proofed it carefully, knowing that his abilities were on display in this debut, and then printed a hundred copies, working deep into the evening.

A knock interrupted him while he cranked his press. He wiped ink off his hands and opened his front door, discovering two leering imbibers of more than enough barleycorn.

"Where's the ladies?" asked one.

"You have the wrong address. This is a newspaper."

A vast confusion settled over one. The other

just chortled and meandered off. Flint closed the door. He would need to put up some large signs proclaiming the offices of *The Sentinel*. Yet he suspected the signs wouldn't do much good. Now and then he heard footsteps on the stairs to the second floor, along with muffled voices and tawdry laughs. He wasn't a puritan — he knew the realities of frontier towns, of settlers almost all male and hungry — and could live with it. But these things depressed him.

He pulled off his ink-stained printer's smock and scrubbed his hands. His fingers had been purpled from the inks of many years, and they looked perpetually dirty. He sometimes called himself Blackfingers, especially in private moments when some dream of a woman looked him over, her gaze settling on his work-stained hands before dismissing him.

The next day he delivered his prospectus to every advertiser he could find in *The Democrat* as well as some cafes that didn't advertise. He figured he had walked seven or eight miles that day, and the same number the next, when he attempted to sell advertising space. He found no takers. Few had bothered to read his flyer. Most just heard him out and shook their head apologetically. Not one merchant bought space. Not even saloon keepers and restaurateurs bought cards, the little boxed announcement ads that kept a name or service before the public. In all his years, Flint had never experienced such desolating rejection. All he had gotten for his labor were blisters on both feet.

He trudged back to his office that second afternoon, wondering whether to publish an issue at all, feeling an unaccustomed weariness. He unlocked his door and found before him on the floor a sheet that someone had slid over the threshhold:

"Sir — I am one of the merchants you solicited but must remain anonymous. I sympathize with your efforts. Many do, for reasons that are obvious. Your opponent's agents made clear that no one who advertised in your proposed newspaper would ever advertise in *The Democrat* again. Meanwhile, Sir, that paper cut its rates, making publicity in that organ a more attractive proposition than ever. I fear, Sir, that any advertiser found on your pages will suffer the unwelcome attentions of the authorities. I sigh, Sir, for the good of the county and our bright shining city. Things are not right. Please do me the honor of destroying this. I write at great risk. Your ally, Cato the Elder."

Flint had suspected as much. He studied the letter again, noting the pseudonym. His informer knew something of ancient Rome and the grave Senate speeches of Marcus Porcius Cato, who advocated a rebirth of Roman republican virtue through ascetic life and simplicity.

So, Flint had a friend. He tore the missive to bits and stuffed it into the parlor stove. An ally gave him heart. He needed one, just one, to carry on. He would produce an issue, and he would charge two bits instead of a dime for it. That would be a fat slice out of a miner's three-dollar-a-day wage, but he thought that the ordinary townspeople would buy at least one issue, even at that price, if only to see what the new fellow in town had to say.

Heartened, he began planning his debut. He would be at a disadvantage in every respect, but especially in the gathering of news. Westminster obviously had an army of informants. But Flint discerned some patterns in that paper: extraordinary coverage of business news, all of it positive and of a town-booming nature; no mention of failures, bankruptcies, departing concerns; no coverage of the miners or their families, or their weddings, funerals, births, ceremonies; their guild halls and meetings; no coverage of any foreign-name groups or citizens; little mention of banks and finance or Colorado economic trends, in spite of all the merchant news; extravagant praise of elected and appointed officials, who apparently could do no wrong; no weekly report of arrests, sentences, court cases, indictments, or any other official news; and an ongoing hostility toward the mine managers.

It would be an opening. He would cover what Digby Westminster scorned. He resolved not to attack *The Democrat,* much as he itched to ridicule it. He would let that monstrous windbag, that hot-air balloon, deflate himself. He would quietly show the citizens of Silver City what the opposition was not covering, get the humble family news that Westminster scorned. Soon, things would improve.

There wasn't much money in all that. At birth, a doctor usually got ten dollars; an editor nothing. At marriage, the preacher got five dollars; the editor nothing. At death, the doctor often got ten, the minister got five, the mortician fifty; the editor nothing. The whole world thought that news should be free. But Flint never imagined he was in the business for the lucre.

Elated, Flint began putting his paper together. There was something heady about being a David against such a Goliath. It would take cunning and skill and, above all, the transparent honesty and editorial courage that had become his hallmark. He would need every advantage, and one of them was to select the right publication day. *The Democrat* appeared on Thursdays. Flint decided that his Sentinel should appear on Fridays. That would give him the last word, and by the time He-goat Westminster got around to a reply the following Thursday, it would be outdated. Flint's views would have six days to sink into the community without being publicly ridiculed or assaulted. Time enough.

Not that newspapers were in business to engage in jousting. He doubted he would reply to Digby Westminster's bombast. He would simply publish what interested him, maintain his dignity, and hope to attract readers. He would live by his wits.

He retired to his spartan little cot, his mind fevered with plans and dreams. But he couldn't sleep. The raucous district kept him awake. Well past midnight, he heard traffic on the stairs just beyond the wall of his flat; laughter, furtive steps, the shatter of glass, mysterious noises in the street and closer at hand.

Then a knock came at his door. He ignored it. Some oaf wanting a woman. But it persisted, and he heard a muffled woman's voice. He swung out of bed, feeling the cold, bare planks bite his feet, and stumbled to the door. Chastity stood without.

"What on earth?"

"Mind if I come in?"

Flint sighed. "What time is it?"

"Two. I'm done for the night. When I draw my shade, that's it. That says go away."

"What do you want?"

"Just to talk. This would be like six in the evening for you. I'm off the shift. Hey, I want to tell you about Silver City. Somebody better do it. You want stories?"

Flint was about to grumble that stories from a creature like her probably didn't have an ounce of truth, but he yawned and stepped aside. She floated in, wearing only her black dragon kimono and pink slippers. This was all a bit intimate for a man of his tastes, and he regretted he had not yet bought curtains or shades. Still, he let her in, and she settled into a kitchen chair while he lit the coal-oil lamp. She looked none the worse for wear after a night in her profession.

"The stove's cold," he said, hoping to stave off a request for coffee at that hour.

"I don't want java; I'm going to bed in an hour or two. But Flint, I want to talk to you. You're alone around here. It's a tough place. You could get hurt. I sort of like you, even if you're as friendly as an archbishop. You remind me of someone who's lost. I want to help. I don't know why — I'm softhearted, I guess. Now's the time. You've got to learn what's going on in this town before you get into a mess. Listen, sweetheart, me and Sara and Marcella upstairs, we're better than ten reporters. I'm going to give you the low-down."

Flint thought sourly that it was a loathsome way to get news, but it seemed appropriate for *The Bawdyhouse Bugle*. "All right," he said, swallowing a yawn. She wouldn't know what made news, but he could be polite for half an hour.

8

Chastity Ford had been irrevocably separated from the world. No bridge would ever join her to any community of Americans. Once she understood that as a young woman, she managed to fashion a bearable life after all.

She had been born into an unusual life. Her father, Guadalupe Ford, a bearded patriarch, had been the famous atheist of Zanesville, Ohio. Ford ran a prosperous farm just out of town, employing the latest theories of animal husbandry and crop rotation. He was no silent atheist, but rather a militant one, who delighted in attending revival meetings and lyceums and lectures to make sport of clerics and uplifters. Lecturers turned pale on the sight of him, recognizing that Ford knew Scriptures better than they did and could argue them to the ground.

Chastity and her sisters had grown up shunned. Their father was a pariah, without a single friend close by, though he maintained a lively correspondence with other radicals in Boston and across the seas. His daughters were outcasts in the elementary school they attended; their schoolmates were not permitted even to talk to the Ford daughters, so the girls became a sorority of themselves and learned to ignore the slings and arrows directed their way by cruel peers and pious schoolmarms. At the time they reached eighth grade, normally the conclusion of female education, Guadalupe Ford and his retiring and saintly wife, Abigail, continued the girls' schooling at home. As a result, Chastity was extraordinarily well-read in English literature, rhetoric, the sciences, math as far as algebra, and philosophy.

Her father had derived certain ideas of self-government from his beliefs. He subscribed to the virtues, holding that if private persons were to live in perfect freedom from the external laws and public understandings and oppressions of the state and God, they must evolve within themselves an internal government suitable to proper conduct. In that sense his atheism was rather like the liberalism of the Founding Fathers, who knew that a society of freemen with little or no public yoke upon them would function only if citizens did not become licentious and rob and oppress their fellows.

Thus Chastity actually grew up within the confines of a moral and ethical regimen far more puritanical than the strictures imposed on their Christian neighbors. Even the sisters' names bespoke the seriousness of the virtues. If this regimen was a burden for a little girl, it was even more so for a blossoming young woman. Not one swain came to the Ford door, and it broke her heart. The pariah father and terror of all pious Zanesville yeomen had created pariah daughters withering on the vine.

It had been Guadalupe Ford's intent to raise his girls strictly, and then upon their maturity at eighteen, release them from his authority, knowing they would govern themselves flawlessly after years of his firm direction. But his habits of tyranny over his wife and children were not so easily put aside, and he couldn't give up his grip. Chastity, the oldest girl, discovered herself imprisoned, yearning for a different world, and rebellious, aching to have a beau.

Then one day when she was twenty, everything changed. She had accompanied her father to Massillon, where he was giving a week-long series of lectures. He often took his oldest daughter with him to usher, sell his books, distribute programs, and collect fees. His lectures were particularly biting and scornful that week, and she knew some hot mysterious fire burned in him. When on the last day of the lectures she found out what it was, her life turned upside down. She returned to Zanesville knowing he wasn't what he professed, knowing she had no home and no future.

She fled within the week, spending the pin money that would buy passage to someplace in the free West where a woman might bury herself and survive. En route to a destination she didn't know, she examined herself and discovered a glorious beauty, an educated mind — and a pain that dominated everything else within her. She arrived at harlotry out of desolation, knowing it was all that life would ever offer her. Silver City turned out to be her first venue, and she found no need to travel elsewhere.

From the start she operated independently, picked her clients, charged stiff and legendary fees, offered her customers hospitality, grace, and unhurried attentiveness, and turned away more than she chose. Abusive gents never set foot in her door a second time.

She rarely accepted more than three gents a night, and she received much of her income by renting the three flats in her building. In spite of a heart that was dead within her, she fashioned a tolerable life, with only a few problems, many of them stirred up by the editor of *The Democrat*, who was one not permitted through her door.

Her principal disappointment in Sam Flint was seriousness, which reminded her all too much of her father. She fantasized about him, wished she could lead him to her own independent ways and beliefs. She gladly would have accepted the handsome young editor into her arms. But you couldn't have everything.

"Couldn't this have waited?" he asked, shaking sleep out of himself.

She settled into his kitchen chair. "I'll drop in at any hour. You'll get used to it."

"Any hour. And we'll just sit here in domestic intimacy, you in your kimono, I in my robe."

"Well, I'm your landlady. You're stuck with me. I've closed up shop and here I am." He grimaced. She knew he would. "If you're looking for a landlady who goes to church and doesn't wake people in the middle of the night, go rent somewhere else."

He glared.

"I'm going to tell you about Silver City. I sleep with all the best men, so I should know."

"Miss Ford, I prefer to develop my own sources of news."

"Two men run this town. They despise each other," she said.

"I know. Digby Westminster and Achilles Balthazar. I intend to interview Balthazar when I can."

"What do you know about him?"

"He owns the biggest mines."

"Yes, and he's the worst man in this place. He lives and breathes profits. He's cold as an ice cave. He stole the mines, connived to get them. He did it with lawsuits, harassment, blackmail, intimidation — he's got a dozen torpedoes working for him. Mine-security guards he calls them, but they beat up anyone he tells them to."

"Then I suppose I'll face a licking."

He annoyed her with his sheer innocence. "You don't seem very worried about it. A lot of miners have been crippled. One was hit on the head and turned into a drooling simpleton. Some disappeared, but no one could ever pin anything on Balthazar.

"Flint, he even looks evil. He dresses like an undertaker. He screws a monocle into his left eye and peers at you from bright blue eyes. He never blinks. I swear he never stops studying you. He'll look at you and recite your most private thoughts. He gives people answers before they ask questions. When miners go to see him, he knows why they've come before they say a word, and he gives them their answer and turns them out of his office before they've opened their mouths. He thinks labor is less valuable than timbers, so the mines keep caving in. So far, something like twenty men have died in his hellholes, all for that rich silver glance ore that's making him a silver king."

"Yes, that's what *The Democrat* keeps hinting at. I've read it for almost a year, Miss Ford. I've a pretty fair idea of how the wind blows here."

"No, you don't. Achilles Balthazar is colder than the South Pole. You can get frostbit from his stare. If any miner protests anything — and lots have tried — he listens, nods, and then fires them. If any county official objects to his way, he listens, nods, and says he'll shut down his mines and wait for the town to die. That's eighty percent of the production here, Flint — he holds the whip. They wanted him to quit dumping his waste water into the creek — it's loaded with poisons, including arsenic. He just smiled, said some arsenic would be good for Silver City. It kills cattle twenty miles below here."

"Well, Digby Westminster's doing a good job exposing all that. He snarls and roars, but it doesn't seem to help."

"Balthazar has more authority around here than God, Flint. He gives me the chills. He's married; they say his wife's mad. Some summer nights you can hear screaming from up there. Have you seen his place? The one up on the shoulder, overlooking this town like a lord's castle? He's got an adult son, Hamlin. He's degenerate. He spends a lot of time around here, wasting the old man's money. The tinhorns like to clean him out of a little but never a lot, because he's threatened to have them beaten by his torpedoes. There are two graves in the Balthazar cemetery lot, a girl and boy. No one knows what they died of.

"When the miners refused to go into the pit until they got better pay and especially safer timbering, he just laughed and shut them out, and when they caved in he lowered their wage for a while. When half a dozen Cornishmen died from a cave-in at the Lucky Strike, the whole town was outraged. Every one of them left a widow and children. The county attorney tried to prove negligent homicide, but guess what? The case was dropped. Just dropped suddenly. Flint, men like Balthazar shouldn't be allowed to do business."

Flint was awake and listening now, and that pleased her, because her next point was crucial. "Flint, Westminster can criticize Balthazar and get away with it because he's got all the county officials in his pocket. You can't. If you say a word, you'll be dragged out of here, and we'll never see you again."

He smiled slowly. "I'm sure that's how it looks to some people. But even evil men are cautious, and never more so than when dealing with a newspaper editor. And a good editor has a way of saying things blandly even when they aren't."

It made her mad. "Don't be dumb. Look, Flint, dearie, take it from someone who's been in bed with them all. Don't crusade, and don't climb into Balthazar's pocket. And listen to me — I'll tell you who swings a big stick."

Flint eyed her solemnly. "Miss Ford, I regard a newspaper as a sacred vessel. It does more than report news. It exists to expose evil and commend the good. It informs citizens so they can come to their own conclusions. If Achilles Balthazar were to mend his ways, I'd commend him no matter how much he's hated here. If I find he's a sinister force ruining Silver City, I'll say so and tell why. If I get hurt, I get hurt."

She sighed. "I ought to evict you before this building gets burned down. You can't get insurance in the sporting district, you know."

"Miss Ford, I'll take your warnings under advisement," he said. It was a dismissal.

She wished he wouldn't be so damned formal. He was a pompous prig. She glared, erupted from her wooden chair, pushed straight to him, kissed him hard on the lips, and retreated before he could recover from his astonishment. She watched him rub his lips, trying to erase the kiss.

"You deserve worse," she said, and wheeled out.

9

As he worked, Marcus Bridge wondered how the new editor took the note under his door. The fellow was an impressive man. Bridge had ferreted that out from the brief visit they'd had when Flint tried to sell an ad, and also from Flint's remarkable, dignified prospectus for *The Silver City Sentinel*.

Bridge had made three spindles on his foot-powered lathe while assessing Flint, and he'd discovered some resonance vibrating between them, though little had been spoken. In the end, Bridge had been forced to put him off, but with the faint hint that he hoped Flint would give Digby Westminster a run for his money. It would be something to watch closely.

Marcus Bridge watched everything closely through gold-rimmed spectacles perched on a ruddy nose, behind which were bright, merry, intelligent eyes seeing more of the world than what was ever immediately in sight.

He had two passions. One was his trade. He was a master cabinetmaker and furniture builder, which he had learned during a long youthful apprenticeship in the Appalachian country of Pennsylvania. His other passion was the forms and shapes and prospects of civil society, which had entranced him as a youth, when he had devoured the Federalist Papers and the classics, including Plato and Plutarch. He was entirely self-educated, and supposed he wasn't half as wise as any properly schooled academic. His humility actually served him well.

But that wasn't the whole of Bridge. In his youth he had discovered Molly Lawrence, a bookish, serious girl whose parents had supposed she would end up an old maid. But obviously Fate had intended Molly and Marcus to share a life, gently debating everything, each from bottomless wells of learning and contemplation. This utterly cheerful and endlessly affectionate union had generated five children, two of whom lay dead and buried of cholera one terrible summer in 1869. But three lived, Augustus, Timothy, and Livia. The boys helped him in his shop; Livia helped her mother and scorned semiliterate suitors.

The Bridge establishment ran from Silver Street clear back to a cliff. In front was a lending library — the practical Marcus supposed he might as well earn a few pennies from his thousands of books, and he charged two cents a day. Behind that was his woodworking shop, redolent of pine and thick caramel-colored glue. In the East he had worked with ash, oak, hickory, and maple, specializing in his own Hepplewhite variations. Here he worked largely with the softer pines of the San Juan mountains, which suited him well. Miners needed cheap furniture, and he made it lovingly, with emphasis on sturdiness. The kitchen tables, wash stands, dowelled chairs, rockers, bedsteads, cupboards, armoires, and benches vanished as fast as he could shape them. He also did a lively trade in cabinets and coffins.

Behind the furniture shop stood the family's generous quarters, always in wild disarray because of the paraphernalia of scholarship strewn about. It was not uncommon for the entire Bridge family to enjoy an intense and cheerful debate about some facet of Plato's *Republic* or John Locke's philosophy or Adam Smith's *The Wealth of Nations*, with Molly the natural arbiter, serving pudding and libertarian ideals and making sure soft-voiced Livia was heard.

Life had gone along pleasantly for almost three years in Silver City, but this Monday Marcus suspected things were going to change. For many years the Bridge family's passions had been nicely compartmentalized. There was the cabinetmaking, which brought a comfortable income as well as a deep pride in achievement, and there were those books and tracts and seductive ideas floating about. The latter had never had any connection with the former. As a businessman, Bridge had been cautious, prudent, affable, bland, and utterly uncontroversial. He had advertised in *The Democrat* because it brought him trade, and the fact that he detested

Digby Westminster didn't enter into it. Injecting morals or ethics into producing, buying, and selling would confound matters. On occasion he had penned letters to *Harper's Illustrated* or *The Nation*, and at times he had scolded senators. But none of that had anything to do with his lucrative trade as a cabinetmaker.

But all that was about to change, and Bridge dreaded it. Like a moth attracted to flame, he circled ever closer to the light. When Flint had arrived in Silver City, Bridge had flown straight into the flame and gotten singed. This Monday, against his every instinct, he would swoop around the flame again.

Every Monday morning, *The Democrat*'s advertising salesman visited the Bridge store to sell an ad. Westminster usually had two reps out pounding the bushes, and one or another always came by. This morning, shortly after eleven, the callow, pox-pocked *Democrat* drummer named Padrick Stemple jangled the bells that announced a customer, and he strode cheerfully back to the shop, his order book in hand.

"Ah, there you are, Marcus. Always making legs. Eventually you'll have a leg up." This was followed by a well-practiced nasal hiccuping that Stemple erroneously supposed was lighthearted laughter.

Bridge did not stop. He had learned that if he stopped for every salesman and pest, he would get little work done. He rhythmically pumped the treadle to spin the lathe, and he continued to peel well-seasoned pine.

"You're here to sell me a larger ad than last time," he said, his eyes following the emerging curve of the leg.

"Well, old boy, I am. We're going to have a little demonstration of solidarity in Silver City," Stemple said. "We're asking every merchant in town to double his ad space this week, just this once, to send a message uptown. You know, Digby's calling that new outfit *The Bawdyhouse Bugle*, because that's how she is. Why, he told us privately that when he visited the young degenerate, a well-known tramp wearing only a kimono hustled out of sight."

"His landlady," said Bridge.

"Well, obviously more than that — his paramour. The man's going to promote vice. He's going to lead the young men into perdition. That's what Digby says. So Digby's planning a little extravaganza this issue. We'd like each merchant not only to promote his wares, but also to include a sentiment expressing a Virtue. Something patriotic if you wish. We can supply the sentiment if you'd like. And he'll write some opinion suggesting that if Flint doesn't leave town on his own, then he ought to be wearing tar and feathers when he leaves Silver City."

"Well, that's fine, Stemple, but what evidence have you that this Flint lacks virtue?"

"Why, it's obvious isn't it?"

"No, not obvious. His flyer explains in a most satisfactory manner why he's located where he is. Can't say that I blame him, business space being so tight. And he emphatically announced that his location would have no bearing on his policies, which I found admirable."

Stemple sniggered cheerfully, letting Bridge know who was naive and who was the sophisticate. "Look, Marcus, he's been caught red-handed, almost. Now, we'd like to sign you up. Good for business. Good to stand with the upright. Good to protect your family from the squalid world."

"Well, Stemple, I don't know. I've pretty much decided I don't need to advertise at all. I've more work than I can handle."

"You won't advertise? Gad, are you mad? Your sales'll dive."

"Stemple, do you see any pieces piling up? Do you see chairs and coffins? Do you see unsold tables and benches reaching the ceiling?"

Stemple confessed he didn't.

"Well, then. I'm going to cut back my advertising. Instead of the four-column-by-twelve-inch ad we've been doing, I'm going to put in a card. Just say 'Bridge Cabinetry. Furniture and all wood products. Competitive prices. West Silver Street.' "

Stemple's face reddened. His drummer's affability fled, and he turned snarly even before he spoke. "I won't sell you a card. Buy the ad or forget advertising in *The Democrat*."

"Sorry, Stemple, I'd be quite content with a card. Just an announcement'll do. I can't see

81

that I need anything more."

Stemple squinted from red-rimmed eyes, trying to look tough, which his gangly scarecrow frame wouldn't permit. "You don't fool me, Bridge. I know what's behind this. Believe me, if you don't change your mind, this'll go straight to Digby. He understands this just as well as I do. Where'll you be when we chase that depraved Flint out of town? Out of luck. You're the one merchant who's out of step. You're the one merchant playing with fire. It's those books. You read too much for your own good."

"You know, Stemple, I never see you in our lending library. I'd like to recommend Adam Smith, *An Inquiry into the Nature and Causes of the Wealth of Nations*. A remarkable discourse against British mercantilism."

"Against mercantiles? Why, now I know you're an overeducated fool. You're one of them businessmen that don't know what a good business climate means. *The Democrat* protects you. No one has to compete in Silver City. It's all arranged and comfortable. The paper fights vice. All Digby wants is a show of solidarity. Next thing we'll be seeing your ads in *The Bawdyhouse Bugle*."

"Have I told you that I'm going to advertise in *The Sentinel*?"

"If you do, Bridge, you'll be sorry."

"How will I be sorry?"

"There might just be a little whispering about you."

"What'll be whispered?"

Stemple sniggered and slapped his order book shut with great authority. "Some people just like to hang themselves," he said, and bungled out.

Marcus Bridge watched him go, knowing he had crossed a Rubicon.

10

Collecting news in Silver City turned out to be one of the most discouraging of Flint's enterprises. The merchants clammed up, and many oozed hostility. He decided, after two bootless days, that this was just as well. He would only be replicating material collected by Digby Westminster.

He turned to the courthouse and introduced himself to Sheriff Drew Poindexter, a sleek, catlike, obscure man who gave off occasional glints of annoyance that probably were the visible sparks of volcanic rage.

"Flint," the sheriff said in a velvet voice, "my records aren't for publication. I don't give them to *The Democrat* and I won't give them to you. I'm a sheriff, not a ledger."

"Those are public records, Mr. Poindexter."

"They're *my* records, and you may as well get that straight right now."

"All right, sir," Flint said, writing that down with his stubby pencil. "I expect I'll have to report that your public records were not available to *The Sentinel*. The public will have no way of knowing what disturbances have occurred during the week, who's been charged, and who's been detained. Customarily these things are always available to the public."

"Well, I'm not customary." He turned away. "And Flint, keep your nose out of official business, or you'll be in big trouble."

Flint nodded and grinned and transcribed the sentence. Poindexter didn't like that, and leaked more volcanic gas.

After that, Flint worked his way through the courthouse, introducing himself to the assessor, county clerk and recorder, clerk of court, and a justice of the peace. All of them seemed tight, polite, and distant, their eyes focusing on some point above and behind Flint. None of them warmed up to him, but he didn't expect that. They were all beholden to Digby Westminster. It would be tough to get news out of them, even official records. When he finally stepped outside, he could almost feel the courthouse sighing relief, as if it had just passed a kidney stone. All this he would deal with in the classic manner: If officials withheld public information, he would report that fact in his paper, issue after issue, slowly eroding support among voters. Citizens rarely like secrecy in courthouses.

Having been shut out by local businessmen and the courthouse crew — the people tightly locked up by the opposition — Flint knew he would need to develop his news in other quarters. Silver City, with its population of four or five thousand, would supply copious news if he went looking for it in the right spots, such as the neighborhood saloons. And he had yet to talk to ministers and lawyers, often good sources of stories. Undertakers could be good, as well, and so could teamsters and freight outfits.

But he knew of one important venue to explore first. He had heard only negatives about Achilles Balthazar, but it behooved a good newsman to see for himself. He hiked up Silver Street, past his flat and the sporting district to the mines, and toiled up a steep path to the Silver Queen, the centerpiece of Balthazar's holdings. It was time to beard the lion.

In startling contrast to the dreary mine buildings, headframes, boiler rooms, and rickety rails spiderwebbing away from the mine collars, Balthazar's supervisory offices had been minted in pomp. The entry to the glistening white building was flanked by fluted white colonnades, and its freshly washed windows gave Flint glimpses of a lush interior with cornices on the wallpapered walls, wainscotting, shining desks, and white marble busts on pedestals.

He entered a reception area manned by a ruddy young functionary in suit and cravat and awesome pompadour, doing sentry duty beneath a cut-glass chandelier.

"I wish to see Mr. Balthazar," Flint said.

"Are you a drummer? He sees sales representatives only on Friday mornings between ten and eleven."

"No, I'm starting a newspaper here in opposition to *The Democrat*. I'm Sam Flint, the editor."

The young fellow pursed his lips into a carp mouth. "He doesn't see tradesmen."

"I'd like to introduce myself anyway."

"I have standing instructions not to admit the press."

"It seems to me that if he wants objective, neutral coverage of mining issues, he ought to see me. I wish to talk to him about wages, injuries and the lack of an infirmary, creek pollution, monthly production, and the declining price of silver. If he's in his offices, I'll just drop in for a moment —"

"I assure you, sir, no one drops in on Mr. Balthazar."

Flint grinned. "Very well, I'll wait to see him. I take it that's his door behind you. You may tell him that Samuel Flint of *The Sentinel* wishes to make his acquaintance and will be waiting here. Perhaps I can catch him when he comes out."

The clerk pursed and stretched his limber lips, allowed himself some smirky smiles, adjusted his gold pince-nez, and returned to his paper shuffling, while Flint settled his carcass in the unaccustomed luxury of a quilted leather armchair.

It didn't take long. In due time the clerk was summoned by a distant oleaginous voice; soon he reappeared with some papers, which he set on his gleaming desk.

"I've been instructed to grant you two minutes. He is merely curious about you. Don't try to extend the interview."

"Well, I'm curious about him," Flint said, circumnavigating the clerk's desk and heading for the sanctum of power.

Flint penetrated the vast office, discovering a Persian carpet under his feet, Audubon prints on the walls, and matching black leather chairs lining the walls. Before him, on a royal dais, stood a massive walnut desk, and behind it sat the man himself, erect in a tall throne.

Achilles Balthazar exuded solemnity, and Flint knew at once that humor would be quite out of place before this altar. Balthazar's gaze ate Flint up in pieces, biting off Flint's face, chest, physique, ink-stained fingers, clothing, and finally, shoes. Flint had never experienced such eyes, big and shining and blue and voracious, sucking light into them yet radiating none. Balthazar was mostly bald, with a noble brow and a tonsure of black hair nesting the shining egg above. His thick mustache bristled like a declaration of war.

"Don't smoke," Balthazar said in a stern voice. "A criminal vice, an affront to health. You wished to have a look at me. Do I confirm your prejudices?"

"I have none, sir. I'm Sam Flint, new in town."

"And you've been hearing about me ever since you arrived."

"I have. But the reason I'm here is that I make my own independent judgments."

A faint humor built around Balthazar's eyes.

"I will confirm the truth of everything they say about me. Have you a pencil and pad? You may quote me."

Flint dug into his pockets of his baggy tweed suitcoat for the tools of his trade, and he waited.

"I run my mines to maximize profits. I enjoy being rich, and I enjoy flaunting my wealth. From my palatial home high up over there" — he waved languidly toward a prospect outside — "I can see much of the gulch and all the toiling ants down below. From my house I can also see above the gulch, across the San Juan foothills. I have vision; the ants in the gulch don't."

Flint wrote it, wondering whether the magnate was deliberately attempting to present himself offensively.

"You are wondering," Balthazar said, "whether I enjoy offending the world. No. But I enjoy giving the exact truth about myself."

Flint felt himself peered into; he had the strange feeling he would scarcely need to ask a question. He noted the two minutes had elapsed.

"We've consumed the two minutes, but I choose to continue," Balthazar said. "You've no doubt heard that I don't value human labor, and that is correct. Miners are ants. I send them into the earth, and they bring up rock and make my anthills. There are always ten more than I need. I install the minimum timbering I can get away with. The object is not to protect the ants but to keep cave-ins from disrupting production. A cave-in, you know, can prevent ore from reaching grass, and I am forced to buy enough wood to keep it from happening regularly, but not a stick more."

Flint wrote that and was about to ask what Balthazar thought of miners, their wives, their children, their dreams, their loves, their rights. . . .

"There is no milk of human kindness in me," Balthazar said. "Ants have families, but they are subhuman. Their suffering is the result of their own dull and stolid natures."

Flint had the eerie feeling that this interview virtually repeated others, and all he had to do was think a question and it would be answered in the ongoing monologue.

"If you suppose that makes me an unhappy man, you're quite wrong. I relish life. I'm not a bit lonely. Each mine is earning a profit, and all three are still producing bonanza ore. I function without love. I don't expect it and don't give it. I care not at all about the opinion of others. If a minister rails at me, it doesn't matter. If the president of the United States commends or rebukes me, it is a matter of indifference. The only opinion of me I relish is my own. Production goes along; I get rich; I have funds to satisfy my every whim. Maybe my whim will be to turn your paper into a mouthpiece of management."

"That's not possible, sir."

"You will tell me you can't be bought. We'll see. I enjoy testing a man's principles. Some poor devils who express high principle have a low threshold. Are you one?"

"Try me," said Flint, responding to the first curiosity about him that Balthazar had shown.

"I've given you two minutes. Now you have an accurate interview."

"I was hoping to get weekly or monthly production figures from you for your group and the rest of the mines, if you have them. They would be of interest to Silver City."

"They're private. I'm sure Silver City would be interested, but Silver City has done without."

"What are your ore values? How many ounces to the ton? And how efficient is your mill?"

"My ore's rich enough to invite theft, which I employ means to prevent. You're attempting to worm facts out of me, but you won't succeed. I'll tell you one thing, though: Silver glance ores can be hard to reduce. That's silver sulfide if it means anything to you. Now, does that satisfy you?"

"How about the other mines? Are they doing well?"

"I head the Mining Association. A word from me sets policy. Our policy is silence." He stepped around his desk, took Flint's elbow, and steered the man toward the door. "Go write it up," he said. "Send me a copy when you publish."

"Maybe," said Flint.

"Don't be indecisive. It's a vice."

Flint found himself propelled into the waiting

room, where the clerk smiled cheerfully.

"Mr. Balthazar gave you five minutes," he said. "That's a record for a tradesman. I think he likes you."

Flint nodded. He knew he had a story. He would get the other side from the miners and run the stories together at the right moment.

11

Flint spent two discouraging days digging for news and trying to make contacts. One minister, who had obviously gotten the word from *The Democrat*, shooed Flint out. "I'll not have you hiding your naked, vice-ridden rag behind church news and sermons," he snapped.

Flint didn't protest. It would take an issue or two to overcome such misimpressions.

He found a lawyer, Daniel Burleigh, Esq., dressed in his waistcoat and shirtsleeves, poring over case books through gold-rimmed cheaters.

"Have you a moment? This isn't really business," Flint said diffidently.

The big bear of a black-haired man settled back in his wooden swivel chair and nodded.

"I'm Sam Flint, editor of a new weekly paper in town called *The Sentinel*. I'm always on the lookout for court news. I just wanted to introduce myself."

"You're the one," Burleigh said, surveying the editor. "You don't look dissolute and vicious." The faintest smile had lifted the corners of his lips.

Flint answered in kind. "I'm a wastrel, a despoiler of innocents, and a mouthpiece for everything corrupt."

"Well, in that case, have a seat. These precedents can wait."

Flint lowered himself into the opposing chair.

"Your alleged reputation precedes you. I always examine the source. If it comes from a rival, I remain the perfect agnostic. I suppose you are where you are because no other quarters presented themselves."

Flint nodded, suddenly relieved. "I'm not sure I'll be able to survive," he said. "But I'm looking for sources of news. The usual ones aren't open to me."

Burleigh steepled his hands. "Hmmm. Those would be the courthouse gang, the merchants, and probably the ogres at the mines. Ah, Flint, you're a masochist. What'll you do, publish national and international news?"

"I'm coming to that. But if I could find just a few like yourself, who might supply stories, I'd be able to run some meaningful local news. Right now, I'm not sure I could even get vital statistics — births, deaths, marriages. . . ."

"You might be useful to me, Mr. Flint. There are times a lawyer would love to publish a story. I sometimes litigate against the powers that be in San Juan County." Burleigh waited expectantly, with a certain cock of the brow.

Flint felt his spirits sink. "I'm sorry, sir. I don't do that. I'll not shade the news or publish untruths if I can help it. If it happens, it is because I was misinformed. Nor can I open my pages to lawsuit propaganda. I do want legitimate news. There's a fine line, but I can usually see it."

Burleigh chuckled. "You know, sir, I was hoping you'd say that. Permit me to express my admiration."

Relief poured through Flint. "You'll help me, then?"

"I didn't say that. If I were a known source of information to you, I'd have tough sledding in district court. My clients would disappear."

"Is it that corrupt?"

"No, not corrupt. No one dips into the county till. Justice is mostly done. Call it venal. Call it cozy. If you were to bid for the county printing at a rate well below Westminster, you wouldn't get it. They'd find some reason. It's a tight little world over there. The favored few run the county. If Homer Shreveport — he's the judge — wants a pothole in front of his house filled, it gets filled. The sheriff and his wife have the contract to feed prisoners at the jail for a dollar a meal — it's a fancy profit for some gruel they get at the Dollar Cafe for two bits. That's how it is. Not real graft; just a lot of comfortable arrangements among the favored." He smiled. "I'm not one of the favored. One survives, in my position, with discretion."

"What about taxes?"

"Ah, the heart of it all. Silver City was never incorporated. That's one way they avoid taxes. Imagine it: four thousand here and no mayor, no property taxes, no constables, no city elections. It's all supported by saloon license fees and gambling and bawdyhouse taxes. They'll be coming to you wanting two hundred a quarter as an inmate of a bawdyhouse. I'm surprised they haven't already. Maybe they're waiting for your first issue so they can say you're in business."

"What? I'm not an inmate. I rent a flat."

"Poindexter won't see it that way. Your landlady's a notorious woman. I'll defend you if you decline to pay, but you'll lose. I'd suggest finding other quarters."

Flint laughed bitterly.

"Now, to answer your question: no, I can't supply news. I'm running a risk even letting you sit there." He gazed amiably at Flint. "But if you should receive anonymous information, trust it."

"All right, I will. You're the first bit of light to shine on my affairs here."

"Forget what you've heard, Mr. Flint." Burleigh stood, and Flint let himself out, eyeing the street sharply. He trudged up Silver Street through a chill October twilight, and by the time he reached his offices he was immersed in gloom.

He lit a lamp and peered at his equipment, feeling stymied. The empty galley trays rebuked him. The California case boxes with all their loose letters sat primly. The press brooded silently. The virginal stack of cut newsprint, the substance of a paper that would never reach the streets, rested quietly. He stared at his type stick, which usually brimmed with ideas, news, and excitement. Now it was an empty piece of metal. He had not yet subscribed to exchange papers and thus could not copy their stories. The telegraph had not yet stretched to southwestern Colorado, and he could draw no current news from one. He could rehash the contents of last week's *Democrat*, but that would trumpet his defeat. All in all, he had a few inches of story: He had paid attention to posters and flyers about town and could inform his readers of the forthcoming appearance of Maurice Barrymore at a local variety theater and the arrival of a traveling medicine show. And he had the Balthazar interview. Maybe twenty column-inches in all.

He could fill all that blank space if he had to: In his trunk were type castings of a serialized Dickens novel. He could create ads. A famous ploy of foundling papers was to fill whole pages with dummy ads to give the illusion of prosperity and popularity. He could fill the rest with puzzles, filler material, a Bible chapter, and windy opinion in ornate language, and call it a newspaper. He could build cards, small boxed classified ads, and blanket his rear page. Politicians resorted to them, but this wasn't an election year. But he hated to resort to such measures. The brutal reality was that he had been shut out and had no news to print. Nervously he examined his purse, finding ninety-odd dollars. Getaway money, maybe, if he didn't make some headway soon. But he wasn't ready to throw in the towel. Not yet.

He heard the slide of a bolt, and Chastity Ford appeared in his hall doorway, wearing her black kimono.

"Time for a drink," she said, setting a bottle of Tennessee whiskey on his kitchen table.

It irked him. "Miss Ford, you may own this building, but you don't have the right to unlock my door and enter as you please."

She smiled. "I'm not working tonight. I sometimes take a few days off. Have a drink with me, Flint. I don't know why, but I like you."

It didn't mollify him. "Look, Miss Ford, the last time you were seen in here in dishabille, word spread all over town, ruining me in Silver City." He saw the dismay form on her face and relented. "I'd enjoy a drink, but please put something on first."

"You're a case, Flint. Everyone else wants me to get undressed, and you want me to dress." She sighed. "All right. I'll be right back. You need another Silver City lesson."

She vanished into the dark hallway, while Flint found two tumblers and some potable water he had purchased from the Chinaman. She returned moments later wearing a puffy white blouse and dark woolen skirt, with a shawl over her shoulders to ward off the chill. Flint was smitten by the sight.

"You're beautiful, Chastity," he said.

"They usually say that when I drop my kimono."

"The blouse frames your face. I like to see your humor, your spirit, without the distraction — the other."

She made a moue. "You sure have a way about you, Flint. You make me nervous."

He poured whiskey, added a splash of water, and handed her a glass. "I should tell you I may be leaving in a week or two," he said. "I don't even have a story after days of hunting — except one I got a few days ago, a talk with Balthazar. And I didn't sell one ad. Not even a card. Westminster's tied up this town."

She eyed him sadly. "Don't leave, Flint. We need you here."

"You're doing fine, Chastity."

"Doing fine? No. They're going to raise my license again. You know how much I pay? Two hundred a quarter. And that's just the official amount. Then I have to shell out more to each deputy — walking money, they call it — or they'll harass me. Haul me off and make me spend a night in their jail. I don't have any rights, and they take half my income."

"I'm sorry. I can't help you. If I had a paper I'd campaign for a property tax — something small but falling equally on all private property, to support the county."

"Well, we're the tax base here, the sporting people."

"It's hard to editorialize against that, Chastity."

"I know. But I hate it. It isn't just the official amount. They come anytime and demand more, and I dare not complain. They just laugh. I tried complaining and they just fined me for it on some trumped-up deal."

"What'd they say?"

"Oh, you know. We prey on people. We're scum. They're just taking back the money we stole. It killed Marcy."

"Who's Marcy?"

"She used to live here, in this flat. They took money from her all the time. She couldn't pay, and they said she owed the county, and if she tried to run off, they'd throw her in jail or pound on her. One of Poindexter's deputies, he was here all the time, cleaning her out and making her cry. I used to come over here and hold her till she slept. She was weeping all the time. She got behind on her rent and I didn't know what to do."

"Was she using hop?"

"No, no, she was just a hard-luck girl who'd run away from a woman-beater, and she just wanted to survive. But the county just cleaned her out and scared her, and then she killed herself. She got some laudanum and did it on the Fourth of July."

That awakened a memory. "And Westminster made a big joke of it in his paper, didn't he?"

She nodded. "It wasn't a joke, Flint. That poor girl cried for two days, and then got the laudanum. Right here. She died right where your press is. That's why I couldn't rent this. It's a bad place."

"Right here? In this place? What happened to her?"

"Oh, they came and took the body, poor thing. They made jokes. Said she was a cash cow that ran outa milk. Said they'd charge her estate for the burying, so they cleaned out what little she had. I don't even know where they took her, poor thing."

Something rose in Flint. Of all Digby Westminster's transgressions, which Flint had read week after week in *The Democrat* when it came to him as an exchange paper, none had been more callous than Westminster's reportage of this tragedy:

"We hear that one of the sodden soiled sisters uptown celebrated Independence Day her own way. The dear thing decided that laudanum would improve the fireworks, and began sipping skyrockets that afternoon, according to the coroner. She won her independence about seven that evening, leaving behind her a large unpaid license bill, which offended our amiable sheriff. The sister, whose moniker could not be determined, is lying in state in the potter's field, where her many fervent admirers can pay respects. Too bad for the county, though. One more cash cow gone."

Flint could recite that item almost word for word. It was one of several such from the type stick of Digby Westminster.

"Miss Ford," he said, choked, "I remember the case, and I remember how *The Democrat* reported it. That's what brought me here. I hated it, hated that callous man. I didn't know I had come to the very rooms where that woman's agony had played out. . . . I'll stay. I'll publish. I'll do it for Marcy's sake."

"Cheers, Flint," said Chastity Ford, lifting her glass.

12

If news was hard to come by, opinion wasn't. Sam Flint figured he had an endless supply of that, and could fashion a weekly paper from it.

He spent some evenings touring the neighborhood saloons where miners gathered for a mug or two of lager and an hour or two of friendship nearly every night. The saloons were scattered up and down the gulch, far from the sporting district. He wanted to talk to the men who for three dollars a day braved the cold and darkness of the pits, the men called ants by Achilles Balthazar and scorned as drones by Digby Westminster. Flint knew that if *The Sentinel* would have any readership, it would be among these rough toilers.

He didn't feel wholly at home among them, and he supposed they scarcely knew what to say to a big fellow dressed in gold-rimmed glasses and a shapeless tweed coat with elbow patches and speaking with a vocabulary too fancy for their tastes. But those things didn't matter. He would get the feel of Silver City from them, over a mug of the sour local brew, and he would learn their hurts and angers and frustrations.

He tried the Silver Glance first, a long log

saloon snaking from Silver Street into the cliff. It had been named for the argentite ore, the silver sulfide these burly men hammered and hacked from the faces at the end of the stopes. The saloon had spittoons arranged along the plank bar, calcimined walls decorated with lithographs of horses and prizefighters, and a brass rail to lift the foot while a man sucked down suds. There he visited with a wiry Cousin Jack named Polweal, learned that a two-seventy-five daily wage barely kept a single stiff alive, much less a family, mostly because prices were high and all the stores charged the same. Goods were plentiful, but everything in Silver City arrived by ox team or mule train over a tortuous mountain trail from the railhead of the Denver, Rio Grande, and Western. The town desperately needed a railroad, and the miners needed lower prices, which they would not get until there was true competition among Digby Westminster's merchants.

Flint told Polweal he was starting a paper and he'd push for those things. Polweal squinted at the alien in the midst of the toilers, ordered a boilermaker, downed the shot of whiskey and sucked the beer, leaked a little moisture from his eyes, and eyed Flint suspiciously.

"If it's a paper you're starting, tell about the pits. We haven't enough timber above us. Many a lad's been laid in his grave by a rock falling in. Not a cave-in, mind ye, just a piece of rock that should've landed on some lagging."

"In Balthazar's mines?"

"The same, and all the rest. The cap'ins, they'd as soon hug a tree as protect mortal life. A tree counts more'n a man with 'em. And there's more, mind ye. Do ye suppose we toil a ten-hour shift, the same as other places? Nah. We don't come up to grass until ten and a half hours go by, a half hour added for lunch. A lad hardly sees the sun."

"Is Balthazar the only one doing that?"

"All of the cap'ins here. But nary another place in Colorado, so I hear. Just here, mind ye."

"It's something to write about," Flint said.

"The cap'in, he'd as soon listen to ye as swat a fly." The man guffawed.

Flint swallowed the last of his suds and left, walked up Silver to the next saloon, the Miner's Friend, and heard much the same thing. A family man with a crippled hand lamented the lack of an infirmary for miners, growled at Balthazar for ignoring timbering and other safety measures including fresh air, grumbled that his two tykes weren't learning to read and cipher because there weren't any public schools in Silver City, and warned that if things didn't get better, the miners would begin highgrading the better ores to do a little private smelting.

There was plenty wrong in Silver City. Flint could see that. He tried another workingmen's saloon, got the same stories, and then drifted into the dives in the sporting district just to talk to a couple of tinhorns. One pocked fellow named Billy the Deuce, who ran a faro layout, confided that the county got over half his profits, and if it got worse he'd pull out and so would most everyone, and then San Juan County would finally get down to taxing itself rather than milking the sports. It wasn't just the license fees, he said. Any deputy could wander in and help himself, get a free shot of rye at the bar, threaten a week in the jug for disturbing the peace and walk away with a fin.

It all confirmed what Flint already knew: San Juan County feasted on organized vice. No mine was taxed, no business, no home, no ranch or rural property. The merchants fattened and didn't compete except to undercut and drive out new rivals; the mine operators shaved costs to the bone and minted money; the sporting clan bore the burden of government but was so oppressed that it threatened to pull out; miners lacked basic services, such as a workingmen's hospital, schools, pensions, and adequate housing. Not one charity operated in Silver City, though sometimes church congregations raised a little cash to help a desperate parishioner.

That was how Digby Westminster wanted it.

Back in his shop, Flint set to work. He poured some melted type metal into the forms that made ruler lines, picked up his type stick, and began the typesetting. If he didn't have news to sell, maybe he could sell reform. The front page of *The Sentinel* wouldn't have stories; it would have a well-thought-out Program.

106

He felt cheerful at last. Reform might sell even better than news. Reform might give heart to the hopeless and helpless. Reform might induce a miner to surrender two bits, almost an hour's wage, for a copy of his paper. That brought a frown: Flint hadn't discovered any newsboys to sell it. The long, snaky gulch would require two or three: one near the mines to sell to the miners, one down in the business area, and one farther down, in the quiet neighborhoods where the gulch ran a little wider.

Gradually he composed a ten-point program:

1. Silver City needed an infirmary.
2. Silver City needed two grade schools and a high school.
3. Silver City should be incorporated; a mayor and aldermen and justice of the peace elected, constables appointed, and the city made responsive to citizens.
4. Silver City needed a railroad and telegraph.
5. Silver City needed a waterworks with a diversion dam located above the mines and water carried to several sanitary hydrants along the gulch.
6. The polluting of the creek running through town should cease, and the mines should cart dangerous wastes to a safe site below the city.
7. The town needed organized charities to help the desperate, especially mining

widows and children.

8. A volunteer fire department should be organized, with equipment supplied by San Juan County.

9. A universal property tax should be applied to all private property, imposed equitably and at a low level that would spread burdens widely so no group bore a disproportionate burden.

10. A small severance tax should be imposed on the mines, mill, and smelter to pay for the waterworks, hospital, creek pollution control, and other burdens on the public.

Flint smiled. How they would howl! They'd buy up every copy just to see what the madman was prattling about. He'd get letters, which he would duly print, and threats, which he would carefully describe. He would be accused of being a tool of this or that interest, a spokesman for the sporting fraternity, an enemy of all that was sacred in San Juan County. A paper full of sound and fury might just sell better than an established purveyor of news, such as *The Democrat*.

He worked hard on his program, burning coal oil deep into the evening. He had never produced a paper like this, a brief for reform without much news and no ads at all. All the while as he set type, he worried over the problem of newsboys. He finally remembered talking to the amiable cabinetmaker down Silver Street a way,

108

Marcus Bridge. And even as they had visited, two sons listened while they sawed and glued. Both were approaching adulthood. Both might sell papers if their father would spare them.

The next morning Flint hiked down to the Bridge store, remembering now that a lending library occupied the street room. He found the father and sons mortising the pieces of a bedstead. They greeted him amiably but did not abandon their work.

"I'm Flint of *The Sentinel*," he began.

"Yes, I remember," said the father. "Marcus Bridge. Augustus and Timothy here. And that's Livia at the door," he said.

Flint beheld a shy beauty surveying him with unconcealed curiosity. He nodded to her. "Pleased to meet you," he said, and she smiled back. He turned to Bridge. "I'll be publishing Friday. I'm looking for newsboys. I wonder whether you and your sons —"

"Newsboys, eh? It's up to them, Mr. Flint. They're well nigh adults."

The youth named Timothy surveyed Flint solemnly. "What will your paper have in it? And what are your arrangements, sir?"

Flint took a breath and plunged in, not knowing whether he was about to win the young man or drive him back to his dowelling and glueing. Briefly he explained his dilemma — he was cut off from news and had turned to reform issues. He listed them and saw Timothy's eyes shine. The youth stopped his labor and listened.

"As for the arrangements, I'm charging two bits a paper. Steep, but I have no ads. You keep a nickel, return twenty cents to me. I'd like one of you around the mines, selling to miners at shift-changing time, and the other down the gulch in the business district, selling to anyone. I'm printing five hundred and need to sell them all. Later, I'll have some mail subscribers. How about it?"

"I'll do it," said Timothy.

"So will I," said Augustus. "I like what you're doing."

Flint arranged for the young Bridges to pick up their papers early Friday morning, and he hiked up the gulch, feeling relieved. He had correctly fathomed that the Bridge family had taken sides, though the father had scarcely said a word.

Thursday morning Flint laid a nickel on a cigar-store counter and picked up a fat sixteen-page issue of *The Democrat*, bristling with advertisements full of patriotic gore. The lead story in the right-hand column carried the headline SPORTING DISTRICT ACQUIRES A VOICE FOR VICE.

Beneath that, a subhead; BAWDYHOUSE BUGLE TO BEGIN PUBLISHING IN SILVER CITY. OWNER MAY BE NOTORIOUS COURTESAN.

Beneath that, a flamboyant story beginning, "A vagrant gypsy printer probably named Flint, though no one knows for sure, has set up his press in a well-known house of ill repute and plans to write and edit a weekly rag. The fellow, known to be mostly bone between the ears, has formed an open lascivious alliance, witnessed by this editor, with one of the more infamous denizens of that district, and will do her bidding. You may expect that everything he writes will cunningly promote tax relief for the inhabitants of that depraved precinct. Money is always at the root of it."

There were three more stories and two editorials, and a raft of patriotic advertising to show Silver City's solidarity against the repellent invader. Flint studied the entire issue, amazed.

Digby Westminster had taken the threat of competition so seriously that most of the issue was devoted to denouncing Flint or promoting *The Democrat*, one way or another. One editorial contained some barely veiled threats: taxes, fees, censorship, and a lot more. Flint knew intuitively that the threats weren't idle, and the sheriff would act soon. He also suspected that Westminster had much to cover up, along with his cronies, and feared *The Sentinel* more than he was letting on.

Flint sighed, expecting that he would walk out of town penniless and wearing tar and feathers in a week or two. He wondered if it was worth it. It was quixotic, after all, to risk everything for a desperate bawd named Marcy who had been driven to suicide.

13

In his luxurious office Digby Westminster read every word in *The Sentinel* two and three times, masticating the ideas, the language, the thrust, the voice. He sighed gloomily. Samuel Flint was more formidable than he had imagined. He was no itinerant rumpot printer with a brain of solid hickory. Neither was he a naif beginning his first publishing venture.

"Unfortunately, this is a good piece of work," he said to his two visitors, Judge Shreveport and Sheriff Poindexter. "I'll drive him out, but it may take a few weeks, and it'll require brains." He eyed Shreveport when he said that. There was little between Homer Shreveport's ears except a lust to enrich the county coffers with fines.

"Yes sir, you're the general when it comes to print warfare," said the old judge, who had once been the mayor of Tuscaloosa.

Digby Westminster smiled. "I've done it before, in the Tammany wigwam," he said, hoping the judge got the whiff of sophistication. "Flint's bright. It'll take finesse."

Flint had fashioned a four-page newspaper out of almost nothing, employing all the devices and arts of the trade. He had a vocabulary and used it. Westminster knew his own was larger; he was a true student of *Webster's Unabridged*. But he reluctantly confessed to himself that Flint employed his vocabulary better and wrote with clarity, succinctness, and nuance. The Balthazar story was excellent. The extraordinary filler material fascinated him. Flint must have had some grasp of antiquities even to know where to find such pithy extracts.

Westminster read aloud and maliciously: "The judge should not be young; he should have learned to know evil, not from his own soul, but from late and long observation of the nature of evil in others: knowledge should be his guide, not personal experience. — Plato."

"I take it as a libel," Shreveport said.

The editor laughed. *The Sentinel* contained a dozen such items, drawn from antiquity, all of which conveyed the impression that it was a serious, sober, intelligent paper that expressed ethical values. Flint's paper was a standing rebuke to Westminster's jibe that it was a bawdyhouse rag. Flint had not responded to that, and Westminster suspected that Flint would not even mention the opposition paper — at least not for a while.

"It's all a fraud, of course. Every word in Flint's rag is calculated to conceal that it's a mouthpiece of the sporting district. Why, Flint has to be one of the biggest hypocrites walking the earth. With my own eyes I saw Flint cavorting with a trollop in a kimono right in his place of business."

Amusement lit the sleek face of Sheriff Poindexter, lifting his cat-whiskers.

His visitors returned to their reading. Westminster made a note to himself: He would not let pass any chance to attack Flint as a libertine and a mouthpiece of Vice. That was going to be standard fare in *The Democrat* issue after issue, until every one in town grasped it. Flint's rag existed to free Vice from its chains.

Flint's Program offended Westminster the most. It was so loathsome that it wrought dyspepsia in him, induced melancholia and mourning and hatred, and inflamed his rheumatism. Every item in Flint's plank caused a medical crisis in Westminster, releasing bilious gases and threatening apoplexy. Flint's Program even inspired black thoughts of murder: The young editor who was disturbing the arrangements in Silver City ought to be horsewhipped out of town and left to croak on a lonely road. But Digby Westminster suddenly felt ashamed of such effusions of emotion, and he sternly set them aside. He smiled at Sheriff Poindexter, who was reading his copy of the rag and didn't notice.

Examined rationally, Westminster thought, Flint's Program posed a furious menace to the good order Westminster had built, to his own prosperity and that of his merchant and courthouse allies. It would subvert everything for which *The Democrat* stood. It was black sedition. This mouthpiece of the vicious classes ought to be silenced, censored, rebuked, bled, and reduced to a whimper. Flint's plan to incorporate Silver City, create a board of aldermen, a mayor, and a town constabulary, not only meant onerous city taxes but also dilution of power. There were many more miners than merchants, and they would elect the aldermen, thus ripping control of the mining town from the merchants and *The Democrat*.

The editor sighed. The call in print for light property taxes equitably applied would be hard to resist. Truth was, the sporting district couldn't be milked for county revenues much more, and badly needed government services were going begging. Westminster and his allies had tried the other avenue — a bullion tax on the mine output — to bring in some revenue. But Balthazar and his cohort had simply shut down the mines and kept them closed until the county ordinance was repealed. Without silver production, there could be no income from a bullion tax. With miners starving, merchants failing, the sporting district unable to supply more, the leading lights — of which Westminster counted himself the chief — would capsize.

It had deepened his loathing of Balthazar, the fiend incarnate, a walking whirlpool of greed, exempt from law, laughing at reasonable taxes. The bullion tax was to be two-tenths of one percent of the bullion value.

And here was Flint, advocating a broad property tax, and just as fecklessly. Flint wanted it for schools and a hospital, trash collection and a water supply — pleasantries most mortals would wish to see. Westminster had always circumnavigated those matters in print, largely because of the costs, and his merchants would suffer, having properties with larger assessed valuations. *The Democrat* would suffer along with the rest. Such pipedreams, popular as they were, had always been thwarted by the county supervisors, who owed their incumbency to his endorsements.

Westminster abandoned his reading long enough to gaze at the sheriff, who was deep in the middle of Flint's rag. He liked Poindexter, a great cat of a man, always flexing his claws and studying the world with his green eyes. The editor knew men by their eyes. Poindexter had carnivore eyes, which made him a leader of men. All officials should have carnivore eyes, he thought. Men with herbivore eyes, soft and gentle and studying dangers, ready for flight, were followers. That was going to be the remedy here. Samuel Flint had herbivore eyes, gentle and amiable. He would run like a deer when the meat eaters arrived at his door.

"Among the merchants, we have one bad apple," he said to his visitors. "Bridge. My ad man, Stemple, told me that Bridge not only refused to double his advertising this issue as a part of our solidarity effort, but his two louts of boys are hawking the rag today. Always one bad apple."

"He reads too much," said Poindexter.

"The man wants patriotism," said the judge.

"Don't worry. After I get rid of Flint, Bridge'll find that he lacks anywhere to advertise. He won't worm his way onto my pages. It'll remind the merchants that we have their interests at heart."

"That lending library won't bail him out," said Shreveport, scratching his shingles, which populated the ballooning waistline under his rumpled shirt. When it came to shingles, the judge was a famous complainer.

Westminster felt a febrile flush building in his tormented flesh and wondered if the ague would pounce on him again. It was Flint who had done it. The man had agitated Westminster's spirit and flesh and shaken his constitution. He poured some bitters from a decanter and sipped, pondering his burdens.

He ached to know how many copies Flint had printed and sold. Even at two bits, he couldn't make money without advertising. That price was steep — a miner barely earned thirty cents an hour — but Flint could count on selling a few issues at that price, just because of natural curiosity. By then he'd be getting ads from all the town's malcontents and troublemakers, and he could lower his price. Something had to be done at once, before the rag rooted into the rocky gulch and grew into a malevolent nightshade.

Digby Westminster surveyed the unhappy courthouse twosome and thought to placate them. "Rest your bosoms," he said. "I'll handle this. It's merely a newspaper fracas, and I've waged plenty of them in Gotham. It's a war of words and ideas, for which I am sublimely trained. It's also a war of economics, of which I have fought with stiletto and club." He eyed Poindexter. "Let me handle it. Newspapers can bleat. Treat him badly and the whole world knows it. Now, collecting his license fees, that's another matter. He'll howl, but the fact is, he's an inmate of a bawdy house. If he takes it to court, Homer, you'll dispose of it in ten seconds. The way to do this is to show decent citizens who Flint is working for, and once it's over, he'll be gone and you'll have lots of goodwill when elections roll around. It's an Armageddon of words, gents, and I aim to employ the Bible."

"Well, the devil loves to quote Scripture," said Judge Shreveport.

That annoyed Digby Westminster almost beyond sufferance, so he rose. "Time for me to begin a riposte," he said, dismissing them.

Sheriff Poindexter smiled, catlike. "This isn't Tammany, Digby. It's not New York, either. It's a mining camp, not the sissy East. Around here, they string people to lampposts. All that's required is a mob."

Westminster's stomach roiled again. "Leave it to me," he said, only mildly uncertain about his abilities.

14

Sam Flint allowed himself a cautious optimism. Everything went well. The Bridge boys easily sold out the first edition of five hundred, bringing in a hundred twenty-five dollars, of which their share was twenty-five. A bonanza for them; far more than they earned in a day of cabinet-making.

"Was there trouble?" he asked when they showed up at his flat.

"Not a bit," Augustus replied. "People snapped them up. They wanted to see what you'd say. They've all heard about you, thanks to *The Democrat*. I sold copies to a lot of merchants, and even one to Digby Westminster and another to the sheriff."

Timothy reported similar success at the mineheads, selling out his stack to curious miners and a few supervisors. A clerk from the Silver Queen offices came out and bought one, immediately studying the story on Balthazar before returning to the white building.

"If it's acceptable to you, I'd like you to try it again next Friday." Flint hesitated. "There might be trouble."

"What sort of trouble?" asked Timothy.

"Bullies. It's an old newspaper tactic. Street fights. I'd rather you avoid that if it happens. Just bring the papers back here if they come after you. I don't want you hurt."

They looked disappointed.

He cautioned them further. "I can't charge two bits for long. As soon as I get some advertising, I'll lower the price. You'll be earning less. Probably two cents apiece instead of a nickel."

"Well, I've never earned twelve dollars in one day," Augustus said. "I'd settle for less."

"Good. I'll see you next Friday morning, early. If you hear anything — threats, compliments, someone wanting to subscribe — let me know."

He saw them out and turned to his mailings. He had printed five hundred twenty-five copies, saving out a dozen for exchange papers, two for his archive, and the rest to keep on his counter for the occasional person who wished to buy one. Normally he kept more for sale through the week, but he doubted he would do much business with his offices in the middle of the sporting district.

He addressed the exchange copies, using stencils he kept for that purpose. These would go to papers in the region. Most editors would begin an exchange, sending Flint their papers. They would all reprint one another's news. He would take the copies to the post office during his lunch break.

That done, he began breaking down his first

issue, tossing each letter of type into its nest in the case boxes. It was a task for a printer's devil, but he could not afford one. He was low on newsprint and would have to order some from Denver. In another month he would have to order a barrel of ink. His only consolation this time was that he didn't have to fill out advertising invoices and try to collect cash all over Silver City from expert procrastinators. Neither did he have to hunt for advertisers. If he got any, they would come to him. Those factors would save him two days of work.

That Friday afternoon, when he was weary after breaking down pages, a bonneted old woman entered. She didn't belong in the sporting district, and her arrival amazed him. She asked if she might purchase a card, and Flint swiftly accommodated her. She was a seamstress, working in her home, and she wished to announce the fact. Flint charged her a dollar for the two-column, two-inch card, grateful to have a genuine ad, his first.

He worked quietly another hour, curious as to how the town took the first issue and especially curious about what Westminster and the county officials thought of it. Flint smiled. To raise the question was to answer it. Next Thursday's *Democrat* would bristle with bombast. That would be all right. It would only publicize *The Sentinel* and awaken more interest in the new weekly.

Flint figured he had Digby Westminster out

on a limb. One could hardly oppose schools, a fire department, a water system, cleaning up the creek that was serving as the town sewer and diseasing the town's residents. Let the old boy fulminate. Nothing quite stirred Flint more than a battle royal with another paper, especially when he was the underdog.

His next visitor was the sheriff. Flint watched the big silky man slide in, peer around, eye this or that piece of equipment, and finally approach Flint. Not a word in the first issue had assailed the man or questioned his official conduct, but Flint knew that didn't exempt him from trouble.

"Well, it's the editor of *The Bawdyhouse Bugle*," Poindexter said. "Very interesting. Quite an issue you put out."

Flint nodded, his hands still dismantling a galley tray of type. The sheriff watched with feral cat-eyes, and Flint could almost feel the man stretching his claws and retracting them into his silky paws.

"Now that you're in business, Flint, there's the little matter of the license."

Flint's chest tightened a bit. This was what he was expecting. "I'm unaware that merchants are licensed," he replied. "Does *The Democrat* pay a license?"

The sheriff smiled. "No, Westminster doesn't operate from a bawdyhouse or purvey vice. We license purveyors of vice." Poindexter was plainly enjoying himself, and in a way, Flint was too.

122

"Ah, yes," Flint said. "I'm told it's twenty-five a month per gaming table, the same for an inmate in a bordello, two hundred a quarter for an independent bawd or operator of a bagnio, twenty-five a month for a dance hall, and fifty a month for saloon keepers. I guess that lets me out."

"Sorry, Flint. San Juan County's licensing you at two hundred a quarter." The sheriff approached Flint's workbench and leaned into it, inches from Flint.

"I don't quite fit," he said.

"We think you do. You're running a business in a bawdyhouse. You're a mouthpiece of that crowd, purveying vice. You got two hundred, Flint?"

"If I did I wouldn't pay," he said.

Poindexter's cat whiskers flexed, and his eyes glowed. "That's nice to hear," he said. "Very nice."

"What happens next?" Flint asked.

"In seven days the county shuts you down. We file a lien against your equipment to satisfy your debt. The county attorney goes to court, and Judge Shreveport issues a writ allowing us to confiscate this nice press. It's cheaper to pay, Mr. Flint. We would hate to see you face all that trouble."

Flint stopped sorting type and faced the man. Poindexter was larger and more powerful, and he wore a steel badge that empowered him to commit mayhem if he chose and immunized him to a counterblow.

"Sheriff," he said, forcing himself to speak quietly and hold his temper in check, "you and I both know this newspaper is not subject to your licenses. If I were operating two blocks away, out of this district, and if my landlady weren't a bawd, you would not be here trying to gouge money out of me. We both know that. So does everyone else in town. My readers know that I am here because it was the only space available. You know that. You also know that not a word in my first issue violates any standard of decency. What you're attempting to do is going to weigh on your conscience and appall voters. It can't be done in secrecy."

"Two hundred, Flint. I'll come for it next Friday. Nice equipment you have here."

"Justice is sometimes slow, Sheriff, but it is sure. What happens in Judge Shreveport's court may prove to be less important than what happens in higher court jurisdictions and among the voters here on the next election day."

"Why, Flint, licensing whores is an old frontier tradition." The sheriff gazed at him from hooded eyes, the predatory brightness gone from them. "I guess pimps and such don't have rights, like regular people."

"I'll quote you."

"I don't believe you heard me accurately."

Flint sensed he had somehow won an advantage. "That's fine. You can deny you said it in *The Democrat*. And I'll print your denial too. The public will be interested."

Sheriff Poindexter sighed, chuckled, and said the unexpected: "I like you, Flint. Don't tell anyone."

"Editors tattle," Flint retorted.

He watched the sheriff hoist his revolver belt up off his hips and catfoot out like a cheerful painter.

Tension leaked from Flint, and an involuntary tremble traced his limbs. That last spark of amiability puzzled him. It was probably only the sheriff's cunning and was intended simply to disarm him, maybe keep a paragraph or two out of the paper.

But it wouldn't affect the course of events. Flint wasn't going to pay a fraudulent license fee, no matter what happened, and he suspected that San Juan County wouldn't press him for it if he stood firm and publicized every move in his paper. Still . . . he eyed his fine 1873 flatbed press ruefully, and all the rest of his paraphernalia. These precious things afforded him his living. Once gone, they would be costly to replace.

He remembered Daniel Burleigh's assessment of the county's officers: not corrupt, but venal and inbred. Flint brightened at the thought. He could survive because they would stop just short of a certain line. If he had nerve, he would withstand the threat. By next Friday, with the second issue out and more money in, he could pay some part of the license, but that wasn't the consideration. A man had to draw a line, and he was drawing it now.

It amused him to realize he rather liked that slinky cat of a sheriff. He thought he'd pay the man a compliment in the next issue. Silver City was actually a safe place to be, and he would say so. His compliment would be sincere, but it might also serve a different purpose, driving a subtle wedge between the sheriff and Westminster. Flint hadn't come here to fight the county; he had come to challenge the blowhard who loved power and lacked ordinary kindness. But they would never get two hundred a quarter out of him.

15

The young bank president had been losing at faro all evening. He didn't mind. Gambling was a diversion, something to spice a boring life. He had been coppering his bets — that is, betting the cards to lose by placing a Chinese copper coin on top of the five-dollar chips he was wagering. These chips he had placed on one or another card painted on the layout in the spade suit, but perversely, his choices kept winning as the faro dealer called the turns, sliding the cards two at a time, loser and winner, from a slot in the side of the case box, which contained the deck in play. After an hour of bucking the tiger, his chips vanished, and the bank president casually wrote out another marker to acquire more.

The ebb and flow of cash was the only thing that interested him. There were times when Hamlin Balthazar wondered why he was alive. He had nothing to do. Even losing didn't interest him. He never paid his markers, although sometimes a tinhorn was able to wrestle some cash out of his daddy. The Balthazars didn't pay tradesmen if they could help it, and they could never understand why merchants and laborers got into such a lather about petty sums.

Hamlin's mother, Consuela, kept a hundred-dollar bill around the house, and when a tradesman insisted on payment for some silly amount, she flourished it and asked for change. A few of the smarter tradesman brought a heap of cash with them to make change, but these she knew, and ambushed them with a five-hundred-dollar bill for their two-dollar invoice. It was fun, but it created turmoil because she had to keep finding new suppliers.

Hamlin had absorbed all that in his twenty-one years and followed suit. One had to deal with legions of tradesmen, such as the tinhorns here in the lush Bankers' Club, his favorite resort in the sporting district. He favored this house over the others because of its green flocked wallpaper with fleurs de lis all over it, its cut-glass chandeliers that sprinkled the light of the coal-oil lamps, and the buxom serving girls in scooped blouses who plied him with spirits, but also because the tinhorns, most of them in brocaded vests and boiled white shirts, accepted his markers.

He had grown up bored in the household of Achilles Balthazar, his wants met for the asking. His daddy took perverse pleasure in indulging his whims, which Hamlin discovered was a type of control. He sometimes wished he had been born less rich so he might have something to do with his life, but he always put such twisted thoughts aside whenever he was in the presence of his sire, a man of no emotion but a calculating mind, with a wide contempt for his fellow mortals and an obsession with extracting wealth out of everyone and everything. Achilles Balthazar's sole diversion was subtly abusing Consuela, in ways she pretended not to notice. She lived in her own world, mostly abusing clerks, waitresses, cooks, coachmen, gardeners, and maids. She counted it a good day when she could goad a maid to tears. It was a trait Hamlin had picked up and used occasionally, for his amusement.

At seventeen, Hamlin had been shipped off to Brown University, but Providence bored him because it lacked vice. Education was for fools. No one needed it beyond learning how to read and cipher. His classes in English literature became insufferable, especially because he was a lowly freshman. Students hazed him, and they didn't respect him. They didn't care that he was a Balthazar and could buy and sell them at any slave auction, or buy and sell the University, for that matter. He flunked, and that had ended his formal education. After that, his daddy had given him a little bank, saying the Balthazars needed it to conduct their business. At twenty he was the president of the San Juan County Bank, one of three in Silver City. Its few clients were mostly mine managers and supervisors who found it politic to bank there. The institution required almost none of Hamlin's time, and some days he didn't set foot inside it at all.

Hamlin pulled a pad of notepaper from the pocket of his velvet-collared Chesterfield and penciled another marker for a hundred dollars.

"No more markers, Mr. Balthazar," said the wheezy tinhorn who styled himself Billy Behind the Ace.

"It's nothing," said Hamlin wearily.

"It's a lot. I've got eleven hundred in your markers. Time you dance to the tune."

"Go see Father," Hamlin said, yawning.

"I did. He says they're not his debts. I should eat them, and if I don't like it I can always go to another town."

Hamlin didn't like the tinhorn. He had black hair, oiled down and parted in the middle; a pocked face; smoky, carnivorous eyes; and a tic that kept one edge of his blue lips spasming. He wondered why all the world's faro dealers were male, and most of them uglier than a mustang horse. Maybe he would remedy the matter. He could start his own hall and employ beautiful women who would wear black velvet and lilac perfume.

"Here," said Hamlin, shoving the marker at Billy Behind the Ace. "I'll play some more."

The tinhorn sighed, shaking his head again. "Mr. Balthazar, you've got so many markers out that you can't even give them away. I know one sporting man who bought some at ten cents on the dollar, thinking he'd catch you sooner or later or squeeze it outa your old man. He gave up. You know how many markers you got floating around this district? Over a hundred. You know what they come to? Over fifteen grand. You know what a sport can do with them? Light a Havana."

"It's nothing. I don't know why you're upset," he said. He could never fathom why tradesmen got so excited about nothing. He'd seen a seamstress burst into tears at the Balthazar rear door, the trade entrance, because Consuela put off a three-dollar sewing bill. Actually, such scenes amused Hamlin. It was nothing but greed. Tradesmen were far greedier than rich men, he was sure of that.

"I'll play with gold, and you can pay with gold," he said, digging into his pockets for a few double eagles. He rarely carried cash, but this night he had a few coins. He placed all five of his twenty-dollar Liberty double eagles on the eight and smiled. Billy Behind the Ace stared at the glinting yellow metal, blinked, and began drawing cards from the case like a cobra mesmerized by a mongoose. The first turn, loser and winner, were a seven and trey. The bet rode. The second turn, a queen and an eight, doubled Hamlin Balthazar's money. Unhappily the tinhorn slid open a small drawer under the layout and laid five gold double eagles next to Hamlin's. The banker smiled and put all ten gold coins in his pocket, enjoying his triumph.

"Hey, you could pay off a marker," Billy Behind the Ace said, his lips twitching.

But Hamlin merely slid his black silk stovepipe onto his shiny locks, buttoned his Chesterfield, and meandered toward the double doors.

"Balthazar," the tinhorn snarled. Hamlin turned to survey the tradesman and discovered himself staring into the large bore of a derringer. It offended him. He yawned. No one would shoot a Balthazar. The play around the saloon stopped. The Bankers' Club had six faro layouts, two roulette wheels, and a dozen poker tables, but it was mostly empty this Tuesday evening.

"I'll pay you tomorrow. Come to the bank," he said.

"Right now, Balthazar."

"Don't be silly. I don't carry cash."

"You can start with the two hundred. That'll tear up two markers. You owe me eleven hundred."

"Tomorrow, come to the bank," he said, and continued out.

No one stopped him. No one ever stopped a Balthazar.

He stepped into the chilly street. That had been entertaining, he thought — so little was. He trotted down Silver Street toward a building that contained four flats. He used to visit all the flats, but one had been taken up by a tradesman. He decided on Chastity tonight and headed toward her door. Her shade was down, which meant she was entertaining, but that didn't stop him. He knocked.

It took a long while, and when she finally appeared, wrapped in her kimono, she looked sulky. "I'm busy," she snapped.

"Get rid of him."

"I said I'm busy. And you owe me eighty dollars."

He pushed past her. It never paid to take no from any tradesperson.

"What the hell!" came a voice from the boudoir.

"Balthazar here. You can go out the rear door."

But the doxy wouldn't give up. "You get out of here, Hamlin Balthazar. You're not doing any more business with me."

He laughed. "Come to the bank tomorrow." Pushing past her, he headed for the room of carnal delights and caught a skinny oaf pulling up some gray longjohns. He knew the fellow. A deputy sheriff. "Out!" Balthazar said. "It's my turn."

The man glared, first at Hamlin, then at the bawd, who occupied the door. Murderously, the deputy buttoned a flannel shirt, drew up some britches, and swung his heavy, holstered belt around his hips, his glare never leaving Balthazar's face.

"Some day, punk, I'll find an excuse to drill you," he growled as he jabbed his toes into worn boots. "If it wasn't you standing there . . . you'd be feeling my fists."

Hamlin laughed, enjoying his power. Being the son of Achilles Balthazar afforded him a certain pleasure now and then.

The deputy turned to the doxy. "You owe me one," he said.

"I don't owe you anything. All you had to do was chase him out. I can't. Who'm I supposed to get help from?"

He didn't answer. He jammed a felt hat over his ears and brushed past Balthazar, deliberately bumping him with his shoulder. It annoyed Balthazar.

He heard the door slam.

"You're not touching me," she said. "Get out and don't ever come here again."

He grinned, dug into his pants, extracted a gold coin, and held it up.

"That doesn't pay what you owe. Get out, you bastard."

He chuckled and started unbuttoning his shirt. She stared at him, dodged around him into her little kitchen, and vanished out the rear door. He raced after her into a corridor. She was banging on the neighboring door.

He chased after her, got a good handful of her kimono, and yanked. It ripped, baring her shoulder. The door opened, shedding sudden light into the corridor.

"Flint, get rid of this swine," she bawled.

A big, lean man bloomed in the corridor. The fellow clamped Balthazar with an iron grip and pulled him along the hall as if he were a feather, and tossed him out the front door, leaving Hamlin teetering in the dark street.

"You'll regret this as long as you live," Hamlin Balthazar said, dusting off his Chesterfield.

"Learn some respect," the tradesman said.

Balthazar laughed until his sides ached. That was the funniest thing he'd heard in years. Then he stopped. "Your name is Flint," he said. "I never forget. You won't either."

16

Flint glared at Chastity, whose kimono hung open. She looked utterly wanton, and the sight of her shot desire through him.

"Miss Ford, please get dressed," he said severely. "I'm trying to run a respectable business."

"Do you know who that was? That was Hamlin Balthazar." She grinned.

"I don't care who it was. Get dressed if you want to visit here. This isn't a bawdyhouse." He was harsher than he intended, but the sight of so much wild, silky, available flesh was almost too much for him.

"Poor thing," she said, enjoying it. But she vanished into the hallway.

He seethed. It was bad enough publishing here; he had no intention of being her protector, and he planned to tell her so. Irritably he abandoned his work for the night. He still had two more pages to tear down. It was boring work, and some tea with Chastity would be better — if she behaved herself. He built up the fire in the range and shook the grate.

She swiftly materialized in a skimpy blue dress that displayed all sorts of movement when she walked. A closer look revealed that she wore nothing under the dress, which in a way only made it worse.

"You're up to your ass in trouble," she said cheerfully.

"Mind your tongue. Once you walk through that door, you're in a place where I make the rules." He was mad at her, though he couldn't say why.

"What you need, honey, is me," she said, settling on his kitchen chair. "You're so proper that some day you're going to burst."

He felt like snarling at her but didn't. He fussed with the teapot, starting some water heating. "I want to get something straight," he said. "Don't come to me every time you have a problem with some male. I'm not your . . . I'm not the person you call on when you're having a problem or someone isn't paying you. Is that clear?"

Her bright eyes danced. "I've never seen anyone grab Hamlin Balthazar by the scruff of the neck and march him into the street. I oughta pay you a hundred dollars for that."

"I should have ignored you, and him," Flint replied dourly. "If you want a — protector, go negotiate with someone."

"You'll do fine, Flint. You're big and tough." She laughed easily. "Hamlin Balthazar, of all people."

"He's that wastrel son of Achilles?"

"He's the one. He's a parasite. He hangs

around the sporting district, losing cash like it means nothing, passing out markers no one can collect. He owes me a lot of boodle."

"Why do you let him owe you?"

"You don't know Hamlin," she said, suddenly serious. "Nothing stops him. Except you, and you'll pay for it as soon as he can figure out how to get you."

"What'll that be?"

She studied him soberly. "He'll hire someone to hurt you bad. Something like that."

Flint stared. "Nice fellow," he said.

"Flint, there's lots of things wrong in Silver City, and maybe one of 'em's me. But all the wrongs put together don't add up to the Baltha-zars. Not me, not the other whores, not the tin-horns, not even that miserable Digby Westmin-ster amount to anything compared to the Baltha-zars, father, mother, and son."

"I know something about the father, even interviewed him. He enjoys being what he is. The more people squirm and condemn, the better he likes it. But what about Hamlin?"

"Hamlin's cheated a lot of girls," she said. "Maybe you should write an article about him."

"An article saying he hurts sporting girls?"

"Yeah."

"By not paying?"

"Mostly just stealing from us. And scaring us."

"You're in a rough trade, Chastity."

"I'm not getting any sympathy, I can see that."

138

"No, I understand. I'm saying that's a risk you take and one you've always known about."

"No, Flint. It's a risk I take because I'm independent. When Hamlin Balthazar comes in, there's nothing you can do."

Flint tamped tea into a strainer, set it in her cup, and added hot water. "Maybe there's worse, Chastity — Digby Westminster and the bloodsuckers who're ducking taxes. They're the ones crushing you into hopelessness. Not having any dreams or hopes is worse than being cheated, sometimes."

"Flint, you live in some theoretical world."

"I agree. But Marcy, who lived right here, didn't die of Hamlin's type of pain. She died of hopelessness, and what drove her to that was the scheme of things that Westminster and his clique impose on the town. They laughed at her. They thought she was a worthless rag, something subhuman, without a soul. They bled her to death and threw her into an early grave. That's why I'm here. I read about it in Westminster's paper. He thought it was amusing. Something about that riled me up so badly that I packed up and came here just to teach Westminster some lessons in ordinary mercy. There's spirit and there's body, Chastity. Spirit can get hurt worse. The worst killer on earth is hopelessness. Everyone needs a dream."

She removed the strainer, and Flint put it into his own cup of hot water. "You're an odd duck, Flint."

"That's as good a description as any," he said.

"You gonna say all that in your paper?"

"I'd like to, but I'm in an awkward position, because you're my landlady and because I'm here, not over in the business part of town. I can't make the paper seem like a mouthpiece for you sporting people. I've spent a lot of effort making it clear that *The Sentinel* isn't what they're saying it is. It's a strange thing. I can't write about your troubles. I could write about your vices. I could call the district vicious and evil. But I can't do what I came here to do as long as I'm quartered here."

"Aw, Flint, what you need is —"

Someone hammered on the street door. Flint ignored it. It happened every night. In this quarter, any closed door promised illicit delights. The hammering turned more imperious.

"Gee, Flint, go answer before they wreck my door."

"It's just a drunk, Chastity."

A crash changed Flint's opinion. The door swung open. Its bolt had been torn out of the wood. It smacked the wall and shuddered. Three men entered, the first two the size of lumberjacks, the third Hamlin Balthazar, delicate, youthful, pristine in his velvet-collared coat. He was smiling.

Chastity emitted a terrified squeal and ducked out the rear door.

"I'll be over, sweetheart," Hamlin called to

her retreating back. "After I'm done with you, Flint." He looked around, seeing the press, the trucks, the worktables, the stacked newsprint. "No one touches a Balthazar," he said.

He nodded to the two brutes, who advanced on Flint with a malicious gleam in their eyes. Flint knew he was in for it. This beefy pair wore suits and cravats, and it puzzled him until he remembered the big mine security guards he had seen at the Silver Queen. Both were fifty pounds heavier and half a foot taller than Flint. He edged backward, wanting to get his big iron prybar that stood near the press, but the one on the right coiled around, planning on coming at Flint from the rear.

Raw fear laced Flint. His pulse sailed. He looked wildly around, ready to run for his life. He saw just one chance and took it. He dove straight for Hamlin Balthazar but never got there. Massive paws caught him from behind, clamping him tight and locking his arms. He was caught in a vise so tight he couldn't lurch free. The other one, his face blank and businesslike, began a methodical pounding. Each hammer-blow shot thick, heavy, brutal pain through Flint. A blow landed on his arm, mauling every muscle in it. His arm went limp. Another blow, heavy as a sledgehammer, landed in his solar plexus, and life stopped cold for an eternity. It took many seconds before he could gulp air again. Other blows pulverized his cheeks and lips. Flint tasted his own blood and felt the sting

141

of the lacerations where his teeth had cut open the flesh of his mouth.

He felt dizzy with pain. He kicked and squirmed, dodged each huge fist, but the hammering never stopped. He caught glimpses of young Balthazar, eyeing him softly, almost gently. Then more blows shot unbelievable pain through him. A knee into his groin was the last thing he remembered. He slid into a red sea of madness, whirling through galaxies and swimming in lava flows. He never quite lost consciousness, but that only made it worse. He knew he was on the floor, and he knew that he was alone, and he knew that he had been beaten by experts. He wanted to die. He wanted oblivion. He wanted anything but what he was experiencing.

He tried to move but couldn't. His arms and legs wouldn't work. He couldn't move his fingers. He couldn't push his feet. He couldn't crawl. He lay in that condition through some long twilight, until he grew aware of ministering hands on him, and he grasped that Chastity was washing him, soothing him. But even her most delicate touch shot black torture through him.

"Flint, Flint," she whispered. "Swallow this. It's some powders."

"What?"

"Dover's powder. Three-grain tablet."

"No, not that," he mumbled.

But she lifted his head anyway, and he swallowed the opiate, hating himself for it. It took some while, but then he began to float through the firmament. He crawled to his bunk, with her help.

"How long've I been hurt?" he mumbled through mashed lips as she tucked a blanket around him.

"Long enough for Hamlin to do me. I couldn't get away."

"I want to die."

"Flint, I'm so sorry," she wept. "I got you into this."

But Flint was sliding into blessed oblivion.

17

The new issue of *The Democrat* interested Marcus Bridge. He had walked to the post office this Thursday morning to collect his mail and discovered Digby Westminster's rag in his box. Back in his shop, he parked his gold-rimmed spectacles on his ample nose and perused the sheet.

Nothing surprised him. Westminster had largely abandoned reporting the news and was devoting nearly the whole of his front page to the budding newspaper rivalry. He would read all that in a moment, but something more immediate caught his eye. Under the heading NEW LINE OF FURNITURE ARRIVES IN SILVER CITY, Bridge beheld Westminster's squalid revenge.

The lengthy story reported that Smythe Brothers Hardware Company, adjacent to *The Democrat*'s offices, was now offering a new line of low-priced, sturdily built furniture imported from Denver and "perfectly suited to the needs of thrifty miners." This line would fill a great need in Silver City, which heretofore had suffered from unreliable, shoddily built, costly, and crude pine furniture of local manufacture. Indeed, the locally built stuff was of such poor quality that it was likely to fall apart. But the new furniture was the toughest made, the strongest, lightest, finest, most comfortable known, and best of all, two-thirds of the price of the local product.

On and on it went, celebrating the new line of factory-built beds, chairs, tables, and wash stands, all available on long-term credit so there was no need to wait. The prices were so low that Bridge knew he couldn't compete; so low that Smythe Brothers were probably selling at a loss to drive the Bridges out of business. Even the cheapest factory furniture could not be sold at such prices, especially when the cost of shipping it from Denver by ox team was included. He didn't doubt that Westminster was subsidizing the cutthroat operation out of his fat advertising revenue, and he didn't doubt that the subsidy would continue until it broke the Bridges.

He growled unhappily. He should have given *The Democrat* the double advertising it demanded, kept quiet, and discouraged his sons from hawking *The Sentinel* for Flint. He knew he would have to go have a look at the new furniture. If it was junk, maybe he could survive. He had always been an artisan, known for his own variations of Hepplewhite. Maybe he could switch to the carriage trade, selling fine hardwood pieces to the affluent if he could no longer sell his sturdy pine pieces to miners. His family was being plunged into crisis, and he would consult with them all over lunch.

The rest of the weekly assailed Flint, chortling, jabbing, leering, slicing, cutting, and above all, condescending. It didn't follow the Marquess of Queensberry rules, either. "*The Bawdyhouse Bugle* published its first issue," Westminster wrote. "It was filled with such piety and wisdom from the ancients that one might have thought it was the work of a pagan god from Mount Olympus. But of course the program gave it all away. *The Bawdyhouse Bugle* wants to shift the burden of county government from sporting house licenses to universal property taxes. That says it all! As things stand now, the cesspools of vice and viciousness must return most of their ill-gotten loot to the county for the public good. Right now, things are so arranged as to achieve a simple and just retribution: The sinners mulct our good citizens; the county makes sure that the vicious contribute to the general welfare. What better tax than one on vice? But the sporting-house crowd's squirming under the burden, and now they have their mouthpiece."

Bridge thought the argument was powerfully written and damaging, and he wondered how Flint could escape it, even if he could somehow find quarters away from the sporting district. It was as if *The Sentinel* had been forever branded with a Scarlet Letter and could do nothing but fold up and slink out of town. That Westminster's argument was a lie wouldn't matter much.

There was much more. A separate piece noted

that *The Sentinel* hadn't published even a shred of Silver City news and seemed incapable of covering the city and county because decent people and officials shunned it. Westminster did a comparison, showing the stories that *The Democrat* had covered last week. The article noted the utter lack of advertising in its rival and boasted that the town's merchants, in perfect solidarity, had refused to pollute their business by purchasing space in *The Bawdyhouse Bugle*. Yet another story described the effort being made by Sheriff Poindexter to impose a bawdyhouse license fee upon *The Bugle*.

"The sheriff informs us that the rag's liable for the fee under county statutes, doing a pimp business in a bagnio, and he has given the pathetic proprietor a week to cough it up or face seizure of his equipment for tax delinquency."

Bridge fumed. The week would be up tomorrow, when Flint would be putting out his second issue. It was all such patent nonsense, such a stretch of the ordinance, that he thought maybe Westminster was overreaching and people would object. If not, the county would sell Flint's press and equipment to Westminster for a dime on the dollar, and the courthouse cabal would triumph.

The rest of the front page was given over to an assault on Flint's Program, with a fiery denunciation of Flint's proposal that Silver City incorporate and establish its own constabulary and services. Ah, how Westminster could denounce! He did the cleverest guttersniping this side of the Mississippi. That proposed shift of power to the miners and ordinary citizens set Westminster to frothing at the mouth. Bridge thought the rhetoric overheated at best and hysterical at worst, and rather less powerful than Flint's calm, reasoned arguments.

If only Flint would remain patient and analytical and stick with reasoned arguments, he'd win the battle, Bridge thought. But Flint was already losing the war. He had no ads or subscriptions; he faced the threat of punitive county license fees, and he had to deal with a public impression, inflamed by Westminster, that *The Sentinel* was a scurrilous sheet. That was too much for even an honorable paper and its honest editor to deal with.

That noon, at Molly's kitchen table, Bridge waited until his family had consumed the saffron-flavored beef stew and her yeasty fresh bread, and then he read them portions of *The Democrat*, beginning with the story about the Smythe Brothers' new furniture line. The Bridge family suddenly turned solemn. Augustus and Timothy stared into their soup bowls. Livia looked stricken. Molly bustled quietly, her face a mask.

"Ideas have consequences," Marcus said. "Always before, we've managed to run our business without partisan entanglements. I'm afraid I abandoned my basic principle and let us become involved in a crusading newspaper's challenge to an entrenched clique running this county. I'll take the responsibility, but we must all decide on the solution. We can pull up stakes. We can fight the competition. We can try to continue. We can support Flint or not. Or we can do something else. What'll it be?"

Solemnly the Bridge family debated the issue. They were good at it. All those years of spirited discussion and examination of ideas and values had focused their minds. And when they had talked a while, it became plain to them all that they lacked facts. They needed to know what Flint would do; whether there would even be a *Sentinel* where they could advertise Bridge furniture, whether Flint could survive economically, and how Flint intended to deal with the continuing assaults on his paper.

The Bridges closed the shop for an hour. Marcus, Augustus, and Timothy walked up the gulch to confer with Flint. The family delegation would make up its mind after sounding out Flint's courage and plans. The road snaked up the gulch, hemmed by the vaulting yellow bluffs, channeling life the way Westminster had channeled public opinion. Near the mines they entered the sporting district, which slumbered in the midday sun — dreary by day, glittering after dark. Marcus hoped his sons would never linger here, or let themselves be trapped in it, or surrender to their appetites. The place exuded sadness. They found Flint's quarters in a sleazy building that crowded the street, its door barely ten feet from the lumbering ore wagons heading up and down the gulch.

Timothy knocked, and for a long time no one responded. But at last Flint opened, and Marcus beheld a man who had been nearly beaten to death.

"Mr. Flint?" he cried. "Is that you?"

Flint nodded them in. They gawked at him. Flint's face was decorated with purple, black, and red flesh. His lips and cheeks had swollen, and his eyes peered out of narrow slits surrounded by angry, bloated skin. His right arm dangled uselessly, its fingers the size of huge sausages. His left arm worked better. The remaining insults to his body were concealed by his loose clothing, but Bridge didn't doubt that the whole of the man had taken a terrible thrashing.

"Tell you about it," Flint mumbled, from between swollen lips.

"My God, man!"

Flint trudged wearily toward the kitchen and slowly eased himself into a chair. Bridge and his sons followed, their thoughts riveted on this tormented figure. Flint mumbled something that Bridge took to mean that they should help themselves to coffee.

"Did Poindexter do this to you?" Bridge asked.

Flint shook his head, which made him wince.

"Is this Digby Westminster's doing?"

Again Flint shook his head, which surprised

Bridge. Then, slowly, in slurred cadences, Flint described his encounter with Hamlin Balthazar and the young man's two thugs. Flint had done the thing no one in Silver City dared do — put a hand on Hamlin for abusing a woman. And Flint was now paying a price so terrible that he no doubt wished he could flee his own body.

"No paper," mumbled Flint. "Can't work."

"Is your right arm permanently damaged?"

Flint shrugged. He didn't know. "Can't set type," he said. "No issue. Maybe I'll leave. Don't know. I'm licked. Balthazar on one side, Westminster on the other."

"That's true of all of us, Mr. Flint. We're caught in the same vise. It's wounding Silver City." He handed Flint the copy of *The Democrat*, which Flint read so slowly that Bridge wondered whether the man could see or digest what he saw.

"Got you, too," Flint said at last.

"Maybe. We're here to counsel with you. If you stay and fight, we'll stay and fight. The Bridges are men. You can't survive alone. We can't survive without an opposition paper, telling the truth issue after issue, no matter what."

Flint smiled sardonically, the smile twisting his puffed flesh into a grotesque, macabre leer. "Poindexter's gonna take my press from me tomorrow, it says."

"It's a bluff. They're afraid of you. Just call their bluff. Tell the world it's an outrage."

151

"With what? I can't set type, can't sell an ad, and can't keep charging two bits a copy."

"Maybe the Bridges can help you."

"How?"

"Flint, we've some friends in this town, especially among the miners. Let me hunt for a printer. Maybe I know a lawyer too. You'll miss this issue, but maybe you'll be well enough to set type for the next. Give us a chance to scout around. Don't quit. We're in this together, and we've a cause worth fighting for."

Flint smiled skeptically. "I'm not going anywhere," he mumbled. "I can't walk twenty steps."

Bridge saw that the visit was wearing Flint down, so he rose.

"I won't shake that sore paw, Flint, but I want you to know — and I'm sure Timothy and Augustus agree — you're not alone in Silver City. You have us, and Molly and Livia, and by next week you'll have more stout friends. You're a man."

Flint nodded and escorted them to the door. The light was tricky, but as Bridge turned back to look, he thought he saw something that moved him: There were tears on Flint's cheeks.

18

Flint floated through a sea of pain and helplessness, buoyed only by the treacherous Dover's Powder that Chastity supplied to him. The opiate rolled back the torture and cast him adrift, his thoughts unspooling, hour after hour, from a dream weaver's bobbin. He feared and loved those three-grain tablets, knowing they could ruin him even while they gave him release from his torture.

He had been hammered by experts. Nothing was broken and no blood had spilled, apart from a little inside his mouth. The marks of the assault would disappear, but the terror of it would never leave him and probably would influence him all his life. He feared that the ever-present memory of the beating would reduce him to cowardice.

On Friday he heard a hammering at his newly repaired door, but he ignored it. He often did. Later, he discovered a notice tacked to the door, informing the world that the contents of the place were under seizure by the sheriff and that the matter would come before the district court on the tenth instant. So the politicians and Westminster would snatch the press if they could. They plainly regarded Flint as a grave threat, if they chose to resort to such dubious measures.

He had missed an issue. It was all over. He would pack up and leave as soon as he could. He was beaten. Why did they pursue? Had his program been so subversive to them? Had he committed lese majesty? Was it fear? Was it vengeance? Digby Westminster would be the type to rub salt into Flint's wounds.

The hours slid past, metered by three grains of Dover's Powder four times a day, while Flint dreamed of Sherman and Grant fattening up on the mountain on good autumn pasture. He would lose everything. Then on Monday — he thought it was Monday but he wasn't sure — Bridge arrived, bringing someone with him. The man beside Bridge was small, cherubic, wiry, middle-aged, and well-acquainted with the jug, but his bright blue eyes shone with innocence, and his direct gaze admitted no sin.

"Flint, are you better?"

"I guess so," Flint mumbled.

"I see they're going to try to nab your press."

"Can't stop them."

"Yes you can, Flint. A little publicity'll stop them."

Flint didn't argue. He felt too dizzy.

"Ah, Mr. Flint, this is Jude Napoleon, a journeyman of your trade, a veteran printer. He comes often to my lending library, and this time I snared him."

The bantam fellow thrust out a hand, which Flint gingerly took in his wounded one. He nodded them in and steered them toward his kitchen. He had no coffee for them, or even a fire in the grate. But he had a hospitable table.

"Your name is Jude Napoleon?" Flint asked, curious.

"The same, sir. My mother named me for the patron of lost causes and hopeless cases, of which I am the principal example."

"And are you related to the Corsican?"

"Only in spirit, sir. Remember, his surname is Bonaparte. But I am a field marshal of rhetoric. I lead armies of words. I write prose that bristles with sabers, muskets, and howitzers."

Bridge said, "Mr. Napoleon has taken up your cause, sir. He'll work for you."

"But I can't pay."

"He knows that. Mr. Napoleon has lived many years without a pillow for his head. Sometimes, when he comes to my lending library for a book, I have him sweep up my shop and put the wood shavings in a bin. Sometimes Molly gives him a bowl of stew. It's all he asks of us."

"Let me curl up in your shop, sir, and I'll be content. But I must warn you — to extract honest work from me, you must keep me from the grape. I have a vulnerability to the grape. Put the fruit of the vine in my hand, and all work ceases until such a time as I can be enticed back to honest labor. It's my version of the grand mal."

Flint had suspected as much. "How do I do that?" he asked.

"Why, sir, don't edit my writing. I can't bear it. Trust me to find the sublime word, the perfect nuance, the penetrating sally, but don't drive me over the brink with base criticism."

"But I can't abandon my responsibility for what appears."

The fellow's face saddened by degrees. "My life is a balancing act, sir. If you were christened with the names Jude and Napoleon, yours would be a balancing act too. I'm both the lost cause and the field marshal, you see. Since I've been named for the patron of hopeless cases, I must act the Napoleon only if a cause is adequately lost. Is yours beyond redemption? Is it beyond mortal remedy? Can only Divine Intervention rescue you?"

Flint nodded dumbly.

"Ah, in my whole precarious life, I've had only two such cases, and now you make the third — and the best. Hopeless cases conjoined with the need for a Napoleon are as rare as quadruple conjunctions of the stellar bodies. I tremble at the occasion. By some miracle of Destiny, our lives are conjoined at this portentious moment, and the result can only be awesome triumph. Leave it to Napoleon."

"But, Jude —"

"You retire, sir. Go back to your bunk and hatch all those black and blue and purple flags covering your face into healthy pink proto-plasm."

But Flint wasn't ready to surrender his paper

to an unknown printer. "One thing: Will you write only truth?"

"As far as it can be ascertained, most certainly. And none other. We'll not have a mendacious rag."

"But do you know anything about the town? My program?"

Napoleon looked pained. "Shall I recite your excellent program word for word?"

Then, to Flint's amazement, the gypsy journeyman quoted from memory several paragraphs of one of Flint's pieces, and gave Flint a perfect rundown of the state of affairs in Silver City.

"Mr. Flint," said Bridge, "I must be off. Here's your salvation, and mine as well."

"But Mr. Bridge —"

"Go to bed. Your weekly will rise from the ashes, a phoenix."

The cabinetmaker vanished, leaving Flint in the company of an oversized leprechaun.

"Now, sir, I shall need a stool. Taken stem to stern, you have the advantage of me, though we are more equal of beam. Your workbench is elevated not only by your lofty idealism but by four legs that raise it to my chest."

Flint pointed mutely to a stepstool beside the press, and Jude Napoleon swiftly placed it at the bench and set to work with the type stick. Flint stared, wondering what madness had penetrated his sanctum.

"Go repair your carcass, Flint. One advantage

of being my size is that I have less flesh to repair and less hurt to suffer. I shall present you with my first thrust shortly."

Flint nodded dumbly and retired.

Some while later — it didn't seem long — Napoleon awakened Flint from his drowsy estate and presented him with the proof sheet of a lengthy article.

"Now, Mr. Flint, you must play by the rules. You may correct typos, you may suffer silently and bite your ink-stained nails, but you may not criticize your printer."

Flint nodded, perched his gold-rimmed cheaters on his nose with his good arm, and began to read.

Under the headline OFFICIAL THEFT IN THE MAKING, Flint discovered a story about the seizure notice.

"The barely elected sheriff of San Juan County, the honorable Drew Poindexter, served notice that county officials intend to seize the property of this newspaper for alleged nonpayment of alleged bawdyhouse fees. County officials maintain that this enterprise is subject to the sin tax because it temporarily resides in the sporting district for want of other quarters.

"This preposterous contention masks the real intent of the proposed heist, which is to silence an opposition newspaper proposing worthy reforms for Silver City. It further masks the intention of county officials to permit the opposing paper, edited by God's gift to humanity, the honorable Digby Westminster, to purchase said printing equipment for pennies on the dollar. This cozy relationship, wherein the blessed Saint Digby and the lord high sheriff are in cahoots to fatten their purses, needs public ventilation, and *The Sentinel* volunteers to perform that task.

"The equipment at risk, press and typesetting equipment, comes to three thousand dollars more than the alleged two-hundred-dollar fee that is to be levied against us as alleged inmates of a bagnio. That elevates the heist into felony territory and leaves accusations of mere misdemeanor groveling in the dust.

"But, of course, the real purpose is mercenary: The honorable Westminster doesn't want any competitor poaching his advertisers. Lord High Sheriff Poindexter doesn't want his lucrative county businesses, including charging the county one buck a meal for jailbirds whilst he purchases the swill for two bits. And the Right Honorable Judge Homer Shreveport doesn't want any new Justice of the Peace courts to reduce his business.

"The real business of these honorable officials and the unofficial Digby is to procure the silence of a cowed citizenry by gagging a dissenting voice."

On and on went Napoleon. The arcane prose horrified Flint; the bald assertions, little supported by evidence, dismayed him. And yet he could find no untruth in it. This man Jude

Napoleon didn't pussyfoot around. He loaded the howitzers, pointed them, and laid a linstock to their touch-holes.

What would be the result of an issue bristling with florid accusation? Flint's body reminded him that pounding on editors was a frontier sport, engaged in as a matter of divine right by any aggrieved party, including women once in a while.

He stared up at Jude, who was smiling serenely. Flint decided the best counsel was to suffer in silence.

"Very good, Napoleon. Not a typo in it," he said, wondering what would come next.

"Thank you, sir. Now it's time to write a billet-doux to Hamlin Balthazar."

19

Flint drifted through the day on his bed of pain, listening to his cheerful colleague — he couldn't imagine giving Jude Bonaparte a title — hum tuneless songs, shuffle galley trays, and bustle about. Sometime this afternoon, Chastity would visit him, as she had been doing for several days. She would supply him with more Dover's powder and spoon some broth into him. He had little appetite but suffered the broth to keep up his strength.

Once again Bonaparte materialized beside Flint's cot, another galley proof in hand. "Ah, Mr. Flint, sir, I've completed a little item about Hamlin."

Flint nodded, shook the cobwebs out of his mind, and sat up, feeling the lance of pain.

"Now while you proof it, I'll go fetch your mail. It's been a few days. I'm looking for the exchange papers. You did send out a batch of exchanges, didn't you?"

"Oh, yes, twenty-five, I think."

"Good. They'll be our salvation."

"Our what?"

"Our ace in the hole, Flint. Haven't you noticed that Digby Westminster doesn't run much news from the exchanges? It's the chink in his armor. He's concealing certain matters. We shall publish volumes of material from other papers." He paused, alertly. "You're in contact with other mining towns, aren't you?"

Flint nodded. He could hardly remember. "Lots of *Sentinels* went out," he said.

"Ah, good. That means news is floating in. We're fighting a two-front war. But the exchanges will be our munitions dump, our divisions and battalions and our regiments."

All of that mystified Flint. The doughty little printer was probably balmy. The man vanished out the door, and Flint groped around for his spectacles, parked them delicately on his sore nose, and began to read.

"Hamlin Balthazar, the famous young banker who rocketed to the top of the elite San Juan County banking world by virtue of his soundness, diligence, genius, and courage, was discovered in the sporting district a few nights past harassing a certain *fille de joie,* who was refusing his custom until he coughed up certain considerable debts owed the unfortunate woman.

"Since his harassment was in the form of physical force, a nearby gallant rescued the lady from her distress and marched the young Mr. Balthazar, he of the peach-fuzz beard, out of that precinct and into the streets. No harm was done to the brilliant banker's person, although perhaps his Chesterfield was the worse for wear. But Mr. Balthazar's dignity was sorely affronted by such irreverence.

"Mr. Balthazar screeched his complaint into the ear of the earnest rescuer and vanished, only to return a short while later with two of his father's torpedoes, who proceeded to administer a terrible drubbing to the unfortunate gallant. The young banker watched the spectacle, preferring to let thugs perform his nasty business and protect his own chaste flesh from being marred. . . ."

Flint read on, enjoying the ornate prose. Napoleon never once mentioned Flint's name or occupation, which Flint didn't like. Flint's policy had always been to name names, his own if necessary. But if he wished to keep the bantam printer around, he would have to suffer in silence. He proofed the piece carefully, discovering not a single typo. Jude Napoleon had a way with words that Flint envied. The story, while making known the extent of Flint's beating, employed drollery and mockery as its weapons of war.

Napoleon reappeared, bearing an armload of rolled-up papers and looking uncommonly cheerful. "Ah, Mr. Flint, sir, we have a splendid array here: From Colorado, we have Ouray, Leadville, Central City, Denver, and Blackhawk. From New Mexico, Silver City, Mesilla, White Oak. I'll examine them directly. How was my little effort to record the assault for posterity?"

"Oh, fine, Napoleon, just fine."

The compact fellow grinned. "Oh, now, I know your kind. You would've preferred names all around. But we're engaged in two-front war, and names can wait." He dumped his papers on the kitchen table and began examining them.

Flint waited while the fellow hummed and rattled pages and whistled. The Dover's powder was wearing off, but Flint was determined not to take more. He dreaded its fangs. Rousing himself from his bed of pain, he hobbled over to the table.

"How do you read an exchange paper, Flint?" Napoleon asked.

"Why, I read the stories. Sometimes look at the ads," Flint replied, puzzled.

"But you should read the legals too. The county advertising tells the true story. Now look here. This is the *Ouray Eagle*, and here in the legals is a list of delinquent taxes and licenses. See here. The annual licenses for all sporting places, including saloons, gambling parlors, and bagnios, are twenty dollars. Exactly the same fee is applied to all businesses. Look here — the Duckbill Forwarding Company has neglected to pay its annual property tax of twenty dollars. And look here — each residence is taxed five dollars per year. It's all a crude, effective property tax, you see. Five dollars for residences, ten for multiple residences, and twenty for businesses of all sorts. They tax by classes of property, not assessed value."

Flint was puzzled. "What has that got to do with anything?"

"Why, Flint, you're blind. If you're going to fight a newspaper war, you should know the weapons. I'm going to write a little story that informs our fortunate readers that our sister silver-mining city of Ouray, scarcely thirty miles over a few ranges, imposes no special tax upon its sporting crowd, just a twenty-dollar license, and I'll supply examples from the legals here, showing how properties are taxed and licensed in that enlightened burg."

"Well, that's nice, Jude — may I address you familiarly? Very nice, but what of it?"

"No, you mustn't address me familiarly. My saint name is private and obscure, Flint. I'm Napoleon, always Napoleon. Now see here. You're a true naif. I think you've never been in a serious newspaper war. We're going to publish this simple fact. And we're going to invite the denizens of our sporting district to hie themselves to Ouray, where they won't be harassed and where they'll be able to keep their ill-gotten loot. And we shall announce that we are cleaning out Silver City of its vicious elements by promoting this exodus. It's a victory for Virtue."

Napoleon was grinning like a hyena.

Epiphanies bloomed in Flint's sore noggin. "Napoleon, you're a fiend," he said. "They'll have apoplexy at the courthouse. Westminster will slide into convulsions. You're inviting Silver City's cash cows to depart."

"Yes, and Westminster can hardly resist. Shall he argue in print that we need these tinhorns and sluts around to edify Silver City? That the county needs its beloved mountebanks, crooks, pimps, thugs, tinhorns, and doxies? Oh ho, Flint, it'll be a rout."

"Assuming the tinhorns and doxies actually pack up."

"Oh, some will, Flint. You can count on it. Some'll abandon San Juan County and flatten the public purse by that much. Oh, I'd love to hear them at the courthouse when that happens!"

Flint laughed, though the act shot wicked pain through him, spasms of pain interlaced with joy. Napoleon was showing signs of military genius.

Napoleon slit open the wrappers of the other papers, smiling benignly as he studied them. He settled on *The Leadville Miner*, perusing its pages one by one. "Ah, here," he said, peering over his spectacles at Flint. "Something here for our other front. We've an obligation to Silver City to bring the Balthazars to reason, eh? They hold the whip hand. When the county tried to tax them, they simply shut down every mine. The entire gulch skidded to a halt and the county beat a retreat. But there are ways, Flint, ways. It's a matter of economics."

Flint couldn't imagine what sort of economics would bring the Balthazars to heel, but Napoleon was pointing to three advertisements. "See here, Flint. There's a shortage of skilled hardrock miners in Leadville. Several mines are expanding their works. They're advertising for powder men at three-fifty a ten-hour day, experienced drillers at three and a quarter, and muckers for three. And look here — some benefits. One week annual paid vacation after two years. Why, that fabled city has a miner's infirmary, some sick leave." He smiled at Flint. "Now that's interesting. We'll just do a story about this. I think we'll run the ads too. Leadville wants miners; it's offering a lot more than local wages and conditions. Who knows? Maybe a few of Balthazar's men'll decide to head for Leadville."

It hit Flint hard. Publishing things like that was truly playing with fire. He didn't doubt that Balthazar would have him beaten again if Silver City suffered any hemorrhage of skilled hardrock miners.

But Napoleon was already studying *The Central City Progress*. "The Storm King Mine's advertising for smelter men at three and a half for a nine-hour shift. Guess we'd better mention it in our roundup of state mining news, and I'll copy the ad and run it. What it comes to is that Balthazar's offering the worst wages and conditions in Colorado. But we don't have to say it. All we have to do is publish the news from other towns."

Flint was suddenly feeling every bruise inflicted on him by the Balthazar thugs. "Napoleon, I'm afraid of this," he said. "You know what they'll do to us, just for publishing a story like this. If their production declines from the want of men . . ."

"Oh, Flint, you just leave it to me."

"I can't leave it to you."

"I guess I'll go sample some grape," Napoleon said. "I'm developing an awful thirst. I thought I was working for a . . . different sort."

Flint was nonplussed. "No, Napoleon! Don't go. My bruises are howling at me. They've infected my soul. Forgive me."

Napoleon stared solemnly at Flint. "I've an awful thirst," he said, "but I guess it can wait. I'm going to compose these stories in a certain way. Just a roundup of mining news. Trust me, Flint, and we'll subdue the beasts. There's no such thing as a lost cause or a hopeless case."

20

That afternoon, Flint made himself get up and toil. He couldn't set type, as his right arm still dangled and his fingers were too swollen. But he could heat up some type metal and pour some ruler lines and slugs for Napoleon. He could proof galleys. He could even turn galleys into pages, manipulating columns of type inside the chases. But he was so clumsy that he gave up, fearing a slip of the hand would pie the type. He ignored the howling of his body and determined not to fall back again on Dover's powder.

Chastity arrived late in the afternoon, curving out of her black kimono again even though he'd insisted she be properly dressed. She looked wanton and gorgeous, and whenever she moved, the dragons undulated.

She stared at him, then at Napoleon, astonished.

"You're up?"

"I'm making myself work."

"You're crazy. You're not ready. Look at you!"

"I've a business to run, Chastity."

"Well, so do I. Who's this?"

Flint's new associate hopped off his stool and

bowed extravagantly. "Why, I'm Jude Napoleon, late of Montreal, a journeyman printer and gourmet of food and flesh. And you, my dear *fille de joie*, are the legendary Chastity Ford, known far and wide as the loveliest demimondaine of Silver City."

"Holy cow," said Chastity. "You sound like some cavalier. Are you related to Bonaparte?"

"No, no, it's all a fraud. My grandfather, a gentleman thief of French and Italian extraction, arrived in Canada in seventeen ninety-nine. His given name was Napoli, and a deft alteration offered to Canadian officials transformed him into a First Consul's kin. A clever move, which his heirs enshrine in memory and attempt to emulate."

"What're you doing here?"

"Rescuing Flint, *ma cherie*. The man needs rescuing, don't you think?"

"I won't say what he needs. He won't admit it, and he gets mad whenever I bring it up."

Flint started to fume, but Napoleon turned the conversation away.

"Mam'selle, consider me your servant, your worshiper," Napoleon continued. "You're a legend. There are few in Silver City who can afford your charms, but you're the *belle idée*, the golden mistress, of all the males of Silver City. As for myself, I'm so smitten that I can barely stand here and set type. I'm something of a vagabond, you know. Itinerant printers usually are. I can't afford even ten percent of your charms, but if I had a dollar I'd give it to you just to kiss your lovely brow, and if I had a dollar and a half, I'd lift your soft and delicate hands to my lips and bestow my kiss upon them, and if I had but two dollars, just ten percent of your fabulous price, I'd ravish your ankle, and for three dollars I'd perform Beethoven's Ninth Symphony upon the nape of your neck. And if I had ten dollars, my lady, why —"

"Napoleon, enough!" Flint growled. "This is a respectable business office."

"Oh, Napoleon, you dear. You make me wish I could charge less," she replied. "I'll keep you in mind at Christmas."

"Go bargain in the hallway, not here," Flint grumbled.

"You're such a goose, Flint," she said. "Napoleon is a dashing lover. I don't get very many of those. Here. I brought you some stew and some more pills."

"No more pills."

She eyed him. "I'll leave one beside your cot. You'll need it."

"Take it away," he muttered, but she set a three-grain tablet beside his cot anyway. Chastity followed her own instincts.

"What brought you here, Mr. Napoleon?" she asked, ignoring Flint.

"My first name, Miss Ford. The names Jude and Napoleon, which were bestowed upon me by conniving parents, doomed me to an unfortunate life as a wanderer and exile. I won't bother

171

you with all that. Just take my word that the extraordinary concatenation of those names settled my fate as surely as a guillotine blade settles the fate of anyone whose neck lies below."

"Ugh!" she said.

"My nostrils inform me that you have a kettle of stew there, Miss Ford. Do you suppose there's enough for two?"

"I guess there is."

"Ah, good. I've been some little while without sustenance. And our friend Flint here can't afford to pay me the usual fifty cents per thousand ems for typesetting. Now if you'd perform the office of chef for a while, you'd have my true, concupiscient devotion."

"Your what?"

"You'd have my undying lust, Chastity."

"Napoleon, this is a respectable place," Flint grumbled, "even if she does her best to undermine my standards."

"Oh, Flint, all those bruises make you worse than ever," she said.

Napoleon settled himself at Flint's kitchen table while Chastity poured her concoction into two bowls. The beefy fragrances only made Flint nauseated — a common condition for anyone on an opiate — but Jude Napoleon tackled the stew in a manly fashion while Chastity watched. He consumed his own portion, and then Flint's, and Flint was suddenly ashamed that he had given not the slightest thought to his new colleague's needs. Napoleon hadn't descended from heaven; he was flesh and blood, and Flint owed the wily compositor and generalissimo for all the labor he was doing.

Contrition passed through Flint. "I'm sorry, Chastity. I haven't thanked you. You've cared for me when I was so sick I couldn't think. Your pills made life bearable. Your soup and tea kept me going. And all I've done since I got up is growl at you."

She turned serious. "We've got to get you back up," she said. "You're important to us." Her hand waved languidly toward the ceiling and the quarters of her other tenants. "Things just get worse and worse around here."

"Worse? Did Hamlin come back?"

She nodded. "I don't want to talk about it. We're so helpless. We can't count on anyone." Her eyes brimmed. "They license us to make it legal, but when we need help . . ."

"Did he hurt you?"

"Not physically. He's cruel in more ways than any man can know, Flint."

Napoleon bounced in his chair. "The villain. The pig. We'll put a stop to it. I employ words like bullets, ideas like sabers, and threats like cannonballs."

She stared blankly at him.

"Mr. Napoleon is a master at certain forms of rhetoric. Maybe we can help you — if we can survive here, which is unlikely," Flint said softly. "Mr. Napoleon is going to try a few things in our columns that may make your life better — or not. We don't know."

"Oh!" she cried, and swallowed Jude Napoleon in her arms. Flint's colleague didn't resist.

Napoleon came up for air a few breathless minutes later, while Flint watched, paralyzed.

"I'd hug you too, Flint, but you'd consider it a criminal assault on your virtue," she said acidly.

"I'm sufficiently bruised, Chastity."

She laughed nastily, gathered her stew pot, and departed. He felt bad, as if his apology and his caring hadn't even registered on her.

"That was almost the full twenty dollars' worth," Napoleon said in awe. "Flint, you don't need to pay me a cent. I'll get my rewards just by being kind to wayward nymphs."

Flint didn't say anything. He was hurting, and he wondered whether to go back to his cot.

The compact printer set to work again, this time with the exchange papers spread out all over the composing bench. He studied the advertising, perused the stories, and squinted at the legal notices, sometimes pausing to add sentences to his story.

Flint had never seen a compositor work with Napoleon's speed. The Montrealer's hands unfailingly plucked the right letter from the case boxes while the man simultaneously read the exchange papers and composed text. Just as the light failed, Napoleon wrapped up a major story. He carried the galley tray over to the ink table, wiped an inked chamois ball over the raw type, dropped a slender sheet of newsprint over the inked surface, and ran a roller over the paper.

"Here, Flint, proof this," Napoleon said. "I'll start building some ads."

"But we don't have any advertising, and I don't want fraudulent ones in my paper."

Napoleon sighed, patiently. "Chastity's right about you," he said. "A prig. If you'll read my opus there, you'll see that I refer to certain legal ads that we're reproducing from the Ouray paper, to illustrate the sort of burdens that enlightened metropolis imposes on its citizens. I'll light this lamp here, and we'll go right on. We've some catching up to do."

Chastened, Flint studied a gorgeous story about the way the neighboring county funded itself, treated its sporting class, and assessed taxes. And at the bottom of the proof sheet was an editorial in which *The Sentinel* invited the purveyors of vice in Silver City to depart for other precincts. In Ouray, it pointed out, a tinhorn gambler would need pay only twenty dollars a year for a table license and not the fortune he paid here. A saloon keeper would be equally ahead, and the female denizens of Silver City's sporting district would be far ahead, not only saving eight hundred dollars but all the rest that had been mulcted from them by deputies and politicians. The result, the editorial proclaimed, would be to free Silver City from its parasitic classes and make the town safer, cleaner, and more prosperous once the sinks of iniquity were cleaned up.

Flint read the story and editorial with admiration, reread it with awe, and read it a third time with wild glee that made him hurt every time laughter shook his belly. There could be no plausible response to this material. The cash cows would leave, and Digby Westminster and the courthouse clique would experience apoplexy. For a few sweet minutes in the gathering twilight, Sam Flint forgot his bruises. A man named Napoleon had, it seemed, descended from heaven.

21

The next day Jude Napoleon set to work on the pièce de résistance of the new issue, a front-page story about mining wages and conditions elsewhere, illustrated by ads from various papers. Neither Flint nor his rival Westminster had fully grasped the power of economic information, Napoleon thought. Give a laborer news of better conditions elsewhere, and he would usually go there. Mortals lived on dreams. Let word reach the East that Oregon was an Eden, or California a bonanza, and a hundred thousand people would cross a continent on foot. Even a plutocrat as imperious as Achilles Balthazar could be humbled by economic realities. The man could not long operate a mine if he offered less than the prevailing wage. Wittingly or unwittingly, Digby Westminster had been helping Balthazar by keeping silent about wages elsewhere.

While the wounded Flint dozed, Napoleon composed a story that surveyed wages and working conditions in various mining towns, especially Leadville, where mines were advertising for experienced hardrock miners at a better wage than Balthazar was offering.

Ah, it was so simple. Napoleon set type almost

as fast as his mind composed the sentences. He was the fastest compositor in the world. It had been his amusement for years to challenge printers to contests. He had made wagers in New York, Toronto, Milwaukee, Keokuk, and a dozen other places, always winning easily. He not only set type faster but set it flawlessly.

But all that bored him, and he had drifted from town to town looking for a true test of his genius but almost never finding one. Mostly he had hired on as an itinerant journeyman in one burg after another, staying a short while before meandering down the road. Routine typesetting stupefied him. He could set a story while reading Shakespeare, his brain performing several functions at once. When he'd had his fill of some miserable weekly, he headed for the nearest purveyor of spirits, bought a jug, and left town well fortified, never bothering to notify the proprietor.

He had encountered only two or three great challenges in his lifetime, but now he faced the ultimate challenge, a truly impossible situation, and his mind frothed and chomped at it, almost running berserk. Some sort of intoxicant percolated through his compact carcass, making him bounce on his stool, dodge and weave, and conduct an orchestra while setting stories for Flint. He would topple Balthazar, *père* and *fils*, and by the time he was done with Westminster and his courthouse clique and toadying merchants, they would be pleading for mercy. After that, Silver

City could govern itself commendably.

But Jude Napoleon knew that his own talents were not the only factor in this war. He had his own army to consider, in the fusty person of Sam Flint. He had gotten a sense of Flint from perusing the first issue of *The Sentinel,* and he liked what he saw. Flint marched to Silver City with moral purpose, outraged at the way the place was run and the way its weekly paper treated unfortunates. Reformist outrage fueled a good fight.

But would the man fight? Would he cave in? One could only shrug the shoulders in resignation and wait. That beating might have pounded the courage right out of the man. Meanwhile, Flint would bear watching and require educating. Imagine stuffing a paper with filler about the wisdom of ancient Romans — a poor choice. Of course a headmaster's son wouldn't know any better. Poetry was superior. Doggerel was better still, a weapon as excellent as a platoon of lancers. *The Sentinel* was going to publish some doggerel in every issue and abandon the Greeks to their tombs.

Napoleon heard Flint stirring in the kitchen and knew the editor would soon be up, nursing a cup of coffee and his bruises. Napoleon never required a bed and was used to sleeping on the hard floor of shops or on a stack of papers or even sitting up. A small throw rug abandoned by the previous tenant had suited him perfectly and would be all he needed during the forthcoming campaign.

Napoleon inked the galleys and made some proofs for Flint to read. The editor was nominally his boss, and Napoleon had to go through all the appearances. But of course it was all to prevent ruffled feathers. Once Jude Napoleon took over a war, he was the field marshal.

When Flint at last appeared, Napoleon thought he detected a change. The black and blue and purple flesh was altering to green and yellow — a good sign.

"*Bonjour.* You look better."

"I suppose I am."

"Can you function?"

"I'll try. Still can't set type, though." Flint tried to flex his fingers but had trouble doing it.

"Here," Napoleon said, "examine my sublime prose and grasp the intent." He handed Flint the story about mining wages and conditions in the area. It was a stupendous piece of work, but Napoleon suspected Flint wouldn't realize it.

But Flint did. "Why, Mr. Napoleon, this survey of mining wages'll strike right at the heart of Balthazar's power here. Maybe you've found the key."

Napoleon preened. "See how it reads. Not a word about Balthazar or local conditions. No hostility. No fulminations. No editorials. No name-calling. No complaints about the abominable estate of workingmen in Silver City. It's an absolutely straight sober story about mining wages, sweetly researched and honeyed over

180

with facts and figures. It should cost the pirate about twenty hardrock miners, and it won't even occur to him that *The Silver City Sentinel* is reforming him.

"There'll be a regional roundup in every issue — straight out of the exchange papers, Flint. Every issue, more news about good jobs in other places. And by the time old Balthazar wakes up, it'll be too late. *Mon Dieu!* How conceit blinds. After he's lost a hundred miners and his production drops, he'll finally begin competing for the labor — higher pay, better hours, safer conditions, an infirmary. We'll all benefit. The working stiffs will even be able to afford your rag."

Flint laughed, and Napoleon took it for approval.

It turned out to be a merry day. The field marshal studied Flint, seeing the man hearten as Napoleon extracted one story after another from the exchange papers. *The Sentinel*'s rich assortment of regional news was about to make *The Democrat* look parochial and narrow.

Thus it went all that Tuesday and all Wednesday. On Thursday Napoleon extracted a nickel from Flint and hustled out to buy a copy of *The Democrat*. Together they read it, enjoying Westminster's rodomantades.

"It appears that our competition, *The Bawdyhouse Bugle*, lasted one issue and sank without a trace. No issue belched forth from the sporting district last Friday, and the estimable Sheriff

Poindexter could arouse no one in the bagnio when he stopped there to deliver a bawdyhouse licensing notice.

"What a relief. This organ of sin is silent ever more. Vice will have no voice. The vicious will no longer vocalize. The tarts and tinhorns will continue to pay back to San Juan County much of their ill-gotten loot, for the public benefit of all decent citizens.

"It was a scoundrel rag, employing the pieties of the ancients and a cleverly written program that sounded noble, but it really concealed the intention of the dregs of humanity to escape the penalties of their immoral ways. We need hardly point out that the fine-sounding program advanced by *The Bugle* was in fact an insidious tax relief program, intended to bleed merchants and private citizens while freeing the most vicious and irresponsible elements from all the burdens of citizenship.

"Virtually all Silver City's stalwart merchants refused to have anything to do with the rag and supported *The Democrat* with generous ads during our moment of crisis, when Silver City and the future of this progressive paper hung on the hinge of fate. But there was one merchant who lacked vision and furtively supported the rag, ignoring us and our generous editorial support yea these many years. But he will be dealt with sternly. This paper will no longer accept his advertising and will support his competitors. We are for a moral and progressive Silver City,

182

purged of its vices and heretical or seditious elements.

"*The Democrat* is profoundly grateful for this blessed delivery from nefarious competition, and we trust that Silver City will prosper now that we have conquered evil."

Jude Napoleon liked that so much he danced from one foot to the other. But Flint sighed.

"I don't like being libeled," Flint said. "I'm tired of being dragged through the mud simply because these were the only quarters available to me."

"Oh, Westminster would have dragged you through other sorts of mud if you'd located elsewhere," Napoleon said. "But this little piece in here reminds me of Silver City's fat and smug merchants. I think it's time to write another story."

"About what?"

"Ah, give me a while, Flint. There's more to extract from these exchanges."

Napoleon began studying ads in the Leadville, Central City, and Ouray papers, among others, humming and chuckling as he made mental notes. The story evolving in his mind would be nothing but a comparison of retail prices in various towns throughout the area, and his preliminary studies revealed just what he suspected. The smug and protected merchants of Silver City, in cahoots with a paper that controlled them, were charging radically more for everything from shoes to apples. He would do a comparison of advertised prices in the area and set up a table. And after that, the customers in Silver City would do the rest.

Napoleon began humming *The Marseillaise* and setting type. A few stories like this would liberate the captive consumers from the grip of the Westminster cabal. Why, the humblest Silver City mucker would like to know that a pound of roasted coffee beans was three cents cheaper in Ouray and four cents cheaper in Central City. And any thrifty wife would appreciate the fact that a ten-pound bag of refined white flour ran thirteen cents higher locally than in Leadville. And a man would certainly appreciate that a box of Vasco de Gama Havanas cost six bits more in Silver City than in Durango. And that a blue chambray ready-to-wear shirt cost two bits extra around town.

A great delight seeped into Jude Napoleon, as it usually did when he was doing something valuable for those who needed help the most. He wasn't just helping Flint; he was spreading joy.

22

Digby Westminster felt the awful armies crawling through his bones again: first the teeth-rattling chill, followed by the delirious fever, and then the murderous weakness. He gulped a double dose of sulphate of quinine, hoping to stem the invasion. It was odd how terrible events triggered his ague. Let him suffer some devastation of the soul and his body would reply in kind.

The occasion of his wounding was the sudden appearance of *The Bawdyhouse Bugle*, just when he had supposed that putrid organ had been buried under a sprinkling of quicklime. But here it was, stalking the innocent streets of Silver City, risen phoenixlike from its ashes. But the mere appearance of a rival rag wouldn't normally trigger the ague in his besieged carcass. No, this issue was the work of a master fiend, a devil's lieutenant.

Flint had gone to the exchange papers for news and had wrung from them information that Digby Westminster had carefully obscured for years. It was as if that young fiend incarnate had an unerring sense of where *The Democrat* was vulnerable and silent. Imagine libeling good Silver City merchants by running price compari-

185

sons with other Colorado and New Mexico mining towns! And some of them farther from a railhead than Silver City too. Imagine tweaking Balthazar's veinous red nose by publishing the wage levels and help-wanted advertising from other mining towns. Actually, Westminster wished he had done that himself, and it grieved him that he had let Flint get the best of him. A certain unaccustomed envy stole through him.

And there was that nasty little story urging people to buy the cheap furniture from Smythe Brothers, because every item was being sold at a large loss in a "sordid political attempt to drive the Bridge family, makers of fine custom furniture and cabinets, out of business because they didn't agree with *The Democrat*." Westminster fumed. The truth of it was, he was paying Smythe a subsidy of seven dollars an item to undersell Bridge and drive the man from town. It was going to get costly, but Westminster intended to foot the tab until the Bridge family quit. He amended that: Maybe they wouldn't quit. He felt a chill rise from his wallet.

Then there was the front-page feature about the attempt by county officials, namely Sheriff Poindexter, to classify *The Sentinel* as the inmate of a bawdyhouse and charge it two hundred a quarter, even though it was an ordinary business enterprise in temporary quarters. "Readers should assume that if this paper is silenced, it was the work of the sheriff and his official cohorts, in violation of several clauses of the state and federal constitutions." The story fired a shot across Westminster's bow: "Should an attempt be made to enforce any fraudulent interpretation of the county ordinance, such as by seizing property belonging to *The Sentinel*, the matter shall instantly go before territorial officials, and impeachment proceedings shall be undertaken against the officials who are abusing the ordinance."

But none of that brought on the ague. What had truly destroyed Westminster's equilibrium was the piece drawn from the Ouray paper, concerning county fees and licenses. It fairly shouted to the sporting crowd to pick up their gaming tables and bottles and beds and march north thirty miles. And just to make sure, *The Bawdyhouse Bugle* ran an editorial inviting the sports to do just that, pointing out that a twenty-dollar annual fee was certainly cheaper than the thousand dollars or so extracted from the tinhorns and tarts and saloon keepers by Silver City licensing and abusive sheriff's deputies. The rag solemnly declared that this would clean the vice out of Silver City at last, and had the effrontery to quote *The Democrat* to the effect that the suppression of vice would be a good thing. "Amen," *The Sentinel* concluded. "And now we've shown the way."

Westminster read it, sighed, reread it, moaned, and sunk into acute dyspepsia. If the kings and queens of Vice followed Flint's counsel, the San Juan County tax base would collapse, and all the businessmen in town, including Westminster himself, would be forced to pay taxes. He groaned. Flint was willfully and artfully driving off the cash cows, destroying the system. Flint was deliberately ruining a moral balance, penalizing Vice to support Virtue. Flint was perverse, wicked, nasty, and fiendishly clever. A sudden murderous rage filtered through Westminster. For the first time in his life, he itched to point a revolver at another mortal and pull the trigger.

Westminster reached for his sulphate of quinine. The ague was burrowing into his bones, and nothing would stop it. He began feeling colder than a three-day-old corpse, and he wrapped a shawl around himself. He peered wildly around his office, which seemed to dissolve before his eyes. All the oak wainscotting, the flocked wallpaper, the polished desk, the quilted leather chairs, the twin brass coal-oil lamps, the *Democrat*'s own wall calendar, began to melt into a squalid heap. But of course it was only an illusion, the nasty work of the ague. He sniffed, blew into his linen handkerchief, and wrapped his black cloak tighter around himself.

The awful thing about Flint's tactic was that Westminster had no reply. Would he say, in print, that Vice should stay in town and let itself be milked? Could he publicly urge the denizens of the sporting district not to be hasty? Could he editorialize to county officials that they must lessen their taxes and harassments of the sporting bunch? Could he do anything other than hurrah the departure of the sinners? He groaned. He loved to assail the tinhorns and tarts, but he didn't want them to leave. He just wanted them to submit meekly to the county's imposts.

The rest of *The Sentinel*'s screeds he could deal with. Were prices higher in Silver City? It couldn't be helped. The town was far from the railhead and at the mercy of the forwarding companies. Still, stories about prices would breed discontent, and he could expect Flint to focus on the lack of competition among Silver City merchants. With that sort of publicity, it wouldn't take long for readers to notice that the price of coffee was identical in every grocery in town, along with everything else. Westminster would have to deal with that too. He would find plausible reasons, and he would appeal to local pride and the virtue of sound economy and the blessed absence of cutthroat competition. But he hated to be on the defensive.

Westminster wrapped a blanket over his cloak to stop his shivering, but he drew no heat from it. He felt as if his furnace had gone out. He finally abandoned his swivel chair and settled on his office couch, where he shook and rattled like the last leaves of November. In the darkness of the moment, truth descended on him. He had been nicely whipped by a genius. The man he took for a simian typeslinger had danced effortlessly around Gotham's Digby Westminster, the pride of the Tammany Wigwam. It was something to conceal at all costs. His standing among county officials and merchants was at stake.

That was how Sheriff Poindexter found the prince of Silver City. The sheriff had a copy of the loathsome sheet in hand, holding it as one does a handful of maggots. He stared at Westminster, a feline smirk on his face, plainly enjoying the editor's discomfort.

Westminster sat up and arranged the cloak and blankets about him. "A slight attack of the ague," he said by way of welcome.

The silky sheriff said nothing. Those carnivorous cat eyes disturbed the editor. The sheriff was always looking him over as if he were a mouse or a bird.

"Well?" said the sheriff.

"Ah! It's nothing to worry your brain about. Mere words. Windy rhetoric. Don't suppose for an instant that the tinhorns and tarts'll abandon town upon the incantation of a feverish new weekly. You know perfectly well, my learned friend, that the bawds are always skeptical of Elysian Fields."

"The what?"

"Paradise. The abode of the blessed after death, used as a metaphor. A metaphor, my friend, is a figure of speech, a reference applied to something it doesn't literally denote. I am alluding to a place where the sporting classes can ply their vicious trade lawlessly. Now, if the tarts think Ouray's the place to set up shop, they all would have left here long ago. They are always trading information. The same for the tinhorns. My counsel is to do nothing. I doubt that even one license will be lost."

"And if half the county revenue pulls out?" Poindexter's cat eyes glowed yellow.

"Then we may have to make some small concessions. Drop the license fee to one seventy-five or something. Make promises, but of course do nothing after that. A tad less milk from the cash cows."

"What'll you say next Thursday? That Silver City needs Sin? That the ladies shouldn't be hasty? That the operators of dives and hop fiends and all the rest should await better days? I confess, it's entertaining. Flint has your skinny carcass over a barrel."

For an awful moment Westminster ached to yell the irreverent rube sheriff out of his office, but he contained himself. "Well, I'm meditating on that. The proper response will require some sophistication."

"Flint has you treed. Ah, Westminster! I love it!" Then he turned serious. "A few more issues like this could mean the end of good times around here, my friend."

"Your alarmist viewpoint betrays your youth, Poindexter."

"I'm forty-four."

"But you're lacking in political sophistication. You leave it to me. By next Thursday, I'll have just the right, measured response."

"I should grab his press. That'd silence him. So what if there's a flap? There'll be no *Sentinel* around to fan the flames."

"It's slightly beyond the compass of law, young man. There are certain limits, certain, ah, oaths of office, public appearances, niceties of procedure, matters subject to the scrutiny of State officials, to be considered. Not the least is due process. I believe Flint has thirty days to pay up his license before there can be a writ of attachment handed down by Homer Shreveport."

The sheriff grinned. "I suppose. But machinery fails, you know. Things get broken. Type gets scattered. A press breaks down."

"Ah, a naive proposition, young man. You don't know anything about the fires in the belly of an editor with a holy cause. Mess with his equipment, and you'll stir up a hornet's nest."

"Well, arms get broken, kneecaps are vulnerable."

"You're loathsome, Poindexter."

The sheriff yawned. "It's all purely hypothetical. We're just weighing a few options, aren't we?"

"Purely. It's all perfectly harmless as long as no one actually acts. Now, my counsel is to let this pass. If you wish to do something positive, stop your deputies from shaking down the tarts and tinhorns. A lean purse won't matter for a few weeks, and after that it'll all be over. Now, Poindexter, I'm at the point of collapse. I must retreat to my quarters and steel myself against the chills and the fevers. I assure you, young man, I'll whip that scamp with a war of words and ideas and some ruthless applications of economics. He's barely able to produce an issue, and it'll all be history in a short time."

Poindexter's cat eyes glowed with unholy amusement. Could it be that the lout didn't believe a word of it?

23

Flint's young body mended swiftly, but his paper's finances didn't. Money matters loomed larger than ever. The Bridge boys had been able to sell only three hundred eighty out of the five hundred papers they had been given, and they told Flint that the two-bit price was too much. Lots of miners had paid that much for the first issue out of curiosity, but fewer were willing to blow a quarter for the new issue. This time, merchants had bought most of the copies, the boys said, and they had seen copies being passed around in restaurants and saloons. At least the issue had been widely read.

Flint's twenty-cent share came to seventy-six dollars — not enough to keep a weekly paper afloat. He put the leftover papers on the front counter, hoping to sell a few more. But few citizens would brave the sporting district to buy it. He still had no ads except a card or two, and no prospects of any. What merchant would buy space in *The Sentinel*? He had no mail subscribers, either and there was no hope of county legal advertising. Meanwhile, expenses were hemorrhaging what little cash he collected. There was always something. He had to buy coal oil to feed the lamps over his work bench, and charcoal to feed the little furnace that he used to melt down his type metal before he poured it into molds that made slugs and ruler lines. His supplies of newsprint and ink were shrinking steadily, and he lacked the means to order more from Denver. He had to have cash at the post office to mail his exchange issues. He had to buy bundles of firewood from the Ute Indians who purveyed them, for his kitchen range and the potbellied heating stove in the front room. His fonts were wearing down under the hammering of the press, and he would need to replace them soon. He had ruined some *M*s and was turning *W*s upside down to replace them. But he was short of *W*s and was using two *V*s side by side as a substitute. He was running out of stencils for his addressing device. He owed cash to the rancher above town who pastured and occasionally hayed his mules. He needed a new printing smock, and his boots needed resoling. And the Chinaman who brought clean water charged two cents a bucket.

But all these expenses paled before the one looming like Mount Everest just after the next issue: the rent he would owe Chastity Ford. He saw no way to pay the hundred dollars he had finally agreed to. It seemed likely that *The Silver City Sentinel* would produce one more issue and then collapse.

Jude Napoleon had vanished after breaking down this issue, and Flint counted it a good thing. The itinerant printer's issue had been dazzling and had shown the way. Each story served not only as news, but as a haymaker punch into the soft gut of the courthouse cabal or the mining magnates. But then one morning Flint woke up to an empty shop. He consoled himself that this was the way of itinerant printers. They dropped in and out of newspaper plants, helpful until the next itch for a binge overtook them, and then they vanished. They were called gypsy printers, and Jude Napoleon was a classic example. They were simply bindlestiffs with a skilled trade and a yen for the bottle. His departure eased another of Flint's worries — that Flint had lost control of his own paper. Now it was all his again, a fact that filled him with relief.

Actually, Flint intended to continue generating stories based on exchange papers. It was a coup. Let the courthouse cabal starve him for news; it didn't matter anymore. Flint intended to produce one more issue, hope that it would trigger some reforms in Silver City, and then load up his wagon. He didn't know where he would go; he only knew he would be desperately broke and probably forced to do some job-printing in every crossroads he drove through just to survive. Well, he could print up menus and posters and flyers if he had to. As well as wedding announcements, church bulletins, political and religious tracts, and boardinghouse rules. He lacked a job press, but he made the big Cleveland do.

Chastity let herself in to his sanctum shortly after Jude Napoleon vanished. Flint was annoyed, as usual, because she was wearing her half-open kimono with nothing else covering acres of lush flesh that made him dizzy. She looked as sultry as ever, and she was distracting him from his work.

"You gonna be a grouch?" she said.

"Not if you wrap that robe a little tighter and higher. I can only take so much."

"There's something wrong with you, that's what. You don't like women."

Flint stopped sorting ruler lines and eyed her soberly. "I guess I'm strange to you. If I felt no desire, I wouldn't care what you wore. In fact, you're the flame and I'm the moth. But I see more in each woman than her . . . physical beauty. I see her character, her needs, her dreams, her abilities. I hope to marry, and I want the union of man and woman to be sacred to us both. I want to reach old age with the same woman, my boon companion and lifelong mate. It's the usual thing. Nothing special in it at all. But it's also sacred."

She was laughing at him. He gave up, feeling bad. He wondered why he bothered. Most women adored knaves and laughed at honorable men and read romances about being abducted by dashing, dangerous pirates. He wondered why a few fools like himself tried to live according to an ideal of honor and gallantry when women were the first to subvert the whole concept.

She stopped laughing. "I know, Flint," she said, gently. "You don't have to tell me that stuff when I tease you. You're a friend. Don't you know I like your respect? That's more than I get from anyone else. They don't care about me, the person. It just gets funny sometimes, thinking about you here, the innocent editor in the bagnio, lusting away. You're no Napoleon." She registered the absence of the printer. "Where'd he go? I mean, the Little Corporal?"

Flint shrugged. "Gone. Who knows? Gypsy printers descend from heaven and depart into hell."

"Oh, I miss him. I was going to give him some free entertainment just because he's so sweet, but now he's gone."

Flint grinned.

"That was some issue he put together. That's all I hear about. My customers usually want to get down to business, or up to business, but now they all want to know what's going on next door. I'm getting business just because you're here and they can ask about you."

Flint laughed, embarrassed.

"You know what I'm hearing, Flint? Eleven gaming tables have left Silver City, and more are going soon. The tinhorns packed up when they found out they could run a table in Ouray for twenty clams a year. And one bagnio, Mandy Bell's joint. She loaded up her eleven ladies and left in two rented ambulances. Guess how the

198

teamsters got paid — the place got turned into a boardinghouse for miners. I hear more every day." She grinned. "That one issue, Flint, is costing San Juan County ten grand a year at least. They'll either quit grinding us down, or we'll all pull out, and then where'll they be?"

"Well, that's what Napoleon figured."

"It's getting better, Flint. No deputy's been in the district all week, skimming cash out of sporting people. It's like they're afraid they'll lose the rest of us. You did us a lot of good. We can save a little. I know some whores, they aren't so desperate now.

"And there's more. That mining story. Some of my customers are Balthazar's managers and I hear stuff. This burg's lost more than twenty hardrock miners, and they can't find replacements. Bunch just quit, got their tally and left for Leadville and Central City."

"What's Balthazar doing about it?"

She shrugged. "He thinks they're all ants, and he'll just wait for more ants to come in."

"Is he competing for labor?"

"You mean paying more? Nah. He doesn't get it."

"But his production must be going down."

"He's working the rest harder. He added a half hour to each shift."

"They'll keep quitting him, Chastity."

"Most mining stiffs are too dumb. They just keep on mucking. That's why they're in the pits."

199

"Has Hamlin been around?"

"Yes," she said shortly.

"What did he say about our piece on him?"

"Look, Flint, just forget it."

"He didn't like it, I imagine. Napoleon has a way of needling someone, and he really took a jab at Junior."

"Flint, don't mess with Hamlin. Your face still looks like a P. T. Barnum poster. Isn't that warning enough?"

"Yes. But I'm not quitting. A paper can't back down. He's terrorized the whole town. Not just the sports. His IOUs have hurt everyone. I can keep that in the spotlight."

"He told me he'd kill you. I think he wanted me to let you know. So I'm telling you."

Flint considered that, soberly. The old man had a hide as thick as a buffalo bull, but the young man didn't like the heat.

"Well, Chastity, that brings up a point. Unless things change, I can only publish one more issue. I'm about broke. Right now, I can tell you, I won't be able to pay your rent. No big ads, no subscribers, and I can't sell any more issues at two bits a copy. Next issue'll be my last one."

"Aw, Flint, you're just getting started."

"I know. But I'm sinking into debt."

She wrapped her arms around herself. "Maybe I can get the sporting people to give you something. Thanks to your weekly, the deputies and the sheriff aren't squeezing them the way they did. We all owe you."

He shook his head. "I can't do that, Chastity. You understand why."

She nodded.

"I appreciate the warning," he said. "I'll watch out for him."

"Flint, do you really think you can make changes around here with one more issue?"

He started to say no, that he'd been defeated. Westminster's economic noose was tightening, and the lack of advertising would kill *The Sentinel* before it could achieve a thing. But that wasn't what erupted unbidden from his soul. "Yes, Chastity, I need only one more issue. After that, things'll get better for you, for the miners, for everyone not a part of the ruling clique."

"Dammit, Flint," she said, "you're my hero. The least you could do is let me hug you."

Gingerly, Flint did, enjoying her eager embrace. He was only dimly aware that she was being very proper about how she held him, because she loved him.

24

Digby Westminster felt besieged. No sooner had he gotten past the fever stage and started to recuperate than every misfit and malcontent among the slimy merchants of Silver City assailed him, as if it were Westminster's fault.

As luck would have it, a gypsy printer had drifted in the very day the ague pounced on Westminster. The august editor had swiftly interviewed the cocky little fellow, who ribaldly called himself Napoleon, and he discovered that the man had something more than sawdust between his ears and could set type even faster than Digby himself. Westminster put the tramp to work and retired to his digs above his sanctum, there to imbibe sulphate of quinine and undergo the usual two- or three-day ordeal.

When at last he descended the stairs to tackle the business piling up on his desk, he found himself in the middle of a typhoon. His erstwhile cronies, the merchants, were lining up to whine, each waving a moth-eaten copy of *The Bawdyhouse Bugle*.

"Look at this!" yelled Jackson Cooke, a grocer. "They've discovered my Jonathan apples and Muenster cheese sell for more than they do in Ouray and Central City, and they're all in a pet. I could sell cheaper, but you won't let me."

A sullen delegation of neighborhood saloon keepers visited Westminster. The price for a mug of beer anywhere in Silver City was one bit, but now their patrons had discovered a mug could be had in most any other Colorado mining camp for ten cents. And worse, saloon licenses ran only twenty dollars a year in Ouray. "And we pay two hundred a quarter," moaned Gustavus Arnold, whose Pride of Silver City was the main downtown thirst parlor. "Something has to be done, and you're going to do it. You're the man with the county in your dead hand."

Westminster heard from cobblers and hardware men, coal dealers and restaurateurs. In vain he argued that it wasn't his fault; if they chose to gouge their customers, it was their fault. It was up to them to set the prices. All he did was insist on uniformity in the ads. Hadn't he for years carefully kept regional news out of his paper to prevent discontent? And did anyone ever thank him for it?

"But you promised to protect us. You promised to get rid of that scandal sheet. You said you'd squeeze it out. You said it was run by an idiot. You said . . ."

Westminster sighed, threw up his hands, and reached for the paregoric. The whiners kept coming and coming, until he was ready to retreat again to his sickbed. Somehow it was all his fault. How could they blame him? But he knew

203

the answer to that, and he couldn't wriggle out of it. He had assured them that he would control competition. He and his advertisers had a sweetheart deal. Any merchant who tried any price-cutting would no longer be welcome on his pages. Until recently, he was the only advertising medium and job printer in town and thus could enforce his ban. Now he couldn't.

But that wasn't the end of it. He discovered more than ninety subscription cancellations on his desk. The restless citizens informed him tartly that *The Democrat* and merchants had connived to milk workers of their hard-won dimes. Could the editor point to a single piece of important regional news in the last year? It took a real newspaper, *The Sentinel*, to tell the story. Some of the malcontents even said they would buy nothing from any merchant who advertised in *The Democrat*.

Outrageous!

Westminster's bones ached worse than his brain. In one of the rare moments when he wasn't being assaulted by fevered merchants, he wandered through his shop, pausing to inspect the typesetting of the nimble gypsy printer.

"I hear discord. What's all that about?" the fellow asked. He obviously was a veteran typesetter, because his hands never stopped plucking type from the case boxes.

"Oh, nothing. We've a vicious new competitor, the voice of the sporting crowd, a fellow named Flint. He's stirring up trouble."

"It sounds like it. I trust you'll remedy the matter."

"Yes, of course. It's been a testing for me, especially since I've wrestled with the ague. I thought Flint was done for. I've cut off every smidgen of advertising, shut down every news source in town. He can't get a story out of anyone in the county — not the merchants, the churches, the clubs, or any official. I had him licked so badly he scarcely knew how to fill a page. But then he latched onto the exchange papers. And he invented a few other perverse tricks."

The fellow's eyebrows shot up. "Sounds like you've been outmaneuvered, sir."

"Just between us, I made a mistake. I took Flint for a dunce and a tool of the vicious classes. But he has a certain low cunning. And he got an education somewhere. I won't underestimate him again."

"What's he for? Why do people buy his paper?"

"It's all a sham. He professes to stand for a broad property tax and city government. Actually, he's a mouthpiece of Vice, in the pocket of the pimps and tarts and tinhorns, and he's trying to shift the tax burden away from those parasites."

"Now you've got me puzzled. Isn't he urging the sports to leave town? He's getting rid of vice. Maybe you want the tarts around so you can tax them."

"Well, you're an outsider, and you might reach that erroneous conclusion. It's much more complex. We have a painful situation. The mine owners refuse to be taxed. We tried it. They simply shut down and waited. That means, my good man, that the only remaining source of county income is Vice, which exists in copious quantities here, this being a mining camp that's ninety percent male. So we taxed Vice, but now this fellow's inviting all our cash cows to depart. It seems we're a little harder on the poor dears than neighboring burgs, and he's pointed it out."

"Well, you're just dodging the property tax. Shifting the burden of government as long as you can. Right?"

"That's a perverse way to look at it, Napoleon. We're trying to nurture the productive classes here. But Flint is anti-business. He's published some price comparisons — you know, what the merchants in other towns are charging — and it's embarrassed our most stalwart merchants. They've all prospered because we've established a comfortable understanding here, no one charging less than anyone else — a policy I enforce by policing the advertising. Everyone profits."

"Well, not everyone profits. The workers don't profit. The clerks don't profit. The businesses don't profit either. Anyone who's a consumer doesn't profit."

The rebuttal inflamed Westminster. "The

people in the streets don't matter. It's the solid people who build a town that count. Now see to your work, or you'll be on the road again."

"What're we going to do about it?" the fellow demanded.

"We haven't made up our mind," Westminster said, loftily, just barely tolerating the impertinent question. "But I'll tell you the key. We've got to quiet this rabblerouser once and for all, before his next issue. If we act now, there won't be any long-term damage."

The fellow grinned. "I enjoy newspaper wars," he said. "Maybe I can help."

Nosy fellow. Westminster sniffed. "You just mind the typesetting, thank you," he said.

That's how Westminster's day went. The next day was worse. No sooner did he descend to his sanctum than a delegation from the courthouse arrived, led by Sheriff Poindexter. Westminster eyed them sourly, seeing accusation in their faces and suspecting the worst had come true.

The sheriff gazed at the editor through carnivore eyes and stretched his claws. "Ah, Digby, my friend. We thought you were going to rid us of that pest."

"I haven't quite succeeded, but I will."

"Perhaps it's too late. There's been a regular exodus from the sporting district."

"Oh, come now. I suppose one or two tinhorns have pulled out and you're upset."

Poindexter talked silkily, never raising his voice. "Twenty-nine gaming tables. Two bag-

207

nios with fifteen women. Several freelance tarts. Twenty-nine tables. Eight hundred dollars of license fees per table. The county lost about seventeen percent of its revenue because of one issue of a little rag you promised to wipe out."

"Ah, it's taking a tad longer than I expected."

"Seventeen percent, and more. We understand one saloon keeper, Bettendorf, is converting to an unlicensed variety hall."

"Well, license variety halls."

Poindexter preened his whiskers. "By the end of the week, we understand, the sporting district will be half what it was. It seems they can make a better living elsewhere. The county stands to lose half its revenue."

"Well, stop the exodus."

Poindexter chortled. "What, make it a high misdemeanor for a cash cow to leave Silver City?"

Westminster laughed politely.

"Well, Digby, what'll you do? You're the man of the hour."

Westminster surveyed the rubes before him and smiled. They lacked his experience. None had ever been schooled in a Tammany Wigwam or in the art and craft of a big city newspaper war. "Gentlemen," he began. "I can promise you that not one copy of the next *Sentinel* will reach the public. The miserable rag will fold, and Flint will slink away in the night."

"And if you fail in whatever you intend to do, he'll write the story, just as he wrote a little story about our amusing efforts to license him as an operator of a bagnio — which I hope the voters will forget. I've been hearing about that. It seems to have peeved about half the miners in town."

Digby Westminster tut-tut-tutted. "Newspaper circulation wars are entirely private affairs, gentlemen. The county peace officers won't be involved. No, not in the slightest. Have faith."

"And what's your plan? I think we should know."

Westminster rose and closed the door. He didn't want anyone to listen in, including the gypsy printer who was setting type just beyond.

"Now in New York and other great metropolises, the circulation wars are fought out on the streets. It's a war among the delivery wagons, the armies on the corners, and the newsboys. You need a certain kind of newsboy, right out of Hell's Kitchen. The victory, gentlemen, goes to the newspaper with the biggest brutes on the block."

The sheriff's eyes gleamed.

"The loser of the circulation wars might put out a fine paper, with lots of ads, and lots of mail subscribers. But if it doesn't have the right kind of teamsters and foot soldiers out on the streets where it counts, the paper vanishes from sight. Now, Silver City isn't Gotham, but the principle is the same."

"And who do I arrest for disturbing the peace?"

"Oh, I'd say that's up to you, Drew."

"And how do we get our license income back?"

"Why, see my next issue. This Thursday, we shall welcome the sports to Silver City. I'll eat a little crow, of course, but a little Vice is good for the town. You'll have to lower the license fees, of course. At least a little, as bait. But after a few months we can run them up again."

The sheriff's claws stretched and retracted. Homer Shreveport stood. "You'd better get it right, Westminster. Or we'll slap a property tax on you."

25

Jude Napoleon spent two days studying Digby Westminster. It really wasn't difficult to detect the man's weaknesses and fathom his strengths. The concave-chested and spare editor of *The Democrat* was largely driven by vanity. His offices were sumptuous, far more regal than any editorial sanctum Napoleon had ever seen, even at metropolitan dailies. Westminster's office was, moreover, designed to convey the impression of power and influence. The vast desk and tufted high-backed swivel chair stood on a dais, putting all visitors at a disadvantage. None of this luxury extended to the shop, where his printers labored with old, inefficient equipment and worn-out fonts. Westminster rarely donned the printer's smock, choosing instead to hand his printers pages of foolscap covered with his crabby scrawl, then wander through the backshop with distaste graven on his face. All that transpired between his rough stories and finished editions was now beneath him.

The other, obvious trait motivating Westminster was simple greed. He loved lucre and wasn't particular how he got it. With lucre he could put on the dog, take officials to dinner, buy his cronies a round of drinks, intimidate bankers, buy allegiance, scare away competition, and rule Silver City — except for the mine owners. In the presence of Achilles Balthazar, the editor was no doubt obsequious and fawning.

Napoleon concluded that the editor had no vision of the public good guiding him. The back issues of the paper showed no interest in the town's acute problems. He lacked any organizing ideal, such as equality or democracy or liberty. His editorial page displayed only squalid efforts to impose the entire county tax burden on the sporting district and to maintain a merchant aristocracy shielded from competition by a newspaper-operated cartel. As far as principles went, Westminster was rubbery as a squid. His frequent assaults on Vice were merely for show, and Napoleon intuited that the vaunted editor and first man of the county made private trips to the sporting district now and then.

All in all, a delightful mixture, Napoleon thought; good clay to fashion for his purposes. Unfortunately Westminster was a relatively discreet gent, and whenever anything important was being transacted in the lavish sanctum, the editor closed the door to the shop. This deprived Napoleon of certain information he itched to learn, namely what the clique behind the door intended to do about *The Sentinel*. Surely they knew that the recent issue had rattled windows up and down the gulch. Miners were howling about prices and studying wages and conditions in other mining camps. The merchants were pained; the county officials, aghast. The cash cows were departing for better pasture.

Napoleon's careful survey of the editor of *The Democrat* revealed still more information. The man had just wrestled with the ague and remained weak and pallid. Moreover, the august editor plainly didn't quite know what to do about Flint and wasn't up to an editorial retort. That looked like opportunity to Napoleon, who studied the empty chase that would eventually embrace page five, the editorial page.

Perhaps the editor needed some assistance this week. Perhaps, in his weakened and confused state, he would even welcome the words and ideas that Napoleon intended to put in Westminster's mouth. Ah, newspaper warfare had its delightful moments!

Swiftly, and with a blithe and mischievous spirit, Jude Napoleon, the Little Corporal of Lost Causes, began fashioning three editorials.

That Wednesday afternoon Napoleon set the editorials, ran off two galley proofs of each, and headed for the sanctum.

"Yes, what is it? I'm busy," Westminster said.

"Well, sir, I know you're busy and behind. We're putting the paper to bed and there's nothing on the editorial page."

"I've been sick. Now don't pester me."

"That's my point. I thought to help out. I've taken the liberty, sir, of composing some editorials. I saw you were behind. Now, of course, I know they won't be up to your standards, but maybe you could revise them into something."

"Editorials, Napoleon?"

"Yes, sir. You're at a crossroads. They required some delicate attention. I don't flatter myself that I can fill your shoes, sir, but I just thought to be helpful and take a stab at it."

"Wasting time on my pay, I'd say. That's a bit impertinent, but I suppose that's what one gets with a gypsy printer."

"Mostly composed during lunch, sir, so's not to interfere with my duties."

Westminster yawned. "Well, let's see them. They won't pass muster. I'm particular about grammar and logic. I'm from Gotham, Napoleon, and I maintain standards of journalistic expression unknown anywhere else in the West." He thrust out his hand, awaiting Napoleon's donation.

"Here's a set, sir. I've my own copies here, and I'll make any changes you wish. I didn't mean to imply that I could possibly be your voice or conscience, sir. I saw only your weariness from the ague, and the looming deadline. . . ."

"Yes, yes, yes."

"I'll read, sir, and you follow along. The first one deals with a delicate subject. The sporting district. I think I've found a solution, sir, begging your pardon."

"Well, let's hear it."

Napoleon began in sonorous voice. "When it comes to the defense of Virtue, *The Democrat* takes the back seat to no one. We have long advocated rigid control of the sporting district and high license fees for its denizens, as a proper way to recover money gouged from its victims. Such funds are put to good use by the county, and thus free virtuous citizens from onerous taxes.

"It has come to our attention that some sheriff's deputies have been abusing the system. In their zeal to reform Silver City, they have attached more than the customary and legal fees from the vicious elements. And while we generally applaud such zeal as a necessary control over evil, we note that this custom has gotten out of hand and the ultimate result is that San Juan County may be losing tax revenues."

"Ah, good, Napoleon," Westminster interrupted. "You've nimbly dodged the matter. I hadn't quite thought of how to put it."

Napoleon smiled and continued. "Now, our upstart rival, *The Bawdyhouse Bugle,* is urging its vicious clients and subscribers to depart these precincts so that they may practice their sinister arts at less cost elsewhere. We believe this is a foolish and nonsensical proposition, fostered by an overly moralistic rag of a paper for the sake of sensationalism. The important thing is to achieve some sensible equilibrium. We need to impose license fees that rigorously regulate Vice, but not so burdensome that the virtuous citizens of San Juan County need suffer new property taxes."

Westminster stopped Napoleon. "We'd better not call it *The Bawdyhouse Bugle*, not when it's telling readers that the way to get rid of Vice is by sending them packing. We've got to be subtle here, Napoleon. Call that miserable sheet *The Sentinel*."

"Why, yes sir. I've made a serious error, I can see that."

"Well, that's true, but for an outside printer you're doing a reasonable job."

"We recommend," Napoleon continued, "that the county lower its license fees sufficiently to keep the purveyors of Vice content. While we don't welcome them here, we recognize that they are a necessary evil, and there is no point in moralizing about it. Men will do what they will do, and it behooves reasonable people to accommodate reality. Perhaps a new fee of one hundred seventy-five dollars per quarter would suffice, but whatever the amount, we believe it is time for Silver City to be more tolerant and charitable toward its depraved classes. *The Democrat* will not engage in an excess of empty moralizing, unlike our upstart competition."

"Yes, yes, that says it," Westminster proclaimed. "You make that important change, and we'll run it."

"I'm glad you liked it. Now, sir, as far as the business arrangements in town go, I've taken the opposite tack. No trimming, no compromising."

"Ah, good! Let's hear it."

"*The Democrat* has always nurtured the businesses and merchants of Silver City as if they were precious roses," Napoleon began. "The result has been universal prosperity and swift progress as Silver City leaps from a primitive mining camp toward permanence and affluence. We have always focused on local news, because all of us here in Silver City must keep the well-being of our city and county foremost in mind.

"But our reckless competitor has been publishing data from other towns that allegedly prove that our merchants are gouging citizens and our prices are higher than elsewhere. Now, of course, this is largely nonsense, a trick of statistics used by the young hothead who runs the opposing paper. The reality is that a merchant needs a proper profit to provide steady service and assure an ample supply of merchandise in good times and bad. Reckless cutthroat competition really cheats customers by making life uncertain. Who knows what merchant will be cheapest from one day to the next? *The Democrat* has enforced, through its advertising policy, a sound pricing arrangement that encourages business to flourish here. Now it may be that sometimes a customer will pay a few pennies more, but that is nothing compared to the benefits.

"The important thing is for merchants to resist at all costs the siren song of the opposing paper and lower prices. It is nothing but a scheme to wreck *The Democrat* and foster radical change in

217

Silver City. We affirm that any merchant out of step with the rest of us will no longer be welcome to advertise on these pages, even after the upstart competition has been driven from town. We have already seen what fate awaits the misfit. The Smythe Brothers are selling furniture far below the price of the rebel cabinetmaker who abandoned his fellow merchants. *The Democrat* and the Smythe Brothers will ruthlessly drive the dissident out of business."

Westminster interrupted. "Ah, Napoleon, don't use the word *ruthlessly* — it's a tad harsh. Just let it be known that we oppose cutthroat competition and prices below those that earn a sound profit. A merchant should net a fifty-percent profit on sales, but don't say it. The ignorant miners wouldn't understand that it's all for the good and bolsters consumption."

"Certainly, sir, I'll make it as smooth as butter."

Napoleon turned to his third editorial, which excoriated *The Sentinel* for subverting the well-being of Silver City, calling it rash, unprincipled, and obviously beholden to sinister outside interests that were calling the shots. Flint was nothing but a tool, as would be shown in future issues of *The Democrat.*

Digby Westminster bought that one too, and Napoleon walked back to the workshop carrying the embarrassment of the Silver City Establishment in his hands. The august editor would be shown a hypocrite and a trimmer, with less constancy than a windvane. Westminster's defense of price gouging would collapse his subscription lists. His squirming to dodge taxes would make him the laughingstock of serious men. Westminster's new attack on Flint for moralizing, when last week he was calling Flint the voice of Vice, would amuse Silver City and win its contempt. The voice of Virtue would be shown to be a scoundrel, more interested in milking the cash cows and protecting his cronies than in any program devoted to the public interest.

Napoleon made up the editorial page and put the paper to bed. Then he approached Westminster once again.

"It's ready to print, sir, and my feet are itching. I guess I'll be drawing wages, eh?"

Westminster sighed. "You gypsies. That's why you're always broke. If you'd like to settle down, there's a job here for you."

Napoleon fidgeted. "I'm too much addicted to the grape, sir. You'd regret it."

"Well, that's typical. Fifty cents a thousand ems times twenty-seven. That's thirteen-fifty. Take this to the cashier up front. You did a job, Napoleon, I'll say that."

"Yes, I did a job. You can count on it, sir."

26

Sam Flint refused to surrender to the sense of futility that was dogging him this Thursday morning. The lifespan of *The Silver City Sentinel* would be only three issues, but he supposed he would do some good. Well, he had come here full of moral indignation and hadn't given much thought to business. And it was business that would defeat him. He would head for another town, look it over, and maybe start up another paper. He had done that often enough. He had never wandered up to the Wyoming or Montana Territories, and he thought he just might go there before winter closed in.

He worked quietly through the morning, copying stories he found in the exchange papers. He selected carefully, knowing that each story could help improve things in San Juan County. He should have remembered to study the legal and other advertising in the exchanges. That was a way to survey the ways mining camps across the West taxed and licensed themselves. But he had become so preoccupied and full of pain that he hadn't thought of it until Napoleon reminded him of what could be mined from such a source.

Everything he selected to reprint would throw

light on the ugly state of affairs he found in Silver City. It was the best he could do. He wouldn't reform the place this time, but he consoled himself that he had already made the world a little less desperate for some of the unfortunates in Silver City. Maybe when election time rolled around, the miners would vote in a new regime, no matter how Digby Westminster fumed and roared.

But it wasn't a victory, and Flint didn't delude himself about it. He resolved to bow out with dignity. His final editorial page would not ooze with recriminations. Instead, it would offer a sober analysis of Silver City's problems, propose some solutions once again, and wish the citizens the best of times. He might even summon up a compliment for *The Democrat*, which in some ways was an excellent paper with aggressive coverage of local affairs.

Tonight he would print three hundred copies — saving some paper to start up somewhere else — give the last issue to the Bridge boys, collect his share of their coins and shinplasters and bank scrip, and depart as soon as he had broken down the pages. He could not come up with Chastity's rent.

In the midst of these thoughts, Jude Napoleon walked in, carrying a copy of the latest *Democrat*.

"Ah, there you are," Napoleon said. "I've been busy giving the opposition voice."

"Napoleon! You what?"

"I hired on over there and wrote Westminster's editorials for him."

Flint sighed. "You switched sides. Well, I couldn't pay you, so I can understand that. I thought you went down the road."

Napoleon laughed. "Switched sides! Here, you big ox, look at these editorials. I did them myself. *The Democrat* is now in favor of Vice, in favor of cartels and letting customers starve, and is denouncing you for being overly virtuous. How's that for a three-day subversion?"

"You hired yourself on to betray your employer?"

Napoleon beamed. "Ah, Flint, don't get grouchy and don't be so moralistic. What I did is help Digby Westminster express his very own thoughts as vividly as possible. There's not one word in the editorials that defies his own thinking. Far from undermining his policies, I expressed them in the most lucid, crystalline, logical, persuasive form. We went over everything, and he congratulated me for expressing his views so sublimely. He's had the ague, you know. He didn't feel like writing, so your obedient servant took the opportunity to help him focus his thoughts."

Flint wasn't convinced. It all looked sneaky and treacherous to him. Grimly, he spread out *The Democrat* on his worktable and read. The front page was largely devoted to puffery of local merchants, with plenty of references to soundness, the high cost of transportation, and the necessity for sufficient profit to make the risk of doing business in a frontier mining camp worthwhile. A lengthy piece hinted at a growing tax crisis in San Juan County, triggered by subversive and perfidious false information being purveyed by the opposing paper, which was the mouthpiece of sinister outside interests seeking to bankrupt Silver City and pick up the pieces for a song. The mocking epithet, *Bawdyhouse Bugle* had suddenly vanished.

The editorial page proved to be just as damaging as Napoleon had indicated. *The Democrat* had abandoned its principles, if it ever had any. Flint wondered if anyone would notice. Probably a handful of thoughtful people in Silver City would take note, and the rest wouldn't care. It always amazed Flint how few people cared about public business, even when it affected them.

When Flint finished his perusal, he found Napoleon examining his own pages. The gypsy printer was reading the type, backward and upside down, a trick most printers had mastered through a lifetime of working with fonts.

"Pretty subdued, Flint," Napoleon opined.

"It's my last issue. I can't meet the rent, and I haven't a lick of advertising except for some cards. Some patent medicine companies back East want to buy some space to advertise their elixers for ague and plague, but I always make them pay in advance. I'm the victim of economics, Napoleon. I came here on a moral mission and hardly gave a thought to business. Now

I'm paying the price."

"Ah, hopeless cases. We'll have to do something."

Flint eyed the compact printer skeptically, but Napoleon merely smiled.

"Let's get this issue out. What's left to be done?" Napoleon said.

"I'm going to write some editorials." He glanced at Napoleon, not trusting him.

"I have a little suggestion," Napoleon said.

"You're going to put words in my mouth, so I'll hang myself too. You're playing a double game."

Napoleon looked wounded. "No, I was going to suggest something that you write yourself. Something that might win the day, after all."

Flint waited, ready to bite off Napoleon's blandishments.

"Mr. Flint, when we were toiling together last week, you told me why you'd come here. You'd seen something in *The Democrat* when you were getting it as an exchange paper, and what you read disgusted you so much you came here: Westminster's piece joking about the suicide of a poor cyprian and how Silver City had lost a good cash cow. You told me how it made your blood boil, this callousness toward a hopeless woman who took her own life. You told me it revealed such contempt for another human being that you could only believe that Westminster was a beast. And then, you told me, it seemed as if Fate had directed you, because you ended up renting the very rooms where such grief and desperation had finally snuffed out a life. And you told me that you'd found out that the county's licenses, the abuses of the deputies, the lack of protection for this helpless woman, had all added up to a murder of a soul. Mr. Flint, if this issue's to be your swan song, write that story up, as simply and honestly as you can."

The bantam waited quietly while Flint registered his words.

Suspicion raked Flint, even though he loved the idea. "You just want to prove Westminster's argument that I'm the voice of Vice," he accused.

"It might be interpreted that way."

Flint weighed it and liked it. "All right, I'll do it. If it's your way to bring me to destruction, it won't matter. I'll do it because it's why I came here and it expresses what I believe. If people want to twist it, that's their privilege."

Jude Napoleon didn't smile. "Sometimes a moment of truth, a confession, changes the hearts of readers, or shames them, or sets them to thinking. That's all a newspaper can do. Write it, and if it doesn't work, blame me. If it works, the credit is all yours."

"It's a challenge," the editor of *The Sentinel* said.

"Flint, my oversized ears syphoned in a few bits of news over there. Westminster's a discreet man and closed his door whenever he was palavering with his cronies, but I still wormed a little out of him. He's under pressure. The county told him to fix the hemorrhage or there's going to be a new tax. The merchants were all bleating about our price comparisons. Westminster promised he'd take care of the matter, but he's been pretty coy about it. I have it figured out, Flint. He's taking the war to the streets. This issue of *The Sentinel* won't reach the public. He didn't quite say that, of course. He simply told me he's familiar with the New York City newspaper wars — you know, teamsters fighting it out, gangs of juvenile thugs hunting down the opposing newsboys to bust skulls and bloody noses. I'm afraid the Bridge boys'll be in for it. Unless we take measures, not one copy of this issue'll reach the public. Digby Westminster is no amateur."

Flint frowned. He had been in newspaper wars before, battles of bullies using fisticuffs, clubs, and even shotguns, waged by rowdies hauling bundles of papers to their destinations. Rough stuff. It all figured. Up until now, it had been a war of words, and some shabby efforts to use ordinances to silence *The Sentinel*. Now it was entering a new phase. In a way, it signaled that Digby Westminster and his courthouse clique had been whipped on the field of ideas and programs.

"I'm glad you told me," he said. "I should have expected it. I apologize. You accomplished something over there. I don't much like it, but I'm grateful for it. They're crossing a line, which means they're desperate to silence me. Silence us."

"We'll prepare," Napoleon said. "There are means. One is to hire a dozen newsboys and sell out before the ruffians can find them all. Another's to change our schedule. Don't publish tomorrow. Let them hunt and sulk and wait. Another's to meet force with force. We're in the middle of a district full of brutes we could hire. Another is to take the war to them, wreck their distribution system, but there's no time for that. Another is free distribution, door to door, at a moment when they don't expect it. Have you any preferences?"

"Yes," said Flint. "This is the last issue. Whether I make a few dollars out of street sales doesn't matter. I'm busted no matter how you look at it. I didn't come here to make money anyway. I think maybe we should collect a dozen boys and have them slide a free paper under every door along Silver Street. We'll have to choose a time when the bullies aren't looking."

Napoleon beamed. "Time for a break, Flint. Let's go talk to the Bridge family."

27

Flint labored quietly over his last editorial, simply the story of his move to Silver City. He wrote in subdued language, not wishing to be flamboyant or emotional, and yet he knew the simple sentences, at once scathing and tender, would touch the spirit of any reader. His plea was for ordinary charity and mercy toward the world's wayward and unfortunate, many of whom had been driven by hardship into desperate lives.

Napoleon quietly set up the press, and when Flint had finished and proofed the editorial and locked it in the chase, using a quotation from Plutarch for filler, the two of them began printing the issue of three hundred. With two of them feeding the Cleveland flatbed press, it didn't take long to print both sides. The finished papers were stacked to dry, and the two printers wiped down the press.

"Well, that's the last one," Flint said, desolately.

"We'll see about that," said Napoleon.

Flint smiled. The patron of lost causes wasn't coming up with a way to stay afloat.

That evening, after a spare supper, they hiked down the gulch to the Bridge establishment. The lending library was still lit even though the shop behind it was dark. A bell announced them, and in due course Molly Bridge materialized.

"Why, it's you!" she said, delighted.

"It's us, and we'd like to talk with you and your sons, if it's convenient." Flint handed her a paper. "It's still wet," he warned.

"Any time's convenient," she said, lighting the way through the shop. Flint noted stacks of unsold chairs. The Bridge family business was suffering.

They entered a brightly lit room that Flint loved. The parlor was strewn with books and papers, often stacked in heaps. Assorted spectacles lay about at the ready. Shelves bulged with books, some of them morocco-bound and gilded with gold filigree. The Bridges' own furniture, hardwood Hepplewhite pieces, adorned the room. This heart of the Bridge family quarters breathed ideas and literary graces and causes won and lost — and something more. From its very walls leaked a merriment and sagacity rarely sensed by the outside world.

Even as the visitors settled on chairs, the Bridge family materialized from remote places, and Livia Bridge appeared with cups and a pot of tea. Flint found himself gazing at her as if she were the giver of all the world's happiness.

"Why, it's our besieged editors," Marcus said, extending a wood-chafed hand.

"Besieged is the word, Marcus," Flint said. Briefly he explained that this would be the last issue of *The Sentinel*. A weekly couldn't subsist on air, and there was more: Napoleon had gathered that rough tactics would be employed in the morning against Augustus and Timothy. They faced bloody noses or worse, not to mention the theft of the whole edition along with any change they had acquired from sales.

"It's a last resort," Marcus said. "When you lose the battle for men's minds, you go to censorship or violence."

"Did you see this morning's *Democrat*?" asked Napoleon. "I'm proud of the editorials. I wrote them. Every word perfectly echoed Digby Westminster's own views. He's had the ague, which was an opportunity for the patron of lost causes."

They stared at the gypsy printer amazed and then laughed merrily.

"Now, what are we going to do about this?" Marcus asked, turning to his sons. "The streets won't be friendly in the morning."

"I'll brave them," said Timothy. "I can give as well as I get."

"Ah, lad, there'll be half a dozen down on you," Napoleon said.

Timothy grinned. "Well, I'll take along some hemlock."

Flint interrupted that. "I don't want either of you fellows to take a beating for the sake of a dying paper. There's nothing much in this issue. I just continued with Napoleon's tactics, showing what other mining camps and counties do for taxes, and what their merchants are charging."

Napoleon interrupted. "There's more than that in it. *Mon ami* Flint wrote an eloquent editorial, simply telling why he came here to start a newspaper against impossible odds. He didn't like Digby Westminster's callousness. Here, I'm going to read you the last paragraph." He opened the paper to page two. " 'The suffering young woman whose hope ran out a few weeks ago did not willingly enter her profession, according to her colleagues. Her hopes dwindled when she couldn't pay her licenses and all the additional exactions imposed upon her by every passing deputy. She was a mortal, a person, a child of God. Her tragic death didn't deserve to be treated as comedy. She didn't deserve to be considered a cash cow, carrying a whole county on her slender shoulders because the greedy didn't want to pay taxes. Lying now in her potter's field grave but not forgotten by this editor, she remains a rebuke to the heartless and callous gentlemen of Silver City, who hastened her death and laughed when it came.' "

The Bridges sat very quietly in a deepening and gracious silence, paying their respects to a nameless dead woman who surrendered to a brutal world.

"We're here to find out how we can put this paper out," Flint said, embarrassed.

"What about right now?" Timothy asked. "Augustus and I can sell it in the saloons."

"Right now?" The thought startled Flint. "Well, why not? I don't think Westminster's torpedoes would be anywhere around. If you can't sell them all — there's only three hundred because my newsprint is low — give 'em away. Stuff 'em under doors. I'll still pay you your two cents."

Augustus said, "It should make a good evening."

"It's more than the money; it's the stirring things up that I enjoy," Timothy said. "Maybe you didn't succeed altogether, Mr. Flint, but you've made Silver City a better place."

"You mustn't be hasty about leaving," Marcus said.

"I can't meet the rent."

"Well, I want to talk to you about that. The Bridge business needs some flyers. We're switching our line a bit now that Smythe Brothers is giving away kitchen chairs and tables and bedsteads. We're going to do more cabinet-work — kitchen cabinets, pantries, armoires, that sort of thing. And some fine carriage trade pieces of Hepplewhite style using some maple, birch, walnut, and oak stock we've accumulated. We'd like some flyers, Mr. Flint. Little ones, letter size, about a thousand, that we can stuff in doors. They'd announce our new lines. We can't have them done in Westminster's shop, and we wouldn't patronize them anyway. But we'd like you to do them. If you'd just hang on as a job printer, maybe you can start up the paper later."

"Job printer?" Flint calculated swiftly. He would have none of the town's main merchants for customers, but he might pick up some menu work from restaurants. It didn't look promising. "I could do yours next week, Mr. Bridge, but it won't pay the rent."

"Well, we'll talk about that later," Bridge said.

"Don't be hasty to leave," Molly said. "Maybe there's ways to come up with the rent. How much is it?"

"A hundred, but I simply won't be indebted to any group —"

"And how much would a thousand letter-size flyers cost?"

"Oh, fifty."

"Well, there! You're staying in Silver City," she announced. "Pay for two weeks, and then pay for another two weeks."

They laughed, but Flint said, "Mrs. Bridge, weekly papers aren't something you can shut down and start up or publish irregularly. There really isn't any hope of an income. Perhaps with the job-printing I could stay open a while, but not to publish. I'm eating the seed corn now. I'm using up paper and ink I can't replenish."

Marcus Bridge stopped him with a gentle wave of the hand. "Mr. Flint, there are times in the affairs of every man when he must act on faith. By your rational calculus you should fold up, and I appreciate that. We're all businesspeople here. But you're on the brink of success. You might still fold, but you might still accomplish your mission — reforming this cynical town and its brokers of influence. That's why you came; that's why you must finish the job. Keep on, sir, even if the next two issues are only a hundred copies each. It's not your circulation that frets Digby Westminster; it's the power of your ideas and program. It's the strength of your indignation that's suffusing the whole town. This editorial you have here, it'll fire up Silver City. But we still need your leadership. Plant the flag, sir, even if you should be the first casualty."

Flint found them all gazing at him, and he couldn't resist their expectations. "Very well," he said quietly. "If you'll give me that job-printing order, I'll have the flyers ready on Saturday, ahead of my rent day. Then I can stay."

Five Bridges and one Napoleon beamed at him, and from them he gathered courage.

The young Bridges returned to the offices with the editors, gathered up sheafs of the still-damp issue, and plunged into the night. Augustus would sell in saloons and gambling joints and restaurants in the sporting district, while Timothy would head down the three-mile-long gulch, peddling papers in neighborhood saloons and beaneries.

"We'll be back with some loose change," Augustus said as the boys plunged into the crisp night, each laden with a canvas bag of four-page papers.

By midnight both young men had returned to Flint's shop. Each had sold out. Flint paid them their share, and they headed down the gulch. Flint felt elated. He had gotten his last issue out without a street fight. The boys had done a good job. They said many a miner had pulled out a dime or a one-bit shinplaster, bought the last *Sentinel*, and read it while sipping from his beer mug. Augustus reported that even the tinhorns and tarts in the sporting district had plucked up their copies.

"Westminster's going to accuse you of being the voice of Vice," Napoleon warned.

Flint looked at the gypsy printer. "That's why I came here," he said gently. "Let those who are without sin cast the first stone."

28

It amused Achilles Balthazar to fathom what people would say to him even before they knew it themselves. It was a matter of superior intelligence. It was also a matter of ruthless mental discipline. Nothing in the world escaped his curiosity. He spent little time thinking about himself, because it led nowhere. But he was sharply observant of others and could tell instantly what sort of person he was dealing with.

He was awaiting his foreman, surly Silas Graham, who would momentarily loom in his doorway and look grotesquely out of place in Balthazar's luxurious office. Graham ruled the pits with his hamlike fists but was as transparent as a child.

Right on schedule the brute appeared, pig-eyed and grimy, and stood respectfully before Balthazar's desk.

"You sent for me, sir?"

"I'm going to ask you some questions, and I don't want opinions for answers."

Graham looked nervous. That suited Balthazar fine. "Production is down twenty-three percent. Why is that?" Balthazar waited for

Graham to talk about the inexperience of the new hires.

"Sir, we've hired thirty-four new men. Most of them've never mucked ore. We lost most of our powder men, and we've put the most experienced men we've got on it, but they're slow, and they can't hardly doublejack like the Cornishmen."

"And why is that?" Balthazar knew that Graham would explain that all the mines in the local area began losing men when the new weekly began to do stories about wages and working conditions in various mining districts.

"It's not our fault, sir. The miners saw things in that new paper — powder men could get three and a half in Leadville, and experienced miners could work eight-hour shifts in Central City. Things like that. So they pulled time and took off. This paper, *The Sentinel*, it's run two of those stories, and we lost men each time."

"So our new labor isn't worth as much as the old. I intend to cut wages to two seventy-five." Balthazar waited for Graham to say that it would only cause another hemorrhage of workers.

"Mr. Balthazar, sir, that would just encourage men to leave. That would mean we're paying the lowest wages anywhere."

"You could have replied that it was a good idea: less money for lower production. I intend to maximize profits." He knew what Graham would say, and he waited.

"They wouldn't be happy," Graham said.

"They'd be bitter. When your men aren't content, they don't try very hard. You get more out of a man by paying him the going wage."

Balthazar nodded, amused. "Graham, a miner is the prince of hirelings. A cowboy gets a dollar a day, if he's lucky. A clerk gets fifty a month. Even at two and a half a day, the men in my pits will earn three times what common labor will earn them anywhere else." Balthazar waited for Graham to become subdued and skeptical and to begin talking about working conditions.

"Mr. Balthazar, I don't know . . . it's a hard thing, going into the pit for ten or eleven hours, freezing and sweating, going deaf from the noise, risking their lives."

The man was so predictable he was tiresome. Why was it that nine hundred ninety-nine out of a thousand mortals were dumb as stumps?

"Graham, what are we going to do about it?"

"I don't know, sir."

"Here's what we'll do. I'm docking you a dollar a day until you have production up to normal. You're going to go back down there and pound on the slackers."

Graham looked stricken. "But . . . it's the newspaper's fault."

"Why?"

"Because the paper lured your best men away."

"I read every word. It didn't lure one man away. It published market information."

"Market information?" Graham looked bewildered.

"Labor competes in a market, same as any other commodity. What that editor Flint was trying to do was win more money for my miners, and better conditions. He thought he could do it by publishing comparisons. He thought the threat of losing my best men would make me pay more. But it backfired, didn't it? I've just made wages and conditions worse. My miners will now earn two bits less, and you are going to pound on every laggard — that is, if you wish to continue here. You were just thinking of quitting."

Graham looked guilty.

"You may quit if you wish, Graham."

"No, no sir, I'll get right down and start in."

"That's a good boy, Graham."

Balthazar rose and escorted his foreman out by the elbow, which was his custom. It saved time and confusion. He nodded to Flint, who had also been summoned and was perched like an owl in the reception area.

The editor approached warily, wearing his usual tweed jacket with leather elbow patches. It amused Balthazar. People even dressed in uniforms to convey their essence to the world.

"Ah, Flint. You may stand there," Balthazar said as he wheeled around his desk. He insisted that people stand. It made them unequal. "You lost, you know."

Flint didn't reply, but he looked puzzled, as Balthazar knew he would. He rather liked Flint, whose brain was slightly improved over the Cro-Magnon. Balthazar also felt a certain wariness of the young editor. Idealists, while perfect fools, could be dangerous, and none more than those with moral courage, like Flint. Most oafs were perfect pragmatists, taking the world as it was and never bothering to reform it. But once in a while a man like Flint came along, and things were forever altered by his presence. Men like him took some watching.

"Of course I understand exactly what your pieces comparing working conditions were about. Some of our senior men did exactly as you expected — asked for their time and took off. You understand wage competition, but you don't understand me. I've just cut the wages in my mines by twenty-five cents a day. The rest of the mines will follow suit. There are perfect reasons, of course. Production's down. I have a bunch of greenhorns in the pits, so I will pay them less. But the main reason was to show you what practical men can do to reformers."

Flint looked disappointed and did nothing but nod. The editor was smart enough not to open his mouth.

"Where you go astray, Flint, is your assumption that there's a scarcity of labor. Every immigrant boat brings a new load of thick-skulled brutes willing to do anything. You might have won if there weren't droves of these ants crawling around. The truth of it, Flint, is that I could offer one dollar a day and still fill my pits. The only reason I don't is because it's not efficient. Good powder men and drillers aren't easy to find, but they can be trained in a hurry, which is what I just told my foreman to do. So there you are, Flint." Balthazar smiled.

"I don't regret trying. If things aren't right, I'll try to reform them."

"Right? Ah, Flint, right for whom? Morals are so slippery."

Flint didn't respond. Apparently he wasn't going to be drawn into a battle of wit, which was smart of him. He knew his limitations.

"Actually, I've enjoyed the last two issues. You've routed poor Westminster, you know. He's come unraveled. I'll surprise you: I'd let my mines be taxed if it were part of a broad, universal property tax. Somebody has to pay for government. But that oaf Westminster and his merchant cronies first tried to stick the sluts with the whole bill, and then the mines. All they wanted was for someone else to fork over. We'll come to your property tax eventually, especially now that you've strung up Westminster from the nearest gibbet. I must say, you've made the place lively."

Flint smiled slightly, as Balthazar knew he would. The editor turned to leave.

"Oh, I'm not done, Flint. We have business."

Flint paused, obviously debating whether to leave.

"You're my tenant, Flint."

That brought the editor up sharply.

"I bought the building from Miss Ford yesterday for four thousand. She did rather well, I think. Made two thousand on it, and she gets to stay on free for one year. I thought I'd double your rent to pay for hers."

Flint registered that a moment, several emotions passing across his face. "Then I'll be leaving town," he said at last. "The rent's due on the first — three days. I'll be out by then."

"Oh, maybe not," Balthazar said. "I require thirty days' notice."

"You have three," Flint said.

"Oh, no. If you were to leave without giving proper notice, you'd run into my mine-security guards again. Your face still looks like a jungle flower."

"You're stealing my equipment, then."

Balthazar was amused. "No, not really. One applies the carrot and the stick to mules. Your type are mules, stubborn beasts. I've applied the stick, and now I'll offer the carrot. I actually like your rag. You get to stay for free."

Flint's gaze fled through the windows, off toward distant slopes. "You want your own paper, your own mouthpiece. I've never been for sale. Even if you should steal my equipment and leave me penniless, I'm not for sale."

It was just as Balthazar expected. He could have recited Flint's speech for him. "Ah, Flint, you poor devil. You're too suspicious. Stay and publish. I promise I won't censor you. Attack me all you want. Westminster does regularly, and I enjoy it. It's the only attention I ever get."

"No, sir, the arrangement's not acceptable to me."

A swift momentary irritation passed through Achilles Balthazar. He wanted to tell Flint to get out and set up his press elsewhere, if he could find quarters. "Well?" he said. "What would you accept?"

"I don't know if I'll accept anything," the editor replied. "I'll have to think about it for a day or two."

"Now, Flint. Decide now."

"I'll let you know when I'm ready," Flint said, and left.

Balthazar watched him go, surprised for once. In all of San Juan County, Flint was the only man Balthazar admired.

29

Sam Flint returned to his shop in a pensive mood. The news that Balthazar had bought the building astonished him. Chastity had a good income from it, and Flint wondered why she had sold it. He knew the purchase had nothing to do with her or with income from rents. It had to do with him. Balthazar intended to control him, one way or another. That meant *The Sentinel* had succeeded in opening up the labor market, and the mine owner didn't like it. The purchase of the building was all the proof Flint needed.

Flint feared Balthazar far more than he ever feared Digby Westminster. The Balthazars employed ruthless tactics, including the sort of drubbing that still resonated in Flint's body and discolored his flesh. The Balthazars would stop at nothing, whereas Westminster, for all his political maneuvering, rarely crossed certain boundaries.

Flint found Jude Napoleon lounging in the kitchen with Chastity. Flint didn't mind. Napoleon worked with such lightning speed that neither man felt under any deadline pressure.

"It's our chaste editor," the tramp printer said, pouring java from a blackened pot.

"You've come back from the lion's den to tell us this building's been bought."

So Chastity had told Napoleon.

"And my rent's been doubled. I'm to give thirty days' notice," Flint said, "or I can stay for free. Balthazar denies it, but he wants a mouthpiece of a paper. Oh, yes, if I should leave without giving the thirty-day notice, I'll run into his mine guards again and lose my equipment. He called it the carrot-and-stick approach."

"The building's being watched. You can't sneak out," Chastity said.

"I'm a stubborn man," Flint said. "I won't pay double rent; I won't become anyone's mouthpiece, and I won't accept free rent, either. I won't be bought, and I won't let the public think I've been bought. If I'm washed up here, I'll get my equipment out even if I have to hire a few dozen miners who aren't afraid of Balthazar's torpedoes."

"Gee, Flint, you should spend a night with the girls," she said. "We've got to pour water on your flaming virtue." She giggled maliciously.

"Don't worry about it," said Napoleon. "Take the free rent. I'll write a story about Balthazar's grab for *The Sentinel* and quote you: 'No dice.' All you have to do is beat the other guys into print. Don't let Westminster write the story first. If he beats you, it looks like you're hiding something."

"He gets all the courthouse news. He probably knew it ten minutes after the deed was transferred. It'll come out in the next *Democrat*, ahead of us."

"Flint, he's giving you a chance to survive. Take the bait and worry about fending him off later."

"No, I won't accept free rent," Flint said, the old stubborn hardness coalescing in him. "I'll offer him my regular hundred dollars, take it or leave it. I'll pay it out of job-printing or maybe sales, but I'll pay it. If he doesn't like it —"

"You walk away and he keeps the equipment and has himself a paper. Maybe he'll hire me," Napoleon said, enjoying himself.

Flint said nothing. He'd never lost his equipment before, though he'd come close once when a sheriff had attached it. He would have to start over as a tramp like Napoleon, wandering from town to town, scrimping and saving until he could be independent again. It would take at least three thousand dollars. He wondered if he was capable of that.

He eyed Chastity, whose kimono was half open, revealing silken golden bosom. Until then he hadn't paid any attention. Now he tried not to. Her available curves always tortured him. "Tell me how it happened," he said, his gaze averted.

"You poor thing, studying my left pinky finger like it just grew an inch. I'm female, but you pretend not to notice." She sighed and wrapped the kimono tighter. "Yesterday Hamlin came over. He just walked in and threw a nice old slam-

246

bam-thank-you-ma'am customer out. That was something. Then Hamlin said his old man was buying the building. He offered me four thousand in cash, which gave me a two thousand profit. And a year of free rent. That was the carrot. But just in case I refused, he said he'd get the goons and when they were done I'd have to put a flour sack over my head to get any business. That was the trick. They aren't subtle."

"Didn't you go to a lawyer? Get a restraining order? Talk to Poindexter?"

She glared at him. "Hey, Flint, you're dumb. Ladies like me have no rights, no protection. The law isn't for us. If some white slaver came in and decided to sell me in Mexico, do you think I could get help? No. Poindexter would kiss me good-bye. Paunchy old Homer Shreveport would think it was funny and try me one last time. My lawyer — if I could even hire one — would tell me I made my own bed and had to lie in it. I'm not a citizen, Flint. Not me, not any girl around here. Even the tinhorns have rights, but whores don't. I don't even have a right to life. If Hamlin killed me, he wouldn't be punished. They'd say, 'She was just a slut.' If you killed me, it'd be the same. You'd get off." She wasn't laughing now. Some dark emotion lay upon her.

"Why are you here then?"

"I don't know."

"Why don't you leave, Chastity?"

She shrugged. "Maybe I like what I do."

He didn't believe her. "You're well-educated.

Guadalupe Ford saw to it and gave you every advantage."

"I know," she said, melancholy in her voice. "It's too late now." She made a moue, letting him know the topic was closed. There was something between the famous atheist father and his cultivated daughter that had wrought this.

Flint wondered about her. She professed to like her life, but it didn't make sense. She was pretty, educated, and gracious. She could have had almost any man for a husband. Was she a rebel against her father? Was she a hop fiend, with a habit that needed supporting? A nymph? Did she have some awful need to debase herself? They never talked about such things, and he sensed a certain line drawn around her that couldn't be broached.

"So you sold."

She flared. "I had no choice! I didn't sell, I surrendered! You know what they can do with a broken whiskey bottle? He paid me cash, in hundreds, and I banked it. I'm lucky to get anything. A lot of men would've just taken it." She sat there steaming at him, looking so gorgeous he couldn't bear her beauty.

"We could all walk out of here," he said gently. "Start over. I have my wagon and mules above town. We could be out of the area in an hour."

"You'd take me with you, Flint? You, the biggest prude in Silver City, and me, a whore?"

"Yes."

She eyed him a long moment, something

tender in her face that slowly faded. "But you won't. You're staying. Your business isn't done yet."

"It's over. No ads, no subscriptions, no income. No one walks through the door with news. I was going to leave anyway."

"We're all prisoners," she said. "Let's face it, Flint. You and me are in the Balthazar jail. Hamlin's going to be coming around a lot more, and I won't be able to say no, and he isn't going to pay me. It's his building now. Achilles won't come around, but just try printing something he doesn't like, and you'll learn you were bought and should stay bought. You'll get some new bruises. He says we're all ants, and that's how he treat us — bugs to step on."

Flint stared into his coffee cup, wondering what Fate would deal next. At last he turned to Napoleon. "You're the field marshal of lost causes. You tell me what you think."

Napoleon beamed. "Ah, Flint, *mon ami,* you should take the free rent and whore a little — beggin' your pardon, sweetheart. You're not done yet. If you walk away now, you've lost. Westminster and his cronies still rule the courthouse. Balthazar imposes his will on the whole gulch. If he offers you free rent, take it so we can continue our little donnybrook. There's no glory in walking away. And quit worrying about what people think. We're gonna tell the world how we got a new landlord. I've a way with words. So do you. We'll waltz, we'll hop and skip, we'll trot

249

around them all."

"Westminster'll call us *The Balthazar Bugle*," Flint said.

"Why, let him. We'll just remind him that his *Bawdyhouse Bugle* label didn't stick, either. We'll have the best of it."

Flint surrendered. "Maybe we could do one issue. Two hundred sheets left. I'm ruled by the paper supply, Napoleon."

"Two issues. A hundred papers each time."

"We'll see," Flint said.

"I gotta go to work, dearies," Chastity said.

The next morning, while Napoleon began building the Bridge family flyers, Sam Flint hiked up the gulch to the mines and into the swank white headquarters of the Balthazar empire. This time the smirky clerk didn't keep him waiting.

"Ah," said Balthazar from behind his waxed desk. "You've come to tell me you'll accept free rent."

"No, I've come to tell you I can't be bought, and I won't be intimidated. I'm going to pay you my regular rent when I can. And I'm giving you two-week notice. I'll be out of newsprint by then and *The Sentinel* will fold."

"Out of paper," said Balthazar. "We can't have that. I'll have some brought in."

The answer revealed the direction of Balthazar's thinking, Flint thought.

"You still don't get it. I won't be your mouthpiece."

Balthazar laughed, his Delft-blue eyes oozing joy. "I always get what I want, Flint. I pay any price that's necessary. You idealists have a higher price than most, but you have a price." He rounded his desk and caught Flint's elbow to escort him out. The mining magnate was an expert at that.

Flint left, not knowing whether his terms would stick. He wouldn't know until he showed up with the fifty dollars for two weeks of rent. If Balthazar left him alone for two weeks, he would have that much time to achieve what he set out to do in Silver City. It didn't look very promising, but it would be a shame to quit before the war had been won. He walked down the gulch, thinking himself stubborn. He had made a promise to the poor creature buried in the potter's field whose suicide had brought him here, and he would keep it.

30

Digby Westminster studied Flint's paper with such a stew of mixed emotions that he feared the ague would pounce again. He could barely stand to hold the rotten little sheet in his hands, much less actually read it.

Flint had slipped the paper into the saloons the night before his regular Friday publication, as if he had known that his newsboys would lose the war on the streets. It infuriated Westminster. He had intended to mop up every copy Flint sent out into the world. In the morning, his hired torpedoes, six roughs out of Hell's Kitchen, found no sign of the Bridge boys. Westminster wondered how Flint had found out. Surely it hadn't been an accident.

Westminster studied Flint's maudlin farewell editorial with special care, this time licking his chops because Flint had destroyed himself with it. Imagine peddling such bathos to manly men, to morally upright citizens. The worthless bundle of rags who dosed herself with too much joy juice wasn't worth anything but a laugh. None of them were. They were just parasites feasting on men's vices. The one that excited Flint's compassion, whoever she was, hadn't had the moral fiber to make a decent life and croaked by her own practiced hand. She deserved being a cash cow. The sheriff should have squeezed her harder.

Oh, Westminster thought, if he were to write it again he probably wouldn't laugh at death, but beyond that he couldn't fault his little piece about the cash cows. It flabbergasted him that the four-inch jest on an inside page had somehow embarked the lunatic young Flint on his silly crusade. Well, now the camp would chuckle at the galoot, who was flying his true colors. Too bad the rag wouldn't be around any more. Westminster would have loved to heckle *The Sentinel* issue after issue.

Still, this issue continued to do serious damage to the delicate arrangements in Silver City. Flint ran another piece about retail prices elsewhere, focusing on New Mexico Territory, and a lengthy piece about mining wages and conditions throughout the West. The word was that a lot of veteran miners were pulling out, heading for greener pastures, and Balthazar was hiring anyone he could get.

Westminster had no sooner finished perusing the sheet than his ad salesman, Padrick Stemple, hurried in. "Lot of ornery merchants out there, Digby. You promised to silence Flint, and you didn't. Now they're all taking heat from customers. And they're sending you a message. I had a tough time selling two column-inches of ads."

That caught Westminster's attention. "Who's not buying? We'll squeeze them out. Any merchant that won't advertise won't get back in. Flint's leaving; they have no place to go. If they cross me, they'll be out in the cold, like Bridge."

"I tried that, but it don't work, Digby. They've got a mess of angry customers. And what made 'em madder was your editorial about how higher prices are good for everyone. It sounded too much like Marie Antoinette telling all the starving Frenchies, 'Let 'em eat cake.' Miners don't see it that way. From what I'm hearing, we'll get a mess of subscription cancellations in tomorrow's mail."

"My editorials aren't to blame."

"Well, you didn't write 'em this time."

Remembrance leaked into Westminster's thoughts. The tramp printer had written them when Westminster was still woozy with the ague. "Go back and tell every advertiser who's not cooperating that he's in trouble," he said. "No, wait. You walk up to Flint's shop and peer in the window to see whether that gypsy printer's working there."

Stemple's thin lips slid back from his wolf teeth, and he left.

Westminster hastily opened *The Democrat* to read the editorial that allegedly had offended the town's miners, uneasily aware that he hadn't written it. He studied all three opinion pieces, a sickening feeling sliding through him. Each of them nakedly expressed Westminster's private opinions all too well. The gypsy archfiend had defended Vice and the county income from Vice and attacked Flint for being too moralistic in a town full of restless males. The editorial urging the merchants to stick with their cartel oozed a subtle contempt for struggling miners and their families. A sad, nauseous sensation crawled through Westminster's belly, up his throat, and into his skull. He'd been had. That miserable fiend had been planted in *The Democrat* to ruin it, flipflop the paper's views or exaggerate them, and make *The Sentinel* look like the town's pillar of virtue. Westminster stared at the traitorous words on his very own pages — supposedly from his very own pen — and seethed.

Sheriff Poindexter cat-footed in and settled himself in one of Westminster's tufted leather chairs, all without asking. The sheriff's eyes studied Westminster as if he were a dead fish. Poindexter sighed, smiled, shook his head, and said nothing, utterly rattling the editor, who wondered what additional blow could possibly strike him this chilly Friday.

"It sure is amusing," Westminster said, "Flint's sudden attack of charity for the whores."

"It don't win elections," the sheriff said softly. "He's saying we killed her. Flint's like the woman that wrote *Uncle Tom's Cabin*. The more you attack him, the more he wins. But that don't bother me. He'll lose. You bother me. Your little piece yesterday about laying off the bawds —

you weren't kind to my deputies."

Westminster wanted to howl that the editorial didn't express his thoughts in the slightest and that he didn't write it — which would have won an arched eyebrow from the silky sheriff. The editorial had been rough on Poindexter, now that Westminster thought about it.

"I had the ague," he said. "When you're fighting the fever, words get put in your mouth."

The sheriff was enjoying himself, Westminster thought. The lawman just sat there, stretching his claws and retracting them, enjoying it.

"A tramp printer did it," Westminster said.

"He's a mind reader, I take it."

"No, no, I had nothing to do with those editorials."

"You didn't read them or approve them, I'm sure."

Westminster sagged into his squishy chair, refusing to be lured down that road one more foot.

"The voters are rumbling," the sheriff announced. "Like a storm high in the San Juans. The county supervisors are poised to send you to the gallows. Do you know what, Digby? The exodus from the sporting district continues night and day. By my calculation, San Juan County's lost over a quarter of its revenue. The whores have seen the light. They're all en route to Ouray. We lost another seven table games. Three more saloons and a parlor house have vamoosed. But that's not the half of it. The rest of those illustrious citizens have banded together and petitioned the county: Lower the licenses to Ouray's levels, or they'll load the wagons too. Ah, Digby, Digby, you told us you were going to win this little fracas. Do you know what? The county's about to pass a little old property tax. Imagine it, Westminster. Every landowner in San Juan's going to pay for law and order and courts and clerks."

"Oh, it won't happen. Balthazar and his cronies'll shut down again."

"Maybe so but we'll have to try. They shut down last time because they were going to be stuck with the whole load, leaving all you nice and upright merchants as tax-free as the day you were born. If I remember rightly, *The Democrat* proposed that little fiasco. This time the ordinance will spread the load."

Westminster nodded, truly humbled. "Ah, what would the taxes be for a business establishment?"

"Oh, some. Who knows? Enough so you'll feel it. I think the supervisors might just tax newspapers double. They don't love you anymore, Digby. Neither do I. *The Democrat* tells me to go easy on Vice and not hurt the little darlings. *The Sentinel* tells me my deputies are practically murderers, robbing some sainted little slut of her hope. Ah, Digby, newspapers are a trial for a hardworking, honest sheriff."

When Westminster nerved himself to reply at last, it was in the softest voice. "It'll all come out fine, Drew. Flint threw in the towel. You read it yourself. He's pulling out. He's not gotten one display ad since he came here, just a couple of cards. It took a while, but we shut him out. He still can't get any news, not from the county, not from the merchants, not from a church. In a few weeks we'll have everything back to normal."

"No, not to normal. Normal is over."

"Well, we'll all speak with one voice now. I'll get everyone in our informal little coalition together."

"It's too late, Digby. Things are happening. This very hour, one of Balthazar's shysters recorded a deed with the county clerk. Achilles Balthazar's bought the building that houses Flint, from the celebrated Chastity Ford. Do you really think Flint's going to leave town, now that he'd got boodle from the king of Silver City? More likely, he'll put you out of business. The county is, ah, sending an emissary to the white palace up the gulch to begin long, honest, candid, frank, affectionate talks."

"I don't think Flint can be bought. I'll say that for the wretch."

Poindexter shrugged. "What difference does it make? If you're Flint's landlord, you'll pull the strings even if Flint doesn't like it."

"But Flint's pulling out. He said so."

Poindexter rose. "That was before he acquired a new landlord." The sheriff stretched. "Think repentant thoughts," he said, and slid out.

After that, Stemple sidled in. "You're right,

Digby. The tramp printer's setting type over there. Getting up another issue. Looks like Flint didn't quit after all."

"*The Balthazar Bugle*," said Westminster, seeing opportunity in it. "If he keeps on going, we have him right where we want him."

31

On Saturday Napoleon printed the flyers, delivered them to Marcus Bridge, and returned with fifty dollars. Flint marveled at the greenbacks in his hand. That afternoon they broke down the Friday paper. On the sabbath he and Napoleon rested and talked theology. That afternoon Flint hiked up the gulch and into the mountains, found his mules in good flesh and hairing up for cold weather, and paid the rancher for another month of pasturage. The walk out of town put life in perspective for him. The eternal mountains, bearing caps of early snow, spoke to him of lasting things. If he were forced to it, he could walk away from Silver City defeated and begin anew somewhere else. He had utterly no regrets. The place was already better because he had tried to cast light upon its darkness. Not that he intended to quit. He would fight to the last penny. But the walk reminded him that the world was larger than the ferment in the gulch.

On Monday a small, sweet miracle occurred. Four merchants wandered into his sanctum. The first of these was portly, bristly Aurelius Golden, co-owner of a large general mercantile and grocery in the business district. He surveyed

Flint's plant sharply, probably looking for signs of vice and dissolution, and then studied Flint, who waited patiently.

"You printed the Bridge flyer?"

Flint nodded. "And who are you, sir?"

"Golden. You think you could print some flyers for me?"

"I can. Today, in fact. I've plenty of letter stock, but not much newsprint. Would that do?"

"It'll do. How much for a thousand?"

"Fifty, payable on delivery."

"All right," he said, extracting a hand-drawn draft of what he wanted and handing it to Flint.

Golden wished to hold a week-long sale, ten percent off on everything in the store, twenty on selected items including ladies' shoes, boots, ready-made shirts and duckcloth britches, sheet-metal stoves, and fifty-pound bags of potatoes.

"I'll make it handsome. You have a logo?"

"Same as in *The Democrat*."

"I'll copy it. I think this'll be effective. I can deliver it later this afternoon."

"We'll stuff it into every door in town." Golden seemed as if he wanted to talk, but he turned to leave.

"Your customers'll rejoice," Flint said. "It's the first break they've ever had."

"You're telling me!" Golden said, his ruddy face animated. "All we hear's complaints and threats to trade in Ouray. They can wagon over there and load up and save a lot."

261

"You're following Bridge, then?" Flint asked softly.

Golden squinted at Flint, as if making up his mind about something. "It's a business decision. Should've made it long ago, but I didn't realize I had a choice 'til now."

"You might not have a choice soon. I'm pretty well whipped. You should know that before you plunge."

"Mr. Flint, no matter what happens, I'm going to compete. I can have my flyers printed over there in Ouray. I'd never thought of it. I think Golden Brothers'll soon double its trade." He eyed Flint again. "I suppose you know that Balthazar cut wages. The other mines followed suit. That makes a real sale all the better. A man can buy one fifty-pound sack of potatoes in my store and almost make up a week's loss from the wage cut. That's the way to win customers."

"I'm afraid I'm the cause of that cut, sir. I thought I'd pressure Balthazar into being more generous, but he cut two bits out of a day's labor instead. He told me the new help was producing less, so he'd pay them less."

"Well, keep at it, you'll lick him eventually. Nothing like information." He eyed Flint dourly. "You whipped us; you whipped every merchant in town, running all those prices."

"Whipping you wasn't my intent. Breaking up Westminster's combine and letting competition work for the benefit of all consumers was what I wanted. I think you'll prosper in the end. We all will."

"I'll prosper. Westminster won't. He's as shifty as a weathervane, but it won't help him any. That last issue of his really took the cake."

"How do you mean?"

"He hasn't an ideal or a principle or a bit of loyalty in him, and that last issue of *The Democrat* proved it. He did a hundred-eighty-degree turn. Now he's saying your *Sentinel*'s too hard on vice, and he's for it. Ho!" The merchant finally smiled.

Flint smiled and said nothing.

"It's all greed and politics in his skull," Golden continued. "He's distantly acquainted with Virtue, though he talks as if he and it were close kin. He's more familiar with Vice, but you'd think he never kissed unfamiliar lips, the way he carries on.

"Actually, Flint, he's the consummate politician, all things to all men. That's what his last issue was about. Years ago he tried to load the whole expense of the county on a few ladies of pleasure, and then he tried to load it on Balthazar, who battled him down like a bluebottle fly. And why? Partly greed, but mostly because he loves being the big spider in the web. I'm done with him. Golden Brothers'll profit handsomely just by routing the competition. Westminster's little cartel doesn't scare me, especially with you around."

Flint was impressed. Aurelius Golden had a shrewdness about him and a willingness to take chances that was rare in the merchant class. "I think your sale'll give you a big advantage," he said.

"I think so," said Golden. "Get them to me by five if you can. I've some boys ready." He peered about the place again. "Must be tough to publish here. You planning to get out?"

"The instant I can. Space is hard to find."

Golden leaned forward. "Now don't you go spreading this: If I get wind of a good spot for you coming vacant, I'll tell you. We can get you outa here. Just keep it under your hat."

Flint was touched. "Mr. Golden, that's an offer I'll treasure."

They shook on it.

Ten minutes after Golden's visit, Jack Bacon, the hardware man, came in with an order for flyers promoting a big sale of kitchenware. An hour after that, Flint had orders to print flyers for a feed store and a cobbler with a line of saddles and tack. Sales were breaking out all over Silver City. Each merchant wanted a thousand flyers, and Flint quoted them all at fifty dollars. By Tuesday evening, Flint would be two hundred dollars richer.

With that, he could buy a pallet of newsprint in Denver for a hundred-eighty plus freight and have the stock in hand in a few days. He could publish! He left the shop to Napoleon and hiked to the freight outfit that would wire his order

264

from Alamosa and pick up the paper there. He was back in business for a few weeks, if he stuck to small editions. No one was advertising in *The Sentinel* yet, but each job-printed flyer amounted to an ad and actually cost the customer more than the space in his paper. He wasn't knocked out yet. Westminster's cartel was crumbling. There would be repeat business too, as long as Westminster barred the rebel merchants from *The Democrat*.

The sudden improvement in his fortunes filled Flint with a strange warmth, as if he had come to a good campfire in cold weather. That was almost literally true. Now he could buy some cordwood for his dead stoves.

This was rent day. He took Bridge's fifty and walked up the gulch to the whited sepulchre, its fluted columns flanking the shining doors.

"I've come to pay my rent," Flint said to the clerk.

"Leave it with me. He doesn't see tenants."

"We've a rent dispute to settle. I'll wait here."

Annoyed, the clerk let Flint suffer in a soft, butt-deadening chair for an hour, and then slid into the great man's office. A moment later he beckoned Flint.

"Ah, Flint, you've come to pay the two hundred," Balthazar said cheerfully, whittling a cigar.

"I told you I'd pay for two weeks at the old rate. Here it is." He dropped the bills on Balthazar's desk. They seemed small and alien and dirty there, like a vagrant moth. Balthazar didn't touch them.

"You don't listen. You may stay there free or pay me what I require."

"I won't be bought," Flint said. "Go ahead and evict me."

"I'd keep your equipment for what's owed."

Flint was glad he'd taken a walk on Sunday. "Mr. Balthazar, wealth is precious, and I'd regret losing it. The means of production are more precious, and I'd have a bad time putting together a new plant. It's worth three thousand. But more precious to me still is my self-esteem. I can walk away from Silver City proud and happy and broke. I've done some good here. This very day, the merchants threw in the towel. There'll be competition. But no man owns me or my paper. That's how it is."

With that, Flint left, leaving the grubby bills on the desk. Balthazar laughed sardonically. "Idealists," he said to Flint's back. "You ruin the world."

Flint walked back to his shop, wondering what would happen. He could only do what he had to and leave the rest to fate. He felt an edge on his emotions, an itch to fight Westminster, Balthazar, and all their greedy troops.

Napoleon greeted him. "I sold another flyer," he said. "The Singer sewing machine dealer. You're afloat. I ought to leave. I'm named for the patron of lost causes."

"Napoleon! Please stay."

The tramp printer laughed. He had already set three of the flyers ordered that morning and was preparing the press for some gang printing. "A little job-printing doesn't support a newspaper," he said by way of an answer. "Or pay gypsy printers."

Stricken, Flint dug for his billfold.

"Put it away. Let's run these off first, Sam. If you've got some cash, go buy some reams of letter stock. Bradley's Clerical Supply has plenty. We're going to work up our own job-printing flyer."

A wry grin spread across Flint's face. He'd been so busy lancing windmills that he had neglected ordinary business.

"And Flint, take it from your field marshal. Many a county weekly's been printed on letter-size pages, especially where a man can hardly get newsprint. Nice little papers that end up in the outhouse. Don't forget it when you're in a financial pinch."

Flint laughed. He hadn't for a long time.

32

An invitation to sup that evening with the Bridge family delighted Sam Flint. Napoleon was invited too. Flint had grown weary of their bachelor beanpot, and almost as weary of cafe slop intended for miners who lacked taste buds.

But the invitation meant more than good food to Flint. The sordid district in which he lived and worked oozed through his walls, assaulting his ears and eyes and soul. Every night the periodic thumping of a bed in the apartment above him reminded him that his neighbor Marcella was at her business. He had heard every ribald remark emanating from the corridor beside his quarters. From his windows he had watched men vomit and women solicit and pairs of yeggs rob. The buying and selling of lust went on around him night and day, ultimately sullying him.

The partial exodus of the sporting clan to Ouray hadn't altered things much. Buildings changed hands, often in minutes. Bagnios became boardinghouses. Gambling joints became variety theaters. Saloons and dives became cafeterias or dime-a-dance halls or pawn shops. What he needed was a plant in a respectable precinct. But why move? He knew he would be broke and out of Silver City soon, into clean, sweet wilderness.

Napoleon managed to clean up for dinner, scraping off a lawn of black stubble and extracting a clean shirt from the bottom of his warbag. Flint scoured ink out of his digits, switched to his last fresh collar and cuffs, brushed his ancient tweed suitcoat, and then Don Quixote and Sancho Panza set off down the gulch.

The jingle of bells as they entered the lending library announced them, and soon Molly Bridge was leading them through the darkened shop redolent of new-sawn pine and furniture glue. Flint noted that the stock of finished furniture had vanished. The flyer had probably done that.

They entered the room he loved, the warm parlor strewn with books and magazines and gold-rimmed spectacles, a room where ideas and viewpoints seemed to hover in the air. Flint had left vice behind him and plunged into a place bristling with the virtues and hopes and dreams of his civilization.

Marcus met them, along with Augustus, Timothy, and Livia.

"Ah, the warriors," Marcus said, shaking hands. "Evict a cat and have a seat. We have more cats than chairs. We've been plotting all day how to get all of your war stories out of you."

"Your furniture's gone. The flyers worked?"

"They did the job. The boys stuffed them

under doors all evening, and customers showed up all day. We've a month of orders to fill. And there's more to it than the flyers, Sam — if I may address you familiarly. It was all mixed up with politics. A lot bought a chair or a table as a way of lashing out at Westminster's price fixing. They said so."

"They must have read Napoleon's stories," Flint said.

"They had. Some of them came in with *The Sentinel* in hand and wanted me to match prices being advertised in Central City." He laughed. "I met the price. Hurt a little sometimes."

"Your paper's the best thing that ever happened in Silver City, Mr. Flint," said Livia in a shy voice.

Flint thanked her and found himself drawn to the lovely young woman. She was about twenty. He had noticed her before, but this was his first chance to get acquainted. Bridge's sole daughter had a glow in her brown eyes and a reserve that hinted of some rich private life going on within her. As Flint listened to her quiet conversation, he realized she was the very kind who enchanted him the most: not really beautiful if beauty could be measured in classic, uniform features of the flesh, but piquant and sweet and wise, a boon companion for any scholar. She probably knew more Latin than he did, and he didn't doubt that she had teethed her mind on John Locke or Edmund Burke. She had a lithe young form too, barely apparent in her winter skirts. But she must be eleven or twelve years younger than he was. Flint checked himself, or tried to. But her shy smile undid his effort to bridle a sudden attraction.

He listened idly to Napoleon orate war stories. They all laughed about his foray into the enemy stronghold as a gypsy printer, and the editorials he had fashioned that perfectly expressed Digby Westminster's unguarded thoughts, which were somewhat different from *The Democrat*'s pieties. But Flint's mind was suddenly elsewhere. He kept glancing at Livia, drinking her in, trying to be discreet about it but not succeeding because she was furtively surveying him. Sometimes their gazes locked, and he felt static electricity crackle. Once she shyly turned away.

Flint found himself telling about the several merchants who were following the Bridges' lead and ordering flyers; about writing for five thousand sheets of newsprint; about deciding to stay on and finish the battle.

"You mean I'll have to spare you my sons when we've gotten busy again?" Marcus asked.

The question made Flint somber. "Westminster's still going to try to throttle us. He's familiar with New York City street wars. The papers there fight it out, and it gets rough. He'll come at us. I'm thinking of irregular publication — getting our issues out at odd, unexpected hours when the bullies won't be looking for you."

Timothy grinned. "We're game."

"That's good, but trouble's going to visit you no matter what we do. I'm going to think this out."

"Defensive war usually fails," opined the field marshal. "You've got to take the war to your opponent. When Westminster gets hurt, he'll quit the rough stuff."

Flint winced. "Two wrongs don't make a right," he said.

Molly called them to dinner, interrupting an absorbing debate, and Flint found himself sitting at a table groaning with such delicacies as bachelors enjoy but once a decade. The scent of chicken dumplings fresh out of her oven, a vegetable medley smothered in some sauce or other, new red potatoes, fresh Brazil coffee, Parker House rolls and sweet creamery butter, and two hot apple pies cooling on the sideboard, dizzied him.

Merriment spiced the meal. The Bridges were expert at joshing each other as they cleaned off the platters. Demure Livia ate quietly, smiled at Flint with warm, glistening eyes, and sometimes repaid the barbed wit of her brothers twice over.

"Mr. Flint," she said, between the main course and dessert, "we know so little about you."

It was an invitation, and he knew she was hiding behind the plural. She wanted to learn about him. So, briefly he described his life, sliding swiftly through his childhood in his father's private academy, the war that transformed him — and then the broken engagement. He decided not to spare himself. Her glowing face turned more sober when she learned he had broken an engagement with a lovely lady only days before the wedding and fled West because he had an uncontrolled itch left over from soldiering for Abe Lincoln. He was scarcely aware that others were listening.

He hurried to the end, describing his life as a frontier newspaper editor with an itch still driving him from place to place and a need to mend the unraveled world.

"Thank you," she said. "I think your fiancée must miss you."

Flint felt bad. Napoleon saw it and spoke up. "Flint's a principled man," he said. "I've never met an editor who'd rather lose than compromise."

Flint felt his spirits sag. He saw himself as a hypocrite, inconstant to one he loved long ago while parading his constancy to his ideals.

"But now he's under the guillotine blade," Napoleon continued cheerfully. "Balthazar this time, not Westminster. Maybe we'll see his head in the basket. I keep telling our esteemed friend he's battling on two fronts. The King of Silver City bought the building a few days ago. He was stung by our stories comparing mining wages and conditions. He lost his best men. His response, of course, was to try to muzzle this big galoot. He doesn't like the idea of competing for labor, but it's a commodity like everything else, and it goes to the highest bidder."

"How is he going to muzzle Flint?" asked Marcus, suddenly alert to a new development.

Flint chose to answer. "He's trying to own me or break me. He called me up to the white office, doubled my rent and then offered me free rent, take my choice. The rest was left unsaid. Oh yes, he also wants thirty-day notice, and warned me if I didn't comply he'd seize my equipment."

"And what did you do?" Bridge asked.

"I dropped fifty dollars on his desk — my former rent for two weeks — and told him he couldn't have me for a mouthpiece even if he stole everything I possessed."

"Oh, hurrah!" breathed Livia.

"That's a hard thing," said Marcus. "Taking your equipment for debt. The means of production. I suspect it's legal too. Maybe you'd better talk to a lawyer. Anyway, what'd he say to that?"

"He said he'd find what my price is, I could count on it. But nothing's happened so far. I gave him what I could afford, and no one has come for my press."

Bridge chuckled. "You bearded the lion, Daniel!"

"The Balthazars have been known to employ brute force," Napoleon said. "As Flint knows all too well."

"I don't think that'll happen," Flint said. "Not if Balthazar wants *The Sentinel*. He's smart enough to know I won't bend."

"Westminster's a yapping pup compared to

274

Achilles Balthazar," Marcus said quietly. "Balthazar'll never tell you he wants your soul, but he's after it."

"That's very true," Flint said somberly. "He may find some way too. I'm not made of cast iron. There are things that might force me to surrender. If he finds a way, it won't be monetary. It'll be because he's threatening to hurt someone."

Later, walking back to his grubby bachelor digs, Flint found himself wrestling with a private hurt. A bright, happy nest like the Bridges' home, with a wife like Livia and children to make a father proud, seemed an impossible dream for a vagrant editor. Why was it that a principled man like himself was always so lonely?

33

Hamlin Balthazar stood at the door, a small, triumphant smirk etching the corners of his mouth. He looked beautiful, like Adonis, his young unlined face so smooth he didn't seem to possess whiskers. Chastity pushed the door shut, but he blocked its swing with his shiny leather shoe.

"Please leave," she said.

"It's my building," he said, pushing in. She couldn't stop him. "I own every board and nail. I own the floor I'm standing on and the ground under it. I own you."

"No one owns me."

He laughed easily and took off his coat. Except for a paleness from the want of an outdoor life, he looked like some Grecian statue, his costly suit luxurious and newly pressed, his paisley cravat snugged into a snowy starched collar. She could have liked this young man, two years her junior, except that his eyes brimmed with hell.

"From now on, I own you," he said in his reedy voice.

"What does that mean?"

"It means you're a slave. I'm a white slaver." The thought amused him, and his eyes danced.

A dread crawled through her, but she kept her

outward calm. "Hamlin, be a gentleman," she said. She forced a smile.

"You're smiling to appease me," he said, enjoying himself. "You'll need to smile a lot. I like smiles."

He wandered through her small parlor, master of it, stamping his ownership on it. "Get dressed," he said.

That surprised her. "Don't you want —" She shrugged.

"We're going to your bank."

"What?"

"Your bank." He smiled. "Where you keep your money. We're going to withdraw it together and put it in my bank."

A coldness ran through her blood. "It's my money and I'll keep it where I want."

"Of course it's your money. But you're going to put it in my bank."

"Why?"

"Because you're mine, and because it's my leash on you. If it's in my bank, you won't go away."

"You're saying you won't let me withdraw it," she said tightly.

He smiled. "You wouldn't want to leave, would you? Just when I've made you mine?"

"I choose my customers," she said.

"No, sweetheart, not anymore. You're all mine."

She registered that, slowly and bleakly. "How'll I live? You never pay me."

"You'll starve if I choose to starve you."

She turned silent. She studied the young man, looking for signs of his intent: for kindness, for violence, for warmth or coldness, for mercy, for cruelty, for respect, for contempt, for lust. She wanted to know a thousand times more than she knew about him, but his hooded face was a mask.

He smiled. "You wouldn't be thinking of resisting me, would you? Or getting help? Or running away? Don't think such things. I own you."

"And what happens if I want to live my life as I choose?"

"You won't have any life to live."

"Are you saying you'd kill me?"

"Oh, not I. I never do such things. Now get dressed."

"I won't."

He sighed. "I've some gentlemen just out in the street. I guess I'd better summon them."

Dread ran through her. "What do you get from this?"

"Fun."

"Keeping a woman a slave is fun? Why don't you find someone to love? Someone who'll adore you. Someone you'll adore."

He gazed gently at her. "There are two forces in the world, love and power. The opposite of love isn't hate, it's power. Both are rewarding. Power has always been more rewarding to me. I really think there's no such thing as love. I have perfect power over you. You're the best of the dollies in Silver City. You're beautiful and you charge the most. I want you all for myself. I'll make you my slave. Nothing offered by love even comes close to the pleasure that ownership gives me. Now get dressed or taste my power."

He said it so softly, so blandly, that it sounded like a preacher's conversation. She went to her window and found two of the Balthazar mine-security guards standing in the street, their breaths steaming in the cold air.

"You have no power," she said bravely. "Every bit of it's borrowed. None of it comes from within you."

He said nothing but studied her from unblinking brown eyes, opaque like an animal's and hinting at nothing.

"You're very weak," she said, gathering courage. "It's your father's money and your father's private police. If you were strong, you'd pay your gambling debts yourself. You'd hold a job on your merits. You'd be just and fair. If you want to have justice or kindness, seek it from a strong person. Without these — these crutches holding you up, you'd be nothing. You are nothing."

He smiled, unblinking. "Get dressed."

She thought of Flint across the hall, needing him desperately, knowing that he'd try to help her even if he took another awful beating. Something in her sagged. She would have to give ground and begin planning some way to escape.

Not even a Balthazar could keep her in a jail that had no bars.

"All right," she said.

"You were thinking about the editor. And then you were thinking you'd find some way to escape my gilded cage. I'm always ahead of you. My father has that trait, and I do too."

"Where will this end?"

He smiled. "In death. You see, I'm already way ahead of you. You'll not let yourself be entirely possessed, and then —" He shrugged.

Numbly, an icy dread creeping through her, she waited for the rest of his prophecy.

"Get dressed," he said softly.

She retreated to her room and mechanically shed her kimono and put on a street dress. He was watching at the door. She drew a mink-decked cloth coat from her armoire and put it on, not really knowing why she was obeying him.

She found herself walking down the gulch beside him, the two torpedoes behind, the cold within her much worse than the chill in the air. She turned into the San Juan Merchants Bank and approached a wicket.

"He wishes me to withdraw my money," she said to the sallow clerk.

"Well, do you have your passbook?"

She produced it.

"A cashier's check'll do — make it to me," Hamlin said.

"Yes, sir," the clerk said. He turned to her. "You've five thousand seven hundred thirty-three here. That's a lot. You wish to withdraw it all?"

She didn't say anything.

"Ah, Mizz Ford, do you wish to withdraw it all?"

"She does," Hamlin answered.

The teller retreated to another counter, where he filled out a form, and then thrust it through the wicket to her. "You'll need to sign here," he said to her.

She simply couldn't. She couldn't lift her hand.

"I'll sign," Hamlin said.

"You're not authorized," the clerk said, frightened.

"I'll sign," he said, plucking up the pen, dipping it in the inkpot, and signing his name.

"I'll have to consult my officers, Mr. Balthazar," the clerk said.

"Write me the check," said Hamlin.

Frightened, the clerk did as he was bidden and handed Chastity's future to Balthazar, who stuffed it in the pocket of his Chesterfield.

Hamlin led her away. "Now I own you," he said.

"No one owns me, Hamlin."

He laughed and steered her by the elbow back up the gulch to her quarters. She had only one wish, running like a wildfire in her, and that was to escape, even flat broke. Escape with only her life if it came to that. He waited while she opened the door and then entered with her. "Go get

281

undressed," he said.

She headed silently for the bedroom. This, at least, she understood. He followed her, but didn't even take off his Chesterfield. When she was naked she headed for the bed, but he stayed her.

"Put on your kimono," he said.

Numbly she did.

He smiled. "There you are. I'll leave some slippers too."

She waited, bewildered, while he summoned his two men. Then the three of them stuffed every item of clothing she possessed into pillowslips.

"I don't want my canary flying around," he said, as his burly lackeys carted four pillowslips of her clothing away.

"You won't borrow clothing, will you? If the ladies upstairs were to lend you some, it wouldn't be good for them."

She said nothing.

"You're not open for business anymore. You won't let anyone but me in here."

She stood, frozen.

"I'll know if you do."

"How am I supposed to eat? Or get firewood? Or buy a pail of water?"

"Maybe you'll starve, thirst, and freeze," he said.

Something raged in her. "Hamlin Balthazar, you can hurt me or kill me, but the thing you want most you'll never have. You'll never own me. And you have no power over me."

"That's what I predicted." He smiled and left.

She stood stock still in her prison, waiting for the presence of him to fade away. She didn't even hate him. Hamlin was being Hamlin. Then she crept to the front window and saw no one. She could walk away — perhaps. He wouldn't expect that, not so soon.

There was no help anywhere. Girls in her trade had no rights and none of the law's mantle of protection. She studied the street, not knowing what to do.

34

Flint was poring through a New Mexico exchange paper, trying to make sense of the mining news in it, when Chastity materialized beside him. He hadn't heard her come in. She looked distraught. In fact, she looked awful, a desperation in her face that he had never seen there before. She wore her kimono, which annoyed him. She was always ignoring his business standards.

"Flint," she whispered, "could you give me something to eat?"

"Why, sure, Chastity."

"I'm so hungry. I haven't eaten since this morning."

"We've some beans cooking. And a fresh loaf of bread. Pretty humble, but it'll fill you."

"Oh, Flint, it sounds wonderful." She headed toward the kitchen at the rear.

"Let's break for supper, Napoleon," Flint said. The bantam printer was working on still another flyer, this one commissioned by the Bottomless Pit Cafe, which was changing its menu and lowering its price a nickel.

Chastity didn't wait; she ladled steaming pinto beans into a bowl and attacked them as if she were indeed starving.

"What's the trouble?" he asked when she had filled herself.

"Hamlin."

"What's he done?"

For an answer, she burst into tears. He didn't press her, and he signaled Napoleon to be patient too. When at last she had gained her composure, her tear-streaked face looked ravaged, as if some black cloud had hailed on her. Then, slowly, she began to narrate her incredible story, clenching and unclenching her hands.

Flint could scarcely believe it. Marched her to the bank, intimidated the teller and forced her to fork over her money, including the four thousand she had just gotten for the building. Taken her clothing. Told her not to flee. Told her she was powerless, his absolute prisoner. Left her hopeless, penniless, and threatened. He listened incredulously, knowing all of these horrors were real.

"Can you help me?" she asked at last.

"Of course we can. And we will. What do you want?"

"To go. Just to get out of here."

"And start over?"

"Oh yes, anything. Just to get away from him, from the Balthazars."

"Have you considered talking to Poindexter?"

She laughed bitterly. "You still don't get it. Women in the life have no rights, nothing."

"You have a right to your freedom."

That brought fresh tears. Flint realized he

knew precious little about her life and what she faced in some places. He waited for her to reach calm again. "Has he abused you?"

She shook her head. "He just uses me, but that's my business."

"But he hasn't hurt you? That's still assault and battery, no matter what you are."

She reached across and patted his hand. "You're so innocent," she said. "Half the deputies threaten to beat me if I don't pay them something or give them what they want."

A bleakness spread through Flint. "You want to escape. You need clothing. Have you tried the girls upstairs?"

"No. He goes up there. He owns them too. I just know they'd tattle on me if I tried to get anything I could walk out of here with."

"How do you know you're watched?"

"Because Hamlin said so."

"Have you seen them?"

"No, but he can buy eyes."

"Maybe I can find some used dresses for you. Where do I look?"

"Flint," said Napoleon, "if the lady wants to dodge, she shouldn't be wearing a skirt. I got stuff in my warbag that'd fit her smartly." He left the table and returned with a shirt and a pair of denim bib overalls. He handed them to her and she held them up to her. They would work.

"Oh, Mr. Napoleon," she said. "Oh . . ."

"I'll hang 'em on that hook there. Better leave 'em here. You can get 'em anytime. And even if

Hamlin wanders around here looking for petticoats, he won't take a second glance at these."

"She'll need shoes," Flint said. "And other things. A hat to hide her hair. A coat. It's getting cold."

"Let's see your foot, sweetheart," Napoleon said. She held up a bare and gorgeous leg with a trim ankle. "I'd better measure," he said. In a moment he had a size for her. "You'll be queen of the road when we're done."

"Where would you go?" Flint asked.

"Ouray, I guess."

"Thirty miles. Hamlin could snatch you back."

"I gotta start somewhere, Flint."

"Gimme a day," said Napoleon. "I'll outfit you. A hobo queen, only when I'm done no one'll guess. And take some advice from the field marshal. Don't go down the gulch and out. Go up to the ranches above us, and then cut over the mountain. Or go to Durango."

She nodded. "A day seems like forever." Tears welled up again. "I don't have anything." Then she brightened. "I'm wrong. I have you." A thought clouded her face. "He'll hurt you if he finds out you helped me. He'll put those men on you again."

Flint had been thinking the same thing and had swiftly come to a conclusion. "We'll deal with it when we have to. The important thing is to get you out of this mess. White slavery — I've heard of it, never seen it."

"Chastity," said Napoleon, "you mind if I ask how you got into this profession?"

It was something Flint had wondered for weeks, but some innate politeness had kept him from asking. He poured some pungent and weary coffee from a battered blue pot and handed her a cup. She sipped gratefully. At first he supposed she wouldn't answer, but then she did.

"I wanted to be notorious," she said.

"Notorious?"

"Like my father. He got rich — well, sort of — being notorious."

Flint watched a lively animation suffuse her face once Hamlin had been abolished from her thoughts. Could this woman be barely twenty-three?

"He used to make three, four, or five hundred a night lecturing. He'd charge a dollar admission and then sell his book after the lecture and then get people to join his Atheist Society for five dollars. The more the preachers attacked Guadalupe Ford, the more he liked it. He was . . . notorious." She smiled, a momentary brightness in her eyes.

Flint studied her skeptically. There had to be more. "I can see Guadalupe Ford's daughter becoming a radical, a champion of free love, or joining a utopian community, but not this."

She didn't reply at first, just stared into her lap and then gazed out the window. "Yes," she said. "There's more. Maybe someday I'll tell you.

Flint, please understand. This is all that's left. It's a rotten life, mostly, but it's better than lying in a grave."

"Has it to do with your beliefs? What you got from your father?"

She laughed bitterly. "You mean because I was brought up against religion I think it's all right to do anything? Oh Flint, you're so naive. . . ."

Napoleon said gently, "Then it was a hurt. Most people are hurt. Not many can live up to ideals. Just remember, you're a valuable person, and no one can be perfect or even good."

A flash of gratitude filled her face, but it faded like daylight at dusk, and soon she was shrouded in twilight bleakness.

In one of those illuminating moments that reveal others, Flint knew that this woman at his table despised herself. And that she would say nothing more — for now.

No one spoke for a long while.

They heard a soft click, and a moment later Hamlin Balthazar walked in, uninvited. He smiled. He wore his immaculate black Chesterfield, his velvet collar freshly brushed, and a black derby. He looked so smooth and young, untouched by life, undamaged by failure. The gorge rose in Flint, and he throttled back an impulse to drive Hamlin's teeth down his throat.

"Ah, there you are, Chastity, plotting your escape. I came to feed you. Even a canary needs to be fed."

"You might have knocked," Flint said.

"My building."

"You might have knocked," Flint repeated, with more edge.

"You're plotting to take my property from me. She's mine. I own her. She's chattel. I'd call it theft if that happened. She can't escape on her own. If something should happen, why, I'll know just what to do." He smiled broadly. "But you know all about that."

"Maybe I don't."

"Plotting," he continued. "You'll get her some clothes and hang them here so I won't see them. You'll feed her and equip her and choose the moment. Ah, you see, I have my father's gift of divination. He's right. You're all ants."

Flint didn't see any point in saying a word. The more Hamlin talked, the more the man might reveal himself.

Hamlin turned to Chastity. "Time to go back to your cage," he said. "I have a little meal and some other entertainments in mind. I'm glad you love only me."

She sat quietly, unmoving. Her face had turned bleak again, almost as if she had aged a decade in a moment. Flint pitied her almost more than he could bear. She looked so small and helpless.

"I put your money in a special joint account," he said. "It'll be safe there. I told Sheriff Poindexter I was going to be your trustee. He laughed and made an obscene joke of it. He hoped I would enjoy trusteeing with you."

"Leave her alone, Balthazar," Flint said almost inaudibly.

"I was hoping you'd say that, Flint. I never need much of an excuse. It's almost like grabbing me by the collar, isn't it? I see the bruises haven't quite disappeared."

Flint sensed the presence of others in the hall, which was all that kept him from leaping at Balthazar and giving him a thrashing he wouldn't forget. But that wouldn't help Chastity escape.

"Come along, Chastity," Hamlin said, an easy smile on his face.

He had spoken no threat to her, but it hung in the air.

She sat rigid.

He turned to Flint again. "A story. You're already writing a story in your fevered mind. All about Hamlin Balthazar, the rights of any American citizen, the protection of the law, the illegality of white slavery, and the evil of slavery of any sort. You'll even mention that you fought in the war to get rid of the Abominable Institution, and here it is in Silver City."

Hamlin's discernment shocked Flint. Father and son could read his mind as if it were an open book.

"Come along, or I'll take your dragon kimono from you too."

Like some marionette, Chastity rose and vanished into the hallway.

291

Hamlin smiled. "Be careful, Flint," he said, following her. "You could be hurt."

"Hey, Hamlin. I'm Jude Napoleon. Pleased to meet youse," said Flint's colleague. Balthazar took no notice.

35

Mournfully, Digby Westminster studied the six flyers on his desk, supposing they spelled the doom of an empire. Each announced a sale. Each had been printed by Flint for less than the cost of the same amount of space in *The Democrat*. Each put the rest of Silver City's merchants on notice that there would be fierce competition henceforth. Each was a victory for consumers, in Westminster's estimation the least important segment of society. Common laborers would reap the harvest of lower prices, while worthy merchants would see their profit margins diminish.

But Westminster was not an unsophisticated man, and he knew full well that cartels could defeat market competition by employing the ever-friendly protections of government. He intended to propose an ordinance to the county supervisors, making it a public nuisance to distribute flyers door to door. He thought he might have trouble getting that one through, but it was worth a try. His own advertising revenues were down sharply, and the new ordinance might just restore them to their prior glory.

He regarded the straying merchants as a villainous and disloyal lot, and his mind seethed with ways to punish them. But not just yet. He had to drive Flint out first. As long as the young reformer flourished up there in the sporting district with a press to print more flyers, Westminster's carefully crafted prosperity coalition would be in trouble.

• He was not a man given to much self-doubt. He always knew exactly what he was doing and approved heartily of himself. But now an unaccustomed doubt plagued him, a strange pain of the soul that kept abrading his confidence. Was he doing the right thing? Had he erred along the way? Was he playing the fool? Was he a lesser man than the formidable Flint? How easy it was to let pride get the best of him. He had never before fretted and fussed this way or felt the nervous tensions he felt now. He responded to this worm of humiliation by reminding himself that he was a formidable man, a New York sophisticate of the first rank, a former sachem of Boss Tweed — and soon he felt better.

There were always ways and means. The purchase of that building by Achilles Balthazar was a heaven-sent opportunity. Now Westminster would make it plain, issue after issue, that *The Sentinel* was a tool of the most oppressive mine manager in Colorado. *The Balthazar Bugle*, he'd call it now, and the nickname would strike right into the heart of every miner who read it. Westminster could scarcely label it *The Bawdyhouse Bugle* anymore. It would only point to his own journal's wobbly opinions about the sporting district and the reality that a third of the sports had abandoned Silver City as a result of Flint's market and taxation stories.

His own weekly was not yet in serious financial trouble, but Westminster didn't doubt it would be unless he stopped the hemorrhage. It wasn't just the loss of ad revenue, either. He'd gotten thirty-seven subscription cancellations. Not enough to be dangerous, but an ominous sign. They were all the result of that offensive editorial written by that gypsy printer, urging merchants to hold the line. That was not anything to be said in public, though of course Westminster had urged it privately for years. Ah, how his misery with the ague had plagued him.

Gloomily, he contemplated the next regular meeting of the supervisors, who were going to consider a property tax ordinance that would spread the county's burden to everyone who owned land. Poindexter had told him maliciously that the revenues from the sporting district were now down over a third, and the county would soon be unable to make payroll or remain solvent without the new tax. This independence on the part of supervisors Westminster had put into office rankled him, just as everything else that was happening these days rankled him. There were moments when he itched to walk into Flint's sanctum and throttle the upstart with his gold-headed Malacca walking stick.

The editor took a deep breath. He would put that upstart rag out of business yet, and once Flint was on the road, some sanity would return to Silver City. Flint was obviously going to publish irregularly to avoid street warfare. Well, Westminster would have to resort to rougher tactics. He knew exactly what to do; no sachem of Tammany Wigwam lacked such fundamental knowledge.

The next step was to pie the type. He laughed. The man on the street wouldn't have the faintest idea what that meant, but any printer would. Every printer had a pie box, which contained miscellaneous type waiting to be sorted and dropped into the case boxes. There would be plenty of moments when *The Sentinel* would be unguarded, and those were the golden times when a sneak would slide in, throw the galley trays to the floor, and scatter type from here to kingdom come. The whole labor of putting an issue together was typesetting. Men toiled hour after hour, setting word upon word, day after day, until at last a paper was filled. And through all of this process, the type sat in galley trays, vulnerable to any sort of touch.

So formidable was the task of setting type and the danger of spilling — or pieing — it, that all papers kept cast-metal feature stories and house ads in reserve, ready to throw into the breach. Any journeyman printer could recite the horror stories, the moments when they were sliding a chase into the bed of a press and it careened to the floor, instantly demolishing a day of hard work.

Westminster pursed his thin lips. His soul recoiled from a remedy so drastic. He had set miles of column-inches himself, and the horror of pied type seared his soul. But war was war. These things couldn't be helped. If he must resort to the most extreme measures, he would. With that resolved, he gained a certain peace. The next issue of *The Sentinel* would never reach Flint's own flatbed press, much less the streets where Westminster's three hired men would lurk and pounce.

With those comforting thoughts to buoy him, he began to plan the next issue of *The Democrat*. He had a few little schemes in mind. Certainly an editorial, warning the politicians that any one of them who voted to impose taxes on the freemen of San Juan County would not receive the paper's endorsement at election time. He would mention that the opposition paper wouldn't be around by then, of course. He didn't know quite how to replace the lost revenue milked from the county's vice, but it would have to be the mines. He would campaign, once again, for a tax on the mines, either on their profits or the value of their bullion.

But the pièce de résistance in this issue would be a splendid little story about Flint, with a few nasty words about the tramp who was working with him. Westminster was a past master at this art. The trick was not to overdo it and destroy credibility. Just a nice little story, loaded with nasty innuendos, all neatly packaged to avoid libel lawsuits, and the result would be that Flint's reputation would never be the same. Westminster called these tactics "the tarbrush." He would set this one himself, knowing that the fonts in his hands would supply inspiration.

So inspired was he that he hurried out of his sanctum to the composing room, pushed aside Austin Bean, one of his elderly typesetters, donned a printer's smock, and began work. He hadn't engaged in any artful character assassination since his Gotham days, but it would all come back in a rush when he felt the Qs and Ps in his fingers. And there would be no repercussions either. A little tarbrushing was routine on the frontier, and the chance of answering a court summons was nil.

"We have it on good account," Westminster began, his fingers flying to the case box and back to the type stick, "that our brother editor up the gulch may have quite a colorful past. Editors and typesetters are members of a close-knit brotherhood, where the news of one soon reaches the rest. Word of those in our exotic trade gets bandied along, hither and yon, reaching this ear and that, even out here in the wildest West.

"Indeed, out here, where the long reach of a copper's arm is least likely, is where our most unusual members often show up. That's how it came to our ear that one Flint, from Friendship, upstate New York, was once apprenticed as a devil, or assistant, in Buffalo, but was drafted into the war. Serving his country wasn't his inclination, and he deserted within a few weeks and just before a great battle, never to be seen wearing the blue again. Now, there's no saying whether this printer's devil is the same as the one residing up the gulch, and of course *The Democrat* makes no such implication.

"But what is known among our fraternity is that this brash young fellow Flint began showing up at papers in Indiana, Illinois, and Iowa after the great war, serving with some skill. But in a regular pattern, after a few days he vanished, often with some valued piece of equipment, even a whole font of type or a galley tray or what we call a chase, which holds the type for a page. But that is common enough, and many a paper has been birthed in such fashion. A little borrowing started many a frontiersman on a great career. Still, word got out among editors to beware a self-proclaimed journeyman printer named Flint or any big, friendly fellow using an alias. Now, whether this Flint has any connection with the one up the gulch is purely debatable, and our readers should make no such inference.

"This Flint, according to the news whispered through our fraternity, was nabbed a few times, fined and once imprisoned in Keokuk, and is actually a convicted felon several times over with warrants outstanding. Nonetheless, he found ready employment, being personable, and managed eventually to nip an entire press in Fort

Dodge and vanish with it. Now, again, we don't intend to imply that the legendary Flint of this account is the same as the alleged editor up the gulch.

"What we do know about this other Flint is that he began publishing weeklies on the frontier, in faraway places where no one asks questions about a man's past. His usual method was to approach a moneyed interest and become its spokesman. He's been the mouthpiece of gambling interests, a tong lord, an opium and hashish dealer, railroad men, cattlemen, bankers, monopolists, and speculators, always slanting the local news in behalf of those who pay him. Now, we're not saying this particular Flint is any relation to the one up the gulch, but it has not escaped our attention that he keeps putting out issues without any advertising in them — a phenomenon unheard of in American journalism. No decent merchant has deigned to buy space in a paper so plainly in the hands of one interest or another.

"Now, any sensible citizen knows that a paper existing without visible means of support must be financed nefariously, by some private interest, for better or worse. It is an easy matter to discover the true nature of that interest, simply by studying the thrust of the paper. It seems noteworthy to us that the building now housing our opposition has been purchased by Achilles Balthazar, and before was owned by a woman of ill repute who was constantly seen in his place of business, wearing very little. All these things fit the history of one Flint from upstate New York, but whether this is the same Flint or not we would not hazard to say.

"Whoever the Flint is who bleats his programs as the mouthpiece of the rich and powerful up the gulch, he has certainly prospered. He now operates a costly rotary flatbed press, a far cry from the little Washington press that vanished from a Nebraska weekly some years ago. And this Flint employs a gypsy printer whose dubious name is Napoleon, the sort of moniker that excites a multiplicity of questions among sober men. If this Flint should be the same as the scoundrel well-known in newspaper circles, then it is quite understandable how a man could prosper without selling ads, and own a handsome press and a whole roomful of printing equipment for which there is no visible bill of sale.

"Of course, all these matters need sorting out. But the good citizens of Silver City ought to read the opposing rag with a large degree of caution, always asking *cui bono* — who benefits? And of course, we urge Sheriff Poindexter to ascertain whether this Flint bears any relation to the mountebank and cad for whom there must be a dozen warrants outstanding. As we say, there's no proof of anything, but an intelligent citizen will read the opposing paper with the utmost skepticism and caution."

Ah, it was exquisite! Digby Westminster felt a

great flood of malicious pleasure flow through him. It was a just compensation for a life spent suffering the ague.

36

For two days Flint and Napoleon didn't see Chastity, but they continued preparing to free her. Napoleon found an ancient pair of shoes that would fit her and bought them from a cobbler for fifty cents. He rummaged around town for a coat and a knapsack. Flint made ready to supply her with food and a few dollars with which to purchase necessaries when she got to Ouray.

Then she showed up the following morning, not in her kimono but in one of her house dresses. Flint took one look into her ravaged face and knew that her ordeal had taken its toll.

"Chastity! Are you all right?"

"I guess."

He poured a cup of ancient java into a cup and handed it to her. Napoleon abandoned his type-setting and joined them in the kitchen.

"You're dressed," Flint said. It was a question.

"Hamlin gave me some of my clothing because I was cold. I told him I was getting catarrh. He brings me some food and firewood every day."

"Can you go out?"

"No. He won't let me. And he didn't give me my coat."

"Why did he take your clothing?"

"He said he wanted me to know he owned me, and the best way was to take my clothes. He makes me dependent on him for everything. I don't have a cent."

"Is Balthazar abusing you?"

She laughed sourly. "If you mean has he hurt me, no. But the way he talks, it could happen. If you mean is he destroying my sanity, yes. I'm scared to death all the time, and I feel so helpless. He loves to tell me what he'll do if he catches me with a customer or if I try to get out. He's diabolical. He speaks so softly, gentlemanly — but the words! The words!"

Napoleon said, "Over there on the hook is almost an outfit, Chastity. I think those shoes'll fit you. I'm still looking for a coat and a knapsack."

She stared at Napoleon's collection. "He'd kill me," she said.

Flint said, "If you let him do this to you, you'll die another kind of death. This is slavery, pure and simple, and the secret of it is to take away your hope and leave only fear. I don't suppose he's promised anything better in the future."

She shook her head.

"Why does he do this? Does he ever explain himself?"

"He says possessing me is the most entertaining thing he's ever done. He likes it. He likes to tell me exactly what to do. He comes in the evenings, and all I do is follow orders. He says making me a puppet is fascinating, the biggest challenge of his life."

"What happens when you protest?"

"His voice gets very soft."

"Chastity, he can't own you, not if you don't let him. He can only threaten your body. But you've got a God-given mind and soul that he can never reach if you don't let him."

She smiled wanly. "I'm an atheist."

"You've an area inside of yourself he can't touch. He'll want to own that area too. He'll try to tell you what to think, what to believe. Don't let him. He'll keep on trying, but don't let him. When he owns your mind and your will, then no one can help you."

"I don't understand," she said soberly.

"Some people just want to possess another. Men especially. They like to possess a woman, not love and respect her. Hamlin wants to make you a puppet. I've met the type. In the army they're dangerous. Fight back, tell him he'll never own you."

"What good would that do?"

"Maybe it will keep you alive when everything seems lost. When you're fighting, you're alive."

Napoleon said, "I'm named for the patron saint of hopeless cases. But I don't know if he'd intercede in your case. You'll have to rescue yourself."

"It's no use," she said bitterly.

It was dawning on Flint that Chastity Ford lacked the inner resources to fight a battle like this. She'd already given up. It was that dark secret of hers. Something corroded her will. "I ought to talk to the sheriff," Flint said. "I doubt that a law officer would permit this if he knew of it."

"No! I'd be hurt! Please, please, don't tell anyone."

"What do you want, Chastity?"

She shook her head. "I don't know."

"Yes you do."

"I just want him to go away and give me my money back."

"What would you like us to do, Chastity? We'll get you out. We'll harness up and drive you clear to Ouray if that's what it takes."

"He'd just come and get me. There's no protection for line girls. Flint, maybe I can work it out with him. He'll get bored and look for something else to do."

"What about you? Aren't you getting bored too?"

"I'm going crazy. I can't even go out, except to the privy. I can't have visitors. I can't even have my laundry done. He says he'll arrange it. I've nothing to do but wait for him."

"Should you be here with us?"

"Who knows? He's got so many rules." She smiled wanly. "Thanks for looking after me. No one else does."

"Chastity, how do you know you can't go out?

Has he got those mining-company guards outside?"

"No. He just buys information. Just about everyone on Silver Street is on his payroll. For all I know, he's paying you too."

"Stop that kind of thinking, Chastity. If you think you have no friends at all here, you'll go to an early grave."

She cried then, softly and desolately. She wiped her tears away, patted Flint's hand, and silently returned to her room. Flint watched her retreat with an aching heart. No woman, not even one who had entered a tawdry life, deserved a fate so cruel.

He sipped bitter coffee a while, wondering what to do. Napoleon stayed silent for a change, the man unable to remedy this lost cause.

"I'm going to talk to Poindexter," Flint said at last. "You mind the store."

"What'll that do?"

"Maybe nothing. But there's a shiny new Constitutional Amendment against involuntary servitude. Maybe he'll get up some courage and act."

Napoleon didn't say anything.

Flint hiked up the gulch, hoping to catch Poindexter in his office at the courthouse. He found the sheriff behind his desk doing paperwork. The man's carnivorous gaze followed Flint into the chair across the desk.

"I don't give interviews, Flint. Especially to you."

"I'm not here on newspaper business. I'm reporting a crime."

That intrigued the sheriff. He set down his nib pen and waited.

"We have a case of white slavery in town. Totally illegal. I'd like you to do something about it."

Poindexter's eyes danced, and the faint ridges of amusement built along his lips. "You mean Chastity Ford, queen of the demimonde."

That took Flint aback. "How did you know?"

"Hamlin came in and told me."

"He . . . what?"

"He said you'd show up to complain."

Flint's mind whirled. "What did he tell you?" he asked at last.

"He said he'd always wanted her for himself. She's the prettiest tart in town. He cleaned out her bank account so she can't go off. He's keeping her a prisoner."

Flint felt a fine rage boiling through him. "So Hamlin's told you he's stolen close to six thousand, he's holding her against her wishes, and you sit here doing nothing. Has she no rights?"

"She's just a slut, Flint."

"She still has rights!" Flint yelled.

Poindexter grinned. "Oh, not really. If you think I'm going to go pinch Hamlin Balthazar and charge him, bring the roof down on Silver City and me, think again."

"You're sworn to uphold the law, no matter what."

"Flint, you pompous ass, get out."

Flint started to protest but didn't. This would be newspaper business after all. He stood up and walked out.

"Flint!" the sheriff yelled at his back. "Go ahead and print it if you want. It'll get me reelected."

Flint didn't reply. He hiked sternly up the gulch, seething with rage at the injustice and callousness of the world. When he slammed into his shop, he found Napoleon grinning.

"I already wrote it," the printer said.

"You wrote what?"

"The Chastity story. Here."

Flint snatched the galley proof and began reading. It was all there: the captivity of Chastity Ford by Hamlin Balthazar; the coerced transfer of her entire savings, including those from the sale of the building to Achilles Balthazar; the helplessness of a woman whose wealth and even her clothing had been taken from her; Hamlin's threats of violence to her person, and his threats to destroy her beauty if she tried to flee; and then, to Flint's astonishment, a good depiction of Poindexter's refusal to protect a woman of the sporting district.

"They'll call us *The Bawdyhouse Bugle* again, Flint," Napoleon said.

"How did you know what Poindexter'd do or not do?"

"Long and familiar study of sheriffs. The man with the badge knows who has the power in this burg."

"He told me to go ahead and write it. Said it'd reelect him."

"Flint, you must be one of about ten men in the West who think soiled doves are anything but parasites. You're the one out of step around here. Over in the saloons, they'll say that young Hamlin finally did something bright."

Flint collapsed into his chair. That was a bitter thing. "Should we kill the story?" he asked Napoleon.

"Flint, if you kill this story, I'd pull out. This is important. The miners and all the rest, they'll laugh at first. But in the quiet of the night they'll be visited by shame, and in a while both Hamlin and Poindexter will learn something about public opinion. I'm here because you're no coward. This should go on page one, if I may say so. We're the newspaper of lost causes. We're also the paper of conscience. I admire you."

Flint looked at the unsmiling tramp printer and felt a great gratitude and tenderness. Let the roof fall, but get the truth out.

37

Flint read and reread the lead story in that Thursday's *Democrat*, riveted to it by its loathsomeness. It slapped him like the odor from the vault of an outhouse. He felt fouled. This was no ordinary assault on a rival; it was a pack of lies of the basest sort, veneered over by some careful footwork that made it seem less libelous than it was. He didn't doubt that any court would find it libelous anyway, except maybe Homer Shreveport's court. But that was moot. He had no means to bring a suit, and the verdict would come too late, long after the indelible stain on his honor.

He wondered whether he could even bear to walk down a street in Silver City now. Whether his friends would turn against him. Whether the Bridges would wonder, and Napoleon would stare shrewdly at him. Silently he handed it to his printer, who read it carefully and then looked searchingly into Flint's eyes.

"If I protest or deny, it'll only look worse," Flint said gloomily.

"I've never seen such a filthy thing," Napoleon said.

"I've got my honorable discharge right in that

311

trunk, but what good would it do?"

"Don't give up. Never give up. Sometimes these things backfire on the author. People will compare what you've written, the good you've done, the courage you've shown, with this, and doubt it. Westminster's motives are certainly on display. People understand that."

"I don't see how," Flint said.

He stared about him. The next issue of *The Sentinel* was all but ready to go, thanks to Napoleon's deft hands. Most everything had been set and was lying in galley trays. Putting the paper to bed was only a matter of building the pages inside the chases. Flint had one overwhelming instinct — to get outside, out of the stinking town, and purify himself in the country air.

"I'm going for a walk," he said. "I can't stand it in this cesspool."

"I'll go with you," Napoleon said. "We'll put the paper to bed in the afternoon and print this evening. Maybe we can think about a reply."

Flint nodded. He wanted to be alone, but Jude Napoleon would be a good walking companion.

"We won't sell any ads anyway," Flint said, surrendering.

He shrugged into his thick mackinaw against the sharp cold and waited for Napoleon to undo his smock and get ready. Then they hiked into the wind, up the gulch, past the brooding mines, past Balthazar's whited sepulchre of an office, past some mining neighborhoods, and at last upon the great plateau that footed the San Juans.

All around them lay a sea of browned grasses, clean and windswept. Ahead rose the vaulting peaks, whited with the first snows, their lower flanks dark with pines. The wind felt fresh and sweet. The snow above was pristine and it blinded him. A slight fragrance of pine and cedar hung upon the breeze, an incense to Flint's lungs.

He was comforted. Mortals lived in their own cesspools, but nature was innocent, and now the innocence of this unsettled West began to work at his spirit, mending and cleansing it. Flint knew that no amount of slime dumped on him could destroy what was in his heart: He had lived his life as honorably as he could, not without evil or weakness or failure, for those were the inheritance of all mortals, but he had always tried to be just and to abide by the great moral and ethical laws of life. Digby Westminster could demolish his reputation, but he could not demolish his soul.

He watched puffball clouds scud over the peaks, shooting shadows down their slopes or slicing them off. A bright, coy sun caught not only his gaze but his spirit and held it. He was not alone here. Beside him walked a faithful friend. Around him was that mystery of mysteries, the Creator.

They hiked silently, and Flint blessed Napoleon for his silence. Later they could decide what to do, if anything. Their hike took them to the place where his mules were pastured, and he detoured across open meadow to see them. Grant and Sherman eyed him suspiciously. No quadruped on earth was as canny as a mule or as gifted at evading work. But Flint carried no halter, and the mules decided that they had escaped the fate worse than death and turned back to their greedy nipping of sere grasses. They had haired out for winter, and they looked fine.

Flint broke the silence at last. "Those are my mules," he said. "Good, stout, big ones. If I'm careful not to weary them, I can pull my outfit with just those two."

"You thinking of leaving?"

"Wouldn't you?"

"Sometimes we are baptised into honor."

"I don't know what you mean."

"If you can endure, with dignity, what has been poured over your head and not flee this place, people will come to the right conclusions in the end. If you walk out, you'll confirm Digby Westminster."

Flint knew that was true. But he didn't know whether he could bear the opprobrium. "Napoleon, do you know of any way to fight it?"

"Do you have your discharge paper?"

"Yes."

"We can make a plate and print it without comment. It'll speak for itself."

"That's a start," Flint said. "It says I was with the Ohio Volunteers. That'll help too."

"Are you, shall we say, spiritually ready for your ordeal?"

Flint was baffled and nodded.

"Westminster has all but called you a thief. The sheriff will look into it and do his worst."

Flint's spirits sagged again. "Jude, I'm finished here, no matter what I say or what defense I have."

"*Mon ami,* you've only just begun. We'll endure this together. Perhaps the thing to do is ignore Westminster. We have our agenda. While he's busy attacking you, we'll be busy promoting the reforms we'd like to see here, eh?"

"It won't work," Flint said, "unless I can answer his most telling thrust. How indeed do I publish without advertising?"

"We have advertising! We publish flyers. All we have to do is say it. Job-printing supports *The Sentinel.*"

Flint smiled. "Just barely," he mumbled. "There'd better be a lot more soon."

"You're an interesting man, Flint. You come here because Westminster made a joke of some poor harlot's suicide. Not for profit or power, but to deal with callousness and coldness. I'm fascinated. As we talk these days, I learn you're a moralist. You publish a newspaper to make the world better. You're a master of the English tongue. You could publish a nice, bland, stately paper somewhere, garner bouquets all your life, find yourself an enchanting wife, and live happily ever after. Instead, you roam from one sorry place to another, bearding the lions and getting yourself exiled. Now, Editor Flint, why is this?"

Flint really had no answer. In fact, in some moods he considered himself a wayward Don Quixote. "It was the war, Jude," he said. "I've never been the same." It was as good an answer as any.

"War does that."

"After it was over I came out here to the wild country. I had to. I breathed it in. I can't settle down. The other night I looked at Livia Bridge — there she was, enchanting, sweet, generous, loving, educated, independent, the sort of lovely woman I could go mad about."

"Well?" said Napoleon.

"I'd only deprive her of a good life."

"Maybe she'd tame you and you'd settle down. Take it from a Frenchman. Don't talk yourself out of Livia. Try."

Flint had no answer to that. He was always mad about some woman or other and always telling himself she'd suffer if she fell for him. It was some mystery of the soul, and it drained a lot of joy out of his life.

They walked quietly back to town, and as they descended into the gulch again, the sweetness of nature vanished. The miners' neighborhoods were quiet, sober, and desperate. The cluster of mines reeked of business and rapacity, and the sporting district oozed cynicism and lust. They turned into Flint's quarters, entered and beheld catastrophe.

From one end of the gloomy workshop to the other, type littered the floor — a thousand thousand *T*s and *P*s and italic *A*s and an army of periods and quotation marks. Flint eyed the mess, knowing exactly what happened. Each galley tray lay naked, its contents forever scattered. Even the galley trays containing his filler material, his favorite aphorisms from the ancients, had been emptied. Well over a hundred hours of skilled labor lay on the floor.

"I guess I should've stayed," Napoleon said, matter of factly.

"No, I'm glad you came," Flint said wearily. "It kept you from being hurt."

He hunted for the galley proofs and found none. The intruders had nipped the stories too, so they couldn't be copied. No doubt the stories were in Westminster's hands. This had been a job for experts. Balthazar's torpedoes wouldn't have known how to do it.

So the war had come to his sanctum. There would be no issue of *The Sentinel* tomorrow, no response to Westminster's brutal attack, no story about Hamlin the slaver and a sheriff who wouldn't enforce the laws. Every one of his galleys was no doubt in Westminster's hands. The man had the whole issue before him and knew exactly what Flint was thinking, planning, and doing.

Flint surveyed the despoiled workshop. Not a thing had been stolen except those things most precious — the labor and the inspiration. It would take Napoleon and Flint at least a day just to pick up the mess, sort the type and put it back in the case boxes, rebuild the nameplate, and set the filler material and all the rest.

"Well, Napoleon, let's put out the issue anyway," he said. "I'm angry enough. This'll be another story. This time we'll bare our fangs."

"I'm glad you didn't give up, Flint," Napoleon said. "Now I'll show you how fast I can work and why I won bets setting type."

Flint had thought to gobble some lunch first, but he found himself quietly sweeping up the fonts and throwing the type back into its niches. He threw the slugs and ruler lines into little piles he would deal with later. There wouldn't be a paper this week, but there might be two next week. It did no good to weep, so Flint worked and fanned the flames of anger that were leaping through him. Silver City needed more than reform; it needed to be purged.

38

Chastity Ford decided there was no point in running off. Flint and Napoleon made escape possible, but she believed that if she put her mind to it, she could somehow penetrate Hamlin Balthazar's armor, drive him away, and even get her money back. She suspected she was in grave danger, but in what form she couldn't fathom. She began studying him during his nightly visits, her mind sharper and more focused than it had ever been. It put her in mind of Dr. Johnson's famous observation that nothing concentrates the mind so much as the knowledge that one is going to be hanged in a fortnight.

Her evenings spent as a marionette were ordeals, demeaning and bizarre, but she put aside her misery and disgust and self-pity and began instead to learn all she could about the young, smooth-cheeked Hamlin Balthazar, scion of the most powerful man in western Colorado. She realized first that he never personally engaged in violence, though he used the unsubtle threat of it — a word or two about his father's mine-security men — to enforce his will. Neither was he any Marquis de Sade. He inflicted no pain and asked for none. In that purely physical sense he had not violated her person and probably wouldn't. He did not want to mar his beautiful property.

His pleasures lay in another and equally perverse direction. He derived his delights from total control over her. He wanted her to be as obedient as a dog, no matter how humiliating the ordeals he imposed on her. Once he made her crawl about on all fours, pick up his shoe in her mouth, drop it at his feet, and bark. It had enraged her. But her flashes of temper only kindled laughter in him, and a sudden erotic interest. He was stronger than she, but used his strength only to ward off her furious assaults whenever he drove her crazy. He always managed to provoke her to a rage, and those were the moments when he tugged her to her bed and emptied himself.

His real gift was a sort of spiritual terror.

"You should really try to escape, Chastity. Why don't you? Flint'll help. I'd love to give you a mile headstart before we come after you, the hounds after the fox. Then we'd kill you."

She had stared, her mind whirling. He wanted total control, but what really excited him was resistance.

"Why don't you kill me, Chastity? I'm sure Flint'd lend you a butcher knife. I deserve it, don't I? I've taken everything away, including your freedom." His liquid brown eyes danced with amusement. It was the ultimate expression of his power, inviting her to kill him and knowing she wouldn't.

Again she had stared at him, pondering the invitation.

As the nights passed, one ordeal after another, she discovered a pattern: He was constantly begging her to be angry, to resist, to flee, to fight. Something in her calculating calm disappointed him.

"You're studying me, looking for my weakness," he said one night, alive with pleasure. "I always know what you're thinking. You wear your thoughts on your forehead. Most people do. I can read them. My daddy taught me how. You simply see what another person wants, and then everything comes clear." He laughed gaily. "Little fox, you just scheme, and I'll enjoy your scheming. Right now, you're working on some way to get your loot back and get rid of me. That's why you haven't flown my coop."

She felt her mind even more naked to him than her body, and the thought always shot a chill of dread through her. It was as easy for him to thwart her as it was to put a kitten in a box. And it was as easy for him to torment her with her own hopes as it was to put food outside of a kitten's cage and watch the little creature struggle to reach it.

During the long empty days, when she felt her imprisonment far more than the evenings, she tried desperately to come up with something that might drive him away. She also slid into a terrible despondency. She deserved this fate. She deserved to die. It didn't matter that Hamlin Balthazar degraded her. Nothing he could do would degrade her more than she already was.

She had known her father.

That last night in Massallon, Ohio, long after the final lecture, he had entered her room, seething with some sort of animal energy. He awakened her roughly and wordlessly destroyed her life. She whimpered at first, and then closed her eyes and stopped. He bolted away as wordlessly as he had entered, a silent butcher of two lives. She had been too numb to cry. The following day, during the stagecoach ride back to Zanesville, he had looked so serene that she wondered if he remembered, if he were two persons. She could not bear to look into his face. She never looked into his face again.

She didn't blame him; she blamed herself. Somehow she had tempted him. No father would do such a thing, especially an idealist and visionary like Guadalupe Ford. She believed that. She gazed into her own mirrored face and knew herself to be a depraved woman. That was what she saw, and from that moment her belief had congealed. She could never give herself to a husband or be like any other woman. As for her father, she knew that all his oratory and reasoning and rhetoric and learned treatises were nothing more than the rantings of a man who hated the knowing eye of God.

She wrestled free from the black visions of the

past and forced her mind to focus on Hamlin Balthazar. Some small bud of courage kept prompting her to try to win her way free and find a better life. She was young. A lot of living stretched before her.

She thought she'd take the one tack that seemed promising. She would become inert. Hamlin's entire pleasure seemed to arise out of her struggles. She decided she wouldn't speak, wouldn't move, wouldn't obey, no matter what his toothless threats. Maybe, just maybe, he would become disgusted with a passive, unresisting vegetable and abandon her for other, more perverse entertainments.

That evening, he appeared as usual, bearing a one-day supply of food and drink. He tried to make conversation, but she didn't respond. He commanded, but she sat, inert. He tried to force her to respond by escalating his threats. "Why don't you get mad? Have you no spirit? No energy? Are you just going to accept captivity?" he demanded plaintively. "Why don't you fight?"

She knew she had him. Willfully, she kept herself as inert as a sack of potatoes. He pulled her about, tugged off her clothes, stormed at her while she lay passively, staring at the ceiling. He wanted her to make love. He wanted her to rage. He wanted her to do slavish tricks. He wanted her to fetch him a drink. He threatened her with an expert beating. He warned her what a broken beer bottle could do to her pretty face. He told her he'd keep every cent. He told her she wasn't worth his attention. She lay across her bed, unmoving. She had him. Then he grew weary of threatening her and began castigating her for being as dead as a stone. But she did not respond. Finally he stormed out, and she knew she would win.

The next night the crisis came, as she knew it would. He appeared as usual, wearing his handsome Chesterfield, his suit, and cravat, looking like a college boy rather than a wastrel. He brought no food, and she took it for another of his toothless threats. She would have to depend on Flint again.

"I hope you're feeling better," he said.

She didn't respond but settled herself in the Morris chair in the parlor.

"Get me a drink," he said. "Tonight you'll obey or face the medicine."

She didn't move. It would have been fun to mock him, tell him that she could control him far more easily than he could dominate her, but that would only excite him to new frenzies. So she stared at the ceiling, at the coal-oil lamp casting yellow light into the dark room, and waited.

"I'm warning you," he snarled. "Tonight it's different, sweetheart. You're going to come to life or die."

Her heart missed a beat, but she did not speak. He bullied and threatened for another five minutes, and then came the bad moment. He plunged his smooth hand into a breast pocket of his suitcoat and extracted a small black revolver. She felt an icy fear flow through her, but she didn't move. Some intuition, some knowing based on close observation these several days, informed her that apple-cheeked young Hamlin Balthazar would never hurt her himself, though he might call in the family musclemen. He was a coward.

He pointed it at her. "Now, sweetheart, you'll do exactly as I say. You're the slave, and don't forget it. Now pour me a drink."

She eyed that black muzzle — it was some small caliber, she knew — and felt herself surrender. She would obey. But no, there was something in his eyes that gave him away. She did nothing.

"You want to die?" he snapped.

She didn't, and she fought every instinct to become his performing pet once again. She did nothing.

He leveled the gun at her, until she could look right up its barrel, right into his unblinking eyes. Her pulse lifted. She was making a mistake!

"Get up," he said softly.

She didn't, determined now to destroy him.

He walked closer and closer until the muzzle was only a foot from her breast. She sat becalmed.

"I'm warning you," he said.

She closed her eyes.

"Open your eyes," he commanded.

She didn't.

"One last warning," he said.

She ignored him.

Then she heard a snap. And four more snaps. She opened her eyes just in time to see him stuff the little black revolver back into his breastpocket. He whirled out.

"Tomorrow, it'll be different," he said as he slammed the door behind him.

She had won. Soon he'd give up. He found no pleasure in dominating an inert object.

The following day, pleasure began to suffuse her. She ate from Flint's perpetual bean pot, but for once Flint and Napoleon were too busy to pause and visit with her. She watched their furious typesetting, knowing something was amiss, and retreated to her place, feeling cheated of a chance to exult with them over her new-found keys to liberty.

The young, innocent-looking banker returned the next night, as always, and she almost met him gaily, so buoyant was her mood. But that would only excite him. She could win only if she remained as inert as ever, finding within herself the courage to do and say nothing, no matter the threat.

"It's going to be different tonight, sweetheart. Tonight it's loaded," he said cheerfully.

She didn't respond.

"Tonight, if I say dance, you'll dance. If I say bark, you'll bow-wow. If I say crawl, you'll crawl. If I say kiss my toe, you'll kiss it. If I say cry, you'll cry. If I say get mad and fight, you'll get mad and fight. I know what you're thinking. Don't forget it. You think you're done with me. Think again. I own you."

She stared out the window, into a sharp autumnal night, the kind when no one tarried on the street. Tonight would test her limits. After that, she could resume her life, maybe without money, but she could start over.

"Go to the bedroom," he said. "Put on the kimono. Tonight you'll be my geisha."

She sat.

He pulled out the little revolver and pointed it at her heart. "This time, you'll obey," he said smoothly. "There are five thirty-two-caliber balls in it, powder and a cap on each nipple. I own you. I possess all of you, including your every thought."

She knew she had won, and so she sat calmly, unmoving. And then she saw in his eyes, too late, that she had lost. She stood, surrendering to him. But it was too late.

39

The muffled shot next door startled Flint and Napoleon. They had been working far into the night, setting type, trying to rebuild the four-page paper from memory.

Flint didn't like the sound of it. He set down his type stick and headed for the front window, hearing Chastity's front door slam as he did. Napoleon followed. At the window they saw Hamlin Balthazar, awash with buttery light from the saloons and wearing his familiar Chesterfield, plunge into the street, stare sharply both directions, and then walk calmly toward the Bankers' Club.

"Hamlin for sure," Flint said, a flood of worry boiling through him. He whirled toward the door, into the hall, and tried Chastity's door. It was bolted. He tore around to her front door, which hung ajar, and entered, Napoleon right behind. The odor of burnt powder smacked them, and blue tendrils of gunsmoke drifted past the sole lamp.

She lay on the floor, her mouth an *O*, her large expressive eyes seeing nothing. A single bullet hole pierced her breast over the heart. Scarcely any blood stained her housefrock, one of the few

Balthazar had returned to her.

"Chastity!" Flint cried. He plunged to his knees beside her and sought a pulse. He thought perhaps he felt one, but he couldn't tell. Faint movements still spasmed her body. Her lips compressed slightly.

"Chastity! Oh, God," he moaned. He hunted her gaze, seeking recognition in it, desperate for life, aching to see sensibility, focus, anything but the emptiness he saw.

"She's gone, Sam," Napoleon said. "That young hound of hell shot her."

Flint pushed at her chest, wanting her lungs to work. She didn't respond. Then he stood up and felt the world turn cold.

"Let's get him. He's across the street," he said.

They sprang out the door, raced to the gambling joint, and stormed in. The dark, smoky hall, lit by a lamp over each poker table and faro layout, wasn't crowded. They stalked roughly past half-empty tables and surveyed the bar, drawing attention by their hard gazes, but Balthazar wasn't there. He had fled into the rear alley hard against the cliff.

"He might be in another club a block away, making an alibi," Napoleon said. "Where to look?"

Flint shook his head. "Let's get Poindexter. Hamlin's not going far. He doesn't know he was seen."

They returned to their flat for coats and then

hiked down the gulch to the courthouse, their breath steaming in the chill.

"Poindexter doesn't work evenings," Napoleon said. "We'll be talking to a deputy."

"Let's get the sheriff," Flint said. "I want to shove his nose into this. I told him just a few days ago that she was in trouble with Balthazar, and he just laughed."

A block from the courthouse, they detoured into a cul de sac where Poindexter roomed. Neither had been in the building, which contained half a dozen quarters, but the tenants were listed in the foyer. They raced up wooden steps and banged on his door for what seemed an endless time.

When the door suddenly swung open, they encountered Drew Poindexter in a woolen nightshirt and a leveled revolver. He surveyed them angrily.

"Chastity Ford's been murdered. Hamlin Balthazar did it," Flint snapped.

Poindexter blinked, stared, and lowered the revolver. "My night men'll take care of it," he said.

"I said Hamlin Balthazar shot her."

Poindexter nodded. "She's just a slut." Then, as if having second thoughts, he posed the question: "How do you know?"

"We heard the shot. Heard her front door slam. We both saw him in the street, running. You can't miss that Chesterfield."

Poindexter seemed lost in thought. "Wait

here," he said, vanishing into the gloomy interior. Back somewhere a lamp flamed to life. A few minutes later the sheriff appeared, dressed and wearing his mackinaw, hat, and gloves.

"All right," he said. "You should've got a deputy. I don't know why you rang me in."

"Because I'd told you she was in trouble," Flint said. "Because you didn't do anything."

"Just a slut, Flint," Poindexter said.

"It was slavery. And it was being done by the one man who could get away with it."

"If you start talking like that, Flint, you'll get yourself in the hottest water you've ever been in."

"We both saw Balthazar," said Napoleon.

"Who're you?"

"I'm Flint's printer. We were working late."

"What did you see?"

"We heard a shot. At the window we saw Balthazar lunge down her steps, look around, and head for the Bankers' Club. We found her dead, shot through the heart. Then we ran after him into the club. He wasn't there. He'd gone out the rear door. We came back for our coats and went for you," Napoleon said.

The sheriff addressed Flint. "Why didn't you get a deputy?"

"Because I wanted you to see the result of your neglect," Flint said ruthlessly. "And because you'll have to deal with the Balthazars. You have two witnesses. The deputy would've come for you anyway."

Poindexter grunted.

They hiked up the gulch through a sharp cold, past dark residential districts, and then into the gaudy sporting area where yellow light spilled out of every window.

Flint led the sheriff into Chastity's parlor. She lay where she had been before, lifeless, her spirit gone to wherever the spirits of militant atheists go. The sheriff turned her over. The back of her gray dress was bloodsoaked. He stood, hunting for a bullet hole, and found it in the wall near the bedroom door. He pulled out a jackknife and pried away plaster and lath, widening the hole until he could see in. Then he gingerly freed the spent ball, which had lodged in a lath on the bedroom side of the wall.

"Looks about thirty-two caliber," he said, examining the deformed mass of lead in his palm. "Small, anyway."

His next words shocked Flint. "This happens all the time around here. The women invite it. There isn't much anyone can do. Maybe it was Balthazar, maybe not."

Rage boiled up in him. "You're doubting our word!"

Something feline filled Poindexter's face. "My job is to consider the possibilities."

"I warned you about Balthazar."

"That's why I'm considering other possibilities."

"You don't want to deal with the Balthazars, that's it. You'll just let this slide by," Flint raged.

"Well, it won't slide by."

Poindexter smiled slightly. "Who says it'll slide by? I haven't told you what I'll do. No one's above the law." He paused, studying Flint. "You've a sentimental view of sluts, Flint. I'll tell you what they are. They're parasites. They'll steal a man blind. They'll coax a sucker into a crib and their boyfriend'll knock him on the head, rob him, throw him naked into an alley. They'll drop some powders into some booze and the next thing you know, you're missing your wallet, your shoes, and your shirt. They're drunks. They eat opium or hashish or cocaine and die of it. Expensive little habits that they support by coaxing suckers into their cribs. They turn good lads into punks, partying, boozing, ruining young men for the rest of their lives. And just for good measure, they pass along a few little diseases. You're lucky she didn't pick your pocket every time you saw her. And you want me to make a big case when one of the worst of them croaks?"

"It's not like that with her," Flint said.

"Oh, it isn't? I suppose she had a heart of gold. I suppose all that loot she collected was going to go to charity." He stared. "I'll have to wake up Mazeppa Roswell and tell him to bring a plain pine box. She don't deserve a box, Flint. We ought to roll her in a horse blanket and plant her next to the other one from this joint. It'll cost the county more money than it's worth." He paused. "You told me Balthazar put her money in his bank?"

"Yes."

"The county'll get it." He eyed Flint. "Thanks to you, the county's in bad shape. Now we'll get a little back."

"Is that it? You'll bury her and close the case?"

Poindexter smiled. "I never said that. The law requires me to find the killer, and I hope to."

"The case isn't closed," Flint said, savagely. "I'll make sure it stays open until justice is done. Hamlin Balthazar isn't exempt from the law, and neither are you."

"Well, it could be anything. Most of the sluts drink, dope, and go wherever they go. Who knows what happened?"

"I won't let go of it, sheriff. Issue after issue."

"No, Flint, you'd better leave it alone. You're not going to second-guess my investigation. Maybe I'll go for Balthazar, maybe I won't. If you start howling for his head, his old man'll ship him to Timbuktu. You're not going to print a word. Maybe you're trying to pin something on Hamlin Balthazar. We've all heard how she ran around your place in her kimono. Maybe, Mr. Editor, you're inventing a story. You keep your type in the box and forget it, and nothing'll happen to you."

Napoleon said, "I'm a witness too. You have two witnesses. We were working. We heard the shot, ran to the window, and saw Balthazar."

"Well, Napoleon, maybe you're inventing a story too. Hamlin Balthazar, the killer. That would be a sensational story. Wise up, gentlemen — and don't leave town."

Flint found himself talking soft and low, almost murmuring. "I don't know how she got into her business, but I know she was a person with inner beauty, a person worthy of your respect. She used to tell me that there was no protection for someone in her profession; no lawman here would help any girl of the line. Why is that, sheriff? Tell me why you'll protect any businessman from murder or theft or assault or extortion but won't defend some poor desperate women, usually forced into this life against their will, and just let their murders go uninvestigated?

"You know what brought me here? A girl killed herself right over there in my place, where the press now stands. She died because she had no hope. Instead of protecting her, your deputies milked her of her last dime, put her in debt, stole from her until you drove her to her grave at the age of twenty-nine. You just called them all parasites — but what about your own deputies? I came here because Westminster laughed in print at the poor woman's death, and said they'd lost another cash cow. . . . Threaten us with phony charges if you feel like it, Poindexter. We're going to print the news."

40

Flint and Napoleon abandoned the typesetting. Morosely, they watched the mortician, who wore a huge buffalo coat, and Poindexter carry the blanket-shrouded body of Chastity Ford to a waiting wagon. A few chilled revelers in the sporting district watched with clouded breath; others hurried by, wanting no part of such a scene.

"Bury her with respect," Flint growled at the mortician.

"I'm always respectful."

"In a coffin. With a service."

"And who'll pay?"

"You'll donate it," Flint snapped.

The mortician reacted as if Flint were daft, and then drove off into the blackness. Poindexter and a deputy rummaged around in Chastity's apartment, and then turned down the wick, locked the doors, and took a skeleton key with them.

"I'm not through with you, Flint," the sheriff said. "If I see a word of this in print, I'll come after you. Don't leave town. You're witnesses."

Flint nodded and said nothing. The pair of lawmen headed down the gulch and vanished in the gloom. So, Flint thought, Poindexter believed him after all and called him a witness. All the rest had been bullying and hot air.

Midnight had long since paraded by, but neither Flint nor Napoleon entertained any thought of turning in. Napoleon shoved stove wood into the firebox of the kitchen range and watched it catch fire, dippered water into the coffee pot, ground some roasted Brazil beans, and threw the coffee in. Flint watched silently, knowing he wouldn't drink any.

Grief had slowly penetrated the deepest corners of his heart. Chastity Ford had become his boon companion, his confidante, and his nurse. She had always been there, brightening his days. His first harsh notions about her had softened into tenderness. She had been driven into her profession by something terrible that he would never know, but in all the weeks he had known her, he hadn't heard her whine or slip into self-pity. She had dealt with the cruel realities of her life with courage and humor, fighting for some sort of decent life. Her dream had been to make a lot of money fast and get out of the life, moving to some city and living quietly. She was succeeding too, until Hamlin Balthazar decided to turn her into his marionette.

The thought of Hamlin Balthazar built a rage in Flint. Some day he would thrash the man, bruise for bruise, hurt for hurt.

Napoleon said nothing, wisely understanding Flint's need for silence. After a while the tramp printer thrust a cup of fresh steaming java before Flint, who didn't touch it.

How often Chastity had sat at that very table, often in her half-opened kimono, so voluptuous and inviting that Flint could barely stand it, and often wondered why he didn't just enjoy her, since she was doing her best to seduce him. There was something in him that resisted. He felt the fool while her big bright eyes mocked him. Once or twice she confessed that his respect for her — if that was the word — was why she tumbled to him.

A thousand visions of her filled his mind now, tormenting him but also allowing him to grieve and remember. He let his mind drift for what seemed a long time, while Napoleon sipped. It had become very late. Most of the lamps in the windows of the district had dimmed out.

"Flint," Napoleon said. "In the morning, write that story."

"I intend to."

"Everything. All about Hamlin's visits. The way he never paid her. The way he stole her money and made her a slave. And how you protested to Poindexter and how he dismissed it."

Flint nodded. It would land him in the jug, but he was going to report it.

"There's a lot of people who won't want this issue of *The Sentinel* to come out, Flint. Have you thought about it?"

"We're well along with it. Maybe by tomorrow night we can print."

"Flint, here's who won't want this issue to come out. First there's Westminster, who won't want you to answer his lies about you. His thugs pied our type once, and they'll do it again, maybe tomorrow. Now we've got Poindexter to worry about. You're going to make him look bad. You asked him to help Chastity get out of a jam and he laughed at you, and now she's croaked. So you've got him to sweat about. He was dead serious. You say a word, and he'll be down on you. Maybe his deputies will learn how to pie type in the morning.

"But that's not all. Now we've got the Balthazars on our neck. I don't know how close Hamlin and his old man are, or whether the old man even knows. But the kid has just as much access to those plant guards as the old man. He doesn't know that we saw him and heard him, but he knows you're going to write about the murder. And he knows the story is going to talk about him, make him a suspect. I think he desperately doesn't want his old man to know about Chastity. We're his only danger, as far as he knows. He'll do anything. A man who's killed can kill again. So we've got him to worry about. Flint, that's a lot of people who don't want this issue out . . . What are we going to do about it?"

Flint knew that his field marshal was forcing him to think about the troubles that could befall *The Sentinel* as early as next morning. Weariness plagued him, and he could scarcely think at that hour. "I don't know. Try to beat them. Get a

339

two-pager out in the morning, maybe. Fight Balthazar's thugs."

Napoleon shook his head. "You and I are no match for half a dozen of those mine guards."

"We could hide the galley trays. I've done that before."

Napoleon sipped coffee silently, as if to tell Flint that he would need to do a lot more than that. Then he started in again. "We have to feint. Maneuver. A dummy issue, bland as oatmeal. Not a word about the murder. Not a word about Westminster's attack on you. Not an editorial pushing our program. Put them off guard. Then follow with the real issue."

"We're down to two hundred sheets."

"That's all right. We'll run twenty-five *Sentinels* so insipid that it'll look like you threw in the towel. That's for Monday. We've got enough stuff set for that. Then we'll run the real issue on Tuesday."

"Do you think that'll work?"

"Flint, Napoleon won Europe by maneuver."

"Yes, and forgot to maneuver at Waterloo," Flint retorted. He found some humor in it, in spite of his somber mood. "And you're still on the side of lost causes, I suppose."

"This cause is not lost," Napoleon said. "We're on the brink of carrying everything."

Now it was Flint's turn to suppose someone was daft. He yawned, his weariness swamping him at last. "I'm going to get up at dawn and start setting," he said. "I don't like the idea of a bland dummy issue. We hardly have a story to put into it, and we've more urgent news than I can ever remember stuffing into one issue."

Napoleon muttered something about being thirsty all of a sudden, but Flint didn't care.

In the morning Flint heated some of Napoleon's leftover coffee, neglected to scrape his face, and set to work, still worn and weary and at the edge of tears. He began by reading the galleys of the stories they had reset, and realized that every story cried to be published. He would put out a ferocious issue that would rattle the whole gulch. His mind made up, he began the work that howled like a wolf in his soul: the whole story of Chastity's captivity, robbery, and murder. Slowly the words began to parade in his mind and find expression in his fingers.

Some while later, he discovered Napoleon staring at him.

"You can't help it, can you, Flint?"

"Help what?"

"Trying to heal the world."

Flint was annoyed. "I am what I am, and if you don't like it, Napoleon —"

"Flint!" Napoleon was laughing. "Flint, you don't see me working for Westminster. Maybe there's a reason."

Flint subsided, feeling grouchy. "I'm writing Chastity's story. I'm sorry, Napoleon, I have to do it my way. I'm bullheaded. A newspaper's nothing if it's not on the side of justice."

"All right. I'm with you," Napoleon said.

Quietly they worked through the morning. Flint finished his story about the murder and turned to other work. Before the type was pied, the galley trays had contained follow-up stories about regional labor conditions and retail prices in other towns. He would have to dig through the exchange papers again. Resetting a paper was hard, disheartening work.

They broke at noon, just as a messenger arrived from the San Juan Forwarding Company at the foot of Silver City. The newsprint had arrived from Denver and could be picked up any time at its freight yard, or the cartage company could bring the pallet for a small fee. Flint nodded. This afternoon, he'd throw harness over Grant and Sherman, pick up the paper, and save three dollars. He would be able to print a full edition after all. Maybe the delay of this edition was a perverse blessing.

"Let's print tonight," he said to Napoleon. "We still have a lot of space to fill, but we'll build a couple of house ads. Maybe it's time to go after some mail subscriptions."

"I don't know, Flint. You're such a famous fellow that maybe no one'll subscribe." Napoleon's eyes danced.

Flint didn't reply. That afternoon they both worked hard, and by mid-afternoon they had an edition ready to go. It contained a small, sober response to Westminster's accusations, quietly run on page three. All Flint wanted the world to know was that he had been honorably discharged from the Ohio Volunteers after the war and that *The Sentinel* supported itself with job-printing. He sensed, intuitively, that these two facts, plus his editorials calling for reform, would rescue his reputation. He wished he had the equipment to lithograph his discharge paper and run it, but he had never been able to afford such luxuries.

"You get the newsprint; I'll stay and guard," Napoleon said. "I'll have the paper put to bed and the press set up and running when you get back. I can print the first two hundred with the stock on hand. I think I'll hide the finished sheets somewhere. I've a bad feeling about this."

"I do too. We'll hide the issue in batches. As long as I'm getting my wagon, I'll take what you've completed down to the Bridges and let 'em dry there when I get back."

But it was too late. As Flint was putting on his coat, a mob of Balthazar's mine-security guards burst in.

41

Flint stood as motionless as a stone, hiding the disgust boiling through him. The mine guards spread through the plant, poking around, studying the press for signs of recent use. He felt like flying into them, but he knew these brutes would simply pulverize him.

Rage simmered in him. Napoleon quietly put down his type stick and waited. Flint was sick of people invading his office as if they owned it. Anyone who didn't like what *The Sentinel* was saying thought he had a license to wander in and destroy property or tear apart his plant.

"All right," he said tightly, "you've had your look around. There's nothing here for you. We'd like to get back to work."

"Nah, Flint," said one, an older man with a smug smile. "You're out."

"What do you mean, I'm out?"

"You're evicted. Out."

A ray of hope filled Flint. "All right. I'll get my wagon and you can help me load the press and the rest. We'll get these galleys stored. It'll take a few hours."

"Nah, Flint. That stuff stays. You go, you and the gamecock over there."

"What do you mean, that stuff stays? If you're evicting me, it goes. That's my property."

"Nah, Flint, you don't get it. Balthazar says you don't publish any more papers. You ain't paid the rent. It stays, all this stuff."

Flint should have been incredulous, but he wasn't. The Balthazars could and would do anything, including felony robbery. "Who ordered this, Hamlin or Achilles?" he asked tartly.

"The kid. He says, 'Clean Flint out of the building and keep the stuff and run him out of town, and if he squawks, give him some souvenirs to remember Silver City by.' "

"I'll go talk to Achilles. I don't think he'd go for this."

"Those are my orders, pal. We're sticking here. You can get your duds and your pots and pans out, but this whole plant stays. Hamlin says your rag's been hurting the company, and it's just a little compensation, this stuff."

"Does Achilles know?"

"Nah. You can go squawking to him all you want, and it won't change a thing. He'll laugh."

"So it's theft. And each of you is a part of it."

Some of them whickered. The leader did too, with all the amusement that rises from absolute power. "I guess you'll go fetch the sheriff," the man said. "And then old Poindexter'll come here and wave his wand and we'll all go away."

Napoleon plucked a sheaf of galley proofs from a spindle. "Come on, Flint, let's get out.

There's no point in arguing it." He spoke in a way that made Flint wonder if the man had a plan. None of these mine guards seemed to grasp that Napoleon had the text of the whole issue in his hands.

But Flint wasn't ready to abandon three thousand dollars' worth of printing equipment. "Why is Hamlin doing this?" he asked.

The spokesman shrugged. "He's a Balthazar."

"Why is he hiding this from his father?"

"Who knows? His father'll back him. You can't drive a wedge between them, Flint. Now if you don't start packing your duds, we'll throw it all into the street. We've moved in."

"I paid my rent for two weeks. Doesn't that mean anything?"

"Not a thing, Flint. You sure are slow."

"Come on, Flint," Napoleon said. It sounded like a command, which just made Flint more angry. But the gypsy printer was already stuffing the galley proofs in his warbag and adding his clothing, including the stuff they had gotten for Chastity's escape.

Sullenly, Flint drifted into the kitchen area and filled his trunks. He had two, one for clothing, the other for kitchenware and a couple of blankets. There wasn't much. Bitterly he hefted his two trunks to the front door while the guards picked their teeth and watched. Napoleon hoisted his warbag to his shoulder and followed.

Flint heard amusement behind him, and then

the front door slammed. Their stuff rested on the stoop.

"You sure didn't put up any fight, Field Marshal Napoleon," Flint said, acidly. "I'm now penniless. My entire press has been stolen from me."

"It ain't over," Napoleon said cockily.

"How am I going to publish? Without a press? Without fonts? Without paper and fonts and chases and trucks and all the rest? I don't even have a type stick."

Napoleon grinned, and it infuriated Flint. "All right, you go your way and I'll go mine," Flint snarled.

"Hey, Flint. Go get the wagon. I'll guard the stuff. Then we'll go talk to the old man."

Angrily, Flint stomped up the gulch and out onto the vast, sweeping meadows and foothills of the San Juans. For once they didn't make him feel any better. It took an hour to tell the rancher he was pulling out, harness Grant and Sherman, and drive back down the gulch. Napoleon was sitting on the stoop, huddled against the chill, but looking a lot calmer than Flint. Silently they hoisted the trunks and the warbag onto the wagon bed.

"You got cash?" Napoleon said.

"I suppose you want your back pay," Flint said, feeling hurt. He dug into his britches for his purse, thick with money, for once. The job-printing had helped. A lot of the cash was intended to pay for the newsprint

347

that had been sent COD.

"No, Flint, let's go get the newsprint," Napoleon said.

Flint glared at the man. "I suppose the Finger of God will print our edition," Flint snapped. "No, I don't know what I'd do with a load of newsprint now. Westminster'll buy it."

Napoleon grinned.

"Look, Napoleon, I'm going to stop at the sheriff and file a complaint. I'm being robbed. He's got to uphold the law. And I'll stop to see a lawyer I met, Daniel Burleigh. I can't pay him, but maybe he'll help anyway. He can go after Balthazar like a swarm of bees. Thanks for your company and your help. You're the best printer I've ever had. I wish I could do more for you —"

"Let's get this issue out, Flint. After that you can talk to Burleigh or the sheriff."

"What're you talking about?"

"Ouray."

"Ouray?" Ouray! *The Ouray Eagle*, just thirty miles away. Flint gaped at the bantam printer. "Do you think they'll let us?" he whispered.

"For a price. They might even get enthusiastic about it. Right now, the thing is to look like we've been driven from Silver City. Don't stop anywhere except the forwarding company. We need the paper."

Flint's mind raced with the possibilities. It was as if the stormclouds had passed by, and the whole world had turned golden. "You up to driving all night, Napoleon?" he asked.

"Armies march in the night. We shall have our surprise attack," Napoleon said.

Flint hawed the surly mules, and the team began its long downslope journey through Silver City. Once again Flint saw the way the town snaked along a single gulch, hemmed by towering cliffs, often barely wide enough for a road, a creek, and a row of buildings. Silver City was the strangest place he had ever been. The mules, discovering they could pull the wagon along without much labor, hurried down the gulch, eager in their harness. Flint stared at the city he had supposed only moments before that he would be leaving, defeated, like a dog with its tail between its legs. The winter sun had already plummeted behind the San Juans, bringing a sharp chill, but Flint reached the forwarding yard before it closed. He completed the transaction in a hurry, paying out much of his precious cash, and then some teamsters helped him slide the pallet of sheets from the loading dock into the wagon, which creaked and lowered under the load. Paper weighed a lot.

"It'll be a cold one," Napoleon said as they started north. "But it's not overcast. We'll keep the road."

"What if they won't accept?" Flint asked, worried.

"Have you ever seen a newspaper that wasn't starved for cash?"

Flint allowed that he hadn't.

They drove quietly into the twilight, paused

349

long enough to build a fire and heat some soup, drank it while it was still scalding, and then pierced into a bleak, wind-whipped night that numbed their faces and hands. From time to time Flint turned the lines over to Napoleon, so Flint could flex his fingers and warm up by pacing alongside the wagon. A gibbous moon rose at last, layering fat white light over the lonely landscape. A thirty-mile wagon trip through a cold November night was no lark. But the almost empty wagon offered shelter, if it came to that, and the gypsy printer soon showed himself to be a master of the trail.

Flint felt his weariness but ignored it. The fever of success raged in him, driving him onward. They rolled and creaked and chattered through the darkness, traversing utter wilderness, wrestling up terrible grades and braking down relentless slopes. Sometime in the night they rested the mules and built a fire and sipped tea, which revived Flint somewhat.

"You up to setting this issue a third time, Flint?" Napoleon asked.

"You have galleys. It won't be so bad," Flint replied.

"*Mon ami,* this is the issue that refuses to die. I can hardly wait to put it out on the streets," Napoleon said. "By the time we get back, they'll think we're history. They'll have called off the dogs. Westminster's hooligans won't be roaming. I doubt that Balthazar's mine guards'll even be around the flat."

"What do you think'll happen when the issue hits the streets, Napoleon?"

"They'll have to act. Poindexter can't avoid it. Judge Shreveport can't escape it. The county attorney can't duck. Achilles Balthazar won't hide his son, not if he hopes to keep his head from a noose, or at least facing charges as an accessory. Those miners would string up Poindexter if he doesn't act. Either that or string up Hamlin without a trial. When we spread this issue all over Silver City, it'll be all over for them. Those miners'll probably run Westminster out of town too." Napoleon laughed.

"Why didn't I think of *The Eagle*?" Flint asked ruefully.

"Because you loved Chastity. You were grieving. And because it takes a Napoleon to win the war," his partner said, "and a man named for the patron saint of hopeless cases."

42

Flint and Napoleon rolled wearily into Ouray at dawn, as tired as the mules that had dragged the wagon thirty miles up and down grades all night. The place had the hectic look common to all new mining camps, raw buildings thrown up helter skelter, with only a hint of future order and gracious streets. But dawn turned Ouray into a magical city, so quiet that the rumble of the wagon wheels sounded like a cannonade. The city was surrounded by layered red rock, making the whole town glow pinkly in the first light.

Flint steered the mules toward a livery barn and had them hayed and watered while he and Napoleon walked to the nearest cafe with lamplight in its windows. There the pair of printers wolfed down a huge hot flapjack breakfast and a gallon of coffee. From the woman who served them, he asked directions to the newspaper, which was just down the street half a mile.

"Well, are you ready to tackle *The Eagle*? Homer Hopwell's the editor," Flint said.

"Let's hope he's an early bird," Napoleon said.

Flint paid the hostler and hawed the unhappy

mules to life, full of doubts now that the moment of truth was upon him. This was a fool's errand; he knew that. Flint tried to remember what the Ouray paper was like. Hopwell would have all sorts of objections. They rattled through the awakening town, past a dozen mercantiles, a smith, two livery barns, and a feed store, pulling up at last before a false-front building with a gallery. A lamp glowed from within.

Inside they found a craggy, lumpy, humped-over fellow, glasses perched on his pinched nose, salt-and-pepper hair combed back and down to his shoulders in the ancient manner. He was building an ad.

"You're strangers to Ouray," he said.

"I'm Sam Flint, with *The Silver City Sentinel*, and this is Jude Napoleon, my printer."

"No! Flint? In the flesh? Am I meeting the most infamous gent in Western Colorado?" Hopwell asked, in a mellifluous voice.

Flint nodded, not knowing what to make of the man's reaction.

"I've been following the fracas over there; hardly can wait to get your rag and Westminster's. What happened to your last one? Never got it."

"Westminster's bullyboys slipped in and pied our type."

"Oh! A desperate ploy. It means he's lost."

"I wish I had your confidence," Flint mumbled.

"Flint, you're a legend around here, a man they

want to erect a statue to and put it in the square."

"I'm what?"

"Flint, you singlehandedly shipped us almost a hundred tinhorns and whores. It was a cause for jubilation here — at least in some quarters. I don't suppose I should speak for the parsons and the wives."

"Jubilation?" Flint was amazed. "I hadn't thought about what would happen here. I was trying to make the world less cruel for a few unfortunate women."

"Oh, jubilation, Flint. Celebration. We were lacking certain amenities here until you went on a tear. A brilliant idea, comparing license fees, property taxes, prices in ads, working conditions. Our county government's much enriched. The miners are now privileged to witness female pulchritude — they were certainly bored before the exodus to our red-rock country. All in all, Flint, you deserve a shrine, a basilica, a commemorative arch in Ouray."

Flint sighed. "It was Napoleon's idea. Give him the credit. It was his idea to come here too. We've been driving all night, and I have something to put to you."

"Well, let me get out of this smock and we'll chew around that potbelly and have at it."

Bluntly, Flint described what had happened. Hopwell lit a pipe, nodded, asked questions, and came to the right conclusion.

"So you want to print here."

"Yes, if we can. I brought paper. I have a little

cash to offer you. Napoleon and I would work at night and not bother you, print the issue on our own paper, and break down the type for you."

"Well, Flint, there's a problem with that. I don't have enough type for two papers. It's a deal just to get my own paper to bed with the fonts I have."

Flint sighed, knowing it had been a fool's errand. But he wasn't about to give up. "Suppose Napoleon and I help you with your current issue — he's one of the fastest men with a type stick in the country. . . ."

"Not one of the fastest; I *am* the fastest," Napoleon said, indignantly. "I win all the bets."

"And we could put yours out, break it down, set and print ours, break it down, and be out of here."

Hopwell knocked the dottle from his pipe and stared through the window into the bright red morning. "Editors oughta stick together," he said. "You're a fighter. I don't see many of those. Most editors have their eye on the ledger and nothing else. I tell you what: There's a better way that'll save us work. I've been reprinting your stuff regularly. That's why the miners around here want to build you a monument. Now, here's what you do. You set those stories of yours — you have galley proofs, you say? — and run your issue. You can pay me with the newsprint you picked up. I'm always short and it's precarious, getting it. You run your issue, but don't break anything down. Afterward, put those stories back in the galley trays, and put a new line at the top, 'Reprinted from *The Silver City Sentinel*,' and I'll just drop 'em into *The Eagle*! Save me three days of typesetting."

"You'd run 'em?" It flabbergasted Flint.

"Listen, Flint, you're the biggest sideshow in Colorado right now, and I'd have the news before anyone else."

Flint grinned. "Well, let's get at it. We'll show you what a couple of journeymen up all night can do."

"I might just pitch in myself, if we don't crowd the type cases too much," Hopwell said. "I can build you a masthead while you're about it if you're not too particular about my broken-down display type."

Flint felt a rush of energy, liquid fire coursing his veins. Napoleon found a type stick, laid out a galley proof to copy, and plunged in. The sticks began to fill his galley tray. Flint slipped outside to put the mules up at a livery barn, and then set type himself. Hopwell built a mast and was plainly having fun. He was a born conversationalist, talking as fast as he set type but never missing a word or a letter in the stories he was copying.

"I haven't had a tramp printer around here in months," he said. "It gets plumb lonely putting a paper out alone. I'm just having a high old time."

They toiled through the morning, and Flint felt an uncommon cheer as the columns of type grew in their trays. It fell to Hopwell to set the story of Chastity Ford's captivity and murder by a young man who thought himself above justice.

"Flint," Hopwell said soberly, "this is the most important item in here. If there's justice in Colorado, Poindexter has to act, and your district court has to try the case. If he doesn't, my *Eagle* is going to start screaming. It's one I want to reprint."

"I want you to," Flint said. "We're up against two bands of hooligans, and there's no assurance we can distribute this issue. If you reprint, it'll reach the public no matter what."

They broke for a quick bowl of bean soup. Flint felt the loss of sleep and wanted only to nap, but his desperation drove him onward. He set type with numb fingers and a numb mind. Beside him, Napoleon slapped type cheerfully. He and Hopwell hit it off, and their banter lightened the afternoon.

Amazingly, the three men reset all of Flint's galley proofs by mid-afternoon and began loading the type into the chases. A lot of space remained, so Hopwell plugged the holes with his own filler material. Looking for filler, Flint began reading Hopwell's own galley proofs, discovered a fine story about the production of Ouray's mines, and decided to use it.

"I'd like to run this, Homer. I'd like to put a reprint tag in front of it and slide in the type."

"Why, consider it done, Flint. We're here to help each other. You two've wrestled with hell

357

over there, and now you've a new friend. I don't know how you managed, fighting *The Democrat* and its control of the advertising, and fighting Balthazar for better wages and conditions. I'm just plain honored, not to say tickled, you came on over the mountains to work in my plant."

"Homer, if ever you're in a pickle, you can count on me to run an issue for you — if I still have a plant. Right now, I can't even say whether I'll publish another issue or get my press back."

Late that afternoon they locked up the chases and began hammering the type flat with hardwood blocks and rubber mallets while Hopwell readied his ancient flatbed handpress, a rickety monster that Flint knew enough to let Hopwell operate. Old presses had personalities, and woe to the printer who supposed he could run any of them. Napoleon trucked the chases holding page one and page four over to the press and slid them into the bed, while Hopwell began inking with a chamois ball.

"How many are we doing?" Hopwell asked.

"Five hundred," Flint said. "Unless that's too much."

"No, we'll have at it."

Flint went out to his wagon, measured five hundred sheets, and toted them in. Then he turned to Hopwell. "What would you like for pay? I've fifteen hundred left."

Hopwell paused and pondered. "You know, Flint, all this is costing me is some ink. You've managed to set most of my issue for me too. My usual run's three and a quarter, and if that appeals to you, make it three hundred sheets."

Flint did better than that. He brought in three hundred fifty and deposited them on top of Hopwell's supply. "There's an edition for you and then some, Homer," he said.

Hopwell nodded. He was engrossed in levering the platen down on a sheet that had been loaded into the tympan, which held it just above the inked type until the last split second. With a shudder, the old press clamped the newsprint into the ink like an old lover, and then the platen rose. Napoleon slid the sheet onto a growing pile of *Sentinels*.

Thus they labored deep into the evening, printing pages one and four, and then pages two and three. At last five hundred of these lay unfolded in a stack, drying, and Hopwell began washing his old press. But the work hadn't stopped. Flint and Napoleon returned their stories to galley trays, and then added a new heading to each: REPRINTED FROM *THE SILVER CITY SENTINEL*. Then they returned Hopwell's filler material to the galley trays.

"Better leave your mast," Hopwell said, "just in case."

Gratefully, Flint slid the big letters that lay between thick ruler lines into a galley tray.

Hopwell finished wiping the press and picked up a paper. "Flint, this'll bring you glory," he said. "It has courage written all over it in pure gold. I'd like one to put up on my wall."

Flint choked up. "Take all you want," he said hoarsely.

"Now, Flint, you can go back tonight and I won't argue. But I think these ought to dry here, and I think two nights without sleep wouldn't do you any good. I've got a pair of bunks in the rear for gypsies. Why don't you fellows get your bedrolls and leave in the morning? We'll go have a bite of supper, my treat. Not often I get to dine with a pair of real, sterling-silver newspaper heroes."

Flint stepped into the twilight so Hopwell wouldn't see his face. He knew why he had been set upon the earth.

43

Dusk had settled by the time Flint maneuvered his wagon to a halt before the Bridges' shop. After driving all day through open country, with vast panoramas to please the eye, distant snow-capped mountains, huge plains, and endless grades, it seemed oppressive to be hemmed into the gulch again by relentless bluffs to either side of the road.

The hour wasn't late, but the autumnal sun had resigned early and retired for the night. Flint clambered stiffly to the frozen earth. Napoleon jumped down easily. The bell of the lending library alerted those within, and in a moment Molly Bridge materialized, carrying a lamp.

"Sam Flint!" she cried. "Napoleon! We thought you were gone!"

Swiftly she led the wayfarers through the shop and into her home, where they were greeted with exclamations of surprise.

"We never expected to see you again," Marcus said.

"I wasn't sure you would. But Napoleon thought perhaps we could print an issue at Ouray — and so we did. We have it in the wagon."

"Ouray, eh? I wouldn't have thought it. Well, tell us the story, man."

"All right. But first, what's your news?"

"Two nights ago the boys went to your shop, wanting to know about the next issue. You weren't there; some of the Balthazars' men were. So we knew you were in grave trouble. Last night Timothy went up there again and found the place totally dark. He tried to peer into a window and almost got robbed. Not a nice neighborhood, Flint. But he couldn't see a thing. Your shop's silent as a tomb."

"Anything else?"

"Why, we've heard rumors all day: You skipped town. You were in debt. Balthazar confiscated your press. You're fleeing a warrant. Someone died there. Westminster's piece exposed you and you ran. That's the one most people agree on. Westminster had the goods on you, and you hardly dare show your face in Silver City now. Some of the merchants have been voicing it. Good riddance, they say. The ones who got flyers from you are plenty worried now, because they know what Westminster's going to do."

Flint sighed. "Someone did die there," he said slowly.

They stared at him, incredulous. Slowly he recounted the captivity and murder of Chastity Ford; their witness of Hamlin Balthazar's flight immediately after the shot, and their pursuit of him; Flint's warning to the sheriff before the murder; their summoning of the sheriff after it; the reluctance of Poindexter to act against the wastrel son of the man who held Silver City in the palm of his hand; their feverish preparation of a new edition after Westminster's scheming louts had pied the type; the invasion by Balthazar's guards and their swift eviction; Napoleon's thoughtful rescue of the galley proofs and their good fortune in Ouray, which resulted in an issue of five hundred, lying in the wagon.

Bridge frowned. "Let's get those papers inside," he said. "Plenty of footpads and thieves out there. They'd look under a wagonsheet any time."

Flint agreed. In a matter of minutes the Bridges, Flint, and Napoleon had carried the *Sentinel* to safety.

"We could sell 'em tonight," Timothy said. "It's early. Miners just coming off shift. Augustus and I could get most of 'em out. Still ten cents?"

Napoleon replied, "Nighttime is when the wolves prowl. The dark conceals crimes. If anyone were to ask me, I'd say peddle 'em at dawn. The day shift starts at six. There won't be a single thug to stop you. Sell to the miners at dawn, and then head down to the shops and courthouse and sell the rest under Westminster's nose. Catch people going to work."

Flint liked that plan better, as did they all. Timothy and Augustus agreed to fold the sheets and be off before dawn, catching the miners on their way to the headframes.

"Oh, it'll be something," Timothy said. "They'll take the story of that woman's murder by Hamlin right down into Balthazar's pits and read it there!"

Flint had already imagined the issue's impact on Silver City over and over. What bothered him was the fate of his press.

"I think we'd better go," he said soberly. "I have to put up the mules and take care of the wagon."

"Oh, don't rush off. We've lots of cabbage left over, and some corned beef."

It was tempting, but Flint declined. "I have things on my mind," he said. "You gentlemen sell those papers and keep your usual twenty percent."

"Aw, Flint, you're flat. We'll just do it," Augustus said.

The offer irritated Flint, but he swallowed back his pride. "I'd prefer that the laborer receives his reward," he said stiffly.

Something in his tone must have settled the matter. Both young men nodded.

Flint left in a black mood, Napoleon behind him. Flint hated the ugly town, cramped into its gash in the earth. It had ruined him. Or rather, he corrected himself, he had ruined himself dashing against it. He had scarcely come here to make a living, but only to joust at windmills. The wagon seat shot cold through his britches but he ignored it. He tugged the weary mules into the street and headed for his shop, wondering what he would find.

"Flint," Napoleon said softly. "Whatever we find, now's not the moment to wallow in defeat. We've already won."

"We'll see," Flint said grimly, hurrying his mules up the gulch with a slap of the lines. They had hauled the wagon thirty miles that day and weren't in a mood for more.

They entered the sporting district, and the tawdriness of it repelled him. Lamplight boiled from every window. Somewhere some "perfesser" hammered the ivories of an upright piano. Men scurried like rats through the shadows. His first mistake had been to settle here, he thought. He drove grimly past staring faces and a few *filles de joie* sitting in their lit windows, negligees carefully disarrayed.

His own building loomed on the right, and he headed for it. Lamplight poured from every window of both floors. Chastity's quarters had been taken. His own were well lit, but drawn shades — new to him — blocked any view within. It gave him a bad feeling.

"Well, we're not going to see through the windows," Flint said.

"Let me go up there. They don't know me. If you go, you'll just be recognized," Napoleon said.

"They know you. Those guards —"

"Flint, I don't think there's a guard in your shop."

Flint surrendered silently and pulled up just down the gulch from the flat. Napoleon hopped down, made his way to Flint's old place, and knocked. A moment later the door opened, and a blaze of light lit Napoleon's face. Flint couldn't see who had answered. Napoleon talked a moment, the door closed, and Napoleon retreated through the night. He climbed up beside Flint.

"That was a bawd named Big Lulu. The name fits."

Flint waited for the rest, bitterness leaking through him.

"They took it all away, Sam."

Flint sighed. A whole printing shop had vanished. "Did she say where?"

"No. She said she moved in yesterday, and she pays someone named Louis the Frenchie a hundred a month. The place was bare. She saw a rent sign in the window and grabbed it."

"Who's in Chastity's place?"

"Another bawd named Little Spain."

Flint slumped into his seat. One or both Balthazars had simply stolen the plant, just as they had stolen Chastity's money after she had sold the building to them. Louis the Frenchie was no doubt a front man for the father or the son.

"You have any ideas where they took the plant or how I could get it back?"

"Silver City's a big place, Sam. But there's a couple of obvious places to look. One is Hamlin's bank. I don't know what's there.

Maybe it can't swallow a whole printing plant. The other is the mines. There'll be dozens of sheds up there that could hide a printing plant."

Flint nodded. "Let's go look at the bank. If Hamlin's keeping his deeds hidden from his father, he'd probably not stow the press around the mines."

Flint hawed the mules uphill. The narrow road offered no place to turn around until they reached the mines, where the gulch widened. He started to wheel the team and wagon around, but Napoleon stayed him.

"This wagon's a red flag, Flint. Let's go on out to that ranch above the town and leave the wagon and put your mules on pasture. We'll be better off on foot. We have to dodge guards and deputies."

That made sense. Flint drove the mules through the upper reaches of Silver City, topped the gulch, and rode along a moonlit plateau bathed in silver. Some other time the pale prospect might have delighted him. Tonight heaviness filled his soul. They reached the ranch a while later, and Flint led his weary mules out to the fields, wishing he could grain them after a hard day. He would square things with the rancher in the morning. He grabbed his warbag and Napoleon shouldered his. They trudged silently into the gulch until they reached the cluster of mines in the white moonlight.

"There's guards, Flint," Napoleon said. "And it's not exactly pitch black. Most of those storage places are close to the shafts, and most of them have no windows. We'll have a tough time."

"Well, the guards'll be wandering around and we can gauge our chances. If we don't freeze to death first."

"I thought I'd bunk with Big Lulu."

"You go where you want," Flint said roughly. "I'm probably going back to the ranch and try to weather the night under my wagonsheet. I don't see much chance here, except to get into trouble. And if we find the press, then what do we do?"

"Why, Flint, swipe it. I can carry a press on my back anytime."

Flint didn't like the way the night was unfolding. "Napoleon, we're supposing that the plant's being stolen from us. But maybe they just pulled it out so they could rent the place. Maybe all we have to do is ask tomorrow, and we'll get it back right away."

The gypsy printer grinned. "Flint, do you believe that?"

Flint shook his head. "We might get it back if Achilles is behind this. But not Hamlin. We're the only two on earth he has to fear. Especially after he reads the paper tomorrow."

They agreed to meet at the Bottomless Pit Cafe for breakfast. Apparently Napoleon was serious about Big Lulu.

Flint hiked wearily up to the meadows again, discovering a sky alive with stars. He spotted Orion off to the southeast, the belt and sword as familiar to him as they were to the ancients. It pleased Flint that some things are eternal and that some truths endure forever. The very constellations named by the ancients were in the heavens before him now. The good things endured.

44

Digby Westminster exulted in his quiet sanctum, where he had arrived before dawn, well ahead of his staff. Flint had vanished. The assault on his honor had done it, along with a little pied type. Westminster grinned. There was nothing like pied type to win a war. Flint had obviously been unwilling to show his face around Silver City after the coy little item in *The Democrat* suggesting that Flint wasn't what he pretended to be.

Westminster had first heard the exquisite news two days before, when his wide-awake ad salesman Padrick Stemple confided that something peculiar was happening at Flint's plant. After that, Stemple had kept tabs, wandering up to the sporting district every few hours. Thus it was that Westminster learned that some burly fellows had carried Flint's press into a waiting ore wagon from the mines, along with Flint's case boxes, paper cutter, trucks, chases, and all the rest, including some newsprint. Stemple waited for Flint to show up, but the man never did, and it appeared likely the press had been seized by Balthazar, no doubt in an eviction.

Soon thereafter, according to Stemple, a tart

named Big Lulu had moved in and was now doing a lively trade. Something odd had occurred next door too; a new tart had moved into the quarters abandoned by the infamous Chastity Ford. Stemple had seen no sign of Ford either, and there were strange rumors afoot. Westminster had asked Sheriff Poindexter about them but had been brushed off, which annoyed the editor.

All of this tickled Westminster. He couldn't help gloating. He'd won after all. This was his greatest triumph. Flint was a formidable man, no doubt about it. This was the sweetest of all victories, because Flint had the skills of a Napoleon. But he had met his Waterloo. The more Westminster thought about it, the more he compared himself to Wellington, the Iron Duke, who had finally brought the emperor to heel. It all fit; why, Flint even had a gypsy printer with the right name.

Westminster donned his printing apron and wrote a juicy, vindictive story describing Flint's hasty exit, no doubt from having his scoundrel past thoroughly exposed. Westminster noted the telling absence of a regular issue for a week and a half and ascribed it to the lack of support from merchants. He rattled the sabre, assailing merchants who had strayed, and rejoiced that San Juan County was now in responsible, sober, judicious hands once again — meaning his own, of course.

This would be a page-one story. He pushed

aside another dealing with a washout of the main road to Denver and dropped the type into the slot. It fit tightly. Westminster knew how to write a story to fill a hole and rarely had to resort to leading dropped between the lines of type to lengthen the story. Tonight he would put the issue to bed; tomorrow, he would celebrate. A victory like this was aphrodisiac to him, inflaming his concupiscient brain.

A deep euphoria filled him. Flint had been a tough one to whip, but that made it all the sweeter. It had been costly, though. The county supervisors were going to impose a universal property tax, and that was that. Flint had driven off too many of the cash cows. Westminster had lost that one, but he consoled himself that for years, under his leadership, merchants and homeowners had been spared taxes. When the change came, every property owner in the county would curse Flint and remember West-minster's leadership.

He reminded himself to write an editorial urging the county supervisors to tax the mines and ranches most heavily, so as not to oppress commerce and growth in Silver City. Maybe he could still shift taxes off his back and those of his stalwart merchants. Yes, he could do that, and the supervisors would surely comply, on pain of not being elected again. Now that *The Democrat* was again the sole paper in the county, he was fanged once again.

Oh, it was a time to celebrate! He wondered

whether to indulge in a banner headline and sixty-point type and decided to do so. Flint's departure was the news of the year. The large type would also point to the renewed muscle of *The Democrat*, and no one with brains would miss the lesson.

Thus did he spend the rosy dawn hour of Wednesday morning, his mind fevered with the punishments he would mete out to certain perfidious merchants and the pleasures of running the county from his sanctum once again. Power was his intoxicant, and little else mattered. The cause didn't matter; he could shape himself to any cause, adapt any principle with the piety of a deacon, if it suited his pleasure.

This evening, after printing his usual thousand copies of *The Democrat*, he intended to go for a little walk up the gulch. He wanted to see for himself the site of Flint's defeat. He planned to knock on the very door and walk in, seeing with his own alert eyes that no press remained there and that the premises now housed a different sort of enterprise. He was sure, of course, that Big Lulu would want to do business, and he fancied that he would resist at first. After that, who could say? He was given to impetuous moments, which he hid from the world. He would never admit to any commerce with Big Lulu.

The morning quickened as the sun cast benevolent rays into the gulch. From his window he observed pedestrians hurrying to work, merchants sweeping their stoops. He heard his printers arrive, the babble of voices. They would find and read his story about Flint's demise, and there would be a spate of ribald jokes, which Westminster disapproved of but allowed. Decorum was a necessity, but so were working conditions that kept his help from drifting off.

Then Stemple barged in without even knocking, a serious infraction of Westminster's rules. The sanctum was not to be invaded. Westminster was about to rebuke the offender, but the porky Stemple dropped a ghastly newspaper onto the beeswaxed desk.

Digby Westminster could scarcely believe what lay before him — a snappy new issue of *The Sentinel*. He felt like a gasbag leaking air. His practiced eye at once saw that the mast was a bit different, and the fonts were not Flint's usual Caslon and were a point smaller. So it had been printed somewhere else! And in record time! It had been distributed this morning, when there wasn't a *Democrat* torpedo on the streets to stop it! A shudder coursed through Westminster. All his dawn gloating had been for naught. The uptown serpent lived.

"Where did you get this?" he asked, his throat feeling as if a fishbone had caught in it.

"Bought it from a Bridge boy. He's still selling out there."

"Well, stop him!"

"What for? He told me he and his brother had peddled almost five hundred."

"All right. Go buy a few. We'll want to study

it. I intend to give Flint worse than he gives me. Get copies over to Poindexter and the courthouse gang."

"He outsmarted you," Stemple said maliciously.

"If you want to continue to work for *The Democrat*, mind your tongue. Now do as I ask."

Padrick Stemple grinned insolently, filling Westminster with loathing. He decided to hire a new ad salesman. The young man retreated, and Westminster began to peruse this loathsome issue — and to work up a proper response to it. He realized he would have to discard his front-page story. More than an hour of typesetting lay wasted.

He started with Flint's lead story, flabbergasted at what he was reading. The infamous Chastity Ford had been shot; she had been literally a captive of Hamlin Balthazar, who had stolen her money and clothing and threatened her. *The Sentinel*'s own staff had witnessed young Balthazar fleeing her apartment next door, moments after hearing the shot. They had given chase and lost him. Sheriff Poindexter had been warned earlier about the white slavery and had done nothing, and he was now concealing the crime from public scrutiny, threatening *The Sentinel*'s editor with arrest if he broke the story. And a poor woman who deserved better was being dumped furtively in a potter's field, with no public notice.

Westminster could barely absorb all that, and

when he finally did, rage choked him. Poindexter was hiding things from him! But there was more, in another related story: In an attempt to hide the crime and drive away witnesses, young Balthazar had employed his father's mine guards to invade *The Sentinel*, steal the press and equipment, and force the editor and his assistant to flee. *The Sentinel*'s press was still missing and was contraband; this issue of the paper was printed elsewhere and shipped back to Silver City. More issues of *The Sentinel* would continue to be published out of town until justice was done.

Westminster groaned. A thing like that could hit like a tidal wave and wash away everything before it. Gingerly he examined the rest: More regional prices and news about mining wages, and a single small item buried on page three, saying that the editor had served in the Ohio Volunteers and had been honorably mustered out; the discharge papers were available for all to see at Bridge Furniture. And that *The Sentinel* supported itself with job-printing.

Not much of an answer, Westminster thought. But some inner wisdom told him it was enough, and far more effective than a long angry denial. So the young wretch had triumphed after all. The rest of the rag didn't matter. Westminster felt an attack of ague coming on and pulled his box of quinine pills from his desk drawer. Why, in perilous moments, did his wretched body afflict him so? The shock had drained his strength out of him, worse than a hemorrhage of his blood.

He allowed himself a dollop of self-pity, though he was against it on principle. He had run Silver City wisely, with a modest genius in fact, benefiting the merchants, keeping the peace, shifting taxes to the most vicious elements, and maintaining excellent relations with elected officials. All of it wrecked by an interloper without a practical idea in his skull. He sighed, knowing that all mortals are born to trouble, but he wished such an oppressive load of it hadn't befallen him. He allowed himself a minute of sorrow, and then he rallied his spirit. Digby Westminster was not a man to surrender to misfortune.

He sank into his tufted leather chair. Things might not be so bad — Poindexter had promised Flint a trip to the pokey for interfering with justice. Maybe that would turn into something juicy, Flint's weak rebuttal of Westminster's accusations would go unnoticed, and Westminster could follow up with a tougher attack. A coup de grace was needed. Yes, things could be salvaged if Westminster was nimble. And that's what politics was all about.

Ague or not, it was time to go talk to the sheriff. Time to take a firm hand and bring the day's affairs around to his benefit. He rose abruptly, commanded his two printers to break down the lead story he had set at dawn and await a new one. Quite possibly, with Poindexter's compliance, he could expose the whole alleged murder story as a fraud and show that Flint was merely a rabblerouser inventing sensational stories as a last resort.

He'd make Flint cry uncle one way or another.

45

Achilles Balthazar read the lead story in *The Sentinel*, closed the door to his posh office, and studied the entire issue carefully. His comptroller, Rudy Attila, had bought it on his way to work and passed it along.

So the punk had finally gotten himself into a jackpot and had tried to hide it. Hamlin had told him only about grabbing Flint's press to teach Flint a lesson — it had amused Achilles. Tradesmen needed lessons. But the punk hadn't said a word about the rest and never mentioned that he was in trouble. Not that Achilles lacked some knowledge. The head guard, Hector Doolittle, had gossiped about Hamlin's little love nest with the Ford woman.

He wondered where the brat was hiding. Hamlin rarely showed up at the house anymore, much to Consuela's relief. She despised the brat, along with the rest of the world. When it came to despising Hamlin, you had to take your place in line. It probably didn't matter where the brat hid out. The sheriff obviously wasn't going to act unless *The Sentinel* drove him to it. Drew Poindexter had a proper respect for the Balthazars and knew perfectly well what Achilles could do to Silver City with a single command.

Achilles hated the whole business. Usually he controlled events, but this time events were forcing him to act. The problem wasn't that pussycat Poindexter, but Flint. Everything had been fine until the big editor wandered into town and began stirring things up. Now all the ants in the gulch were marching.

Achilles allowed himself some irritation. He rarely let emotion govern him, but Flint was an exasperating case. Achilles had good reason to rage. The editor had no idea how seriously his stories about wage and working conditions had afflicted every mine in San Juan County. The stories had also crippled Balthazar's alliance of mine owners. No sooner had those stories appeared in *The Sentinel* than the most experienced Cornish hardrock miners quit and headed elsewhere. Good powder men and double jackers were hard to find, and hard to replace. They had learned their skill in the tin stanneries of Cornwall, England, and had become the elite men of the pits. Without them, mine production had fallen by half or more, and every mine in the district was hurting.

No concessions! That was his public stance. But Balthazar knew that his fellow mine managers weren't toeing the line and were secretly paying the few remaining powder men in Silver City premiums to stay on. Balthazar was doing the same, furtively paying half a dozen Cornishmen four dollars a day, and half a dozen top drillers three and a half, in spite of the proclamation of the San Juan Mining Association that its members would hold wages at two seventy-five. Balthazar himself had rammed it through. He could hire muckers at any price. There wasn't much to learn about shoveling ore or cutting drainage ditches or wedging timber into place or laying tram rails. But not the imperious powder men. Put powder in the hands of a mucker and he'd hardly loosen a bushel of rock if he didn't blow himself up first. It galled Balthazar to be at the mercy of the ants.

There would be no prosperity in Silver City until Flint was whipped. Balthazar chastised himself for underestimating the editor. Idealists were the most dangerous people on earth, and stubborn idealists were worse. Suicidal idealists like Joan of Arc would rally armies; routine ones like Flint could make short work of a whole mining empire.

The difference between Flint and Westminster was the difference between a bull elephant and a spider, Balthazar thought. Westminster was the spider, spinning webs, stinging prey, and winning private advantage; Flint was the trumpeter, calling the world to arms. Balthazar regretted ever supposing that Flint was another mere tradesman. If Balthazar's mines were to survive, he would have to deal with Flint in a manner so decisive and final that the editor would never trouble him again. It should be easy — Balthazar had all the high cards — but somehow he knew it wouldn't be.

Balthazar reread the rest of the paper, knowing he could trust every word Flint wrote. The mining magnate examined the part about Poindexter's indifference to the crime and his desire to keep it secret. That was interesting. The pussycat was afraid to pounce.

It was Balthazar's gift to plumb the thinking of others, and he turned to the question of what Hamlin would do and where he was hiding. Achilles knew at once that the brat was too arrogant to flee; he was lying about, probably in the sporting district, where he had a den or two. Achilles knew also what Hamlin would have in mind after reading *The Sentinel* — killing the witnesses, Flint and his printer. That was the dumbest idea in the brat's skull, and if he succeeded he'd stretch rope for sure. Achilles had to get to the boy and stop it, that was plain.

Achilles already knew what was fermenting in Poindexter's skull. The courthouse gang, including Westminster, was going to try to discredit the story, bully Flint, accuse him of yellow journalism, and run him out of town. That was dumb too. None of those ant-brained influence peddlers understood the mind of an idealist. Flint would rather be a cause célèbre than earn a nickel.

Achilles found himself wondering why he even bothered to rescue the brat. Let him hang. He'd been a worthless piece of goods from the beginning. But try as he might, he couldn't let Hamlin

382

dangle from a hemp rope. Achilles finally decided he had to act. For the first time in memory, the Balthazar reputation mattered.

The question was what to do about Flint. He already knew Flint's mind. Idealists were the easiest of all to read. Wherever he was, he would continue the fight. He even announced his intention to publish *The Sentinel* elsewhere — Ouray, probably — until he could return to Silver City. Achilles also knew that Flint couldn't be bribed. Achilles could offer him his press back if he left the state for good — and watch Flint laugh at him. Still, every man had a weakness. There were always ways.

Achilles's whirling thoughts swiftly settled into plans. He had built an empire with an incisive mind and he would now deal with these looming problems in the same manner. He felt his spirit lighten, as it always did on the verge of action.

He opened his door and summoned Dorset, the loathsome clerk.

"Get me Doolittle immediately," he said.

Dorset leaped up and vanished, his pompadour coming undone.

Then Balthazar settled into his swivel chair and awaited his chief of mine security, the man whose task was to keep the ants from stealing silver ore, Du Pont powder, cables, or anything else they could lay their hands on. Hector Doolittle understood his task and proceeded with more than the usual intelligence for a gorilla, building a small force of a dozen men to patrol the Balthazar properties around the clock.

The chief appeared promptly. He was heavy as an anvil, massive as a steam boiler, ruddy and shrewd-eyed under his usual black derby, and he walked like an ape.

"You haven't kept me informed," Achilles said.

Doolittle squinted and sagged slightly, remaining silent.

"What didn't I know? Why do I have to read about my son in this paper? Why didn't you tell me?"

"I thought it was a family affair, sir."

"Family affair! You're paid to keep an eye on things. Well, what don't I know that you know?" Achilles slapped the offending paper. "Start with the slavery."

"Well, sir, Mr. Hamlin asked us for help. It seemed, well, a bit comical. We escorted the lady to her bank to withdraw her funds. We cleaned her place of the clothing. We kept an eye out to make sure she didn't run off. We bought spies in the district to keep an eye on her. Because we were directed to, sir. Flint, that editor, was fixing to get her out of town. But Mr. Hamlin wanted to keep her like a pet Chihuahua, so we kept her there, that sort of thing. It was too small a matter to report to you, sir. And we're used to Mr. Hamlin's requests. It's just his high spirits, sir."

"And you were accessories in several crimes."

"Well, sir, we're under your supervision,

and Mr. Hamlin's."

"Ah, so you're blaming me. You might have come and asked me. He's a swine, you know. I raised the rottenest brat west of the Mississippi." Achilles was growing annoyed. "I should turn you over to Poindexter."

Doolittle blinked and squinted.

"And you never told me you stole Flint's press and stuck it in my powder shack — which makes me an accessory too. I learned it from Hamlin two days ago. He thought it was funny."

"Why, sir, Mr. Hamlin wished to drive Flint out. Apparently the editor annoyed Hamlin, sir."

"You never said a word to me."

Doolittle shifted from one foot to the other. "We respect the privacy of all the Balthazars, sir."

Achilles bore down. "From now on, Doolittle, you tell me everything. I don't care what it is, or whether it's Hamlin or Consuela or anyone else, you'll tell me. Is that clear?"

"Perfectly, sir."

"Now go find Flint, that's the first task. And keep Hamlin from shooting him. I know the brat's brain better than I know mine. He's thinking that if he kills the witnesses, he's free. I really ought to let him hang, but I won't. Get Flint, wherever he is, and get him before Poindexter or Hamlin get to him."

"We'll manage it, sir. How about Flint's assistant?"

"He's just a gypsy printer, isn't he?"

"Yes, sir."

"He'll drift off. I want Flint. And after you find Flint — or before, if you stumble into him, find Hamlin and bring him here and don't let him sneak out. He and I are going to have a little conference. How many of your men are on duty?"

"Four on this day shift, sir."

"Put eight on this. I want Flint in here before noon."

"We'll do it if we can, sir."

"You'll do it, period. And Doolittle — do it privately. I don't want to hear about a street brawl with Flint. Lure him, do what you have to, but don't start trouble. I've a mind to turn you all over to Poindexter and prefer charges. Accessories in theft and white slavery, my God, what a bad joke."

Doolittle turned very solemn. "If we've made errors indulging Mr. Hamlin, sir, we'll avoid such errors in the future. We thought we were doing it out of loyalty to your family."

Balthazar rarely laughed, but now he laughed derisively, and Doolittle slunk away. The man leaked petty pomposity.

Offer Flint protection. Keep Hamlin from shooting Flint. Work on the editor for a while and see what makes him tick. And above all, keep *The Sentinel* mute while the dust settled. Balthazar had no worries about *The Democrat*, which would whore its way along. Time cured everything. Achilles had learned that long ago. Delay trouble and you've won. Silence Flint and the world would forget. That and do some quiet dealing with Poindexter. Maybe ten thousand to keep the county afloat, and a trip abroad for the punk. He would see about all that. Maybe it was time for Flint to be a houseguest and meet Consuela Balthazar.

Achilles laughed and laughed at that.

46

The piercing cold ruined Flint's sleep, even though he had pulled tight the pucker holes of the wagonsheet against the wind before he spread his bedroll in the wagon bed. He had put the mules back on pasture and prepared for a tough night by dipping into his trunk of spare duds. But the extra clothing hadn't done much good.

By dawn he felt stiff and numb and ached for some hot java. He had whiled away the long, sleepless hours by thinking of Livia Bridge. She had been much in his thoughts during his quiet moments, the image of her brightness, her quick delight in his work and world, her conversational resources drawn from more books than Flint would ever read.

It wasn't just her vibrant beauty that galvanized him, but the endless possibilities of companionship. Why was it that so few men and women were friends and confidants? Even mates were rarely friends, although they spent lifetimes together. Flint thought it had something to do with the roles they each played. But Livia didn't really fit a traditional role, and that was what had drawn him. Could it be that some day they might sit across the breakfast table, or a dinner table, sharing so much of the same world that they would be not just lovers but boon companions? Maybe that was how the sacred union of man and woman should be and was meant to be — not just a domestic connection but a communion.

He stretched, trying to drive the cold and soreness from his aching flesh. He would see Livia this morning, and that warmed him. The Bridge boys would have some cash from the newspaper sales, which he needed. He was down almost to nothing.

He wondered whether to rustle some firewood, heat some water, and shave. The biting northern wind made up his mind for him. As much as he disliked entering the world with a stubbled jaw announcing his sloth, he would do it this morning. He was to meet Napoleon at the Bottomless Pit anyway. They would hold a council of war, and decide on the next step, after reviving themselves with a fine, steaming, pungent, enspiriting cup of Arbuckles' best. Flint knew of no Elixir of Happiness, but he thought a good cup of java was a reasonable substitute.

He bundled into his mackinaw and headed for Silver City, curious about the impact of his surprise issue. It was going to astonish more than a few people who thought he had fled town. The thought brightened his spirit more than any three cups of coffee could. The story about Hamlin Balthazar would wend its way into every corner of Silver City. A thousand miners and their families would expect Poindexter to act, would insist that justice be done.

At the cafe, Flint found Napoleon reading. He had picked up the exchanges at the post office and was quietly perusing them for news, as though *The Sentinel*'s workbench was still awaiting him.

"Did you sleep, Napoleon?"

"Don't ask impertinent questions, Flint."

"Have you learned anything?"

"The Bridge boys are selling the last papers. I watched Timothy unloading them to the men going on shift. No one's troubled the boys. We caught Westminster flatfooted. He's probably gloating in his lair. Look about you."

Flint did. He spotted three issues of *The Sentinel* and several intense conversations among the miners who were sharing the issue with their fellows. They were locked in serious talk.

Flint ordered a double stack of flapjacks, thinking he could gnaw his way through several pounds of them, and turned back to Napoleon. "All right, field marshal, we've got them running. But we have no press and no home, enough paper in the wagon to do a couple more small issues and pay Hopwell with some newsprint. We're in trouble with Poindexter now, and he'll be coming. I don't relish being jugged on some trumped-up charge."

But Napoleon wasn't really listening. Flint turned to see what Napoleon was staring at, and discovered one of Balthazar's men working past the tables in their direction.

"It seems we've been found," Flint said. "If anything happens to me, meet at the Bridges'. If you need cash, draw some from the sales money. Tell them I said so."

Napoleon grinned. "He's cutting a swath. Look at the way those miners clam up."

The man loomed over Flint, squint-eyed, looking like an anvil wearing a derby. "Flint, Achilles Balthazar wants to see you."

"Tell him I'm not available."

"Listen close. He says Hamlin's itching to kill the witnesses. That's you. Mr. Balthazar's trying to find the punk and keep him from doing it. He has your press. Hamlin stuck it in one of his powder vaults. He thinks maybe something can be arranged."

"You tell him I don't bargain," Flint replied coolly.

"Yeah, he said you'd say that. Look, Flint. He thinks the sheriff's going to rough you up. You've made Poindexter look real bad, neglecting his duty and hushing up stuff. Mr. Balthazar isn't against you; he figures he can hide you, let it blow over."

Flint wavered. Then Napoleon pushed him toward a decision.

"Go gab with the man, Flint. I'll be around."

"All right," Flint said. "I'll see what he wants."

The ruddy mine guard squinted cheerfully

and pushed through the crowded cafe, Flint following. Minutes later the man ushered the editor into Balthazar's office.

"Ah, there you are," Balthazar said, "the homeless editor."

Flint hardly knew how to respond to a man whose son he had just exposed as a probable murderer. He nodded.

"You're finding it hard to talk to me, of course. You have the goods on Hamlin, and you're wondering how I'm taking it."

"You have my equipment. It's been stolen and I want it back."

"Ah, I have a lever with which to pry you."

"No, sir."

"I thought as much. You remind me of Joan of Arc. Admirable in a way. You'd rather burn than recant."

"Mr. Balthazar, I was invited here to discuss my equipment."

"That's the smallest fraction of what lies on the table. Hamlin took your equipment without my knowledge or consent and for the purpose of silencing you." He shrugged. "But you were not to be silenced, it seems."

"Not ever, sir. I'm asking for justice. There was more to Chastity Ford than her profession. More than your son saw in her too. He thought he captured the beautiful, famous queen of the demimonde, but he could never capture her mind and soul. And when he found he couldn't have all of her, he killed her. I'm sorry that you're afflicted, but the need for justice cries out."

"He's a swine, a chip off the old block."

"Pardon me?"

Balthazar laughed. "You'll get used to the Balthazars. Hamlin's a dumb pig, and I'm just a hog. I'm offering you protective custody."

"What are you talking about?"

"My brat wishes to kill you. He'd never dream that I'm hiding you in my home, and I won't tell him. Poindexter wants to harass you. He's going to hold you for a few days and tell the world you invented the story to sell papers. Be my guest. In a few weeks, I'll return your equipment and get out of your way."

All this was too much for Flint, and he found himself looking for motives, trying to grasp what this was about. "Why?" he demanded.

"Ah, you're full of doubts. The father of the murderer is protecting the accuser, not only from his own lethal son but an angry sheriff. It's perfectly simple. Hamlin's a pig, but he's my pig. I intend to negotiate with the county attorney and ship Hamlin to Shanghai."

"Then we've nothing to talk about."

"Ah, yes, Chastity Ford. From what I heard, you're right. An educated, bright rebel, playing the demimonde because she thought it would scandalize the world and make her a fortune."

"Mr. Balthazar, you've reasoned it all out. But I'm different. I'm full of grief, and I've wept for a strange and marvelous woman. I'm so angry I'll fight even when I've lost. It's not cold reason but passion that rules me, and there's no way you'll ever change that. It's also a passion for justice. Hamlin had me beaten by your guards for the offense of pulling him off Miss Ford when he was abusing her. I've never had such a pounding. My flesh still hurts when I think of it. And now you expect me to negotiate. Forget it. Take my press if you must. It'll merely be another theft. Hamlin stole her money, including the proceeds of the sale of her building to you. It seems to run in the family."

Flint seethed.

"I was afraid of that. I know your mind better than you do. Alas, Flint, we're opposed. A pity. I wish you'd accept our hospitality for a few days. I've Poindexter to deal with and Hamlin to ship out, and I also need some discreet silence from the newspapers. If I can't get it voluntarily, maybe I'll get it involuntarily."

"What are you saying? Am I a prisoner?"

"No, Flint. The moment I freed you, there'd be a crusade in every issue about it. You can walk out of here. But you won't be protected from anything. Not Hamlin, not the sheriff, and not my guards. You'll do better at my house. Of course Madam Balthazar is a witch, and she'll make you as miserable as possible. She has it in for tradesmen."

"You're referring to your wife?"

"Absolutely. Let me show you something." Balthazar turned to a table behind his desk and plucked up a cartoon pinioned under glass. "We lived in Cleveland. I ran a foundry. The Balthazars were as famous there as we are here."

The silver magnate handed the cartoon to Flint, and he beheld a Thomas Nast-type drawing of the three Balthazars emerging from a sewer through a street manhole. Mrs. Balthazar wore a pointed hat and carried a broom. Balthazar sported fangs, a bulbous nose, and a bulging coin purse. They were stepping on the body of a laborer.

"Isn't it a gem? Caught us perfectly. It was in the *Plain Dealer*."

"Why do you deride yourself? You're the strangest man I've ever met."

Balthazar smiled. "Actually, I simply enjoy using your bourgeois language to mock myself. I learned long ago that success comes to those who don't shackle themselves with all the balls and chains of religion or civic virtue. I really consider myself a pure pragmatist. I do whatever works. But it's more fun to label myself as you see me. It's become one of my amusements."

Flint didn't believe him. "If you were happy, I might understand you. But the Balthazars aren't. You're all desperate, especially Hamlin. You haven't any friends or confidants, and you despise each other. Well, you can't escape justice. It comes slowly sometimes, but it never fails to even up the accounts."

Achilles nodded grandly, but Flint saw a flash of pain.

"I believe you came for your press. Enjoy my hospitality for a week, and you'll have it."

"I don't bargain about justice," said Flint.

"I know," Balthazar said, "but I thought I'd ask. For the record — when you go to the law — I've offered you your equipment, offered to protect you, and sheltered your goods after eviction."

Flint turned to leave, wondering whether he was still at liberty, but the squinty guard let him pass. He plunged into blinding sunshine, free and at risk.

47

Flint blinked in the bright light, glad to be free. But he knew he had willfully thrown away thousands of dollars of equipment and would have to start over. It saddened him. He wished he weren't so intractable. It was a fault. He could have compromised a little, waited it out, gotten his stuff back — maybe — and picked up the cudgels again. Hadn't someone once said that retreat was the better part of valor?

But it wasn't in him to do that. If it had been some minor issue, he might have bent a little. But a defenseless woman had been murdered. There still was the attitude in Silver City that some people didn't count and didn't deserve the protection of the law. Swift, sure justice was his goal and he didn't intend to sell his soul by languishing at the Balthazar mansion while the father shipped the son to a foreign shore.

He pitied the Balthazars. In spite of all their wealth, they couldn't be happy. Achilles's bravado, his mockery of his own family and himself, his pretense of enjoying the ugly condemnation of that cartoon, all veneered a bitter life. His rotten family had been fashioned out of all the wrong ideals, including cynicism, selfishness, greed, and the illusion that all the world was as rotten as they were — that plus a belief in their own immunity to the laws of God and man.

Flint peered about sharply, aware that Achilles Balthazar was right: He was in danger from Hamlin. But the mines and the mill hummed busily, and no one paid him any attention. It occurred to Flint that he was homeless, broke, and at loose ends. He didn't really know what to do next.

Impulsively he hiked down the gulch to the Bridges' home. They would have news. There he found them all, including Napoleon. Livia smiled at him and headed for the teapot and some cups.

"Did you get the press back?" Napoleon asked.

"No. Achilles wanted my silence. It's lost, I'm afraid. He'll keep it. I won't stay silent for a minute about a murder."

"What's he trying to do?"

"Hustle Hamlin out of the country. Keep me from landing on the issue again. Silence me for good."

"Ah, Flint, he should've known better."

"That's what he said. He called me a Joan of Arc and said I'd rather burn than recant." Flint felt melancholy. "That's not it at all. I don't want to be a leader or a saint. I just want to see justice. A woman I cherished is dead."

Livia, returning with a tea set, eyed Flint somberly and said nothing. There were questions in her eyes.

"We sold out the issue!" Timothy said. "We each took a hundred out at a time and then came back for the rest. We got more cash than we charged too. Lots of people paid with a one-bit shinplaster or a quarter and didn't want change. See, it's fifty-five dollars." He showed Flint a grimy wad of ancient paper and worn coins gathered in a bowl.

That looked like manna from heaven to Flint, and he began to sort it. His share, after the boys took theirs, came to well over forty dollars. He paid them and divided the rest evenly with Napoleon, handing him the grubby paper coins and a few metal ones. "It'll have to last us a week," he said to the gypsy printer.

"Any Napoleon can live on nothing but reputation," Napoleon bragged.

"Some people sure were excited," Augustus said. "That issue's going to be read from one end of the gulch to the other."

"Well, at least Silver City knows about Hamlin," Flint said. "But it won't change much. The courthouse gang'll triumph, Westminster will still rule, and the Balthazars'll continue to be Scrooges."

"Flint, my friend," said Napoleon. "One thing I admire is your integrity and principle. One thing I don't admire is your bouts of pessimism. You've already won."

Flint laughed cynically and sipped some of

Livia's pungent Earl Grey tea. It slid like nectar down his raw throat.

"Now take it from the man named after the patron of hopeless cases. The next step is to consolidate your victory. A little audacity is needed, but nothing more."

Flint stared at Napoleon as if he were daft. "Napoleon, Samson recovered the strength to pull the house down on top of himself and Delilah and the Philistines. Is that what you mean?"

"No, you've won. All you have to do is chase 'em a little."

"Napoleon," said Marcus Bridge skeptically, "you're a most entertaining fellow."

But Napoleon was serious, it seemed. "They don't think you've lost. They think you won. Here's a bit of information: Achilles Balthazar and all the rest of the mine managers are paying secret premiums for certain skills, especially the powder men. And even at that, they've lost production. You won. They'll have to hire competitively. Sheriff Poindexter's been exposed as a cruel, lax man and one now letting a murder slide by. He's lost and he knows it. Digby Westminster's lost too. His merchants abandoned him. Now that some have started sales, the gouging will stop. His courthouse gang's on the rocks. There's going to be a light tax on real estate, spread over the whole county. You won that one. His piece defaming you is a joke, and it'll destroy his paper. You won that one. We

400

won it with this last issue, and every yeoman in Silver City, every merchant, knows it. Take heart!"

That so astonished Flint that he gaped at Napoleon. Then he laughed. It was the greatest bloom of happiness he had felt in a long time. "All right, field marshal, what's the maneuver?"

"Go visit them. Start with Poindexter. Tell him that he'll enforce the law or there'll be another story in the next issue. And don't worry about his threats. He won't touch you. The eyes of Silver City are on him. I'll be ready to run up to Ouray and print another issue if he should get a little crazy and hold you there."

"Visit the sheriff?" Flint could hardly grasp the audacious idea.

"Right into the lion's den. He's toothless. He knows that better than you do. After that, drop in at *The Democrat*. Old Digby will welcome you like a glass of hemlock."

Livia giggled. Timothy guffawed.

"And what do I say to this man who defamed me, deliberately lying through twenty column-inches of fantasy?"

"Why, say you want a total retraction in the next issue."

"And if he refuses?"

"I don't think he will, Flint, unless his conceits have blinded him to the feelings of his advertisers."

"But he can't retract. It would destroy what's left of the credibility of his paper."

"That's right. You suggest he put it up for sale or fold it."

"I should suggest that — when I don't even have the press or equipment to publish? When I have twenty-two dollars to my name?"

"Yes, suggest it. Your howitzers are loaded, Flint, and he knows it. Issue after issue of *The Sentinel* will march out of Ouray, each one putting the lie to his rag. He has no choice. His paper's already destroyed. He's been receiving cancellations all week, and his ad revenue's collapsed."

Flint felt seduced by all this, but his sense of reality kept him from believing a bit of it. "Napoleon, they know I'm broke and don't have a press and can't even do job printing. You just can't tell me that I've routed all the powerful politicians, defeated *The Democrat*, and forced the Balthazars to ante up decent wages and working conditions. No, I'm sorry."

Napoleon sighed. "I feel a good bout with Bacchus coming on," he said. "I thought maybe you wanted to win. Why, with twenty dollars I can have a week-long toot."

Something in that shamed Flint. He remembered a promise and warning given weeks earlier.

"You have nothing to lose, Mr. Flint," said Livia.

"And everything to gain," said Molly Bridge.

Flint reddened. "I've been timid. I didn't sleep much. All right, I'm off. I have one request:

If Poindexter finds some excuse to throw me into his cells, you put out the next issue up in Ouray, Napoleon. Can you handle the mules?"

"Flint, I know the minds of mules better than my own. They're smarter than horses, wilier, more stubborn — but greedy. The key to the soul of a mule, Flint, is his greed."

Flint sighed, shrugged into his coat, and plunged into the cold weather. They had stuffed his head with dreams, but as soon as he had descended the gulch to the business district and courthouse, icy reality would take over. He remembered something from history, about Napoleon's phantom armies, his reports of great victories, keeping his enemies off balance. Such was the emperor's reputation that word of his arrival was all that was needed to send enemy troops fleeing. Napoleon indeed!

Suddenly Flint laughed. He couldn't help it. He knew he had moral courage, but what was that against political power and money? He had some public opinion behind him now, but the other side had all the arms and ammunition. He headed for the courthouse on his fool's mission, hoping the sheriff would be baking himself at the pot-bellied stove instead of making his rounds in the bleak winds.

Well, he thought, the jail would be warmer than trying to bed down in his icy wagon that night. He reached the courthouse, walked down to the end of the building where Poindexter had offices and a six-cell jug, pushed open the door, and entered.

The sight of Flint was too much for Drew Poindexter. "You!" he shouted, "you!" He leaped to his feet.

"It's me, all right. You've read my story. Now what're you doing about it? Have you got a lead on Hamlin? The public wants to know."

Poindexter, hunched like a watchful cat, eyed Flint through carnivore eyes and pondered the questions while two deputies stared.

48

The first inkling of success filtered through Flint's mind as he saw the sheriff recoil. Maybe there was something to Napoleon's audacity. Time seemed suspended as Flint waited, pencil poised over a wad of newsprint, for Drew Poindexter to answer him.

"I'm doing a follow-up story," Flint said relentlessly. "Have you made any progress? Are you looking for Hamlin?"

Poindexter's mouth formed and unformed words.

"Throw him in the jug, Drew," said a deputy. "He needs to learn manners."

Flint turned to the deputy. "That'll go into *The Sentinel* too. It's what you do to criminals and suspects, not what you do to editors."

"Get out," the sheriff said.

"I'll have to report that you're not doing anything or enforcing the law," Flint replied, not budging.

"I should wring your neck."

"I'll quote you. From what I hear, just about every voter in Silver City wants justice done. They trust *The Sentinel* more than they trust you, it seems." Flint scribbled on his pad. He was starting to enjoy this. "Now, for publication, let's have a report on your progress."

Poindexter turned to his glowering deputies, who stared back at him, almost as if this little ballet were an effort to decide something between them. "You're the alleged witness. It could be nothing but a big newspaper hoax, a little sensationalism to sell your rag."

"It happened next door," Flint replied. "And there are two witnesses, both ready to swear it under oath. Now, if you're doing nothing, I'll leave you to your potbellied stove and write the story." He turned to leave.

"Wait," said the sheriff. "You can tell people we're investigating and expect to solve the case soon. We have several suspects."

"Several suspects! And none of them Hamlin Balthazar! Why, I'll report it. Even his father knows he did it. He's looking for Hamlin. He told me he intends to ship his wayward son to Shanghai for a few years, and maybe arrange for a donation to the county after talking with you. I thought that was rather quotable. It's not every man who discusses bribery in advance."

"He said that?"

"Rather careless of him. I think Hamlin's hiding out, probably in some cubbyhole in the sporting district. You could nab him with a door to door search, as easily as not."

"Balthazar said that about Hamlin?"

"That's right," Flint said, a sense of total victory building in him. "What are you afraid of?

That he'll shut down Silver City? It's too late. Because of my last issue, the whole county knows about Hamlin. He's licked. You're all sitting around here quaking in your boots about a man who knows he's licked. He's not going to close any mine. He's hurting; the mines aren't making money and won't until he bids for labor at the market rate. If he tries to muscle his way through this, the whole state of Colorado'll be on him."

Poindexter's cat eyes studied Flint unblinkingly, but the editor didn't mind. The sheriff wasn't even flexing his claws. "Hold up your story for a day or two," he said. "I'll have Hamlin in the jug. And I'll want statements from you and that printer."

"You can reach me anytime through the Bridge family. I'm temporarily without a roof, but I'm here."

"And when you write it, Flint, you make sure that you get it right: I uphold the law."

Flint grinned, and the sheriff blinked.

"I'll check on your progress tomorrow, Sheriff," Flint said.

He left them, nothing but utter silence behind him. It had been easy, and Napoleon was right. Flint marveled. There was something in a truthful story — written fearlessly and distributed to a public who trusted a paper's integrity — that became a living force able to move mountains. He lamented his own lack of faith. He had seen only the shambles of his own paper, the reality of his vagrancy and pauperization, and had scarcely realized that the edifice he had fought so hard was crumbling.

He paused in the corridor. Maybe the doors that had been shut to him would be open now. He found the office of the county attorney, Solomon Drake, and entered. Drake looked up testily from a casebook he was examining and peered over some silver-mounted half-spectacles at Flint, noting his pencil and pad.

"I'm Flint from *The Sentinel*. I understand the county's planning on a property tax. Let's talk about it."

"You're Flint," the man said warily. "All I've heard around here for weeks is Flint this and Flint that, but I've not had the honor. Your reputation precedes you."

"I didn't know I had one. I'm simply looking for information about the proposed property tax."

Drake eyed Flint, surveyed the naked limbs outside his window, and came to some sort of conclusion. "I've been drafting the ordinance," he said. "It'll be up to the supervisors to enact it. So far, it hasn't been scheduled."

"How will it work? Maybe *The Sentinel* will endorse it."

Drake laughed shortly. "What your paper endorses isn't a matter that interests me, but it does interest certain others." Again he pondered, as if making up his mind. "We haven't the means or the time to assess the county. Most of the property's never been traded. We have no market price to base an assessment on. So I've been asked to come up with something very simple. It'll be five dollars for any residence; ten for boardinghouses; twenty for any business or hotel; twenty for any ranch or farm; fifty for any mine. That'll give us more income than, ah, we got from the prior system . . . which has, ah, failed to yield much since you, ah, editorialized about it."

"That's the property tax. Will there also be licenses?"

"Yes, twenty dollars annually for any saloon, gambling hall, or bagnio. Ten dollars per inmate or independent operator." A faint smile collected around the lawyer's mouth. "Does that satisfy your objectives? The licenses are a means of control. We wish to be able to deny one to certain obnoxious sorts, hop fiends, mountebanks, bunco steerers. . . ."

"Yes," Flint said, remembering why he had come — a wretched woman's suicide that had been the fruit of her hopelessness. "I can support all that. So can Balthazar, in case you're interested."

"Achilles Balthazar?" It shocked the attorney.

"The first time I met him, he told me about the attempt to shift the burden of county expense to the mines exclusively. That was the time he and the rest of them simply locked the doors, you know."

"How well I know. You never saw such a

scramble to repeal a law around here."

"Well, he told me perfectly frankly that if it had been part of a general property tax scheme that would spread the burden fairly across the county, he wouldn't have minded."

Drake gaped. "He said that, did he?"

"He said it. You'll have no trouble from him if you spread the burden the way you say."

Drake exhaled like a balloon leaking gas. "I'll let the supervisors know. The whole thing's been tabled until we could get some sense of Balthazar's feelings. He won't discuss it."

"Go ahead and pass it," Flint said, feeling almost heady with victory. "When is the next meeting of the supervisors? I'd like to cover it."

"Next Monday afternoon. They dread it. I don't know of a soul who relishes taxes."

"Neither do I, Mr. Drake, including myself. But I don't know of a soul who scorns basic services, including the recording of deeds. And law enforcement. And a court system where we can find redress if we need to. Bleeding the sporting district may have seemed noble, but it put people in their graves and discouraged reform. A broad tax resting lightly offers the least pain. *The Sentinel* won't rejoice; any tax is painful. But we'll celebrate the end of organized cruelty and hope to awaken a humane instinct in our readers."

"Quite a speech, Flint," Drake said dismissively.

Flint nodded and retreated. He sensed he had

pushed too far, and the man was no ally. Flint weighed a visit to Homer Shreveport's chambers, if the court wasn't in session. The man had been a stooge in all of Westminster's webs and schemes and had bent justice without quite breaking it. But Flint decided not to. The paper was the best place to comment about a judge's conduct.

He rebuked himself for supposing he had a paper. Right now he had a little newsprint and the use of a shop in Ouray. But he was a pauper.

He plunged into bright but toothless sunlight, aware that his sleeplessness was wearying him. He was brimming with stories. Still, every word spoken to him this rare morning had been so important, he would remember everything. This one time, his mind itself would be his notepad. He intended to walk the block to *The Democrat* and confront Digby Westminster in his sanctum, but as he passed Golden Brothers Mercantile, he thought to sound out a merchant. Aurelius Golden had bought flyers and might buy more — if Flint got his plant back.

He found Golden selling a buggywhip to a harried-looking woman. Flint waited until the transaction had been completed.

"Why, Flint!" Golden exclaimed. "I've been reading about you."

"In *The Democrat*?" Flint asked warily.

"Yes, and in your paper. Quite a story, you printing it out of town. You have your press back?"

"Neither my press nor my reputation."

"Ah, Flint, you're good as gold. There isn't a sensible man in Silver City that believes a word of Westminster's screed."

That amazed Flint. In his imagination he had seen that pack of lies sink into the minds of countless vindictive citizens. "How could that be? It wasn't rebutted, except to invite anyone to look at my discharge."

"Flint, everything you've done and said in print made your reputation, not what that cunning old fool tried to do."

Flint sighed. "Well, that's one reason I came in. I wanted to get a sense of where I stand."

"You stand tall, Flint, and I think Westminster's finished. As far as I'm concerned, he can pack up his outfit and vamoose."

"But what about the tax issue? I'm proposing something that's been political poison around here."

"Flint, I hear the annual tax on a business is going to be twenty dollars. If that's so, no merchant in town'll object. Why, Westminster squeezed a lot more out of us for his political machine. We fork over fifty a year just so he could wine and dine the supervisors and keep old Shreveport happy."

"He bribes Shreveport?"

"No, no, no. Just Westminster's Wigwam stuff. He's got that Tammany Hall background, you know, so he was always spending something on old Homer, fat cigars, T-bone steaks at the

Overstreet Hotel. Greasing wheels, he called it. Nothing but high living. But that's dead. I don't know of a merchant in town who designs to fork over another fifty to Westminster or buy more ads than he needs when the devil turned out to be a flat twenty-dollar tax."

When Flint left the mercantile a while later, he felt as if the world had turned upside down.

49

Flint paused before the grand double doors of the posh building that housed *The Democrat*. Its facade was red brick, its name discreetly etched into a bronze plaque, and its casement windows regularly washed. It oozed power and solidity and sobriety, but also a certain aura of invincibility. Flint wondered what sort of fool he had been to take on such an institution.

But appearances sometimes hid realities, he thought, climbing the cream-enameled steps and entering a vestibule graced by a cut-glass chandelier. Digby Westminster's sanctum lay to the rear, conveniently barricaded by the advertising and circulation office. Flint could see the great man through an opened door and proceeded in that direction, gathering his courage. He had just achieved some victories, but this time he was likely to take an awful licking. Still, Napoleon's counsel prevailed: It was a time for utmost audacity and brazen attack.

Westminster sat in his royal swivel chair, in waistcoat and shirtsleeves, obviously in a brown study. Well, Flint thought, the man had a lot to ponder. Flint rapped on the doorjamb.

Westminster wheeled about and saw Flint,

and his expression glaciated into a new Ice Age. That suited Flint fine. He entered unbidden and stared at his tormenter, libeler, and rival.

"I have nothing to say to you, so you may depart," Westminster announced.

Flint didn't blink. He let time pass, like the ticks of a clock, watching Westminster grow taut and nervous. Unless the man was totally devoid of conscience, Flint thought, guilt was percolating through him.

"Mr. Westminster, you'll want to publish a complete and generous retraction," Flint said. "Not only about me, but about the insinuations that my paper was the mouthpiece of Vice in Silver City and of the Balthazars. You never believed it when you wrote it, and you never believed what you insinuated about me."

"Impossible! You may leave."

"No, I intend to stay a while. You'll publish it because you have to. Not a soul in Silver City believes a word of what you've said. You've totally discredited *The Democrat*. Unless you retract, there won't be anything left of your weekly."

"That's nonsense. And every word was true."

Flint laughed. The response seemed pathetic. He had thought he'd be bearding a lion here, not an old fool inventing excuses. Westminster responded to the laughter as if he had been slapped across the face with a glove.

"I hear people are cancelling subscriptions. You scarcely have an advertiser left. I just talked to one. He says the devil you all fought turned out to be a twenty-dollar-a-year tax, while you were demanding much more just for your machine. He doesn't view your leadership kindly. Politicians aren't in vogue here."

"Flint, I'm feeling the ague. I'm subject to attacks, you know. Anything that stirs me up, I'll pay for it with a bilious fever, chills, and sweats."

Flint didn't relent. "Do you know how it feels to be defamed by a powerful, well-connected editor? How it feels to be labeled a mouthpiece of vice when I was just the opposite? How it feels to be —"

"It's just newspaper warfare, Flint. All's fair in love and war."

"No, all's not fair. I didn't send bullies out to wreck your street sales or pie your type. I didn't libel you. I didn't attack *The Democrat*; I challenged the programs and arrangements you were promoting. I took the high ground, and I'm going to survive. You took the low road, and you're facing extinction."

"I'm feeling a fever, Flint. You have no idea how the ague wrecks a man." He slumped sourly. "I won't publish one word of retraction. It'd be suicide."

"Retraction's the only thing that'll save you. *The Democrat*'s already dead. No one trusts it. They might, if you show your readers you're turning over a new leaf."

"Unthinkable! Are you mad? You haven't even got a press! I'm the only paper in town, and

I'll be here long after you've slunk away."

"I've a plant elsewhere. All I need here is an office, and that won't be a problem. I'll get my own plant back soon enough. Balthazar won't want to face grand larceny charges. Holding my equipment is simply a lever he tried to use on me — and failed. No, Westminster, don't delude yourself. I'm going out to sell ads, and I'll get them."

"Ha! You won't sell a one. You think the merchants'll advertise in a rag that forced them into cutthroat competition?"

"Most will," Flint said. "A few won't. I've nothing to fear. Some have told me they're grateful and doing better than before."

"Well, go sell ads, then."

"I'm not done with you," Flint said gently.

Digby Westminster rose to his feet and pointed at the door, almost apoplectic. "Out!"

Flint didn't budge. "There are reasons for me to keep on publishing," he said quietly. "One is to make sure that a broad, fair tax is imposed, one that won't shift the burden of government onto a few cash cows."

Westminster cackled.

"The other reason is to make people aware of the cruelties around us. Because of you — or of a callous view of unfortunate women that you trumpet — some poor souls took their own lives and lie unmourned and forgotten, except by me. I remember them and honor them."

"Ah! You see! The mouthpiece of Vice!"

Flint grinned. He was enjoying himself. "Yes, and the mouthpiece of the Balthazars and mining interests too. I didn't think it was a good idea to place the entire tax burden on the mines while every other citizen pays nothing."

Westminster reached into his desk drawer and extracted a pasteboard box of powders. He wheeled around the desk, past Flint, toward an area of the shop where an employee could find water or coffee. Flint watched, knowing that Westminster had terminated the interview by fleeing. The man did look unwell, and Flint regretted agitating him. But some things couldn't be helped.

He sensed he had won. Quite probably *The Democrat* would fold. Obviously Westminster didn't have the decency or courage to retract. That was a pity, because those accusations would haunt Flint for as long as he stayed in Silver City. There would always be a few who would whisper about him, and believe any malevolent thing. Some people were carrion eaters, feasting on the ruined reputations of others; debunkers who could never see the good or beauty in another's life.

Flint buttoned his mackinaw, took one last look at this stricken enterprise, and plunged into the clean, sweet air and the heady sunlight.

Napoleon had been right. The morning had turned into a rout. But Flint didn't exult. His thoughts kept straying to the unmarked grave where Chastity Ford lay, unceremoniously dumped there without funeral or prayer — not that she would have approved of a prayer. He didn't feel triumphant, and he wasn't even sure he had a victory.

A need was blooming in him. It was past the season for bouquets, and he didn't know of any hothouse where he might find one. But he knew the undertaker, Roswell, would sell funeral wreaths of some sort. He walked slowly down the gulch, through districts he had scarcely seen, coming at last to the establishment in a widening of the chasm. The board-and-batten building had been calcimined white. An elderly, well-coifed lady fluttered into his presence when he opened the door.

"You have a bereavement," she said. "I'll summon Mr. Roswell."

"No, don't do that. I'm looking for two funeral wreaths."

"Oh, I see. And to whom shall we deliver? I haven't heard of any —"

"Two wreaths, please."

She exuded faint disapproval, no doubt because she had no names as gossip fodder, but Flint supposed she would have objected far more if he had explained himself. In a moment she returned with a pair of black wreaths, fashioned from cloth flowers dipped in waxy substances.

"They're quite expensive, two dollars the item," she said.

He paid wordlessly, peeling off grubby four-bit notes from his roll of shinplasters, and took the wreaths. She didn't look happy.

Quietly, he walked down the gulch, carrying the wreaths. Silver City buried its dead in the only possible place, on the flats at the foot of the crevice that embraced the city. The gulch debouched on an alluvial plain where shipping outfits kept stock and warehoused goods. He didn't see the cemetery.

Ten minutes later he found it, a mile north of the gulch. Silver City hid its dead. He wandered through it, passing fenced graves, some with white pickets, others with elaborate black-enameled iron protecting them. These were the resting places of the respectable, the comfortable, the recognized. Clergymen had buried these people. He searched for a place where the outcasts might be buried. The cemetery wasn't large; Silver City hadn't existed long enough for that.

In a far, sunken corner — subject to flooding, he supposed — he found a row of unmarked graves, mostly just elongated hollows. He felt acutely lonely as he studied these pathetic scratches in the yellow earth. Dried brown grasses thinly lawned the area. He sensed that these graves were barely three feet deep, and the first good flash flood would open them.

He found two fresh ones, but which was Chastity's he didn't know, and he wasn't at all sure which of the graves was occupied by the poor suicidal Marcy, the cash-cow victim who had inspired Flint's odyssey. He was going to have to guess. It was the final indignity. He had come to honor Chastity and the unknown woman, and he couldn't say whose graves would receive his wreaths. There was only the solace of intention: No matter whose bodies lay under that thin yellow mantle, he would be remembering those two women.

He rested there a while, glad he had come, glad he was bringing some small remembrance to these two. An unfamiliar wind whipped him; the gulch had its way of sheltering people from the true bite of winter. He didn't really know what to say or do, so he placed the wreaths on the newest graves. He couldn't tell whether he was at the head or foot of them. He found some small cobbles and pinned the wreaths under them against the relentless wind. These few in a potter's field had a home; he didn't. He thought about Chastity and where her choices led her, and the other woman, who had never had a choice to begin with. He found himself loving them both.

Then he prayed for their everlasting souls.

50

Flint tarried at the graves, mostly wondering where Chastity's spirit abode and wishing her well. Most ministers would assign her to the deepest layer of hell, but that seemed unjust to Flint. God would be kinder than mortals and would consider her upbringing. Hadn't St. Paul argued that those who didn't know God were a different case from those who did? Chastity had done what she could to survive. She had experienced some sort of tragedy; Flint knew that much. Who was he to criticize her? That was something he knew in his bones. Let others cast the stones.

He abandoned his vigil in the middle of the afternoon, comforted by his solitary visit to the graves of those whom the world had scorned. Had anyone in Silver City ever come here to grieve? He hiked up the gulch, feeling the chill in the shadowed gash that harbored the town. His audacity had carried the day, but he was not done. Yet another audacious act came to mind, this time aimed in another direction.

When he reached the law offices of Daniel Burleigh, the attorney he had talked to shortly after coming to Silver City, he turned in. Flint had sensed some sympathy in the attorney, or at least disgust at the way things were run in San Juan County. But the attorney was also playing his cards close to his vest and couldn't help Flint then. But now maybe he would.

Flint waited in a vestibule while Burleigh consulted with a woman client. The editor had grown weary and wondered whether he could stay awake while he waited. But then he was admitted.

"It's Mr. Flint," Burleigh said, extending a big hand and offering a hearty handshake. "I remember you well. I was hoping you'd come. What may I do for you?"

"Well, it's this way," Flint said, settling into the chair across from the lawyer. "I'd like to start some sort of action against both Balthazars for taking and keeping my entire printing plant. It's in a powder bunker at the mines, and Achilles Balthazar won't return it. He regards it as a lever to control me."

"Ah, grand larceny, a criminal act if ever there was one," Burleigh said.

"My problem is, sir, I have little cash. I can offer you the princely sum of five dollars, and the rest would have to be an IOU."

Burleigh didn't even weigh the matter. "It just so happens, Mr. Flint, that five dollars will buy you something. We've both criminal and civil possibilities here. If you authorize me, I'll file your criminal complaint with Sheriff Poindexter. If there's merit in it, he'll be forced to act. He'll have very little choice. He'll get bench warrants against the Balthazars and go after them."

"If Homer Shreveport will supply the warrants," Flint said skeptically.

Burleigh smiled. "We can begin a civil action, but that'll cost more money. You, as plaintiff, will allege wrongs done to you. Poor old Shreveport won't have any choice but to issue summons, and the sheriff won't have any choice but to serve them, and Balthazar will have to answer sooner or later, unless he's gifted at dodging a process server. But given your straitened circumstances, I'd suggest we begin with a criminal complaint. It won't cost you anything but a bit of my time. If you authorize me, with a form here, I'll take the matter straight to Poindexter."

"Will it get my press back?"

Burleigh smiled. "I don't suppose Achilles Balthazar would enjoy two or three years in the pen."

"Won't the courthouse gang try to delay this? Hope to get rid of me by keeping my press from me?"

"My impression is that the old regime's finished, Mr. Flint. You whipped them. You're printing elsewhere. They're being scrutinized from one end of Colorado to the other. In any case, the law provides remedies if they fail to act."

Flint found himself enjoying this big, bulbous-nosed, cheerful attorney with the no-nonsense air. "I've come to the right man," he said.

Burleigh smiled and slid the form forward. It gave him limited powers of attorney. Flint signed it and peeled five dollars in grubby shinplasters from his roll. They seemed to pollute Burleigh's shiny desk.

"Well, that was quick. I won't take any more of your time," he said, rising.

"Whoa up. We're not done. As I said, I was hoping you'd drop by. You have another legal matter pending."

Puzzled, Flint slid back into his seat.

"You were libeled by *The Democrat*. I think you should do something about it."

Flint recoiled. "I have no money."

"Set that aside for now. You've a clear case. In spite of Westminster's fancy footwork in the story, he libeled you. All we have to demonstrate is that he invented the criminal from New York with your name and used this to defame you. It'll take time. Some correspondence with the War Department and a few sources in New York and so on. But it's not even a difficult case to argue."

"Mr. Burleigh, I'm living on the dimes collected from street sales."

"Ah, yes. An important point. You've been damaged. Your reputation has suffered. Your suffering simply means we can ask for plenty of compensation, not only from Westminster but from the Balthazars."

"But I'm flat."

Burleigh's eyes twinkled. "I'd like your permission to file the suit. I think it'll topple Westminster. He's a garden-variety guttersnipe, and he's earned it. We'll see about pursuing it later. My instinct is that he'll either settle or flee Colorado."

"Will filing impose obligations on me I can't meet?"

"Nothing that I can't handle or delay."

Flint pondered it. "My printer, an itinerant named Napoleon," he said at last, "counsels audacity just now. He tells me the emperor captured Europe with it. Napoleon tells me he's my field marshal. His first name is Jude, and he tells me he's named for the patron of hopeless cases."

Daniel Burleigh reared back and laughed.

Later, after a comprehensive interview, Flint slid into the nippy winter twilight, simultaneously joyous and worrying how he'd ever pay Burleigh for a full-fledged lawsuit. Here he was, broke, without a press, without an office, without many allies, levering San Juan County into his reforms. In all his life he had never dared to be so adventuresome, and it tickled him just as much as it scared him witless.

He trudged up the gulch, watching lamplight bloom in windows and shoppers hurry home. It reminded him that he faced another cold night, and that his circumstances could only be described as desperate. What good did an audacious day do for a vagrant? He thought to find Napoleon — he wanted to recount his triumphs and maybe share a cheap supper at some beanery. After that he'd head for his wagon and suffer through another bitter night. The Bridges would steer him to Napoleon, so he headed there.

The jangle of the lending library bell brought Marcus this time.

"Ah, Flint! How did it go?" the cabinetmaker cried.

"Beyond my wildest hopes," Flint replied, and swiftly recounted the day's triumphs.

"Well, you've won. That's plain. It's a day to celebrate."

"Maybe," Flint said cautiously. Audacity was one thing; a solid victory was another. The whole thing could unravel. "I'm looking for Napoleon. I need to talk to him."

Marcus Bridge laughed heartily. "Then come inside and talk with him. He's sharing a mug of stout with us."

That didn't surprise Flint, and he headed through the pungent woodworking shop. He found the spirited field marshal, mug in hand, in the parlor along with the other Bridges.

Someone thrust a mug of the dark brown beer in Flint's hand, and the heat of the room permeated him. He hadn't slept for so long. Now with the first sip of stout, a weariness stole through him, and he knew he could not stay awake. But they were all clamoring for his news, and so he told it, encounter by encounter.

When he told of his trip to the cemetery he again discovered a solemnity in Livia's eyes, as if she were weighing a man who would befriend disreputable women. He decided to talk about what had brought him to Silver City in the first place, even though they had read about it. Sipping the mellow dark brew, he quietly told the Bridges of reading an exchange copy of *The Democrat* one day and finding Westminster laughing at a suicide and calling it the loss of a cash cow. For the next weeks his disgust had worked on him. If the life of a human being meant anything at all, or if every mortal had value in the eyes of God, then Westminster's callousness was wrong.

"And you came here just because of that?" Livia asked, amazed.

"I was weary of where I was, in Arizona Territory. But yes, I thought I might make the world a better place."

"You came for that and not for any business reason?" asked Marcus.

Flint nodded, suddenly embarrassed. He was nothing but a fool, a Don Quixote.

"Then I'm glad you found us," Molly said.

Livia smiled, and Flint's world smiled with her.

Flint wanted only to escape and sleep, but Napoleon stayed him. "I've been busy," he said mysteriously.

"I was hoping you'd join me for a bit," Flint muttered. He needed cold air or he'd fall asleep.

Napoleon ignored him. "I've been selling ads. Got a fistful. Twisted a few arms. Some merchants aren't fond of *The Sentinel*, but most are. They've had their fill of Westminster. I charged half Westminster's rate, and that pleased 'em. I told 'em we're printing out of town and we'd have a paper out on Friday."

"You sold ads? And they bought some this time? What does it come to?" Flint asked, scarcely grasping it.

"Over three hundred — if the rascals pay. I thought I'd head for Ouray in the morning and start building them. Between us, we've stories enough to fill the hole. Trust Napoleon, Flint. The emperor always paid attention to logistics."

But Flint wasn't listening. He was exhausted and couldn't prop up his eyelids a moment longer. The last thing he remembered was the warmth of a blanket.

51

Flint and Napoleon took off for Ouray in the morning, under a cast-iron sky that spat crystals of ice and sawed off the mountains. The weather worried Flint. He needed to put *The Sentinel* on the streets of Silver City in a timely way, if only to prove that it lived. A tough snowstorm could halt traffic for a fortnight, and as he steered the big mules north, he entertained himself with desperate plans to send the paper south on the back of a snowshoer.

On the way out of town Flint had stopped at the law offices of Daniel Burleigh. There he learned that the attorney had filed criminal complaints with the sheriff, and that Poindexter would get grand larceny warrants for both Balthazars plus six John Does for the mine guards who had participated in the theft. Burleigh cheerfully reported that the unhappy Poindexter took it like a double tablespoon of cod-liver oil.

That gave Flint another story. He and the redoubtable Napoleon carried the stories in their heads this time, and typesetting would go more slowly in Ouray because they would have to compose them as they set the type. Flint hoped that Hopwell wouldn't mind.

He had the property tax story from Solomon Drake; a story about his interview with Balthazar, who was keeping the press and trying to rescue Hamlin; a story about the sheriff's inaction and Hamlin's continuing liberty; a story about his interview with Digby Westminster; and several stories about the merchants, some of them Napolcon's. Not a lot, but all important. He would add some opinion. This issue would have some fat ads, but it would still require a lot of filler and exchange news.

The relentless north wind, driving ice crystals into their faces, soon numbed and chafed them both.

"Why don't you warm up under the wagonsheet, Napoleon, and we'll take turns driving," Flint said.

Napoleon grunted. "This army has gloves," he replied mysteriously.

They nooned in the lee of a rocky cliff, and the veteran wanderer soon had a fierce fire warming their fronts while their backsides froze. The foreboding skies were laying a skiff of snow upon the land.

Flint worried his way north, his mind writhing with unaccustomed anxiety. What if Hopwell refused them? What if Westminster's street bullies were ready and waiting this time? What if the Bridge boys suddenly quit? What if Balthazar's private army caused trouble?

"Relax, my friend," said Napoleon. "Trust the emperor."

"Well, he landed on St. Helena, didn't he?" Napoleon laughed.

They reached Ouray as night closed in and in the nick of time, as the wagon was miring and the mules had reached their limit, dragging it through muck. Never was lamplight so welcome to Flint, who sat numbly on his seat, shivering in wet duds. Hopwell had shut down for the day, so Flint unhitched the mules, walked them to the livery barn, and ordered baits of oats. Then he and Napoleon headed for the nearest and warmest cafe, the Peerless, where they drowned their chills in java and devoured platters of beef and listened to miners gossip.

After that they tracked down Hopwell, who was enjoying his third mug of pilsner in a local thirst parlor, and shanghaied him. The editor didn't mind; he wanted all the news and was as eager to help as before. They worked out the same deal: Flint would pay with newsprint. Hopwell wanted the stories and would use most of them as exchange news after Flint and Napoleon were done. He listened eagerly to all the latest events, pronouncing them the best stories in the state.

He lit the lamps in the shop and left *The Sentinel* staff to its work. Wearily, Flint faced the awesome task of setting a whole issue in just a few hours. He grimly plunged in, while Napoleon began building the ads from the notes he had with him. Flint surveyed Hopwell's half-filled chases and realized he was going to have to remove body type and headlines that had already been positioned in the pages and put it back into galley trays, although there was an Ouray story or two he could reprint, especially one about a big strike of high-grade gold ore.

Thus the pair of vagrants labored into the night. Once in a while Flint headed to the window and peered into the mysterious dark. It didn't reveal much, but the ground had whitened. By the wee hours he knew he had reached his limit. He was making errors every sentence. Only two or three days had passed since they had done the previous issue here, thirty long miles from home, and he had scarcely slept.

"Let's break for a while, Jude," he said. They were barely a quarter of the way through the forbidding task. He couldn't remember being more tired in his life.

The bantam printer didn't argue.

Within minutes Flint had his bedroll stretched out on one of Hopwell's cots at the rear, pulled off his icy, wet boots, stuffed some pine logs into the range and turned its damper down, and that was the last he knew.

He didn't want to wake up in the morning, but it gradually seeped into his fogged mind that Napoleon and Hopwell were talking in the shop. Guiltily he swung out of the cot, not knowing the hour. When he reached the composing room floor, he was mortified to learn it was after eleven.

"Let you sleep," Hopwell said. "You needed

it. You've been in the middle of a war, son. Waging the durndest little press fracas I've ever heard tell of in all my years of word slinging."

Flint rubbed the stubble on his jaw, staring at Napoleon, who seemed none the worse for wear, and at the impressive columns of set type in the galley tray.

"I've been setting your stories, but I can't remember half of it all. You're going to have to fill them out, add some 'graphs about what I missed," Napoleon said. "Go eat, and then we'll go over it."

Flint marveled. Napoleon was a man to take the initiative. Even an incomplete story was better than no story.

Flint stepped out into a blustery winter day. Three or four inches of snow lay on the red rock cliffs, enough to cause serious trouble going back. But maybe some traffic would cut it down before they left this evening. He headed for the livery barn to order another bait of oats for the mules and then wolfed down a hurried breakfast of flapjacks.

They set stories all day, proofed while they rested, and late in the afternoon Hopwell slid the first two chases into the bed of the handpress, inked them, loaded the newsprint, and began to print another four-page *Sentinel*. Together they ran five hundred copies and a few extra. Napoleon had guaranteed a five-hundred-copy circulation to the merchants who bought ads for the first time.

By the supper hour they were wiping down the press, moving the columns of type to galley trays, restoring Hopwell's partially completed pages to their original condition, and returning the filler material. Flint brought in more than enough newsprint from his dwindling supply to repay Hopwell.

"You'd better stay over, Flint. It's gonna be a cold, mean night, and you'll drive through gumbo," Hopwell said.

"I've the need to get back there," Flint said. "I want this issue on the streets on schedule — proof that *The Sentinel* lives." It meant driving through a pitch-black night over mountains and terrible grades. But he didn't feel in control, imagining terrible events were taking place in Silver City. All could yet be lost. Stars filled the heavens once again, and there would be enough light on the whited ground to allow night passage. He had a raging thirst to get back, and he couldn't deny it.

"I think we'll go," he said. "We've slept. Homer, you've helped us again. I'm in your debt."

"Sam Flint, I'm proud to. It puts a little spring in my legs."

Gingerly they loaded the still-damp edition into the wagon bed, covered it with oilcloth, wrapped their bedroll blankets about them, and headed into a wintry night and a vast, involuted silence.

"You go back there and sleep," he told Napoleon. "We'll take turns again."

The gypsy printer crawled under the wagon-sheet, and Flint steered the quiet, unhappy mules into the somber night. At least, he thought, they weren't hauling a loaded wagon. They had done that often enough, and Flint had rested them frequently when they were dragging the press, chases, case boxes, newsprint, and Flint's personal stuff. Tonight he would rest them just as often because of the mire, which would wear them out faster than the heaviest load.

The rhythmic clop of the mules and groan of harness through the hushed night brought peace to Flint at last. The night seemed magical. A gibbous moon climbed the dome of heaven, spreading its silvery light over the vast white panoramas. The San Juan mountains loomed chalky and black and somehow forbidding. Stray clouds chased the moon and sometimes obscured it, a gigantic game of hide-and-seek playing itself out above him.

The mules didn't seem to mind the night passage. Traffic had flattened the snow in the ruts, and the surface of the trace seemed hard enough, save a few mirey places Flint negotiated carefully. One could scarcely lose the way on a night like this.

All the tension of the last weeks slid out of him. This issue would do the trick. *The Sentinel* had arrived in Silver City to stay. Now, with advertising and some avid readers, he would find new quarters far from the sporting district, keep on pushing for a better, happier community, and begin to prosper. He relished the thought of some type metal rivalry with *The Democrat*.

He would visit the Bridges often. They had always welcomed him. He had eyes for Livia, if she would have him. He thought she would. Something galvanic flowed between them whenever they talked, and he always felt a rush of something sweet and breathtaking when they were together. She was younger, but what difference did that make? The important thing was that they were born friends, boon companions, each with a scholarly bent and a swift grasp of the ways of the world. Maybe, if dreams came true — and he believed they did — they would become partners for life.

He drove two hours through a grand night, without feeling any chafe of wind. He rested the mules, and then Napoleon drove two more hours. Flint thought they would make Silver City before dawn, a better speed than he had expected. He took over once again, after checking Sherman and Grant's hooves and feeling their fetlocks for heat. The mules seemed fine.

He traversed a long flat not far from Silver City, reaching a place on the south end where pine forest stretched down from the hills. An abandoned prospector's log-and-sod cabin stood there, along with an ancient pole corral hewn into a gulch. The place had been used off and on by storm-stranded travelers for several years.

As he passed it, a horse and rider bloomed like some sinister night mirage or apparition. Flint watched, astonished, as the rider trotted straight toward the wagon, a ghostly visitor closing fast.

In short order, the rider rode alongside, staring at Flint. The man wore a buffalo coat and a woolen hat with flaps. He rode a big horse that might have been a sorrel, but the moonlight was tricky, and the rider held the reins with one gloved hand. The other held something metallic.

"Flint," yelled the rider. "Get down. And that printer too."

Flint knew the voice and, utterly stunned, knew that he had only moments to live.

52

The voice belonged to Hamlin Balthazar.

It all came to Flint in a rush. Hamlin intended to kill the witnesses and go free. How the young man had identified the wagon Flint couldn't say, but probably he had ridden to Ouray and seen it parked in front of *The Ouray Eagle*. Then he had returned this far, less than two hours from Silver City, and lain in wait.

Flint knew his only hope was to spread doubt.

"Who's that?" Flint asked with a muffled voice. "Who're you?"

"Get down, Flint."

"Is this a robbery? You can have my purse," Flint said. "I don't want trouble."

Flint hoped that Napoleon was awake and lying low. He didn't dare turn around and look. Neither of them was armed.

Hamlin laughed. "The last thing I need is your purse. Step down now."

"Oh? You must be rich. Either that or an honest man."

"If you don't get down this instant you're dead. Get that printer out of there."

Flint felt his pulse begin to race. He braced himself. "It doesn't seem to make any difference

439

if I get down or not," Flint said. "Looks like I'm going to be dead either way."

He wondered if he could flip backward to the momentary safety of the wagonbed. He was out of ideas. He rose slowly and faced Hamlin. "I wish I knew what this is about," he grumbled.

Hamlin laughed. His horse sidled under him, and Hamlin wobbled on it. He was not an expert rider. "Don't pretend, Flint," he said.

"Who'm I talking to?"

"Flint, it's fun to see you buying time, calculating, trying to find a way out. I enjoy it. I have the gift of reading people's minds. You're seeking seconds, looking for a chance. Trying to alert that printer in there. You're squirming. You're also staring into the bore of a revolver. Sweat a little, Flint."

Flint felt a faint shifting of the wagon on its springs. Napoleon was stirring slowly, avoiding any creaking. Flint didn't dare look back.

"I don't know why you think I'm this Flint. Maybe it's a mistake. You feel good about killing just anyone? Is that it? A mad dog shooter?"

"You're a case. Your mind's all fevered up. Nice moon — I can see who it is, and you know it."

His only chance was to step down and rush Hamlin, maybe scare the horse. The shot might go wild. Slowly, his pulse trembling, he stepped onto the hub of the front wheel and clambered to the cold ground.

Hamlin laughed easily. "If I told you to stand

on your head, you would, Flint. Anything to buy another second."

That was true, Flint thought. He felt his limbs go dead, paralyzed with fear. This was worse than the moments before attacking that high ground at Fredericksburg. Worse than anything he had known.

The bore of Hamlin's revolver aimed straight at him, as large as a lead pipe. Behind Flint, the wagon creaked slightly. Hamlin's horse side-stepped and whirled just as a shot shattered the night. Flint dove straight at the horse. It squealed and reared as Flint slammed into it. Another shot deafened Flint, this one inches from his ear. Flint clawed at Hamlin's leg, yanking Hamlin half out of the saddle, and felt the brutal smack of the barrel over his shoulder.

Flint yanked again, this time pulling Hamlin out of the stirrups. Napoleon landed on Hamlin as the boy hit the snow. Flint dove for the boy and pinioned him. The printer was yanking the boy's arm back. Hamlin howled and dropped the revolver.

A *whoof* of air erupted from Hamlin. He kicked and bucked, but suddenly the kicking stopped and Flint realized Napoleon had pinned the boy's legs. The revolver lay in the snow, black and sinister, three feet from Hamlin. Flint felt his pulse slow, but his own wildness boiled through him.

He crawled off Hamlin and dragged him to his feet, his fists itching to pulverize him. Blood-red rage exploded through Flint as he shook the punk until his teeth rattled. The boy whined and gasped. Sheer revenge flooded Flint.

"We've got him," Napoleon said calmly as he picked up the revolver.

Reluctantly, Flint let his rage seep away. No one would object if he pounded Hamlin to pulp — the boy deserved worse — but Flint thought the noose would be enough. He lowered his big fist, feeling cheated.

"Dumb worthless punk," Flint said roughly. "You think killing us wouldn't be laid at your feet. You might think you have an alibi, but let me tell you something: You'd sit in Poindexter's jug and they'd grill you twenty-four hours a day until you sang. And they'd grill anyone who's covering for you. You kill us? You'd hang in a fortnight."

"I'll give you ten thousand dollars, Flint," Hamlin said. "Just let me go."

Flint laughed harshly.

"Twenty thousand. I'll make my pap fork over."

"He doesn't think you're worth twenty cents."

Napoleon was loosening the latigo of the stock saddle Hamlin had been riding, and with this he trussed the man's arms. The captive gave no further trouble.

They herded him into the wagon and tied him there with cord.

"You're just ants," Hamlin said. "Wait until my pap deals with you. You haven't seen anything yet. You'd better let me go."

"You're going straight to Poindexter, and we're going to swear out complaints for attempted murder."

"Aw, I wasn't going to do that. I was just going to scare you. All I wanted was the new issue. I don't like what you're saying about me, and I'll sue you."

Flint sighed. There was the defense, already percolating in the punk's skull. Well, it would be up to Judge Shreveport. The thought wasn't comforting.

Flint watched Napoleon tie the reins of the saddle to the back of the wagon. Then he crawled into the wagonbed and began patting down Hamlin, who was tied just behind the front seat. Napoleon was looking for a concealed weapon, a hideout, a knife. Flint wished he had had the presence of mind to do that, but he was an editor, a newsman, not a copper.

Satisfied, Napoleon slid back away from Hamlin. "You try anything and this little thirty-two-caliber murder weapon you stupidly kept will go off," he said.

Flint stared into the silvery night, uncommonly alive to every freshet and noise. "Napoleon, maybe there's something more in the shack," he said. "Some evidence."

Napoleon grunted and trudged across the snowy grasses. In a moment he came back empty-handed. "No, nothing. The punk has a few brains," he said. He began hunting in the snow where the struggle occurred and finally picked up something that reflected moonlight, snapped it, and slid it into his pocket.

"What did you throw at the horse?" Flint asked.

"My Barlow knife," Napoleon said. "I had to open that puckerhole first. I'm glad you kept him occupied. I'm no knifethrower, but a gypsy printer named for the patron of hopeless cases will try anything."

Flint would have laughed any other time.

He reckoned dawn wasn't far off. The yawning mules lowered into their collars and pulled again, and the wagon creaked slowly through the cold night.

"Where is Miss Ford's money?" Flint asked the boy.

"In the bank."

"Why'd you take it?"

"Who says I took it?" he retorted.

"Your guards," Flint said. "Why'd you kill her?"

"Who says I did?"

"You will. She was a special woman."

"How do you know?"

"She was my friend."

Hamlin laughed. "Guess we know all about that."

"No, you know nothing about that or what a friend is, because you never had one."

"When we're done with you, Flint, you'll be a grease spot."

Flint drove quietly through the night, while Napoleon guarded Hamlin. Dawn rose swiftly. One moment it was dark; the next the world was bathed in wintry gray and then in sunny brightness. Hamlin settled into glum silence.

Wearily, Flint steered the mules into the long gulch that hid Silver City from the world, and the wagon creaked its way past quiet cottages and occasional neighborhood saloons and grocers. At last the business district rounded into view, and beyond it the courthouse on its tiny parcel of flat land. Flint drew up before the jail entrance on the north side and grunted at Napoleon.

He found Poindexter within, standing at the potbelly stove and awaiting his coffee. The sheriff stared from a carefully masked face.

"I've got Hamlin."

Poindexter blinked. "It's too early. I don't function without a cup."

"In the wagon. He tried to kill us."

"You choose inconvenient times."

Poindexter followed Flint out the door and into a nippy morning. The sun had yet to reach into the gulch. Poindexter peered at the trussed youth lying in the wagonbed and then at Napoleon.

"All right," he said.

Napoleon hoisted Hamlin to his feet and helped him step down while the sheriff watched. A deputy wandered out and joined him. They steered Hamlin into the office and dropped him into a chair. The deputy unwound the latigo and untied the cord, handing them to Flint.

"The latigo's his. It's from his saddle. I'll get it — it's in the wagon. You'll have to find out about the sorrel."

Flint got the saddle and tied the sorrel to the hitching post. The mules looked surly. He returned to find Hamlin in leg irons and manacles, at last looking vulnerable and glum.

"I'll want the whole story, Flint," the sheriff said. "And yours too," he said to Napoleon.

That took a half-hour longer than it should have, but in the end, Flint felt sure that the sheriff would do his duty.

"All right," the sheriff said to Napoleon. "Any more?"

Napoleon shook his head.

The sheriff turned to Flint. "It took courage to go against a man with a gun." It was a compliment.

"We did it together."

"You've done a lot of things together," Poindexter said amiably. "We'll see you in court. I'll have to issue a summons so you'll testify."

Flint nodded and turned to leave. He had a paper to distribute. "I've work to do," he said.

"Flint, I hope you're fair to me. I'm going to keep the peace and enforce the law and I hope we can cooperate."

"I write the facts, sheriff."

"Stop at *The Democrat*, Flint."

It was an odd request, but Flint meant to

honor it. He and Napoleon clambered aboard the wagon, and Flint steered the weary mules toward the rival paper.

53

Flint and Napoleon rattled *The Democrat*'s fancy brass doorknob and were met with silence. They peered through windows in the composing room, finding bare wood where only two or three days ago printing equipment crowded the floor. A tour of the building's naked windows revealed that nothing remained in Westminster's posh offices. Indeed, only the incised bronze plaque at the front of the building suggested that the paper had ever occupied those precincts.

Flint was puzzled. "Maybe Westminster hit hard times and moved to cheaper quarters," Flint said.

But Napoleon was grinning.

"Burleigh'll know," Flint said. He didn't really believe that Digby Westminster had abandoned Silver City. *The Democrat* had been solidly entrenched, affluent, and powerful. Why would its editor flee with the first adversity?

"Trust the field marshal. He's gone, vamoosed, hightailed it."

Flint felt too tired to rejoice. He still had an issue to distribute, and bills to collect after that. Merchants had marvelous ways to dodge the invoices.

Burleigh's door was still locked, but as they turned to leave he admitted them.

"Two traveling sons of guns. I thought you might be my first clients," he said, ushering them in. "Let me start the fire."

They waited impatiently in the chill as the attorney crumpled some *Democrats*, pushed the paper into his black Oakwood potbellied stove, added some kindling, and scratched a lucifer.

"I guess *The Democrat* was useful for something," Flint said.

"Well, I'll tell you what you want to know in a moment. I want your news. I suppose you have a paper in the wagon."

"It's outdated," said Flint. He apprised the attorney of Hamlin's attempt on their life, the capture and delivery to Poindexter, and the sheriff steering them to the empty office.

Daniel Burleigh leaned back in his swivel chair, contemplating. "The day you left," he began, "I filed the libel suit in the county court. It wasn't hard to draw up. His courthouse pals must have told Westminster instantly. I don't think he ever did get a summons, but he certainly got the news. Yesterday four big Pittsburgh wagons and ox teams showed up at his plant, Kinnear Forwarding Company, and loaded him up. The rates are cheap to Denver; they usually go east empty, so Westminster got out of here for very little. He's on his way to Denver; he hasn't been served yet. Do you want to pursue it? This court's writ runs in all Colorado. He's probably still in the county if he's with the freight."

Flint shook his head at once. He would have liked a full retraction, but Westminster's flight amounted to a retraction of sorts, especially when it became publicly known that Flint had filed the suit. "Let him go," Flint said. "But let the suit hang a while just to make him behave."

"You son of a gun. You don't need my counsel. The rest of my news is that I've also filed an action against the Balthazars and their guards. I think Poindexter's deputies are afraid to serve Achilles, but they'll have to. And now that they have Hamlin, they'll breakfast him with that, along with the murder charge. We'll be hearing something soon, I suppose. How'll I find you?"

"Leave word with the Bridges."

"You've won, Flint. The town'll benefit. You broke 'em."

"I'm still facing Achilles, and I don't seem to own a press."

"Ah, it'll all come together." Burleigh eyed them somberly. "The pair of you took on the local Gibraltar. I don't know how you did it."

Flint nodded toward his printer. "The man's name is Napoleon."

"But not Bonaparte," the gypsy said, oddly modest and subdued.

"Mr. Burleigh, as soon as I collect for some ads, I'll pay you."

"Mr. Flint, your credit's better than

Vanderbilt's around here. Take your time. You're the only newspaper in town. I'll take a copy of the latest and deduct a dime." He laughed heartily. "You sons of guns."

Flint delivered a couple of copies to Burleigh and then hawed his sullen mules up the gulch through a brightening day. He reined up before the furniture shop and lending library and eased down, feeling numb. Wordlessly, Napoleon opened the puckerstring at the rear of the wagon, and they hefted the unfolded issue inside while Marcus, Timothy, and Augustus watched silently.

"I guess I can spare the boys a few hours," Marcus said. "We're doweling a table together." He nodded them in, and soon Flint found himself telling the whole story once again while the Bridges listened, solemn and rapt.

"He almost killed you," Livia said.

"Napoleon saved us. He stirred up the sorrel."

"You've won," Livia whispered, her eyes shining.

Something in that pleased Flint mightily. "Not yet, but soon."

"We heard Westminster pulled out," Marcus said. "Augustus walked down the gulch and had a look. It shows what right thinking can do."

Flint wanted to object. It took a lot more than thinking good thoughts. Napoleon had taught him a few things about newspaper wars. But Flint held his peace.

"We'll sell out the issue," Timothy said.

"It's already outdated. If I had a press I'd run a special supplement."

"Well, we'll just shout the news," Augustus said.

"What're you going to do now? Have you eaten?" Molly asked.

"We'll try to collect some cash for the ads. That means we'll deliver a copy — proof of advertising, it's called — and talk some merchants out of some lucre. And try to sell them another ad."

"You must be tired, especially after Hamlin. I'd be in a room unable to face the world after staring up a gun barrel."

"Sometime this afternoon, Mrs. Bridge, I'll start on a two-day sleep at some local hostelry. After that, I don't know."

He and Napoleon climbed wordlessly into the wagon again, this time heading for the Bottomless Pit Cafe, which was a good description of their condition. They found it still crowded with miners who had come off the night shift and soon would be going to bed. They commandeered a small table and waited for the serving woman. Flint was about as tired as he ever got and was feeling melancholy, though he couldn't say why.

"I know you. You're Flint," said a man at the next table.

Flint beheld a burly miner in a denim jumper, his flesh pale from the want of sun, and dark circles under his solemn eyes.

Flint nodded.

"Well, your rag did it. There's not a lad goes into the pits that isn't a friend of yourn. Some writer you be, taking on the tigers."

"Did what?"

"Why, licked old Balthazar good."

"What happened?" Flint was simply baffled.

"Where've you been?" the man asked, disdainfully. "That moneybags finally gave in a little. Tally's starting at three a day again, more for powder men and drillers. Muckers are a dime a dozen, but a powder man like me — well, Flint, old Achilles, he found out a thing or two. We don't grow on trees. He's been holding on to some of us with a little under-the-table cash while talking about cutting wages. But now he's surfaced. It's four a day for a powder man, three and a half for good doublejackers."

"Well, I didn't have anything to do with that."

"Why, you did! You began writing up the tallies all over the state, and a lot of good men left. He's been advertising in all them other weeklies: Come to Silver City, good pay, good conditions."

Flint and Napoleon stared at each other. They hadn't been looking at the exchange papers recently because they had no offices. "You say Balthazar's been advertising?"

"All over creation. We got a few new men, one from Central City, and a good powder man from Blackhawk. It wasn't just the tally. It was changing the hours too. We're not in the hole ten and a half anymore; we're down for ten, and then up to grass. He don't take off time for a pasty now. There isn't a man but thinks your little rag pushed him to it. Thanks to you, we're seeing a wee bit of sunlight."

"When did this happen?"

"Well, it's been happening for a little while, my friend. I think the old skinflint threw in the towel, is what I think. We're getting a wee bit better timbering too. Not that it's enough. He's still putting the sets on six-foot centers and not laying in enough lagging — that's the planks over the beams — to keep a bloody lad safe in the rotten spots where the rock above you's like daggers waiting to drop, but it's a piece better. And the muckers, they're not leaning on their shovels so much. Give a man a reason to work, and he'll muck."

Flint felt a quiet exuberance rising in him. Had those pieces begun by Napoleon done the trick? "Sir, the credit isn't mine, it belongs to this gentleman here, a fine journeyman printer named Jude Napoleon. He started those stories about wages and conditions in the area."

"Well, then, Napoleon, there's many a lad that'd drink to your health. You come by any miner's saloon, and you'll never spend a dime." He squinted at Flint, as if daylight was too much for his eyes. "Goes for you too, Flint. Now we've got a fair-enough weekly. Between Balthazar and that rag of Westminster's, a plain working man got ground right down. We can spare two bits for a mug of ale or a ribbon for our ladies, and the merchants are even fighting each other a bit for our custom."

Flint sipped his java, enjoying the victory. "I don't know your name," he said to the miner.

"My name's not important. I'm just a stiff that goes into the pit six times a week."

Flint sighed. "Well, I'll be getting a new office. You stop by any time things aren't right, and I'll write it up. Or you can write it up yourself."

"I'd as soon hold a live fuse in me hand," the man said cheerfully, turning to leave.

Flint wolfed down a breakfast steak; Napoleon polished off a stack of flapjacks; both sipped java.

"I'll put the mules on pasture, then I'll start collecting. Owe you a big piece of change. There should be enough to rent something."

"*The Democrat*'s old place?"

"Never. I'd feel the ghosts."

"Flint, I'm taking off. Got the itch."

"What!"

Napoleon shrugged. "You aren't a lost cause, and you don't need a gypsy veteran of the newspaper wars."

"But I need a good journeyman printer!"

"Plenty of those, and you can train a few devils. No, Flint, you don't need me. I'm like a knight, looking for someone to rescue. Maybe I'll find a fellow like you." He grinned. "But I don't think so. There'll never be another Sam Flint. As for me, I'm a man of the open road, a man with a pent-up thirst, a man looking for another fight. Say good-bye to the Frenchie."

Flint felt tears rising and fought them back. "But your pay — we can get it from Timothy or Augustus. They'll be done soon."

"I might do that, Flint. You go put Grant and Sherman to bed."

Out on the street, Flint shook hands with Napoleon and tried to see him, but he couldn't — the gypsy printer was a blur.

54

Flint wrestled the California case boxes into place and surveyed his new plant. It seemed a miracle that he should have a perfect shop, well-located in the center of the gulch, scarcely a hundred yards from the Bridges' store. The family had swiftly built him a front counter and workbenches and had furnished the back room for him with their fine pine pieces. They had even fashioned a gilded sign, announcing THE SILVER CITY SENTINEL in black letters. It hung proudly over the whited front door, which stood four steps above Silver Street.

The place had been occupied by a firm of mining engineers and geologists, who decided the abandoned *Democrat* plant had just the space they wanted. Flint pounced on the vacancy immediately. This narrow board-and-batten building stood in a respectable quarter, and the fifty-dollar rent he could handle easily.

He was still so tired he could scarcely remember recent days, but this night he would sleep in a new bed in his own quarters. No worries would disturb him.

Two days earlier Daniel Burleigh had reached him with news: Achilles Balthazar was dealing.

He wanted Poindexter to drop the charges against himself — but not Hamlin — in exchange for the return of the equipment, which he said he was merely storing for Flint as a courtesy. He agreed that the mine guards should plead guilty and be fined twenty-five dollars. But Burleigh hadn't been satisfied. He demanded two hundred dollars for Flint's losses, and he got it. The attorney took fifty out for himself and left a hundred and fifty for Flint to use starting up the weekly again.

Just that afternoon a mine wagon arrived at the new address, and the burly guards wrestled all of Flint's equipment up the four stairs and into the building, placing it where Flint directed. The trouble was over. He had his plant back. The rotary flatbed stood ready.

He intended to start publishing on a regular schedule again, sticking with Fridays. But Silver City was a large town, and he would need a journeyman printer or two devils and at least one accountant and ad salesman. Flint retracted that. There would be an accountant and ad saleswoman, and she intended to learn how to set type and write stories too. Livia would be a natural at anything she did for the paper. The thought brought a blossoming of good cheer to him, weary as he was.

Flint already had a story for the next issue. The county property tax ordinance had been enacted. A deputy had already collected twenty dollars from Flint and given him a receipt. The process was ongoing all across town. It wasn't an onerous burden, yet the total would support the county better than before and permit some things that couldn't be considered earlier, especially a school. He would do some editorializing about that. He wanted a telegraph connection and a post office at both ends of the long, sinuous town, and better sanitation, among other things. There never was a shortage of things wanting, especially in a raw frontier town. But they all had price tags and had to be tackled one at a time.

There were other tasks awaiting him: He intended to cover Hamlin's trial closely. He would have to testify. It occurred to him that Napoleon hadn't stayed on, and Hamlin might escape the noose because there would be only one witness; it would take two to hang him. Still, no one knew that. Maybe Hamlin would confess and plead for a mitigated sentence. Flint intended to report it all, fearlessly. He had no stomach for hangings, but this ruthless brat deserved the noose if anyone ever did.

He swept the shop, remembering how Jude Napoleon had done it each night. Flint had never seen the tramp printer again. Napoleon had taken a final week's pay out of Timothy's circulation cash and had vanished. Flint mused that the man was really an angel dressed as a mortal, sent by God to rescue him. It made a pleasant fantasy, but the fantasy never got farther than Napoleon's night with Big Lulu.

Nonetheless, the gypsy had been a godsend, arriving at the right moment and employing tactics Flint hadn't considered. In his own way, Napoleon was the image of his namesake. Flint knew how to wage wars of ideas, wars of opinions and programs, against opposing papers. But this fight had been different; this had required the skills of a man who knew the hard edges.

Whoever Jude Napoleon was, he seemed a miracle, and Flint knew he would remember the bantam printer with awe and thanksgiving. Now he believed in miracles.

Flint contemplated a supper in the Bottomless Pit but wondered if he could stay awake. As he put the broom and dust pan away, he heard a knocking. It had to be one of the Bridges. He opened to Livia, who stood there smiling, wrapped in a heavy woolen cloak, a soft cloche hat covering her brown hair. Her breath steamed.

"My mother sent this," she said, handing him a wicker basket covered with a napkin. "It's supper."

"Come in, Livia. I was just getting settled."

She smiled, and he felt that smile pierce clear through him. "Not tonight, Sam. Our supper's waiting. She said if she invited you, you'd fall asleep again. Two nights in a row!"

"I'm sorry," he said, embarrassed. "I'm worn out."

"Don't be sorry! We know how hard it's been. Anyway, take this — it's chicken dumplings my mother loves to make when she can find a chicken, and some other things, including some pie. She had to use dried apples, but it tastes fine because she puts in a little cinnamon. And if you fall asleep in the middle, we won't have to rescue you." She laughed gaily.

"Livia —" he said, his gaze meeting her shining eyes. "Thank you. And thank your mother. I couldn't have gotten along . . ."

"What time do I start?"

"Oh, anytime."

"Well, I'd be embarrassed —" She left the rest unsaid.

"Eight o'clock," he said, rescuing her.

"Sam? Thank you for the chance. It'll be a miracle for me, you know. I've always dreamed of doing something like this. I like ideas and words. I hope you'll be happy you hired me."

"Livia, you'll be writing some of the best stories in the paper, and you'll be the best editorialist. We're going to do fine together."

"Well, that sounds good!"

She hastened home. He carried the basket to the handsome pine kitchen table that Bridge family genius somehow made elegant and plunged in. But his mind wasn't on his food, and only vaguely did he know how savory it was.

He was thinking about what brought him here. An ugly, cynical story about a desperate creature whose suicide had been mocked in print. A small thing, but one that enraged him. It led to large events, much larger than Flint imagined when he first drove Grant and Sherman up the gulch, peering at a raw, cramped new city with only one street.

He had come to set some mean attitudes straight. Nothing could be more quixotic. He hadn't come to make a living and hadn't expected to stay. But now, a few weeks later, he found himself the David who had toppled two Goliaths. And he was in love.